dead
water

C. A. FLETCHER

orbit

orbitbooks.net

ORBIT

First published in Great Britain in 2022 by Orbit
This paperback edition published in 2023 in Great Britain by Orbit

1 3 5 7 9 10 8 6 4 2

A CIP catalogue record for this book
is available from the British Library.

ISBN 978-0-356-51384-3

Typeset in Garamond by M Rules
Printed and bound in Great Britain by
Clays Ltd, Elcograf, S.p.A.

Papers used by Orbit are from well-managed forests
and other responsible sources.

Orbit
An imprint of
Little, Brown Book Group
Carmelite House
50 Victoria Embankment
London EC4Y 0DZ

An Hachette UK Company
www.hachette.co.uk

www.orbitbooks.net

dead
water

The ravens look down on Sig as she breaks water and clips herself on to the red ball bobbing in the light chop, regaining her breath: she's too big for prey, too small to be a fishing boat with the chance of scraps tossed over the side that might drift in and land where the ravens might hop from rock to rock and pluck them from the salt water.

They're about to move on when they see dark shapes in the depths below her, submarine shadows that lazily swim towards Sig on a converging angle. There are three of them and even the smallest is easily four times as long as the swimmer, who hangs there steadily getting her breath back, normalising her breathing as she floats by the buoy, unaware.

The ravens wait.

Maybe there will be breakfast to be picked off the water's edge after all.

VARANGIAN: OATH BREAKER

They should have sent more.

And he was right not to have told them how fast his axe was. They also should have taken more note of the knife and the sword he carried with it.

He filled the waterskins before he threw their bodies in the well and headed north into the desert.

More would come. No need to leave them fresh water to drink. Let them pace themselves by what was left in their own waterskins.

At the time it had seemed like a good idea.

And more had come. Chasing them as they picked their way homewards from waterhole to oasis to well, and every time they came he met the pursuers with axe and sword and left the bodies bobbing in the water to confound the followers.

Lords of the Water they might be, but if he could slow them down by leaving that water undrinkable, they might get home.

Again, it had seemed like a good idea.

His master, the emissary, suffered a second knife wound the third time they were attacked. It was bad. It might have healed.

He told the older man it likely would, and because he had sworn a blood-oath to protect him with his own life, his master took comfort and believed him.

But just as the emissary had been charged with delivering a message, his guard had sworn another blood-oath to the emperor and was charged to return with the reply at all costs. And tending his master would slow him.

Faced with breaking one oath or both, he steeled himself to break the word given to the lesser authority, and did him the kindness.

He did it while the wounded man slept because he had liked him greatly and wanted him to go easy. But still, he left his body with the others in the well.

He meant no disrespect and told himself the emissary would have understood that he had had to break the lesser oath in order to be true to the greater. He also hoped he would have approved of the fact that in death he was doing a last service to his own master.

If his horse had not stumbled on a drift of shale and broken its leg as it threw him on to the ground, he might have made it.

He gave it the kindness as fast as he could, but though it swung sweetly his axe sang a jarringly wrong note as it hit the stones beneath and chipped the blade. He took that as more of an ill omen than the fallen horse.

He scowled, shouldered the last half-empty waterskin and limped his way north, trying not to think that his bad luck was punishment for a broken oath.

They found him two days later because the birds had started to wheel above where he lay. By this time, he was close to death and run so mad with thirst that his mind was already halfway out of his body and so close to the cold seas of his heart's home that he *kept mistaking the vultures wheeling overhead for the remembered ravens of his happier life. When he first saw the men who found him, he thought he recognised some of those he'd left in the wells, and he understood in a blurred moment of relative clarity that he was stuck between the worlds of the living and the dead. He even glimpsed the familiar face of his master at the back of the angry crowd before the light slipped through his fingers and he plummeted into the welcoming dark of unconsciousness.*

The men who find him did not give him the kindness.

They gave him water.

Part 1

FIRST LAND

There is one knows not what sweet mystery about this sea, whose gently awful stirrings seem to speak of some hidden soul beneath.

HERMAN MELVILLE

Chapter 1

Islander

A pair of ravens ride the brightness on the thin morning breeze above the islands, wheeling high on the updraught as the wind makes first landfall since sweeping off the barren rocks of Labrador more than two thousand cold sea-miles to the west.

From this height, the main island makes a shape like a hogtied bullock lying on its side, neck stretched for the knife as its mouth gapes wide in a final bellow of protest. The rocky tangle of the skerries to the south looks like a flying gargoyle snapping at the rearmost hoof of the doomed animal.

The island is not big and lacks the mountainous majesty of its wilder Hebridean siblings to the north. The two low humps of land don't quite amount to eight miles nose to tail and barely two miles at the widest point, and the tallest hill only squeaks above four hundred feet if measured to the top of the deep heather covering it. It is, however, both first and last land, a barrier island standing guard with its face set to the North Atlantic and its back to the Highlands of Argyll thirty-five ferry-linked miles away.

The birds spot movement in the water and arc across the

ridge of higher ground towards it in case it means food. As scavengers and klepto-parasites, the carrion birds aren't fussy about where the next meal comes from.

Something red and white and splashy is disturbing the gunmetal deckle of the inshore waves in a westward bay to the head of the main island, where a long curve of shell-sand makes the back of the bullock's neck. The beach is deserted.

The ravens dip a wing and swoop lower still.

The red is a buoy, one of two at either side of the bay, and the splash is a swimmer, a lone figure in a wetsuit who jack-knifes into a slow and very controlled duck-dive. The ravens see the long black swim-fins break water and wave a brief farewell in the air, just like a whale sounding, and then the swimmer is gone.

Sig is unaware of the ravens above her as she kicks slowly but determinedly away from the light, head down as she matches the angle of the line tethering the buoy to the unseen lobster pot far below. The pot is beyond her reach on the one lungful of air that is all the life she carries with her, but that's not why she does this.

She's not swimming towards something. Freediving without oxygen tanks is a thing she does for its own sake. It's the closest she gets to a small escape, one she can live with, a way she can find a place where the constant pain in her broken body goes away for a while. More than that, in freediving like this Sig finds – for a minute or two – not just the purity of the practice itself but the end of magical thinking, the death of extraneous thought and a place where the past is finally, mercifully silent. And of course the small escape carries with it the possibility of the larger one if she should lose focus. That's what gives it the hard straight edge, like the bone-chilling cold in the water around her: in the freedive, nothing matters but the present and the exercise of the rigorous self-discipline needed not to drown in it.

She fins calmly downwards with slow, stiff-legged kicks for the first ten metres as the buoyancy of air-filled lungs pulls her body in the opposite direction, back up towards the surface. At the ten-metre mark, the all-round pressure of the water is twice what it was at the surface, and her lungs are now half the size they were. She has trained for this and can read the signals her body is sending her, which calms her enough to no longer feel the panic she once did when the physics change abruptly as she hits twelve metres, as the buoyancy that's been pulling her upwards back to safety disappears and the sea begins to pull her in the opposite direction. She has come to think of this as the invisible trapdoor to the deep: she stops finning and puts her arms at her sides like a skydiver, letting gravity pull her downwards.

For the next ten metres, she glides deeper into the gloom, feeling a great calmness as she becomes one with the liquid world all around her. And although she is alone, she does not feel lonely, not in the way she has grown used to in what she thinks of as her land-mammal life. Here she feels more and more like a sea creature the further down into the comforting squeeze of the water column she goes. A solitary sea creature, alone, but – here, at least – comfortingly and correctly alone. It's like meditation for her, this daily practice. And where some meditate to achieve an inner quiet, Sig does it to hear herself. It is here, away from the world, doing this one hidden thing with no one else to rely on, that the chatter disappears and she is able to remember the one voice she misses. Time has worn away the precise memories of other voices she's lost – her sister's, for example. Down here, alone in the dark, she's fallen into the habit of giving herself the necessary calming reminders in that other lost but not forgotten voice.

At thirty metres, there is a red tag on the line and the pressure is triple that of the surface, and the only sound in what is now the last quiet place in the world is her heart beating about once every three seconds as it slows to half her normal resting rate.

Below the red tags are four more white tags spaced a metre apart, and then another red tag. They're depth markers. Once there were more, all the way up to the ten-metre mark. She has slowly built her capacity over the months by snatching them off the rope one by one, going deeper and deeper as her resilience increased.

This is where she feels the urge to push on and see how much further she can go. To reach the next red tag, deeper than she's ever been.

NO. ENOUGH. NOT TODAY.

The moment she feels that urge, her discipline kicks in hard and she imagines the voice telling herself to turn head to tail. She begins finning again, this time steadily heading upwards towards the light, fighting the impulse to kick frantically as she moderates the oxygen burn to make the most of what's still usable in her lungs. She has to get back through that trapdoor. The screaming ache in her lungs at this stage used to scare her, but now it's an old friend, a way-station on her return to the surface and the waiting air. She knows that for one more day she has managed not to push it further than her own self-defined safety boundaries, and she smiles as she rises unhurriedly towards the waiting buoy overhead. This was the right decision for today. Maybe in a couple of days she'll push it deeper. Today she has a promise to keep. Today isn't the day to flirt with checking out.

SMILE.

Smiling is also something she has disciplined herself to do. It no longer comes as naturally as it once did. She believes the positive feedback of the physical act of smiling calms both the mind and the body and goes some way to muting the pulmonary alarm bells that are now jangling with an ever-growing insistence.

The ravens look down on Sig as she breaks water and clips herself on to the red ball bobbing in the light chop, regaining her breath: she's too big for prey, too small to be a fishing boat with the chance of scraps tossed over the side that might drift in and land where the ravens might hop from rock to rock and pluck them from the salt water.

They're about to move on when they see dark shapes in the depths below her, submarine shadows that lazily swim towards Sig on a converging angle. There are three of them and even the smallest is easily four times as long as the swimmer, who hangs there steadily getting her breath back, normalising her breathing as she floats by the buoy, unaware.

The ravens wait.

Maybe there will be breakfast to be picked off the water's edge after all.

Below the birds, Sig rolls on to her back, her face a white flash in the black neoprene hood.

She sees the ravens hanging in the vault of air above her, a pair of ragged black crosses beneath a lead-lined sky, black feathers whiffling untidily in the wind like battle-torn pennants.

She watches them as she waits. Only when she is sure she is safely re-oxygenated and her pulse is respectable again does she trust herself to unclip and start to swim the home-stretch of her daily routine. She keeps her eyes fixed on them as she arches her spine and stretches out into a regular backstroke, arms reaching far into the wavelets ahead and then pulling deep scallops of water as her legs churn like a machine, powering her towards the other buoy at the north end of the bay.

Her heart's pumping normally again, and the water is no colder than it was yesterday. That's not why she shivers.

The familiar ravens look ominous and unchancy today. And because it's early and she's alone and over deep water, even Sig – who has spent a lifetime honing her mind to be as perfectly rational a tool as humanly possible – has to remind herself she isn't superstitious, that she can't afford to be, and concentrates on something she can control, like counting strokes and not getting cramp and above all not wondering what she looks like from the birds' viewpoint or – worse – to anything watching her from the unknown depths below.

She doesn't see the change in the water surface thirty yards to her right, the upward bulge in the sea travelling towards her. She doesn't see anything until she finishes her set of one hundred backstrokes and rolls into position for the front-crawl.

Then she sees them.

The shock hits her with a sledgehammer of adrenaline, spiking her heart rate and stopping her breathing in the same moment.

She abruptly stops swimming and hangs there, unmoving.

Dead in the water.

Chapter 2

MacBrayne's ferry

The MV *Isle of Mull* is built to carry seventy cars and up to nine hundred and sixty-eight passengers at full capacity, with a crew of twenty-eight. This deep into the off-season there are five vehicles in the car hold, and even though the crew is a couple of men light, it still outnumbers the passengers roughly three to one.

Within a year of being built, the *Isle of Mull* was found to have a significant deadweight problem which made her lumpy and querulous in challenging sea conditions. She was taken back into dry dock and sliced in half just in front of her funnel so that twenty feet of new hull could be welded in, which cured her weight issue and even sped her up a bit. Unfortunately, she then had a major collision with her sister vessel the *Lord of the Isles*, which resulted in extensive repairs to her bows. Somewhere between the teething troubles and the collision, she gained a slight and ongoing list to port, the maritime equivalent of a limp.

She isn't a lucky ship.

Tom Goodge knows all this because he's reading it off the internet via his smartphone as he waits for the handful of passengers ahead of him to get their food from the ferry's cafeteria. It's a distraction both from the noise of the crying baby and the dagger-like looks his exhausted stepmum keeps throwing his way as she argues with his dad about something he or Tom – or possibly both of them – have done wrong again. Reading about the boat's as good a way of keeping his head down and not getting pulled into their drama as anything else Tom can manage right now, but he's doing it in the sure and certain knowledge that she's going to lash out and hook him in if she can.

The line shuffles forward. Tom, who has grown four inches since he turned thirteen less than a year ago, is always hungry these days. The hot breakfast choices behind the Perspex sneeze-guard take his attention away from his phone, and he begins to plan his selection, hoping his dad and stepmother don't take the final rashers of bacon.

They go for eggs on toast and slide their tray towards the till. Tom steps up to the rail. The girl in the paper cap behind the heat lamps has a nametag that reads Agnieszka. She smiles at him and gives him the last of the bacon.

Behind Tom, Kevo Byres catches sight of himself in the glass covering the menu sheet. He doesn't read it. He's not interested in things like that. Writing and shit. He studies himself instead. He guesses he looks okay. He smiles, then closes his mouth. Fuck it. If he doesn't smile too much when they meet, Shanna probably won't notice the missing tooth anyway. Apart from that, he reckons he's looking pretty good. Better than before he went away, really. He's muscled up a little and doesn't blink so much.

He didn't know he blinked a lot until she told him. He certainly didn't think his eyes fluttered when he was angry. Fluttering your eyes sounds like something a fucking doll does. Something weak. And he's not weak. If he was weak, she'd not have waited to tell him about the blinking and the fluttering until there was armoured glass between them, that's for sure. Anyway, forgive and forget. That's done. New days now. He's worked on it. Long hours after lock-in with nothing else to do anyway, practising not blinking till his eyes burned, feeling the pain and doing it anyway, a head game, still point of the turning world, eye of the tiger, the thousand-yard stare – pure dead fucking zen, man. He'd like to check out his hair, but he's planned this trip carefully, and the plan involves not taking his hoodie down in case it goes bad when he gets to the island.

It won't go bad, but just in case.

He's keeping it simple. Things don't go wrong when he keeps things simple. Things go wrong for Kevo when they get complicated. He's not going to let things get complicated any more, and so everything will get better. That's what he's learned. It's all broken down into steps. Not easy ones, but simple ones. Keep it stupid, simple. Or whatever. He kens fine what he means. He's made a promise. He's not going to do what he did any more.

He turns the Stanley knife in his pocket, enjoying the rough criss-cross of the chequered grip against his fingertips. It calms him.

The smell of boiled vegetables, stewed coffee and fried food isn't great, especially since the whole bouquet is finished off with a piney chemical top-note from the spray used to wipe down the tables between sailings, but he hasn't eaten since dinner twelve hours ago and the truth is he's spent so much time eating in a locked-down unit that despite his better judgement his subconscious recognises the bouquet of insti-tutional cooking and is barking like Pavlov's dog.

The kid ahead moves forward to the till to pay with his parents. Dad's a sad-looking bloke with a nervy-looking wife who clearly wears the pants. Kevo's dad wouldn't have let himself be talked to like that in public. Mind, Kevo's dad wouldn't have paid for Kevo's breakfast, so the moody-looking kid should get a fucking smile on, he reckons.

The doll behind the food troughs asks Kevo what he wants. Sounds German, maybe Polish.

"All day breakfast," he grunts.

"No more bacon," she says. "Sorry."

She smiles at him and says he can have extra square sausage instead. Kevo doesn't know what she's being so cheerful about. It's a fucking canteen. He's not going to tip the fuckin' Heidi for pretending to be nice.

He looks down at the industrial bangers and the dried-out rectangles of pink processed meat.

"Aye," he says, remembering not to smile. "Whatever."

Chapter 3

Cetorhinus Maximus

Sig sees the shark fins break water on the seaward side of her. On reflex, she kills the music in her headphones, wanting to have all her senses alert and on point. The fight-or-flight reflex hardwired into the oldest, reptilian part of her brain kicks in and tells her to start moving again, thrashing her way to the shore as fast as she can. But she hears a flap and splash behind her and turns to see another huge fin between her and the safety of dry land. The fin juts a metre and a half out of the water, sharply angled backwards, the narrow point of an obtuse triangle. It appears to be following the blunter fin of a smaller shark, cutting a lazy circle around her.

She calms her breathing, using the same discipline she has learned to rely on whilst freediving, and makes the rational part of her brain override the reptilian: the two fins are actually one large fish, a dorsal and a tail fin. She's swimming with basking sharks, *Cetorhinus Maximus*, emphasis on the *Maximus*. These supersized creatures are not here to bite a chunk out of her or anything else: they're giant gill feeders, sieving the water for plankton as they swim through the sea with their mouths wide open. Sig is several orders of magnitude larger than a micro-organism, and thus way off their menu. Fish aren't noted for their facial expressiveness, but Sig has always thought of them, with their cavernous gape, pokey bottle-noses and small perma-stunned eyes, as the mouth-breathers of the ocean: large, slow and a bit challenged by complexity. But they are still unquestionably huge, and she doesn't want to get hit by a tail swipe, so she just floats and lets them complete a lazy circuit of the bay. She's never seen them this far in and is surprised that they weren't put off by the sound of her energetic crawl, but then she has seen them close enough to touch from the safety of a boat with a heavy diesel chuntering away, so maybe they're so big they just don't care. The days are gone when they were hunted in these waters for their disproportionately large livers and the oil they provided, and there's nothing else large or dangerous enough to predate on them here.

By now, Sig has stilled the hissing danger signals from the old back-brain and lets herself be in the moment. This is her sea as much as theirs. She's a strong swimmer, graceful and powerful as she cuts a straight line across the water – it's only on dry land that she's awkward and shoogle-footed.

She's well aware that solo freediving is a dangerously bad habit, but she's addicted to it. It calms her mind and for a paradoxical moment takes her out of herself by having nothing to concentrate on but being calm enough not to breathe. There's nothing else that does that for her these days, and she's tried all the alternatives, some to excess. But these basking sharks offer a different kind of calm. Swimming this close to such extraordinary creatures is a privilege, and she'd be a fool not to be in this, of all moments, and just enjoy it.

The ravens are not the only witnesses to this encounter. Lying in the heather on the slope above the beach there is a third pair of watching eyes. Walter John Stroyan – birdwatcher, widower, holder of guilty secrets – has also forgotten to breathe. He thought about standing and shouting a warning to the swimming girl the moment he saw the first fin break surface, but he knew it would do no good, that he was too far away and that she wouldn't hear him anyway. She swims with earphones in, he knows that. He knows the red Zippo-sized lump clipped to the backstrap of her swimming goggles is a waterproof iPod. Walter John knows all about Sig and her habits. He is as regular as she, every morning taking up his position on the hill, unseen, just before she bumps down the track in her old pale blue Land Rover Defender and locks her dog in as she takes the metal brace off her leg and limps down to the water. Her movements are lopsided and awkward until she starts to swim, when she is lithe and powerful and – to Walter John – irresistibly addictive.

From the very start, he realised her dog knew he was there. Maybe it sensed him, maybe it smelled Milly. Milly was calm for a spaniel, getting too old to be frisky but robust enough for a morning walk each day. And well-trained. His wife had seen to that. Milly sat patiently beside him in the heather, not straining at the lead in the way a more excitable dog might.

The dog in the Defender barked at them through the slit of window she left open for ventilation. After the first few days it stopped, but any time he drags his eyes from the slender figure of the girl and checks the vehicle, he can always see the silhouette of the dog standing with its paws on the dashboard, staring in his direction, one ear up, one ear down, which is its permanent state. It's a fell terrier, long legged, black and tan like an Airedale, with the same broken coat but without the overly blocky nose. He knows it's called Rex because he's heard her call to it. He also knows he's safe from the dog as she locks it in because there's a protected family of otters that

19

breed here, and the dog will fight them – or anything else, for that matter – given half a chance. It's the same reason he keeps his sweet Milly on a lead. Just in case.

The otters also protect Walter John and his covert watching habit. The high-powered binoculars which go everywhere with him are for them. Not the girl. Not Sig. He's not pervy, a word he heard on the TV. He's not even very lonely. After all, he has Milly. She's the sweetest-natured thing, docile, obedient and always looking at him with a panting smile. So he's not friendless at all, really. He just likes watching. Watching the island and the things on it. And of all the things on it, Sig just happens to be the one by which he's most fascinated. He came for the otters and found her by mistake. She's the standout, the anomaly – the black swan. And like a swan, he senses that her poise is achieved only because beneath the surface things are churning away. Her muscular legs, her long arms, the glistening wetsuit . . . maybe he is getting a little pervy, he thinks. Maybe he should just talk to her. Maybe this is how old men go pervy, telling themselves they aren't. Maybe he needs to take the lid off this and let some normal air in.

Now Rex is barking again.

The terrier has seen the sharks and is going berserk, scratching and scrabbling at the door and bouncing off the windows in a furious attempt to get free and out there.

In objective time, the sharks patrol the bay around her for maybe ten minutes; but here, down at sea level with her eyes stuck at wave-height, it feels like hours. Sig has noticed this about the way adrenaline works – on her, at least: subjective time seems to go much slower. She knows that it's a function of the way the stress acts on the two sides of the autonomic nervous system, that bit of you that takes care of the body's unconscious actions, the friendly autopilot operating quietly in the background. There's the parasympathetic part that works with functions that don't need immediate actions – things like sex, digestion and defecating. She thinks of it as the chill side. The other, sympathetic, part is the distinctly un-chill part of the system that deals with hot functions that require quick responses. When the fight-or-flight reflex is triggered, the hypothalamus chokes off all parasympathetic activity like an emergency cut-off valve and allows the sympathetic system to flood all available channels. She knows her adrenal medulla has released a massive bolus of norepinephrine and adrenaline into her system, and until it's flushed out again time slows for her, because her muscles and mind are primed to work faster and stronger than normal. She knows all this in precise medical detail because it's the same battle-ground on which she chooses to fight every time she breathes up before freediving. Swimming keeps her fit and uses up enough energy to make sure her mind has a fighting chance of a good night's sleep and some peace at the end of the day, but freediving has made her an expert in reading her body.

The time, real and perceived, passes and the sharks bask off into the distance. She watches them dwindle away into the choppier waters beyond the bay and feels a pang of sadness. Floating amongst them was a rare moment out of time, something to be cherished because it is unlikely to happen again. She shivers and realises the adrenaline has now flushed from her system, and her body is allowing itself to notice that it's been in the water long enough to be getting really cold.

She looks at the buoy ahead of her. Normally she'd touch it and turn, or on a day when she felt like switching things up she'd dive at that buoy instead. She'd hang there, holding on, getting her breath sorted and calm enough to see how far she could dive on one breath today, before frightening herself with her guilty habit. And, as if to emphasise this, a red fishing boat noses round the headland. Two thoughts arrive simultaneously: she thinks that its motor might be the thing that made the sharks move on, and she knows that the unseen man in the boat is watching her. She has no real reason to feel guilty, yet she does. It makes her angry enough to resist the urge to turn from the buoy without touching it and plough a blisteringly fast furrow back towards the distant shore. Instead, she ploughs a defiant sprint towards it which warms her up a little. Once she reaches it, she grips the tether and hangs on to get her breath.

It's her damn buoy anyway. She's nothing to feel guilty about.

Matt McWhinnie is peeling an apple with the razor-sharp fisherman's knife that lives in his back pocket and scowling into the screen of the brand-new Raymarine sonar fish finder that he spent most of Sunday adding to the red-hulled fishing boat that is his pride, joy and principal source of livelihood, the *An da Shealladh*. The scowl is not a normal look for him. His is a face made to smile, and though still on the younger side of forty, his eyes have deep laugh crinkles weather-beaten into their sides. The fish finder is meant to sound an alert as well as show any clouds of fish ahead of the boat, but it doesn't seem to be working. At first, he automatically assumed the problem was his hearing aids – which he's worn since childhood – but he'd checked the batteries and they're fine. He's in a T-shirt despite the fresh breeze, revealing a wide-shouldered swimmer's body and a single tattoo on each arm, a fantastical bloated fish on one, and a stylised man in a flat cap and vest with his fists up on the other. Any Glaswegian would recognise the line drawings as having been copied from the mural at Hillhead station. In the mural, the flat-capped scrapper is titled "Bonny Fighter". The bloater is titled "Queer Fish".

Matt does not have the titles tattooed on to his arms. He just likes the images because he likes the work of the artist who made them. Anyway, the fighter's pretty self-explanatory and the other arm's an in-joke for those who might get it.

It's not meant to be in your face.

Matt's sense of humour extends to the name of his boat. *An da shealladh* means "second sight" – the name's written on the back, in big white letters flanked by line drawings of two hands, each holding two fingers up, one hand facing out, one facing in. Tourists think the two fingers are some kind of roguish "F— you" to the world. People born deaf like Matt note the little motion marks and realise it's the boat's name in sign language. When asked why he'd chosen that particular name, he always said it was because he was fed up with folk endlessly asking him if it was true his family really did have, as rumoured over many generations, the uncanny ability to see things in the future. Some of the older people even used to whisper that the recessive deafness that occurred in his family line, sometimes skipping a generation, was a cosmic balancing for the mystic gift, as if being able to see further into the future had to be offset by the loss of another sense.

The question about his family's supposed fey powers dogged him through his childhood and beyond, following him from schoolyard to the back-bar of the pub, and it irked him. So now, if people ask if he has the second sight, he just says yes and then points to the boat. It's a distraction and it defuses the question. That way, he doesn't have to tell them it doesn't work like that. If that doesn't satisfy them, he tells them that the old stories about his family are just that: stories.

He doesn't tell them that, like all the best stories, there's more to them than it might seem at first glance – that deeper truths often wear the mask of fiction.

He woke up with a bad feeling this morning, which is the

way it does work: it doesn't happen a lot, but when it does it always feels like a deep and dispiriting shadow being dragged across the day ahead. Often, it's a mirage that usually disappears after the first cup of coffee. And even if a bad thing does happen, the uncaffeinated premonitions almost always end up having rational explanations. He makes a point of searching them out when they are as strong as this one and has decided it's probably because he subconsciously knows he's botched something with the new transponder he carefully spent Sunday fixing to the hull of the newly painted boat, because it's currently sending the Raymarine only intermittently clear pictures of any fish moving ahead of him. Nothing fey about that. Part of him thinks he's messed with the boat's luck by painting it red, but he likes the bright splash it makes on the grey seas, and the old white and yellow paint job that his grandparents and parents had favoured before the boat was his had been long overdue for improvement.

He looks up and registers movement in the bay to his right. He watches for a long beat, ambushed by the suddenly intensifying sick feeling falling between him and the bright red of the distant buoy and the figure in the water. Sometimes – the happily few but very bad times – that sense of shadow is so tangible it's like a physical thing, not just a sensation in his mind. Right now, it's so strong that he can almost see the gloom like a rain squall passing across the sea between them.

Sigrid.

Her solo freediving is deeply selfish bullshit in his book, and he doesn't need any ESP to know that there is a nontrivial likelihood that one day he or someone else will be pulling her body from the water. He also knows he has no right to stop her freediving alone. It's actually technically her lobster pot the buoy marks, even though it's he who checks it and keeps tally of what she is owed when he sells the lobsters on. She's never shown an interest in taking on the fishing side of her husband's affairs. And she's never even cashed one of the carefully totalled cheques he leaves in her post-box every three months.

He's told her what he thinks, in language blunt as hers. The most forgivable thing he remembers saying is that her claim of finding peace in the world by literally dropping out of it was a lunatic contradiction in terms. It's not an argument she was a bit interested in then, and now – given the less forgivable things he said to her – it's one that they're unlikely to continue with since they don't talk any more.

No, solo freediving is in his – and any sane person's – mind nothing more than slow-motion suicide. With a side order of Russian roulette. It's only a matter of time.

It shouldn't make him angry. He shouldn't care. But that bad feeling he woke up with is hanging in his head like a dark cloud, squid-inking his day.

He snaps his knife shut, sticks it back in his pocket, takes a bite out of the apple, and spins the wheel and heads for the girl on the buoy.

Chapter 4

I got a feeling

The coffee is as criminal as Sally Goodge thought it would be, but the months of broken nights she's spent resenting getting up to feed the baby and then feeling guilty about it have exhausted and reduced her to a state where she'll take the acrid burn of stale, over-roasted beans like it's a punishment she deserves. If she just thinks of it like medicine instead of a scalding beverage, it's not so bad. And if she stays as she is – wedged in leaning against the wall between the bolted-down cafeteria seat and the equally immoveable tabletop – maybe her throbbing head won't roll off. Lack of sleep always gives her headaches and though her husband has tried to reassure her that they're not actual migraines, she's pretty sure they are. And if they're not, then they're head-splitting enough to do until one comes along, however much of a medic he might be.

If she wasn't scared of waking the baby currently sleeping fitfully in the papoose wrap strapped across her chest, she might move to the softer seating in one of the lounges because the two Telco engineers sitting kitty-corner to her two tables away are clearly scoping her out. She knows they're

Telco engineers because their matching red parkas have HIGHLAND TELCO emblazoned across their backs in a lime green typeface that's making her eyes strobe. And she knows they're scoping her out because, well, they're guys, and even hungover like a half-dead dog she's self-aware enough to know that she's worth a look.

Her phone jolts into the first bouncing chords of a ten-year-old banger from her school days – an old in-joke ringtone she keeps meaning to change, not least because she shouldn't be thinking of the ex who programmed it as his personal sound, let alone pick up the call knowing he's on the other end of it. She kills the Black-Eyed Peas and slides an earbud into her ear. Stupid, she tells herself.

"What?" she says, eyes scanning the room around her to make sure it's free of husbands and stepsons.

The display says UNKNOWN NUMBER, which is what she programmed it to read. She's stupid, but not that stupid.

"Hey Sal," he says. "How's Jock-land?"

His easy drawl pours into her ear like honey. Worse than that, it pours like he knows it's honey and he's sure it still works.

"We said no more contact," she says quietly.

"I know," he says. "I know. But I just wanted to make sure you're okay up there North of the Wall. You know – wildlings, White Walkers. Anything could happen ... "

"Joe," she says. "We said we weren't going to do this."

"I know," he says.

Silence hangs between them for a long beat.

"But you picked up," he says.

The baby stirs against her chest, grizzling a little as it pushes itself away from her and then relaxes and goes back to sleep.

"I'm hanging up," she says. "We agreed."

He doesn't say anything.

"It's not fair," she says. "We don't want this. I don't want this."

"So hang up," he says, voice easy.

She listens to the silence again. She doesn't hang up. No harm if they say nothing. If she's very still, she can believe she hears him breathing gently in her ear.

"Come on," she says, hating the fact she can hear her voice thickening as she lowers it. "This isn't—"

The silence cut and went fuzzy.

"Joe?" she says, heart lurching treacherously. "Joe—?"

"Coverage," says a voice behind her. One of the Telco engineers is grinning at her. His beard is out of control. What it lacks in grooming it makes up for as a crumb-catcher. It's like he's wearing half his crusty bacon roll around his face. His pal swivels in his seat and joins in. Clean shaven. Blue eyes, black hair – shockingly good-looking, in fact – reminds her of that actor Cillian something in the TV show about old-time Brummie gangsters.

"Too far from mainland. You'll not get a signal now, I'm afraid," he says with a smile, almost apologetic. Like it's his fault and he wishes he could make it better. Damn, those eyes are something.

"In a dead zone," says Shaggy Beard. "Surprised you got a signal this far out, in point of fact."

"Right," she says. "Thanks."

"Hope it wasn't anything too important," says not-Cillian. His grin is a challenge. He doesn't give a monkey's about whether it was important. He just wants to chat her up. She's met guys like him. They flirt just to keep their hand in. It's not serious, until it is. They're trouble. She knows the type. Sees it in the mirror every morning.

"No," she says, nodding, wanting to be out of this conversation. "It's cool."

"Won't get coverage until we're about half a mile out from the island," says Shaggy. "Be different next week, though; we're on the way to upgrade the exchange box there."

"Right," she says again. This is not information she needs to know.

"You're not local," says not-Cillian. "On your holidays?"

"No," she says.

"I'm Jamie," says once-not-Cillian-but-now-Jamie. "This is Malc. Can I get you another coffee?"

He's flirty.

"No thanks," she says, giving an eye for an eye as she stands, ignoring the pulse of pain in her head as nicotine deprivation adds its own special sauce to her overall exhaustion. She really needs to find somewhere to have an illicit cigarette before she kills someone.

She isn't flirtable. Not by a phone engineer, at any rate.

Jamie watches her go.

Malc watches Jamie.

"She's got a new baby strapped across her, for Christ's sake," he says.

"Yummy mummies?" grins Jamie. "You'd be surprised."

Chapter 5

The girl on the buoy

Matt keeps his eyes on Sig's head, slick as a seal in the neoprene hood bobbing alongside the corroded red buoy.

"You okay?" he shouts, throttling down the engine and letting it chunter quietly as he keeps the boat as steady as he can against the inexorable push of the tide.

Sig stares back up at him, holding on to the buoy.

"Nothing to worry about," she shouts.

Matt nods. Takes a beat. Like he's not going to say it this time. Then he shakes his head.

"You can't keep doing that."

She feels her chin come up in defiance. Something about him has always made her push back, though that pushing back is not what has led to the gulf that now lies between them.

"No law against it," she says.

"Common sense is a law, Sig."

He sometimes says things as if they're carved out of stone. From her own childhood she recognises it as a farmer's trait as much as a fisherman's, seeing the world as a series of great simplicities – the weather, the soil, the sea. Matt was more sophisticated than that, she knew. Maybe because he grew up having to compensate for his deafness by picking up on other cues, he was more attuned to greater complexity in the wider world than most, yet out on the water – and, in the past, around her kitchen table – he retreated behind this barrier of stark and over-simple certainty, from behind which he would fire terse utterances like the one he'd just shouted across the water at her.

"It's not," she shouts back.

"Darwin's Law," he says.

"That's not a thing, Matt," she says. "It's really not."

She's beginning to feel the cold now. Her hands are going numb, clutching the buoy rope while the rest of her stays still, leaching warmth into the sea around her. She should get moving.

He keeps staring at her, even as he ducks his head into the wind shadow of his coat, held wide to protect the flame from his zippo as he sparks up the rollie. He sucks in a lungful and slowly lets the smoke out into the freshening breeze.

"There are cleaner ways to top yourself," he says, his voice closer to a growl than a shout.

"Name one," she says. Sometimes the urge to break that barrier leads her to poke at him in a kind of defiance.

He spits a shred of tobacco off his lip and shakes his head.

"I don't want to argue," he says, voice almost lost in the wind.

"But you came over," she says. "But you turned the boat around and came over."

Matt nods. Like she made a fair point. Like they could be having a reasonable conversation. As if they could ever talk normally with one another now.

"He wouldn't want you doing this," he says.

And there it is. The first low blow.

"I'm not," she says.

"I'm not a fucking idiot, Sig," he says. "I looked it up on the internet. I know you're breaking all the rules here."

"I am not committing suicide," she says.

"Freediving without a buddy? Without a team? No one does that."

She's suddenly very exhausted by all this. It could be the cold, or it could be this ground they are going over again. Or it could be he's making her feel guilty about the only thing that seems to centre her these days, something that's only her concern now, and this pisses her off despite knowing he means well.

"I'm in control," she says. "You don't have to keep nagging me."

"You're in control until you're not," he says. "I know you: when you run, you always want to improve your time, when you climb you want to go higher and harder. So what are the chances that you, being you, are not pushing yourself to go just that wee bit deeper every time you do this?"

He raises an eyebrow as he stares her down.

"Ran," she says. "And climbed. As in, past tense. This is what I do now, Matt. What I can do. And I really, really don't want to feel bad about it."

"And I really, really don't want to be the one to find you fouling my nets one fine morning," he says. "Plus, my gran wants an eye kept on you."

Playing the Kathleen card is the second low blow.

"I'm getting cold," Sig says. "We done?"

He should stop now, he thinks.

"Angus and Seona told me," he says. "You didn't sign the papers."

"That's your business, is it?" she says.

"You should have," he says.

"Don't want to be a guardian," she says.

"Or an aunt," he says.

"I'm only her aunt on paper," she says.

"And it only kicks in if Seona and Angus die before she's an adult," he says. "Fuck's sake, Sig! They're healthy. She'll be way past grown up by the time they toddle off. It's nothing. Just words on paper that'll make them feel a bit easier . . ."

"Why don't you do it?" she says.

"Wasn't asked and I'm not kin," he says. He points at the buoy. "Is it because of this?"

"Don't know what you mean," she says.

"You thinking of toddling off yourself?" he says.

"Her grandparents understood," she says. "It's all good between us. I'm looking after her while they go to the Modh. No bad blood. Don't stir."

"No," he says. "They just said they understood because they're nice folk and didn't want to make you feel bad. They're kind. Like—"

He bites off the rest of the sentence and looks away. She stares at the back of his head.

"Like who?" she says. The shiver in her voice is just the cold water. She needs to move.

"Like you, Sig," he says, looking back down at her. "Like you used to be."

And suddenly she's had enough. She lets go of the buoy.

"Good luck with the fishing."

She hits play on her iPod and pulls the goggles back over her eyes as she turns and ploughs back towards the beach. Matt watches her for a few moments, then spins the dog-end of his cigarette out over the water and turns back to the Raymarine.

Sig hears the change in the note of the engine as the *An da Shealladh* turns away and moves out to sea. She stops and takes a half-minute breather on her back, watching Matt follow the sharks. She feels relieved. As if it's really any of his business what she does. She doesn't mind the nagging itself. She's pretty numb to most things these days – sadness is its own kind of armour. What she minds is the intimacy the nagging implies. Maybe because that intimacy reminds her too painfully of what brought them together and the unfillable hole that now exists where it once was.

She knows Matt sees things differently, because if he saw it her way he'd not be worried about her freediving. She doesn't have the energy to argue with him any more, partly because too much has already been said and partly because he's stubborn and contrary and – in his own way – frustratingly unfathomable.

She rolls forward and begins to crawl the last hundred metres to the beach, trying to clear her head and get back to the happier headspace she'd been in with the sharks. Before Matt interfered. Before he put words to the thing behind the thing she's doing every time she pushes herself a little further down that rope. It's her business and not his. And besides, she tells herself, she didn't do it today, because today she has promised to look after someone else, and even Matt would probably agree she's a woman of her word.

If only he hadn't put that other word out into the fresh morning air. If only he'd let her leave the unsaid unvoiced. Because it's not a plan or a firm intent. It really isn't. At best it's just subtext, she thinks.

Chapter 6

Golden girl

Rex stops barking when he sees Sig walking out of the water. This is the moment when she changes, when she goes from sleek sea creature to wonk-kneed land mammal. It is high tide, so the wet hard pack gives way quickly to the drier beach drift beneath her feet, the treacherous soft sand she hates. She concentrates on staying upright as her feet hirple her body towards the Land Rover, one shifting footfall at a time. She's used to the pain in her patched-together knee and the ache of the tendons making up for its reduced mobility, so she doesn't even notice herself grimacing in concentration.

She sees the flash of neon orange off to her left, and her first thought is that this is more of the marine plastic against which she fights a daily one-woman war. Her scowl deepens and she makes a dutiful sideways detour to pick it up. It's the same startling colour as a trawlerman's glove she found half buried in the tideline a couple of months ago and unconsciously she must be expecting another one because she's surprised to find it's a water bottle jutting out of the side-pocket of a small military looking backpack instead. The pack is camouflage patterned – and by the time she gets to it she's decided it's army surplus because no actual soldier would pair it with such a garish water bottle.

She stops and looks round, instinctively looking for an owner, but there's no one in sight, and when she looks back down at her feet, hers are the only footprints in the sand. If someone left it on the beach, they're long gone, because the tide has been in and out since they were here. She reaches down and lifts it. She's not surprised it's soaked. It hangs slackly from her right hand, balancing the fins she's carrying in her left. It's not anywhere near full, but there is stuff in it, heavyish hard-edged shapes clunking in the bottom of the bag.

The harsh *kraa* of a raven makes her look up and see the two birds circling high above her. Just for a moment she's strangely tempted to put the backpack back down and leave it where she found it. Then she suppresses the irrational shiver that grips her and heads for the more friendly noise of Rex's increasingly excited barking. Some tourist has likely left their picnic, she thinks as she limps back to the Land Rover. She'll open the bag later and see if there's any ID or something. Right now, she needs to get out of her cold wetsuit and into something warm. That shiver was a warning. She's been in too long.

Rex leaps up at her and licks her face as she opens the Defender door and begins running tight circles around the vehicle, pausing to cock his leg at intervals, as if guarding the perimeter while she changes.

Walter John Stroyan sees the tense lines on either side of her mouth as she peels off the tight neoprene hood and lets her hair shake free.

Golden girl, he thinks, as he always does. My golden girl.

Though he knows of course that she is not his, the morning intimacy of this one-sided meeting each day is the thin streak of sunlight that gets him through the increasingly grey afternoons of his life. It's an innocent pleasure, one that cost nobody anything, really. It isn't something he needs to feel bad about, but then – if it truly is innocent – why could he not talk about it to anyone? A secret pleasure, but not a forbidden one, surely? Just looking. Looking was no crime.

Peeping, says the voice in the back of his head. Peeping. You're a sad old peeper.

She reaches back and yanks the long pull-tab of the zipper downwards in one smooth movement that splits the black wetsuit and reveals the nakedness beneath, a forbidden glimpse of pale muscled skin that runs thrillingly from the nape of her neck to the muscular cleft at the top of her buttocks. Stroyan inhales sharply and knows this is the moment he should, as he always did, drop the binoculars from his eyes and look away up the beach.

That is his daily sacrifice to whatever gods oversaw the deepening eccentricities of lonely old men. He did not watch her strip. Not ever. He always looked away. He had never seen her naked. Maybe from the corner of his eye he'd seen movement, but he had never looked directly at her as she peeled the suit off as she was now doing, staggering painfully from one foot to the other as she pulls herself out of the synthetic rubber skin. He had never seen her breasts or the taut curve of her stomach, and he certainly hadn't lingered over her legs or the rounded bottom she unconsciously presented to him as she bent and picked up the wetsuit from the ground and tossed it into the back of the Land Rover. He had never done any of that before today because he had sworn to himself that he wouldn't ever do that – it would have been a vile thing to do, a terrible intrusion.

And yet today he watches. Dry mouthed, heart fluttering on the forbidden knife edge between fear and excitement. It must have been the sharks, he thinks. That was what had changed. He had thought she was going to die and had not been able to warn her and now she was not dead and instead was . . . this. Alive. Naked. A woman. Elemental. The thing entire.

He feels a pressure against his fly and realises he is having an erection. The shock of that almost-forgotten stirring breaks the spell and he finally drops the binoculars and looks away, mind thick and woozy with desire.

He doesn't watch as she quickly towels off and then bends again, strapping the metal and Velcro brace around the scars that harrow irregular tracks through the otherwise unblemished smoothness of her right leg. He only looks back at her once he is sure she's cinched the men's 501s tight round her waist and shrugged into the long-sleeved thermal T-shirt that she seems to live in. Only once the temptation is wrapped back up in her strangely androgynous covering does he allow himself to see her again.

But this time she turns and seems to see him.

His heart stops as she pauses, face angled towards the landward side of the bay. He freezes, caught, guilty, not knowing whether to drop into the heather or just do the normal thing and wave a greeting. Waving hello would inoculate him, surely, mark him as the normal man he really was. But would a normal man even have to think about whether to wave? His hand stutters as he begins to raise it, and then the moment is gone, and she turns away to call her dog in as she throws her kit and the salvaged backpack inside and swings up into the Land Rover. Walter John is left in the heather, stuck in an undignified and bungled half-crouch, neither fish nor fowl, not waving but drowning, in his own mind nothing but ridiculous.

He straightens as she efficiently circles the vehicle and bounces up the track away from the bay. Only then does he notice that he'd let go of Milly's lead. He looks around. Sea. Sky. Heather. No dog.

"Bugger," he says. "Fuck."

It's the first time he's used a profanity since he'd buried his wife. Even though it is only his ears that hear it, it suddenly feels like he'd defiled something that should have been clean.

There is scarcely a cloud in the sky, but it feels like an ill omen.

Like he'd called in bad luck.

Chapter 7

Under the funnel

Kevo is stretched out across four seats, dozing and watching the clouds overhead. It's uncomfortable since the seats are hard plastic bucket chairs, but he's used to discomfort and still not really used to the freedom of being outside again, and he likes the fact no one else is out here on the deck. It also makes him invisible to those coming up the steps.

He's jolted out of his doze by the sound of a man's voice, followed by the scuff of feet hurrying up the metal steps behind him.

"Tom . . ."

"Dad, leave me alone. It's fine."

He can see through the gap between the chair backs that it's the kid from the line at the food counter, the one with the not-so-happy family and the little baby. He hunches over the railing, looking out over the sea, his back to Kevo.

"I was just saying that wasn't kind."

The man's voice again. On second hearing, it's not just English – which reminds him of his parole officer – but it's got a kind of disappointed whine in it, the sort of thing that, if he let it, might set Kevo's teeth on edge. He's met a few screws who had that passive-aggressive schtick down pat. Kind of guys who figured it was easier to act disappointed than come right out and say what needed to be said. Kevo preferred the ones who were just aggressive: with them, you knew where you stood.

"I am not her childminder."

The kid's feisty, though. Through the gap in the seats, he sees the man come and stand next to him at the rail. Kevo sees what the boy does not – that the man raises a hand to touch his back and then thinks better of it and takes it away.

"Tom . . . Ruby is your sister."

The kid's back is humped in such a clear show of resentment that he really doesn't need to say anything to make his position clear.

"Half-sister," he says. "Half-sister. At best."

Beat of silence as the dad takes this in.

"What do you mean 'at best'?" he says carefully. The kid shrugs.

"Doesn't matter."

"Tommy. Mattered enough for you to say it . . ."

Tommy. Something defeated in the way he says it almost makes Kevo feel sorry for the kid.

"Dad," the kid says, a different kind of weariness in his voice. "I'm happy you're happy."

"No, you aren't," the dad says. "If you were, you would be more . . ."

"More what?" Tom says. His father shrugs.

Kevo is kinda regretting he hadn't sat up and made his presence known when they first arrived. He doesn't want to be caught eavesdropping like this. Other people's problems? He has his own shit to fry.

"You know . . ." says the father.

"Helpful?" Tom shoots back.

41

"No. Cheerful. I was going to say cheerful."

The boy sighs and shakes his head.

"I said I'd come. I'm here. I didn't actually say I'd be cheerful."

Kevo sees the guy rake his fingers through his hair.

"Now you sound like a child," he says.

"I am a child," he snorts. "Your child. Not her childminder."

They both watch some sea froth past the side hull below them.

"Maybe you shouldn't have come," the dad says.

"Maybe."

Passive-Aggressive Dad sighs and goes all whipped-puppy on him, voice lowered in defeat.

"I thought this would be good."

The boy doesn't go for the bait. He just grunts and lets him twist in the wind. Dad sighs some more.

"Well, I don't really know why you came if you're going to be like this."

"Mum asked me to."

The dad's head comes up in surprise.

"Your mother?"

The kid turns. Kevo can't see more than his shoulder and the edge of his face as he confronts his father.

"Yeah, Dad. She's a nice woman, remember?"

"Tommy," the dad says, but his kid rolls right on over him.

"And she's feeling pretty crappy, what with one thing and another. In fact, the only thing that could make her feel worse about her life is if she felt she was poisoning my mind about you. Forcing me to take sides."

Christ, Kevo thinks. I really should have sat up before all this. I don't need to be hearing their sad family shite. But he's on the kid's side now, no question. Kid's what? Twelve, thirteen?

42

"Bean. Come on. You used to be such a smiley, sunny boy . . . It does feel like you have taken sides."

Bean. Must be a childhood nickname. Manipulative fucker's pulling all the stops.

"Oh, I have," the kid says. "I'm on Team Don't Run Off With Someone Half Your Age And Make Your Wife Feel Guilty About It. But hey, Dad, that's just something I came up with all on my own. Mum didn't have to force that on me one bit."

A gull floats past them, hanging in the air like all the things remaining unsaid in the silence that follows.

"Ruby's under the weather," says the father. "Sally's on edge. This is a big step for her. It's her first child. She's never really lived outside a city, so moving to the island . . . "

"Dad," says the boy, Tom. "I know all that. And I came because Mum thought it would be good for me to help you settle in and have an idea where you were going to be living. What I don't know is why you aren't dealing with the baby, because it's clearly under the weather and you're the nurse. I mean, that's actually your job. As in what you're trained for."

The guy's a medic? Kevo wasn't expecting that.

"She's just running a little temperature," says the dad. "I've given her Calpol. I'm not worried about her. I'm worried about how you spoke to Sally—"

The tannoy squawks to life, cutting the conversation short. The announcement tells them they're about to arrive and all drivers should return to the car deck and wait in their vehicles.

The kid takes this as his cue to escape the conversation and walks past his father, who waits a couple of beats and then follows him down the stairs.

Kevo sits up, pleased to be able to break cover. He stretches and then stops dead.

Sally Goodge sees that the runty guy with the chipped

tooth is shocked to find her sitting hidden in the lee of the funnel, smoking her illicit cigarette, holding it well clear of the infant strapped to her chest in the baby-carrier. They exchange a look.

"Families, eh?" he says.

She nods as she spins the cigarette out over the railing into the sea below.

"Yeah," she says. The baby starts grizzling.

"Should be a law against them."

Chapter 8

One of everything

Rex stands on the seat next to Sig, looking back as she drives away from the beach, small frame still taut with excitement. She reaches across and strokes the rough fur bristling on his back.

"It's okay, boy," she says. "He doesn't mean any harm."

She's known the old widower has been watching her for a long time, up there on the hill every morning, come rain or shine. She'd even wondered for a moment if the backpack she'd rescued was his, until she saw the lack of footprints around it. She really isn't that fussed about him watching.

It's one of the many things she hasn't cared about since it happened.

He's just a birdwatcher, maybe an otter-watcher, like she's just a swimmer, and she figures they're just each doing their thing, same as the gulls and the rabbits and the ravens do theirs, each a separate part of the island's varied ecosystem. She thought about it briefly when she first spotted him, and she genuinely doesn't mind if he catches a glimpse of her ass while she changes. She's been told her attitude to nudity can be a bit Scandinavian for these other Northern islands, but the person who told her that is long gone, and nobody else's opinion matters much anyway. It's only a body, just like anyone's. Just with a few more scars. The only self-consciousness she retains about it is a kind of battered pride that the damn thing keeps on going – in fact, perversely keeps getting stronger again – despite everything.

And she knows the birdwatcher had been a patient and kind man who looked after his wife through a long final illness. The island is small enough for her to have heard a lot of people saying that about him as they tutted at the sadness of the woman's decline. It would probably have surprised those same folk to know Sig had time for kind people because she appeared to have little time for anyone really, being herself a loner.

People who live alone and keep to themselves get a reputation for sourness in a small community, but the truth is Sig bears no grudges against anyone except herself.

In a happier life, she'd likely tell them she felt kindness was a seriously undervalued quality. One of those easily disparaged words, like "nice". But this was not that happier life, and – since it now never would be – she could see some virtue in the argument that "nice" and "kind" were qualities too soft-seeming to have much currency in a hard-edged world.

Rex huffs and turns around to sit next to her on the bench seat of the Defender, panting as he watches the single-track tarmac ribboning through the heather ahead of them. She scratches between his ears.

"Good dog," she says. "Busy day today. Evie. Your friend. Coming to stay. Evie."

He cocks his head and looks at her. It's easy for her to pretend he understands why she's grimacing at the thought of her unwanted guest.

Five minutes later, the Defender bounces off the hardtop

on to the uneven ruts of her own driveway. The unmade-up track curls round the small hummock in the land that hides the low house from the road. It's one of the many things she liked about the place from the moment she saw it. On an island with no real trees, even the most remote house shows itself, but not theirs – now hers. Low to the ground, a long L-shaped single-storey made from two old black houses with new wriggly-tin roofs that have been connected to a more recent boathouse that angles around the only slipway on the western shore of the island. *Caladh falaichte* is the name of the house, which means "hidden harbour", though it's no real harbour to speak of, just an old stone boat ramp that adds a smidgin of extra protection from the grey ocean to that already afforded by the rocks that guard her tiny scoop of bay.

Sig parks up close to the kitchen door that is in fact the main entrance to her refuge. Rex circles the building while she walks around the corner and hangs her wetsuit under the outside shower. She turns the water on to rinse it while she goes inside to make the strong coffee for which her body is now jonesing. It's not just an unbreakable ritual for her, the hand-grinding, the filter folding and rinsing, the hand-pour over the grounds in the glass carafe, the tantalising wait while it drips through – it's the only remaining indulgence of her day.

She has the coffee made by the time Rex finishes his patrol of the perimeter and pads back inside the house. It's a room that shocks people who enter it for the first time. They expect the cramped quarters and dimly lit interior that the old, landward face of the house suggests. In fact, it's newly washed in light each morning because the rubble-built stone wall that used to face the sea and protect generations of crofters from the winter storms has been replaced with a huge floor-to-ceiling glass window. The window – or rather, the three heavily engineered panels of sliding glass and the reinforced frame that not only houses them but supports the tin roof above – is the most expensive thing Sig has ever bought, all but obliterating the money she had received in what was, in the circumstances, an unwelcome insurance payment. But while she regrets a lot about life, she does not regret that purchase for a moment. The windows let the light in, whether she wants it or not, and that's a good thing.

If she didn't have them, she wouldn't have been able to stay on the island and remain sane.

The two ancient black houses have been knocked into one long room with a door at the far end that leads to the boathouse beyond. At the near end, where she stands over the Chemex trying not to twitch as she waits for the coffee to be done, is a kitchen area with one stool. In the middle of the room is a long worktable that serves as kitchen table and desk and anything else she needs it to. There is one work chair pulled up into the semi-circular scallop cut into a well-worn jeweller's workbench placed at the end of the table. Beyond that is one armchair, facing the window, and at the end of the room, by the boathouse door, one box-bed which, though a double, sports only one pillow: a keen-eyed visitor would see that there is only one of everything in the room. She knows Evie – who has the uncomfortably sharp vision of youth on her side – has in fact christened it the House with Only One of Everything. Evie was just the right stroppy age to be able to claim the licence to say outrageous and iconoclastic stuff, and acute enough to pick the right words to sting a bit as they stuck. And it was true that Sig aggressively favoured the quiet life, on her own, with only one of everything – including one companion, which in her case was Rex. Which made her having promised to babysit Evie all the more of an unwelcome imposition.

She'd agreed for two reasons. First, technically she was Evie's aunt by marriage, though everyone had made it clear that no one expected her to take the girl in when her parents died. Sig was only a very recent and still faintly exotic arrival, and she had not been a part of Evie's childhood. She hadn't even really had time to establish a settled relationship with Evie's parents. They'd been polite and welcoming enough, but even before her own loss she'd felt there was still some work to do with Evie's mum before they felt comfortable with each other, and then the first bad thing happened to Sig and it was probably too late, and then Evie's own bad thing happened and it definitely was. Evie had been taken in by her grandfather Angus and her grandmother Seona, and Sig had been left to deal with her own sorrow in her chosen and purposely solitary way.

The story might have been different if Evie's loss had preceded Sig's, but it hadn't. And two tragedies in the same extended family gave the more superstitious and gossip-prone of the islanders a small dose of schadenfreude as they muttered sadly about bad things coming in threes and eyed Sig, the incomer, with a mixture of sympathy and morbid anticipation. She'd overheard Mary-Kate the shopkeeper talking about this to one of her fellow gossips in the pub one night. She'd turned and told them that a number is just a number and that she didn't believe in superstitious nonsense like that, and they were nuts if they did. She also told them bad things don't come in threes: they just come. She'd been calm and polite about it.

On a small island, a lot of potential conflict is avoided by people not saying exactly what they believe. Sig's directness was allowed for on account of her recent loss and her Scandinavian upbringing. She stopped going to the pub.

Seona and Angus had recently gently asked if they could

put her down as a guardian for Evie if anything happened to them, and she had been as surprised as they'd been to hear the reflexive "No" coming out of her mouth. They'd been too polite – or maybe shocked – to ask why, though she'd seen the question hovering in Seona's eyes, and she'd filled the silence by saying she was the wrong person and they had not pushed, which was a relief because in that moment she had no good reason to give them. And she definitely wasn't going to give them the bad one. The one Matt had got a little too close to today, the one he was only half right about: Sig was sure she wasn't suicidal, but nor was she risk averse. And whatever she was doing in her solo freediving would, in one way or another, solve the dilemma for her. She'd push the envelope until it broke, or until she got snapped back by it, maybe into scaring herself straight. Flirting with the risk put an edge on things. It required a discipline and a commitment to a purpose she didn't feel in the rest of her life any more. It was way too tangled and dark for her to be able to explain to Angus and Seona, but it made sense to her as long as there was just her to satisfy. Taking responsibility for someone else would mean justifying it to them too. She didn't want to disappoint anyone, and she certainly didn't want to give Evie another parental figure to lose. And in the end, it probably came down to the fact that she, Sig, didn't want to get close to anyone else. Getting close was letting your guard down, and that was how the pain got in.

Fuck it, she thought. Maybe Matt was right. Maybe she'd just become a coward. Maybe she'd stopped being kind. It wasn't a good thought, but as long as she was the only one who knew, she could live with it.

And she wasn't really unkind. She had Rex and they took care of each other well enough, and so she'd said that of course she'd help out with Evie whenever they needed. She might be a coward, but she wasn't a monster. As if to show no hard feelings, a week later Angus and Seona had asked if she could babysit Evie while they went to the Modh, and so here she was, heading to pick the girl up. It was the right thing to do, but it still felt like penance, and that rankled just a bit.

The other reason she'd agreed was the things she and Evie shared, which were the accidents.

Sig's accident was the reason she walked with what Evie called a shoogly foot. It was also the reason she wore the scars on her face, the scars she didn't care about any more. They were her own fault and one of the things she felt least guilty about.

Evie's accident was genuine, an everyday tragedy, the loss of a daughter that tore the heart out of her grandparents, a thing all the worse for its ordinariness and something for which the young girl bore no responsibility at all: an oncoming car jumping lanes in the wet, one sickening impact killing her parents and knocking her into a wheelchair, possibly for the rest of a life at present being lived with her mother's parents. The accident hadn't been her fault. Not the tiniest bit. Not like Sig's.

Beyond the boathouse door is a bathroom and a toilet. But these days she has almost entirely abandoned the bathroom, preferring to wash, when she feels the need, in the outside shower on the seaward face of the building. She slides the window open and steps outside, turning the water off and leaving the rinsed wetsuit to dry, swinging gently on the hanger like a soggy black phantom.

She pours her coffee and sits at her table to examine the lost backpack, noting how the battered water bottle in its side pouch perfectly matches the vase of startlingly orange crocosmia at the centre of the table, a tall bunch of flowers that provide the major splash of colour in her pale and light-washed lair. She savours the hot bite of the first, best swig from her mug. As happens every day, it feels like the caffeine is mainlining into her brain and flushing out any residual cobwebs the swim has not managed to clear.

Sig unzips the main compartment of the camouflage pack and pulls out the contents. The first thing is a shallow blue and definitely un-military pink Tupperware box, which seems to confirm her suspicion about it being a forgotten picnic, but the next thing she takes out is a long trowel that looks like it's been crossed with an unnaturally wide-bladed serrated hunting knife. She puts it on the table next to the box and reaches in for the last item, which is a plastic sandwich bag containing a dull-looking metal container about half the size of a cigar box. The box is deformed and split, as if wrenched open or trodden on. From its weight she guesses it's made of lead. It's got a rough letter T on it in a different metal.

She opens the Tupperware box and finds it doesn't contain a sandwich but a book of sorts – more like a few pages of stiff vellum about twice the size of a passport, sandwiched in a folded rectangle of mottled leather that is closer to a wrap than a book cover.

She looks closer, and suddenly she doesn't like having it in her house. The vellum sheets are bound in with a kind of rustic brutality, with a thong that passes through them and two holes at either end of the spine. The thong has a stopper on it, like a bead, but the bead that she first thought was ivory is, on closer inspection, a tooth. It smells musty – not bad, just old, like it's been in a damp cellar forever, except it's so dry and brittle that it clearly hasn't. It's the kind of creepy gothic thing that Evie would like. She moves it to the edge of the table, somehow glad that she doesn't have to even touch it. Thinking of Evie makes her look at her watch. Ferry will be in soon. She'll put a "Found" note up in the island shop when she picks her up, put the word round.

As she gets to her feet, Sig sees that the crocosmia needs more water. She fills a jug at the kitchen sink and pours half of it into the vase at the centre of the table, and then she leaves the jug as she checks her watch and heads for the door.

"Rex," she says.

He jumps off the soft seat where he likes to curl up in front of the window and cocks his head at her.

"Car," she says. "Now. Let's get this over with."

She must remember to get loo paper. And milk. Probably bread. And maybe bacon. Or sausages. No – Evie's vegan. Or is it just vegetarian? So cheese, maybe. She should have made a list and now there's no time. Shit.

The thing the House with Only One of Everything lacked altogether was an owner who was built to be a hostess.

Chapter 9

No harm in being polite

Milly the spaniel, sweet natured and biddable as she is, is not coming back, even though she hears Walter John whistling and calling for her on the hill above the narrow inlet where she has found something dead that smells, to her heightened senses, delightfully rotten.

She will return to her master in a minute, but right now, for the moment, the powerful mixture of odours coming from the body lying twisted and face down, half out of the water, is too seductive to be ignored. A waterlogged Flecktarn-pattern camo parka helps the corpse blend into the surrounding terrain, but the heady tang of rotted flesh and the necrotic brain matter now marinating in the salt water pooled in the catastrophically split and dented skull has irresistibly drawn the dog straight to it.

"Milly!"

The voice is getting further away. She licks, then tugs, at the content of the skull, tugs and chews, almost giddy with the rank and briny rot that squishes across her tongue as she does so. The body has an expensive-looking metal detector wand twisted across its back, held in place by a shoulder strap.

There are earphones attached to it by a loop of curly cable. They float like a sea anchor beside the booted feet, gently flopping back and forth in the swell that lifts and drops the lifeless body as the dog tugs at it.

"MILLY!"

She can tell from the deepening tone of the shouts that she is a bad dog. She had better go find her master.

But not before she has one more bite of the treat.

Walter John has exhausted himself and begun to lose hope when his spirits are lifted by the sight of the dog bounding up from the shore. He sees two rabbits break right and left ahead of her, startled from where they were sitting hidden in the heather. He whistles and waves, and then she bounces up and round him and is delighted to hear him say she is in fact a good girl, a very good girl. She can hear the relief in his voice. She sits when asked and lets him clip her back on to the lead that she hates.

By the time they return to the road, Walter John has decided the only way to deal with his other problem – whether Sig saw him waving or not – is to address it head on. He must stop watching her surreptitiously and the only way to make sure he remains blameless and true to his word is to go and see her.

That's what he will do. He will tackle this directly, before he becomes the sad old peeper he fears he is well on the way to being. He will drop by her house and say he saw the sharks and was worried she had been spooked by them. If you thought about it, the sharks were a godsend, a break in the pattern, the perfect excuse to talk to her. It was good. A chance to clear the air.

Truth is, it had been getting harder and harder not to look at her changing over the recent weeks, and now he has given in to temptation he has to make sure he never does it again. It can't become a habit. That way a kind of madness lies. A kind of madness but a certain damnation. It is not the way he wants himself to turn out in the end.

So, he will go and see her, introduce himself properly, and then talk about the sharks.

When he gets to his house, he feels the blank windows staring at him in accusation.

"I haven't done anything," he says as he lets himself in just enough to loop the car keys off their hook. Christ forgive him, but he is losing his marbles. Talking to himself.

In his inmost self, he knows he's really talking to his dead wife. He starts the Peugeot and reverses out into the road and turns towards Sig's house.

Ten minutes later, Walter John is still involved in a silent argument that he seems to be losing, despite the fact he is talking to someone who only exists in his head. Because of this, he forgets to indicate a turn as he slows at Sig's driveway and narrowly avoids being rear-ended by the post-bus which he has not seen speeding up behind him on the single-track road, hurrying towards the ferry. He waves a flustered apology and makes the turn through Sig's gate.

He is happy to open the door and let Milly run free the moment they get there. Her breath is worse than he can remember, and she'd twice farted with such noxiousness that he'd gagged, even the second time when the car windows had already been rolled down to let air clean out the first one. It was like she was farting heavy gas that sat low in the cabin and was impervious to the wind rushing in. The smell was so pungent that it seemed to have a solid, sticky presence all its own. No wonder he had been too distracted to see the bus creeping up behind him.

That's why she was so long in coming back, he thinks. She'd been eating a dead seal or something. She'd done it before, although the results had never been as vile as this. She will sleep out in the garage tonight. He is getting too old to be scrubbing her runny shit out of the fitted carpet any more, and the linoleum in the kitchen is so old and crazed with cracks that he would never be sure he had cleaned properly.

Sig's Defender is not there; no one is home. That presents a dilemma. He could just go, but the post-bus has seen him turning in. If he leaves and the driver of the-bus tells Sig she had missed a visitor, then all the weirdness he's trying to avoid will just grow bigger. So maybe he should wait.

But if he waits, there's no knowing how long she might be. It's probable that she's just headed to the ferry to pick up any new mail from the shop, which is where post and packages are left until the bus delivers the ones not already picked up on the next day. But that might still be an hour, or more. And maybe she has other errands to run. So perhaps it will be best if he leaves a polite note.

There's never any harm in being polite.

Chapter 10

Hell on wheels

It's a nightmare at the pier. It looks like half the island's population is upping sticks and leaving as they mill around talking and joking and greeting the latecomers as they arrive with their backpacks and wheelie cases and other odd-shaped bundles.

In the far corner of the waiting area, a minibus-load of teenagers have spilled out on to the tarmac and have undone their bundles, revealing the musical instruments inside. They are now starting a jam session that Evie Kennedy – on any other year other than this, her strange fifteenth – would have been part of. She sits with Katie, her best friend since forever amongst the other friends she's known just as long, nodding along to the dancing beat of the accordion and fiddles, getting aching apple cheeks from smiling so hard to show she's happy and totally okay about the fact she's not going to be getting on the ferry with them. Which of course she is. Totally okay. It was her choice, after all. Everyone tried to make her go until Katie – who could be irritating but was usually brilliant just when you needed it – had turned round and put them all straight.

"She knows us but she doesn't know all the other folk that'll be there and she's not comfortable being in a hall full of weirdos and strangers having to explain what happened, so leave her alone, okay?"

So now they were all about to go and she wasn't and that was fine.

It's a thing, the traditional Celtic music, out here on the islands. Every year there's a gathering, called the Modh, and everyone goes and competes and listens and attends classes and has a good old time. There's even dancing, and when she was younger, in the before time when Evie was normal, unnoticed by fate and the loved child of two living parents, she had been good at it, even winning medals. Her parents took her to the Modh when it was on Jura and they had had fun. At least that's how she remembers it, although what she remembers is filtered through the photographs her Granny Seona and Granpa Angus like to look at every now and then. There she is, in the pictures, as she was. Frozen in time, caught in the dance, tiptoed and cross-gartered in a short kilt and velvet waistcoat with bouncing hair almost as pale as the lace jabot flouncing round her neck as she whirls. The blonde curls are gone now, one side arbitrarily buzzed off while she was unconscious in pre-op, the other side evened out in a hospital haircut as she recuperated. Adding insult to injury, her hair has remained stubbornly short ever since, taking forever to grow out and, where it has grudgingly lengthened, it seems to have decided to be dull and straight from now on, with no memory of the curls that had bounced happily through her before-life. Also gone is any imminent (or foreseeable) possibility of tiptoes, replaced by the certainty of the wheelchair she sits in. That photo was the good old days, when she could dance, when her legs worked and she had parents. In that picture she looks light as thistledown as she bounces in the air. Now she's a burden, a reminder to her grandparents of what they've all lost. They love her, she loves them, but all that love can't hide the fact every one of them is tired – not of each other, though there is an element of that too – but mainly just tired with having to keep on keeping on.

That's why she encouraged them to go to the Modh without her. Angus is an accordionist, and he loves it. The break will do them all good, and Evie is even looking forward to escaping the retirement bungalow that has been so lovingly fitted with everything she might need, from handrails to ramps and a whole new wheelchair-friendly wet room instead of a boring old bathroom (as Granny Seona brightly said, covering up what Evie knows is her regret at losing the bath she loved to soak in with a good book): she's looking forward to going to stay with Sigrid in the House with Only One of Everything, although she has worked on another alternative if Sig shows the slightest sign of resenting having to look after her.

The reel comes to an end and Katie's mum sticks her head out of the minibus window and suggests they all put the instruments away and load up because the ferry's coming in.

Katie taps her on the shoulder and nods at the old man walking towards them.

"It's your old folk."

Her grandparents are walking towards her, Angus watching the always-surprising bulk of the ferry as it appears around the headland, starkly changing the scale of the landscape as it does so. Granny Seona keeps looking in the opposite direction, back to the coast road. Evie knows she's worrying that they'll have to embark before her ride shows up. She worries about everything these days.

Evie looks at Katie.

"Good luck—" they both say, and then "Jinx!"

They grin at each other.

"You'll have fun with your auntie," says Katie with a rueful smile. "She's a weirdo just like you. Must run in the family."

"Sig's not really my aunt."

"Evie. Her husband was your mum's brother . . . "

"Not by blood."

"An aunt's an aunt."

"Yeah, but she doesn't really want to be," says Evie. "You know what she's like. She's a loner."

"She's pretty cool, though," says Katie.

"She is cool," says Evie. "That's why you've got such a crush on her."

"Have not," says Katie, just a bit too quickly, suddenly remembering why her pal Evie can be so irritating.

"If you say so," says Evie, shrugging like it's nothing. "She's just not very . . . "

Her brow knits. She can't find the word.

"Warm?" says Katie, after a pause. "Not warm and soft like an auntie who bakes cakes and things."

"Yeah," says Evie. "She's definitely not that. She's different."

"On this island, different is good," says Katie, sketching a wave as she turns to join the bunch of kids now cramming back on to the minibus. "Smell ya later."

Granny Seona walks up and squeezes her shoulder. Evie looks up and sees she's still looking back at the coast road in a distracted fashion.

"She'll be here," says Evie.

"Oh, I know" says her grandmother, just quickly enough for Evie to know she doesn't quite believe it.

"And even if she's late, you don't have to worry about me," says Evie, reaching back and squeezing her hand. "I'll be good."

"I know, but she said she'd be here," says Granny Seona.

That querulous shiver in her voice is one of the things Evie needs to escape for a couple of days. It's fear, and it didn't used to be in her grandmother's voice, not in Evie's memory of it in the life before. And there's no point to it now. The worst had happened. There really isn't much left to be scared of.

"Gran," she says. "You get on the ferry when it comes. I'll stay here. Not like I can go anywhere. She'll find me."

"What if it rains?" says Granpa Angus.

Evie jacks her thumb over her shoulder.

"I'll just hang out in the shop," she says. "It'll be fine. Mary-Kate won't mind."

Chapter 11

How the darkness gets in

He doesn't mean to let Milly into Sig's house. He wouldn't have if he'd been paying attention, but the wire spiral on the back of his notebook got snagged on his pocket lining as he tried to pull it out. He'd already knocked on the door, even though he knew the place would be empty. He's surprised that the door pushes open, and then he sees Milly snuffling inside at his feet, and before he can grab her, she's in.

"Milly!" he hisses.

She trots off into the room as if she's gone deaf again, and he has no choice but to follow. Again, even though he knows the house is empty, he calls out as he enters.

"Hello?" he ventures. "Sorry! My dog's pushed her way in ..."

Nobody replies. He steps further in. There is nothing there but light and more light washing in through the dazzlingly unexpected wall of glass on the seaward side.

"Wow," he says. He hears himself, hears the surprise in his own voice, and wonders what makes him say it. He can't remember ever saying "wow" in his life. It just isn't the kind of word he uses.

But then this long room isn't what he'd expected. It isn't the kind of room he normally finds himself in. It's like something he'd seen, but only on a TV screen. It isn't only the light or the closeness of the sea just the other side of the glass. It isn't the sparseness, the clean lines of what decoration there is. It's the feeling of the room itself. It isn't a sterile sparseness, and the worktable that runs down the length of the room holds an ordered jumble of tools and paper and things, but it does feel ... focused. Focused and spartan. Like a place where things get done. On purpose. Not a place where life just happens, accidentally – which is what his house feels like these days. Just a place he stays in to keep the weather off while he eats food he doesn't much enjoy or watches a TV that shows an incomprehensible bright world beyond the island that he has no real interest in understanding any more. His house, he realises, feels like a waiting room. A between place – interstitial and unloved – made for passing through, before passing on.

The purpose in this room draws him in, overcoming his natural reticence. Even as he moves past the kitchen island, his hand trailing along the cool slab of thick grey slate seems to pick up an extra hum of energy.

"Hello?" he calls again, clearing his throat and looking towards the far end of the room, in case there is an unseen inhabitant beyond the door.

There can be no harm in looking at the work on her table; he knows that she makes things she sells in a gallery in Sweden, but he's never really seen her work. His wife had seen some on her workbench when she'd brought Sig and her partner a home-made cake to celebrate when they'd first moved in and renovated the blackhouses. She'd told him it was very detailed, very good. She'd been like that. Welcoming, encouraging. She'd known how to put people at ease, how to be a good neighbour and friend. Walter John had not known how much he relied on her to hide his natural diffidence, not until she was gone. Sitting in the small island church, he had looked around and realised that, although he knew all the faces, they had each been brought into his life by her. It wasn't that they were "her" friends and not his, but she had been the prime mover, the magnet that attracted them. And of course, they have been kind to him as a widower, but he knows that the kindness is tinged with a duty to the departed, rather than a primary affection for him. It was understood why she had done what she had done at the end, and the fact she had waited to do it while he was away for the day, the very first day he had not cared for her in more than two years, that fact was understood too, forgiven, and, in a way, admired. Easy enough to admire when they hadn't had to find her, but that was not her fault: she was not to know that the health visitor whom she had expected would cope with that shock had missed the ferry. She'd tried to do it perfectly and as kindly as she could manage.

He doesn't mind it much, being her left-over. He just wishes he could make a better fist of it. She'd always said old men got sad and bitter because they forgot to water the tree of friendship when they were young. Tree of friendship was the kind of thing she said. A bit soppy, really. But that soppiness had filled his life with a warmth he now misses, just as much as it had filled their house with friends "just popping in" for a chat, just as much as she had brought wildflowers or clumps of heather in to brighten the place.

After the stints she'd endured in hospital on the mainland, and after the funeral, the idea of flowers had a whole different meaning to him, and her beloved collection of vases and jugs remains dry and empty, no use for anything except gathering dust and dead spiders. She'd loved the bright crocosmia that seemed to spring up in the ditches around the scattered houses on the island, the same orange flowers that Sig has placed in a big jar in the centre of the table.

Thinking of her, he unconsciously reaches out and touches them at the exact moment Milly sees the movement beyond the window and goes wild. He jolts at the sudden frenzy of barking, the ancient part of his brain reacting instinctively to the raw, primal alarm sound of it. He knocks the flowers, which are just a bit too long for the jar they stand in, and it tips.

He would still have caught it and stopped what happened next if the tail of his eye hadn't caught sight of what Milly was warning him about.

The black-clad shape of a woman twisting in the breeze, a dark shape defying gravity, triggering the memory he tries to forget, suspended one foot off the ground, backlit by the unforgiving light at the edge of the window . . .

The vase tips, slipping through his dry-skinned fingertips. The flowers spill across the table like jackstraws.

For a long, long beat, the only sounds in the world are the glug of the water calmly emptying into the tray in the centre of the table and Walter John choking as he clings to the table's edge, trying not to have another heart attack as he struggles to make sense of what looks very like the ghost of his dead wife hanging by the neck, just as he'd found her in the garage when he returned from the dentist.

Of course, he realises, as the irregular bumping of his heart evens out a bit, it isn't his wife, and it isn't a ghost. Ghosts don't exist, for a start. And his wife had had feet. Two of them. Sig's wetsuit doesn't have any. Now he can see what it is, he chunks out a half-laugh and sinks to one knee.

"Jesus," he says. "Jesus Christ . . . "

His eye had made a suicidal ghost out of a wetsuit, and for

a horrible, heart-stopping moment his world had tilted off its axis. He'd let his imagination and his guilt about his wife play tricks with his head. This is what he tries so hard not to do, not to let that imagination run free, because that is where a sort of madness lies. That is how the darkness gets in.

All he needs is a couple of seconds to get his breath back. And for the dog to stop barking. And then everything will be right as rain.

"Milly," he wheezes. "Shut up!"

She doesn't, now adding a deep rumbling growl between barks.

"Milly!" he says, hoisting himself back up on to his feet. "Fuck off."

It was the first time he's ever sworn at the dog. He is a man who prides himself on not swearing. She turns and looks at him.

He doesn't look back at her. He's just seen the ruin he created on the worktable, now strewn with wetness and flowers and pooling blackness. He says "Jesus Christ" a couple more times and sinks back to the floor.

Milly starts growling again.

It could have been worse. Not much, but maybe. That's what Walter John tells himself. The water hasn't splashed much, and almost all of it has been caught by a shallow Tupperware container.

He'll clear up the flowers in a minute, but right now he has to move fast. Because the water that has filled the Tupperware is black, and he can see there is something like a book just beneath the surface. He has to get the book out of the water, but he doesn't want to spill the inky stuff on the clean table.

"Shit."

He is swearing more today than he has done in the last five years. He runs around the table and pulls open the sliding glass door. Then he goes back, carefully disentangles the brimming Tupperware from the tangle of flower stalks lying across it, and very gingerly carries it across the pale scrubbed floorboards, over the door frame and out to the edge of the old stone jetty a couple of paces beyond.

"Shit shit shit," he says as he carefully tips the dark liquid into the clear water below. He puts his fingers on the book to stop it sliding out, and grimaces as the breeze flips some of the water back across his trouser legs in a fine spray. When the tray has only the soggy book left in it, he puts it on the ground and goes back inside to get some kitchen roll from the drum on the countertop.

Milly trots down the slope to the water and watches the black ink swirl and spread like a cloud. If Walter had been watching, he might have thought how concentrated the inky blackness must have been because it quickly obscures the clear view of the stones and pebbles and pieces of broken china on the seabed below.

Milly is intrigued by the ink spreading itself like a cloud below her. She sniffs close to the water. A wavelet splashes her nose. She growls and licks the wetness off her muzzle.

Walter John comes out and crouches over the sodden book and sets about trying to dry it as much as he can with the paper towels. As he handles it, he can't help noticing how old it is. It looks like a real antique. He really hopes it isn't something priceless. He prays that it can dry out and be as good as new. He wonders if he should rethink his earlier qualms about leaving without saying anything or writing a note, even though the post-bus had seen him turning into the drive. The post-bus might easily never mention anything to Sig. Walter John might just have been using her driveway as a place to turn around. Maybe he'd forgotten something and was doubling back home to pick it up. That's something he can say. There's no one to tell anyone else he isn't telling the truth. He can say he'd forgotten Milly, left her back at his house. Or her lead. Yes. Old men forget. He might easily have been turning around to get her lead. Even though he knows as he thinks it that he could never actually do it, he does think maybe he can put everything back and Sig might think the jar had just fallen over in a sudden gust of wind. Except the room had the windows closed. But that jar they're in, it has quite a narrow bottom for such tall flowers. It's feasible. No one has to know. He could easily have been turning round to get Milly's lead.

Where is that dog? he thinks, looking round.

"Milly?" he says, standing. "Milly?"

The dog is gone. The water below him is clear, as if the sea has already begun collaborating with him, cleaning up the evidence.

A mile or so around the ragged coastline the dead body in the camo parka remains, face down in the water, flopping gently back and forth in the swell. A rabbit sits alert in the heather above it, watching. If the corpse wasn't floating in a kind of perpetual wave-jostled motion, it would be easier to see the small spasm that cricks the neck a couple of millimetres, and flexes the smallest finger on the right hand.

It's a tiny motion. The rabbit doesn't react. It's just a rabbit. Even a sharp-eyed raven might miss it.

Chapter 12

Warp and weft

The ravens weave a daily fabric of vigilance and memory across the land as they fly criss-crossed patterns of an intricacy no one on the island has the patience to notice. It's always been like this. The time they inhabit is different to the one humans live in. It's not that it runs at a different pace, the passage of the years felt relative to a different lifespan; it's that these birds float across the sky on a plane that intersects humans' but is unnoticed by them.

The birds, on the other hand, notice everything. That is their purpose, both how and why they stay alive. They see, they remember and they understand. The island is a barrier island, bulwarked against the thunderous might of a northern ocean, and they are its sentinels.

Since their daily patrol shuttles back and forth across every inch of the sea-girt land in paths as regular as loom work, an alert observer might have called them Warp and Weft, though of course they might just as easily have been called Thought and Memory if noticed in earlier times.

They have a selection of roosting points on which they can choose to enthrone themselves depending on the weather and the direction of the prevailing wind. Right now, conscious that their stomachs are still empty, they are perched on a favourite rock, a pale slab of speckled grey dolerite that juts out of the heather high enough on the island's tallest point to give them a good view but just low enough to stay tucked in just below the ridgeline where they can keep out of the wind when it comes – as it now does – from the north-east. From up here they can see a good slice of the island and the sea beyond, a wide arc that goes from the straggle of new sheds around the jetty of the fish farm all the way past the north cape to the few houses dotted intermittently along the lonelier Atlantic coast.

Of course, they don't mind the wind as a human might, but when they choose to sit they like to do so without having to brace themselves against the unpredictable buffeting of any passing breeze. When they decide to be still, they take that decision very seriously. It's a kind of balance, as much as anything, making themselves the still point of their turning worlds.

A birdwatcher might see the ravens on their throne and think they were seeing the same island that the ravens saw, but they don't. It isn't just that the birds' eyes are sharper and see further, it's that they are wired to a different array of senses. These ravens mark changes that would be entirely undetectable to an ordinary mammal or bird. Change, to long-lived birds like these ravens, is always to be noted, not just because a disturbance in the status quo might well be a harbinger of danger, but because that "balance" must be preserved in all things if at all possible. It's as if the ravens have a sense memory of how things should be and an active mind that allows them to react to things when they are off-kilter. How the ravens sense these changes isn't directly explainable in human terms, but it's analogous to the simpler sense of balance mammals achieve once they learn to walk. And if the world lurches, the ravens note it. And try to adjust.

Looking down at the distant roofs of the fish-farm sheds, they feel the change. They scan the landscape and the sea for a new shift in the pattern.

Because the pattern they are charged with observing has altered. The ravens have already seen a thin line of darkness spill out on to the island, thin and almost imperceptible to start with, like a single drop of ink rolling down a sloping page. They first saw it yesterday as a man in a camo parka took something out of the ground that should have stayed tucked safely away for ever. They saw him examine it and open it and put the contents in a pink plastic sandwich box, unaware of the darkness that appeared to leak from the hole he had cut in the ground. They saw it seem to loop and snag his feet as he walked furtively away, making him stumble and fall and smack his head on a stone, the only stone on a bare slope of moorland, as if the darkness had waited for just the right moment to trip him. His bag, the bag containing the source of the leaking darkness, tumbled on down to the beach while he got to his feet, his head now leaking a different dark, arterial red into the world as he staggered the other way, dropping straight over the lip of a small cliff, leaking life into the hungry water lapping gently below. Leaking life but not lifeless, because some of the old darkness had already soaked into him and is leaching out like a bloom into the narrow inlet where his red-anoraked body bobs face down on the tide, waiting.

They can't see what the next change is, which makes them all the more uneasy. There's little to see that's new since the day before. A distant boat on the water, a car winding along the road, and someone smoking outside one of the fish-farm sheds. Grey smudge of a rabbit lapping rainwater from the rocks that lie close to the body.

One raven cocks its head in a very human looking squint, trying to get a clearer view. The other makes a dissatisfied noise – a high, knocking *tok-tok-tok*, and then lofts back into the air and dips towards those distant sheds. It can't tell if it's the dog or the fish farm or even the rabbit that's disturbed the pattern, but something has changed. It will go for a closer look. Besides, its stomach is still empty and there is always the possibility of scraps around the processing shed at the fish farm.

The other raven has taken to the air almost simultaneously and tilts its feathers in the opposite direction, heading away from its companion. It's as if they've made a plan to split up on a search of the island.

As they fly away on their diverging courses down over the heathered slope, each raven gives out a harsh series of *kraa*s that sound like warnings to anything that can hear them in the landscape below.

Chapter 13

Behind the eight ball

The black and white pool ball on the end of the stick rattles in her hand as Sig shifts down into third gear, helping the Land Rover meet the rise in the road leading past what she always thinks of as the lonely Catholic church, neatly penned in its bright square of fenced-off grass in the midst of the drab brown of the moorland.

He'd put the eight ball on the gear shift. They'd found it in a flea market in Paris on their way back from a climbing trip in the Dolomites, the worn ball already drilled out and probably reclaimed from the gearstick on a car junked long ago. She'd said it was kitsch and he'd bought it anyway when she wasn't looking, and the next time she saw it it was back home in the battered Defender he'd bought for her wedding present. It was a private joke about how they first met.

She'd felt embarrassed because she hadn't bought him anything to match it. He'd told her not to worry, he'd be getting his present in instalments over the decades to come. Besides, he'd said, someone in her family should give her a wedding present, and since one was unlikely to be forthcoming from her parents – who had not attended the wedding – and since he was now officially family, it was kind of his job. Almost a legal obligation, he'd said, waving the wedding certificate in her face and scooping her up in his arms as he lifted her into the driving seat, forestalling any more protests. He'd always lifted her, even if it was just his voice on the end of a phone call.

Her absent parents were Christian Scientists, which was a sufficiently unusual thing in the broadly rational Sweden where she'd grown up to have marked them out as mild oddballs in the small community where they lived. It hadn't been a big thing in the early years of her childhood, more a matter of raised eyebrows than any real prejudice, and she'd never felt singled out at school. Her mother was admittedly brittle, which gave her a reputation for being a bit cold and standoffish, and she was never more than a couple of steps from her Bible. Her father was a fractionally warmer presence in her life, but one who focused more on her mother's fragility than what Sig increasingly felt was the cause of it, which was her sister.

Ebba was nearly two years younger than Sig and began life as a funny and healthy baby who grew into an energetic toddler and then a small child who seemed to charge through life at extra speed, as if she was always trying to catch up with Sig, whom she adored without qualification. They'd shared a room since the moment Ebba was born, and when she was old enough to have nightmares Sig was the one who comforted her and swore she'd always protect her. Ebba had loved chasing games and snowball fights and running pell-mell on the beach in the wind. They played heroes and monsters, games where they were Viking warriors, fearless shield-maidens afraid of nothing in the world. Their mother had hated the way they tore around the house and the garden, and she disapproved of and discouraged their love of velocity and the outdoors while encouraging them to join her on stately "nature" walks that made them both frustrated and itchy to run off into the woods and play hide and seek. She frowned on the imaginary battles they fought as fearless shield-maidens, because these games were, to her, unchristian and too much in love with the older folktales and the human-sized pagan gods who wove their bright blasphemous strand all through them. They were absolutely forbidden from climbing trees, so they spent much time outside off the ground, straddling branches and hiding from their mother, the joy of naughtiness rising in great bubbles of barely contained mirth inside both of them. Sitting in those forbidden trees, they made up more stories and games and worlds into which they could escape together. They built a perch out of pallet wood lashed on with bailing twine, which grew into the skeleton of a treehouse they called Valhalla before their mother found it and had their father remove it for safety. They just waited and found another tree in which to build a new hut for heroes to hide in. Ebba was the worst giggler and was always the one who got them caught, but Sig never minded. It was just what Ebba did. Minding about Ebba giggling would have been as pointless and silly as objecting to the birds singing as the sun rose each morning. Her laughter was like that, just the pure sound of nature revelling in itself. Ebba was only ever still while painting and drawing, which she loved, though she was very specific about her drawing book and would only use one side of the sheet, despite her mother's frugal insistence that she used both sides so as not to waste paper. When Ebba drew people, their hair was always streaming behind them, as if caught in the slipstream of their own velocity, as if everyone was like her. After the illness – when she was gone – Sig sat alone on her cold, stripped bed and rode the horrible vertigo caused by the sudden realisation that Ebba had just crossed a line between being a person and becoming a story, a story that she would have to fight to remember as clearly in the future as she did at that very moment. The idea that she would ever forget a single detail of her sister's short life seemed both impossible and inevitable, and this deepened her pain and despair and made her get her sister's drawing book and start writing things down on all those empty sides that Ebba had fought over with their mother. In that moment, it felt like she'd left them purposely blank for Sig to write in, and that's what she did, late into the night, building a world of words where her memories would remain as sharp and bright in whatever unimaginable future lay ahead as they were to her then. The first thing she wrote was under a picture Ebba had drawn of herself. Sig didn't really know why she wrote those words, but as soon as she did she knew they were both true and carried more freight than seven short words were meant to bear: "Strong winds were blowing through her hair".

Only years later did she hear the same words in a song and wonder if she'd heard them as a child and absorbed them unconsciously. It didn't matter. They fitted Ebba like no one else.

Her mother had drifted into the girl's bedroom in the early hours of the morning, and when she saw the writing in the sketchbook she had torn it out of Sig's grasp with one hand and smacked the side of her head with the other, the flat palm hitting her so hard that Sig thought she'd burst an eardrum. It was the first and last time her mother hit her, but it sealed the moment as a punctuation point, not just in Sig's relationship with her parents but as the end of a long three-day sentence in which she'd watched them pray for Ebba, who had developed a case of mumps that metamorphosed quickly into an increasingly painful attack of mumps-derived meningitis. The meningitis threw her into convulsions and made breathing harder and harder. As extreme Christian Scientists, they had not had the children vaccinated and didn't see the need for the timely antibiotics that the adult Sig later discovered would likely have saved Ebba's life. Eleven-year-old Sig had pleaded with them to call the doctor, and when they tried to explain how God would do the right thing she'd left the house and run the snowy mile to the farm next door to get the grown-ups there to call the ambulance.

Ebba had been gathered by the time she got back to the house. "Gathered" was her mother's word.

Her father tried to explain that God had taken care of Ebba, and that all was well. Sad for a moment, yes, but happy too, because Ebba was now going to be at peace and happy forever.

Eleven-year-old Sig had told him that God could go fuck himself.

Her mother had gasped and left the room in tears. Her father had followed, trying to calm her.

The paramedic had looked at Sig and nodded her head in agreement.

After the ambulance had taken Ebba away, Sig had walked out of the house, crunched across the snow and climbed the tallest bare-branched tree in the garden, fully conscious of her mother watching her from the kitchen window. Sig sat there, high and solitary in the cold of the evening until it grew dark, trying to keep her mind safely blank by imagining how she must look like a big raven roosting above the garden. Trying not to think of how she had broken her promise to always protect her sister. When no one came out to call her in, she knew her mother had forbidden her father to do it, and something else broke inside her at the thought that he was weak enough to have agreed.

There had been a court case as her parents were charged

with letting their extreme beliefs delay the help that could have saved their child. It had been a local, even a national, scandal but Sig had sleepwalked through it because it was, in comparison to the loss of her sister, an irrelevance. There had been social workers and foster care for a while, then a period back at home with heavily supervised parenting, and then sixteen-year-old Sig had left what no longer felt like a home anyway and gone to a residential college to do her exams. By that time, she'd had more than five years of growing and thinking for herself. It was as if Ebba's death and the smack to the side of her head that had followed it had sent her careening down an entirely different direction to the one her parents had taken. She'd decided that any time she faced a choice between self-help and science or waiting for an angel or some other imaginary supernatural power to show up, she voted rational all the way. The first thing she did on arrival at the college was get herself vaccinated for everything she'd missed. The second thing she did was swap the gold crucifix and chain her mother had tearfully given her for an ice-hockey stick and a used set of pads. She'd then majored in sciences, learned to rock-climb and played every sport she could fit in, and got good enough results to go on to university in Stockholm to study Materials Science and Structural Engineering. A holiday internship at a big architect's firm in their model-building department turned into a full-time job on graduation. She worked as a structural engineer in a department that specialised in reclamation and renovation of older buildings, and she balanced a largely indoor occupation calculating loads and tolerances with an active, almost obsessive outdoor life at weekends. Sig was self-aware enough to know that her choice of a profession devoted to stopping things breaking and collapsing, and reclaiming lost things, might not be entirely accidental. She suspected she was a broken thing herself and was fatalistic enough to believe no one else was going to put her back together.

Then she found him. She'd met him on a mountain, and though it was far from the island that was his home, she'd seen the sea in the blue of his eyes and had not been surprised when he told her later that he was a fisherman by birth and a diver by profession.

She'd got herself stuck trying to climb a chimney in a high granite scarp beneath a tricky overhang and was taking a breather, trying to figure out how to avoid having to ignominiously retrace her steps downwards, when he had appeared above her.

He'd asked if she was okay, and she'd ruefully admitted she'd messed up and got herself into a bit of a dead end. Stuck behind the eight ball, in fact.

He'd assessed her position and grinned.

"Only one thing to do if you're stuck behind the eight ball," he'd said. "Move."

And then he'd pointed to the one handhold she couldn't quite see from her vantage point and calmly talked her up and across the overhang to join him.

They'd shaken hands and then sat there on the ledge, looking out at the gulf of air below them. After a moment, she heard him laughing quietly.

"What?" she'd said.

"This," he'd answered, sweeping his arm across the view. "All of this. All of that. Just makes you happy to see it, doesn't it?"

His eyes were striking, but it was his laugh that did it. It reminded her of an earlier, simpler sound of happiness, one that she had almost forgotten, despite her vow never to do so. It rumbled deeper and huskier than an eight-year-old girl's giggle, but somehow it sang the same song.

Until that point, the thing she'd liked most about climbing was doing it solo. It had become a sort of meditation in physicality and problem solving. From then on, what she loved, and what they did, was climb together, as a team.

Within 12 hours of that first meeting, they'd kissed. Within the next 12 months, they'd met up on every holiday she could take from her job and co-ordinate with his shifts as a commercial diver on the oil rigs and found new mountains to climb with each other. And within 18 months, they were married and figuring out how to make their lives work together. They came back to the island which was his home. He began fishing again and working as a maintenance and installation diver on the various fish farms that were opening up on the west coast of Scotland, and she went freelance with her structural engineering skills, had intermittent success, and began silversmithing – a discipline which kept her hands busy and her mind clear and occupied. Having fallen in love with him, she then fell in love with the island and the home they renovated together.

The silversmithing was a satisfying and exacting thing to do, like engineering and model building in miniature, and a lot of the pleasure she'd discovered in her internship returned as what had begun as a hobby began to take over from her notional profession. She specialised in boxes that looked like houses and opened up to reveal rooms within rooms, and rings and bracelets that looked like the crowded roofscapes of imaginary cities, precisely made tiled pitches and gables bristling with chimneys, huddled jigsaw-like amongst domes and spires and minarets. Her work sold through a gallery in Stockholm, and she realised after a year that he had done an extraordinary thing in creating the space and security for her to be the thing she'd always wanted to be, a maker of her own worlds.

They bought Rex because they agreed it was probably too soon to think about kids, and she thought it'd be good practice to see how they managed a puppy, and his sister and little Evie or his cousin Matt would look after it when they went on climbing trips. And then she got pregnant.

As happy endings in stories go, it was perfect.

And as happy endings in real life go, it went all too quickly. As he had. As his sister and brother-in-law had.

And now here she was again, she thought. Stuck behind something she couldn't move around. She screwed the eight ball tight on the gearstick to kill the rattle and accelerated into the lonely stretch of road winding towards the harbour.

Chapter 14

Changing

S hanna Nisbett knows she's going to die. Her heart's beating so hard and so fast that it feels like she's being given a bad kicking from the inside. Like it's going to burst a rib or something. She should have given up smoking. She should have cleaned up her act years ago. She should have packed earlier. She should have left more time.

She's going to miss the ferry.

It's always like this: she means to get things done on time, to prepare, to be calm, to plan. But then she doesn't. It's a failing. She knows it. She just can't kick it, this habit, this last-minute thing. It's mad, pure dead mental. And now she's going to die. She's going to die and miss the ferry and not get the train to Glasgow, and her sister will die too, dead and cold and alone in a hospital bed the same way she'll be dead and cold on the lino in this kitchen, dead from looking for her wallet, dead from leaving everything to the last minute.

God, she's such a fucking numpty.

She got the call from the hospital in the ghost-light of the pre-dawn. Her first fuddled thought was that the jangling ringtone would disturb the B&B guest she had staying in the room at the other end of the passage, but she instantly forgot about him when the professionally calm voice on the other end of the line said her sister was in The Royal Alexandra in Paisley, fallen out of a window while cleaning it, they said. Stupid with sleep and shock, Shanna had asked if she was going to be okay.

The nurse had said to come soon.

She'd felt the sick cold stab of it in her gut. Come soon or don't hurry was what the voice on the phone meant. She wasn't going to be okay. Shanna said she'd be there and sat and stared at the phone long after the hospital had gone off the line. Then she'd checked the ferry time and made a pot of tea. As she stood at the counter, she saw the B&B guy's car was not back in front of the house. He was obviously still out, she thought, taking his pictures: he'd told her he would be out very late because he was an astronomical photographer who'd come to take time lapses of the night sky from the wild areas of the islands where there was no light pollution. He'd seemed nice enough, and he paid cash, but she felt there was something a bit sketchy about him in his camo parka and his backpack full of kit, like he was one of those military wannabes who was too soft to actually join up. Anyway. If he was still outside he wasn't having much luck with the stars, she thought, looking at the fine drizzle spitting out of the low clouds over the moor beyond the kitchen window. Then the kettle pinged and she forgot about him and she thought of phoning Allie at the fish farm to tell her she was not going to be able to come in today. Shanna decided it was way too early to wake her, so she sent a text as she smoked an emergency cigarette, then finished half a pack without pouring, and when she did pour the tea had gone cold and now she is late and she had better leave a note for the B&B guy explaining she had to go and asking him to lock up when he leaves, and then she runs for the car.

If the bloody thing doesn't start, if it plays up the way it had been playing up, off and on and at all the wrongest times in the past month, she'll definitely die. The pounding blood in her head tells her that. One more millibar of pressure and her skull will burst. Fuck, she needs a drink.

The wallet is only in her bloody pocket. Fuck's sake.

She runs back to the house and gets her bag. She hadn't known what to pack, so she'd shovelled in the latest load of laundry straight out of the dryer: underwear, T-shirts, jeans. Crumpled but clean – what she feels like most of the time anyway – but she has neither time nor inclination for ironing, so that'll have to do.

Little voice at the back of her head says she can't wear jeans to a funeral; bigger voice up the front says Annie is not going to die. She's tough, Shanna's big sister, not a quitter.

Mind you, Annie also isn't the kind of person who cleans her windows in the middle of the night, much less falls out of them. She is the rock. The sensible one. The one who doesn't have to go and hide on an island. But thinking like that will wait, surely. Shanna's mind strips down into one-thing-at-a-time mode, something she's well used to. A lifetime of leaving things to the last minute has honed this one skill: if she just does the next thing before worrying about the one after it, she can usually skate through. She can get away with it. It's how she lives. One thing at a time.

That's what she tells herself as she cranks the key and waits for the engine to decide how much more shit her day is going to contain.

It starts first go. She exhales and guns backwards into the road, before chunking into first and accelerating for the ferry.

The single-track speeds under the car as she focuses on the next bend, then the one after.

She relaxes just enough to let one last weasel thought in:

it isn't just Annie in hospital that she isn't looking forward to facing. It's the mainland. Real life. Because she's not been living, not really, maybe not ever, certainly not here. She wouldn't have ironed the clothes even if she'd had time. She hits the horn and parps a sheep into a passing space and swerves past.

She checks her phone with one eye as she drives, in case there's an update.

Dead battery.

She'd meant to charge it. She scrabbles for the lead and jams it into the adapter in the cigarette lighter.

Can't even keep her phone alive. As if that isn't a fucking omen or something.

She doesn't really know how to do life, not properly, not Shanna Nisbett.

She's just been getting away with it.

Chapter 15

The missing tooth

Kathleen McWhinnie has walked the sheep path that hugs the northern end of the island all her long life. Now she is nearing the end of that journey, she is rigorous about paying attention as she takes what is, health permitting, her regular stroll. She is happy to be in the open air. She feels released. She has not been out this far for a week, anchored at home by a flu bug that made her feel, for four days at least, exactly as old as she is. But in the last two days she has been on the mend, and the sun at her window this morning called her out of bed and into her walking shoes. As her mother was, and her mother before her, she's a great believer in the cleansing power of a soft breeze and clear sunlight. Fine weather's just as good for airing people as for pegging out the wash, her mother would say.

Kathleen takes in every detail as she walks, always trying to see it fresh, made new as it is every day. Being deaf, she has always had to rely on her other faculties to make up for that lack, and she's trying to keep her eyes young, trying to find that sense of wonder in the small things. She walks to keep herself fit and limber, though being deep into her eighties that's a relative thing. She's no fool. She takes her time. And why should she not? No one is waiting at home any more, her lovely Donald tucked away under the neat clipped grass in the island cemetery these past three years, and the old sheepdog Bobby too blind and lame to do much more than stagger outside the back door to do his business on quivering legs. Nevertheless, Kathleen patrols the wild north cape in rain or shine, a mile out, until she's level with the old Viking seamark that jags into the sky on the ridgeline, then a mile back, dependable as the tide.

She can sometimes feel her heart bumping as she goes, usually when leaning into a stiff wind when the weather's soft, but she doesn't worry too much about it. Either she's keeping herself in good fettle, or she's wearing herself out. If it's the former, good for her, she thinks. And if she should suddenly drop in the heather and not get up again? Well, even better. She can't think of a cleaner way to go. Having seen her Donald die slowly on his feet as the dementia nibbled away at him by degrees, until he was full gone but still standing, she knows fine which door she'd choose for the exit. As if anyone really gets a choice, unless they're a poor sad suicide. Like her childhood friend Jean, the wife of poor and even sadder Walter John. She feels intermittently guilty about the widower. She knows she should see more of him, but when the guilt gets too strong she bakes a cake and has her grandson Matty deliver it. She can't put her finger on it, but the old man has changed in his solitude. As if grief and loneliness have curdled him a little. He was never a strong personality – not the kind of person it was possible to dislike, but not a man who you warmed to especially – but now she feels uneasy around him, not because of anything he's done but because the sadness pooled around him feels like a hole through which worse things may come.

Her mother claimed that her own mother and all the long line of dead women before her had had the power to foresee harm and misfortune, and thereby had a responsibility to protect the island community when they could. They'd also been able to foresee their own deaths. She said they'd found that a comforting thing, enabling them to get things straight before they passed. Kathleen's mother had clearly not had the gift, otherwise she wouldn't have stepped in front of the bus during the blackout in Glasgow all those years ago, and Kathleen herself had spent her life studiously not claiming any such superstitious ability on her or anyone else's behalf.

Not that she has any intention of dying this morning. She's enjoying the light, the way it changes all the time, the sun, the sea and the hill in a constant interplay of cloud shadows as the balance shifts back and forth. Donald once told her that her beauty was like the landscape, constantly in movement, endlessly surprising as the weather moved across it like emotions. The old fool. Though he'd been young enough and just back from university in Glasgow when he'd said it.

It was the same unexpectedly romantic streak that had led him to insist on reading the Edwin Muir poem at their wedding, and then again at their golden, the one that began by saying that hers was the right human face, and ended with the lines she liked most, because they were not, to her ears, boastful or excessively overblown, but suitably modest. Those lines were in her head now as she paused to scan the scenery and get her breath, the ones about the hearth and the land and the sea not being beautiful or even rare in all their parts, but rather in just being themselves – as she and they were simply meant to be.

She was turning slowly around to let her eyes softly brush the familiar circle of the horizon when she stopped, shock jerking her into stillness before her conscious mind could tell what was wrong, the half-smile of recollection dying on her lips.

This face, the face of the landscape she knew so well, was not as it was meant to be. The alteration was so shocking that it took her a long moment to see what was wrong, what had changed. Maybe it took a beat longer because it was an absence rather than an addition. And what was missing, what was no longer where it had always been, was the seamark, the old Viking cairn that usually spiked the ridgeline, the ancient navigation aid that had been helping sailors and fishermen thread the zig-zag channel through the outer skerries ever since they travelled the wave road in dragon-headed longships.

Its absence was as shocking and wrong as a missing tooth in a well-loved smile.

Chapter 16

A bad day for the fish

Matt follows the basking sharks for a while, until they surface again, and he sees the big fins break water ahead of him. He watches them long enough to roll and light a cigarette and then turns back towards the north cape of the island, where his familiarity with the waters and the season tells him there's likely to be fish.

He enjoys the rollie as he throttles away, recycling the exhaled smoke through his nose to get the full kick. He grabs the battered thermos that lives beside the wheel and takes a welcome jolt of strong black coffee. He's given up smoking – on land. He only sparks up on the boat these days. It's not something he's proud of, this small vice, but he once saw a black and white movie where the old actor who played Colombo on the TV told an angel that the thing he missed about being human was that first hit of nicotine after a strong hot cup of coffee; though Matt knows he's no angel, he has to agree with the sentiment. Peter Falk. That was the guy, he thinks, as he takes another slug and then notices the Raymarine is picking up a cloud of fish seaward of the boat.

He takes a final drag on the rollie and spins the butt over the side with a practised flick of his fingers, and then turns the wheel towards the signal.

He grins. It's not going to be too bad a day for the fish, despite his earlier sense of foreboding.

On the ridgeline on the north cape, Kathleen is crying in short, sharp, shocked sobs. Her heart is thumping in a hard, irregular beat and her leg muscles burn with hurt from the scrambled ascent she has just completed. She hurled herself up the steep hill without thinking, pulled by the urgency of that terrible absence of the seamark.

That is not why she is crying. She is too distressed at what lies at her feet to spare a moment for what her body is telling her.

The seamark used to be as tall as she is. It was that tall since forever, a thin cairn made from stones carefully laid in place and then left undisturbed so long ago that the lichen that grew infinitely slowly on the lee side, protected from the prevailing wind, streamed behind it like an old man's beard. When she was little, her parents had taken her for a picnic and she had snapped off a strand. Her father had grabbed her hand and slapped the bare back of her legs for it. She can still feel the shock of it. Then he had sat her on his knee and explained how many hundreds of years it had taken that lichen to grow from a grey-green scab on the rock to a long hair like that, and that to break it off was an affront to history and the ones who had gone before. Pure vandalism, he had called it, but then he had given her a barley sugar and said he shouldn't have smacked her so sharply because she had acted out of ignorance. And now she knew, she would never do it again. And she hasn't.

But someone has. Someone, in the week she had been ill,

has been here and – accidentally or on purpose – taken the cairn to bits. It has the look of something done methodically, at least at first, because the stones seem to have been stacked in a rudimentary horseshoe shape on one side, but then there is a tumbled pile in the middle of it where the cairn had stood. It also looks like someone had been digging at the cairn footing.

She is finding it hard to breathe. This is a crime that calls out for more than slapped legs. This is perhaps the worst thing she has ever seen. It's like a hole punched in her life. It is a violation, a wrongness she cannot bear. She feels the weight of the desecration crushing her. It's too much to carry alone. Without wiping the tears streaming down her face, she fumbles for the mobile phone her grandson made her promise to carry with her wherever she goes, and presses the button that he has assigned to himself.

She concentrates on not falling over and trying to breathe better as she waits to see if he is in range.

Matt doesn't hear the phone ring, but he feels the vibration in his pocket. He takes his eyes off the sonar and sees who is calling. She doesn't normally call in the day. Like all pensioners, she is still haunted by the conviction that it's cheaper to call after six, even when making a video call. She'd resisted the newfangled iPhone he gave her until she realised he could talk to her in sign language. She's been an enthusiast ever since. But her face right now is anything but enthusiastic. She looks distressed and is breathing hard, almost panting. His heart bumps in alarm. He places the phone on the mount above the wheel and squints at the picture on the screen – he can't see where she is, only a blur of heather behind her.

He jams his hip on the wheel to hold the boat steady,

bumps his fists end to end, then slaps three fingers of one hand into the palm of the other, making the sign for "Gran", then waggles the interrogative index finger in the sign for "What is it?"

He ducks his head closer beneath the weather cowling and tries to hear what she is saying.

"The seamark . . . "

Matt can barely hear her over the chunter of the idling diesel and the wave slap on the side of the boat.

"See who?" he signs.

She doesn't answer, not that he can hear properly. The line suddenly sounds dead.

"Gran?" he signs, ducking his head away from the engine, trying to block the noise with his body mass. "Gran? Are you okay?"

He's shaken. She has never sounded worried, his gran. Even when Grandad Donald was getting so hollowed out by the bloody Alz that he was little more than a shambling six-foot baby with a man-nappy – and all the attendant needs of feeding and cleaning up – she was tough as nails and didn't shirk a bit of his care. Nor did she ever complain, though Matt could see it rubbing her down to a shadow and so did as much for her as she would allow him to do. Proud and solid as the rocks around her house, she is. Never worries.

Matt has few heroes, but of the ones he does admit to, his gran is top of the list. Even over the competing noise around him, the small voice he can only just hear has a note in it that is new. New and worrying.

"Gran?" he signs, making it a question with his eyes.

No reply.

On the headland, Kathleen is on her knees staring at the jumbled ruin of the cairn.

"Matty, where are you?"

He straightens in relief. Instinctively the fingertips of his hands come together to make a prow and move as if being lifted and dropped by the waves.

"On the boat," he signs.

The pain in Kathleen's chest is both a new and an old friend.

"Come in, son," she says. "It's no day to be out on the water. It's no day for the fish . . . "

The screen on the Raymarine in front of him shows she is wrong – two fat shoals worth of wrong, in fact – but despite that he is already turning the wheel and gunning the engine for home. Matt lives in the modern world, more than most on the island, and likes to think he hasn't a superstitious bone in his body, but when Kathleen McWhinnie says it's a bad day to be on the water, it's time to head on in. And more than that – even if it wasn't, she sounds in trouble.

"What is it? Are you okay?" he signs.

"Something bad . . . happened," she says. The pain is cinching tight around her chest. It's squeezing so hard now she can barely get breath enough to talk.

"Something bad . . . "

"What? Where are you? What's happened?" he signs.

"Don't know, Matty," she says, voice gritty and hoarse. "But it's not . . . someone's knocked the—"

Kathleen's left-handed, so when her arm goes fully numb and starts spasming the phone tumbles out of her fingers and bounces off the rocks at her feet. And at that moment – as in so many of the moments in her long life when stress or shock have brought the unwelcome gift on her – she closes her eyes and flashes forward and finds she's not here, not on the hill, not in the light of day slowly collapsing into the heather, but she's indoors and it's dark and lit only by the hell-red glow of the electric fire, and she's full of hate, so full of hate that it's like another person's jammed inside the one body with her,

95

rammed in so tight her skin is about to split open, the hate so sharp and ready to spill she can taste it rising like bile in the back of her mouth, and her Matty, her lovely Matty, is in front of her and he's soaked and dripping water on to her good carpet and he's reaching for her and she flinches away and slashes at him with the poker she seems to have gripped in her hand and the noise the noise the noise fills the room, the terrible noise that she, profoundly deaf since childhood, can hear so loud that it feels like it's splitting her in two as it rips from her own throat. And then she flashes back and in the outdoors and the light, and there's only the one of her and she's falling forwards ...

And then a new thing – an unfamiliar thing – happens, as a darker sight comes on her and she knows this is the last thing, the thing she's always known she'll see because it's more than seeing, it's feeling and just as real as real: So she's falling forward in the now, but then she's falling back as the thing sputters in and out of her head. She's falling forwards and it's daylight and she's falling backwards and it's night, she's falling forwards and it's on land and she's falling backwards and it's at sea, she's falling forwards and she's dry and she's falling backwards and she's wet, wetter than she's ever been, and she's falling forwards losing her grip on her phone and she's falling backwards holding an anchor to her chest, and she's dropping back into a dark sea that brutally just swallows her, and with an almost merciful gentleness she's dropping forward into the springy heather beside the ruin of the seamark and is still here, still just here. Of course she's still here. The last vision is the darkest vision, the one that's hung over her all her life, unseen but anticipated like death itself.

She can't seem to move. Maybe the phone is close enough for him to hear her. And though she's now lying in brightest sunlight, there's something she must say before the dark cloud she can feel at her back takes 'her. Maybe she's got enough breath inside to warn him of what she's seen with the second sight she's spent her whole life pretending wasn't there.

"It's bad," she croaks. "Oh Matty, son. It's bad. And worse is coming."

Part 2

THE STONE BOAT

VARANGIAN: THE LORDS OF THE WATER

The desert clans call themselves Lords of the Water.

And water in this dry accursed southern land is what wind is to the northern seas of his true home. Without it, you cannot travel easily. Not for long distances. He has spent hours, days, pulling at an oar, praying for a wind that wouldn't come, so he knows slow progress is always possible, with difficulty.

But he would settle for slow progress from his pursuers.

He had come to this bread oven of a landscape to guard the emissary sent by the emperor he served in the great city on the Bosphorus.

They had made their way south and east, at the end threading their progress from well to waterhole to oasis, following a map drawn by men who knew the fragile string of beads along which the caravans travelled.

The emissary, his master, had come to explain to the people now pursuing him that they should not attack those caravan routes that passed through their lands because the goods belonged to the emperor.

The emissary had told them he had come without an army to explain this, out of courtesy. He explained his emperor was a just man who preferred talk and trade to war.

He was prepared to allow them a small tithe if, instead of attacking the caravans, they protected them.

He came in peace and friendship.

He did them the courtesy of not bringing an army to take their lands from them.

They smiled and listened and said they would need to think about it. Talk to their clans.

They shared food and water and hospitality.

Their faces were hard to read.

Their smiles harder to believe.

Their questions, which were few, were not really about the caravans at all. Like any traders in the Grand Bazaar, they seemed happy to talk about anything but the matter in hand. He had seen this often. The traders softened their customers with friendly questions that built the false sense of a bond that put the customer on the wrong foot when the nut of the matter was finally brought out to be cracked.

They didn't ask about the emperor. Or his emissary. They asked about him. The emissary's guard. Was he a man or a giant – or a djinn, perhaps? Was he a Circassian? They had never seen hair yellow like that. Why did he wear it in a long plait like a woman? Why were his eyes the colour of the deep blue sky at dawn, just before the sun baked the colour out of it?

And the marks that writhed all over his skin, skin pale as the belly of a snake – what did they mean, and why so many?

Were the jagged marks that intertwined with the snake-monsters words of power, or just pretty shapes?

The emissary explained that his guard came from a land so far in the north that there was no sun, only moon, and no sand, only water. And that the snakes were not snakes but the ice dragons that lived there too.

He had smiled and kept his mouth shut.

He did not correct his master.

He saw no reason to tell these people anything true.

They admired the redness in the ruby in his left ear.

He let them come close to see it.

They offered to trade for it.

He said no. It was a mark of honour, signifying that he served the emperor. He regretted it was not his to give.

They smiled and understood. As if it was nothing.

They asked to see his arm rings.

He shrugged and handed one over. As if it was nothing.

They complimented the silverwork. One of them wondered why, if the emperor was so powerful, his guards did not wear gold rings. The emissary explained the Northmen were children of the cold moon they lived beneath, and like children they did not fully understand the world, and so thought that silver was the most valuable since it was the moon's metal, just as real people who lived under the yellow sun knew gold was the real metal of power.

They had all laughed and nodded.

They laughed because they believed he was big and strong but slow. Slow to move, slow to understand.

As if he was certainly something.

But nothing to worry about.

They asked to hold his axe and they admired the strength it took to lift it, but said — politely, always politely — they did not think it a good weapon because it could never be fast as a sword or a knife.

He thought it prudent not to disagree.

And then the days passed as the clans were consulted, and one afternoon they all came together and, though they still smiled, they cracked the nut with one sharp blow.

They thanked the emperor for his offer and his kind forbearance in not sending an army, only the emissary and the tattooed giant who guarded him.

They still smiled as they explained they were happy with their lot and took their pick of the caravans as their tithe anyway, as was their habitual right. The emperor might be an emperor, whatever that was, but they were Lords of the Water, keepers of the wells, guardians of the oases. And without water the caravans would not come. So the emperor should be happy they did not attack all the caravans and be satisfied with the leavings they allowed to trickle north to wherever it was he was emperor of.

Because wherever that place was, it was assuredly not here.

And they smiled and sent them on their way.

"They will attack us once we are beyond the protection of their hospitality," he had told his master as they packed their belongings.

"Nonsense," his master replied. "They have given us a message to deliver. They would not have done that if they meant us harm."

"Sending our heads back is a message," he had said. "And they are thieves."

"Which is why we came with no show, and nothing they could want to steal," his master said. "The emperor is a wise man."

"They liked my arm rings," he said. "And this ruby."

His master had not believed him.

And his master had been right. They were not attacked.

Not the first night, nor the second, and when they camped on the third night, at the first waterhole they had come to, he laughed and told him, See? He had worried too much.

They had come out of the dark after midnight, six of them.

Chapter 17

Dead zone

Sig and Rex are enjoying a companionable quiet as the Defender speeds along the single-track road winding across the moor to the ferry. The agricultural clatter of the diesel engine is so familiar that it's more like white noise to them both, easily filtered out.

Halfway down the unpeopled stretch of road, an old stone bridge crosses a stream where it forks around an islet before rejoining itself and broadening as it continues on the last half-mile of its way to the sea. One of the island's two cemeteries sits on the small hummocky islet that nature has worn into the rough longship profile that gives it its name – *An long-cloiche* – the stone ship. Sig had always liked the name because as a child she and her sister had looked out at other islands in the sea beyond the family farm and had decided that they looked like a small fleet of rocky ships. *An long-cloiche* is the old cemetery which has been there forever, or at least since people believed it was a lucky thing to do to bury their loved ones in a place where the water flowed on either side and thus helped carried their souls off into the West, to the isles of the blessed. It was a sanctuary, a place of ancient safety that could not be stepped on by even the most malign supernatural beings that their more superstitious forebears could imagine peopling the darkness of the long winter nights. He'd told her that, and that the old Gaelic expression for dying used by the poets translated as "going into the West".

Not that he'd gone into the West himself. He'd taken the ferry and driven east, across the width of the mainland to the oil town where he got on a helicopter and flew off to the rigs in the North Sea.

They'd had just the one big argument in their time together, and though it was a substantial one, if it hadn't been the cause of him going off-island to do a fortnight shift on the rigs at short notice, it probably wouldn't have lain so heavily on her.

He had after all sat with her having a picnic on that very island, surrounded by the irregular jumble of old gravestones that gapped and tilted every which way, like teeth in an old man's mouth, and sworn he'd always be there for her, for better or worse, hell or high water, now and forever.

"Forever?" she'd said.

"Forever ever," he'd said and smiled and kissed her.

"We don't get forever," she'd said later, lying back in the heather and looking up at the clouds sailing across the blue above them. "We get one life. 'For life' will do fine."

"Sig," he'd laughed. "Don't always be so literal. I'm trying to be romantic."

She'd rolled towards him and apologised and told him he wasn't doing a bad job of that at all, and later still he'd rolled away and told her that when she was old and grey and he was gone he'd just have to sit up here on the top of the graveyard and watch out for her until she joined him and they both went into the West together.

He was admittedly superstitious – not obsessively so, but he explained it was congenital and not something that someone whose ancestors had probably been fishermen since the longships sailed these waters could help. And he claimed that though some of the more obscure superstitions were nonsense (no women on a boat, nail a horseshoe to the sternpost), some of the others were just rags of common sense and local knowledge, patched up into a story as an easily transmittable mnemonic to be passed down the generations. ("Don't cross the outer skerries at the north of the island on a waning moon in case the old witch gets you because she doesn't come out in the full moonlight" was really just a sensible bit of advice about not getting the keel ripped open on a low tide). And besides, who didn't love a good story?

Sig, the rationalist, secretly loved the lyrical streak in him, not least because it was somehow unexpected in such a practical man. He, in turn, delighted in teasing her about her failure to believe in anything supernatural.

"What about ghosts?" he'd asked her one Halloween, as they sat in the dark staring into the fire.

"Don't believe in them," she'd said.

"Pity," he'd said, putting an arm round her. "Not that it matters. What matters is: do they believe in you?"

Rex's sharp bark comes out of nowhere and startles her.

"Hey," she says. "Hey."

The terrier scrabbles round to stand with his paws on the back of the bench seat and starts whining urgently at something. Sig's eyes flick to the rear-view to see who's on their tail. She expects to see a familiar vehicle waving at them, or else some flustered tourist late for the ferry flashing their headlights to get past, but it's early in the season for tourists and there's nothing on the thin ribbon of tarmac unspooling behind them.

She reaches a hand over and scratches the rough fur on the dog's back.

"It's okay, Rex," she says. "It's okay."

She feels him tense and then spring away from under her hand as he leaps into the back of the Defender and begins to bark furiously at whatever it is that she can't see. He's braced and bristling at something behind and off to the side at the rise of ground that obscures the unpeopled north cape of the island. Sig slows and ducks her head to see what he's seeing.

There's nothing but a low hill covered in an unbroken swathe of heather.

"Come on, Rex," she says.

He turns an excited circle in his own length – looking at her and then prancing back up to the side window and redoubling his barking.

Despite herself, she feels unnerved. She pulls into the next passing place and gets out on to the tarmac. She snags the small leather bag that lives on the shelf next to the speedometer and unzips the Leitz Trinovid binoculars nestled inside. She walks quickly to the back of the vehicle and leans against it to steady herself the way he taught her, the dog still barking animatedly through the window beside her as she scans the hill through the high-powered lenses. There is nothing moving except a raven circling high in the sky to the north.

The German optics bring everything into razor-sharp focus, but there's nothing she can see on the hill; no injured sheep, no walker, familiar or unfamiliar. In fact, unless Rex had taken a sudden and irrational offence at the vast expanse of heather, it's hard to see what he's barking at. She checks both ways on the road and then unlatches the back door, letting the weight of the chunky spare tyre bolted to the outside swing it open against the slight slope of the passing place.

"Go on, then," she says, looking at the dog. "What is it?"

Rex stands braced on the floor of the vehicle, a dog at bay. He stops barking but doesn't jump out as she expected him to do.

"Rex," she says, checking her watch. "Seriously. What's up?"

He cocks his head at her as if she's the one behaving strangely. With his one ear up and one ear down, this is usually a look that charms her. Right now she finds it unnerving, maybe because his whole body is quivering with tension, or maybe it's that and the fact that he won't get out of the Defender despite being so clearly agitated.

"Fine," she says. "Be like that."

She swings the door closed with a decisive clunk and gets back in the driving seat. Rex is now back barking through the rear window again.

She checks her watch a second time, sighs and then pulls hard on the wheel, arcing across the width of the road and three-pointing back the way she came. As soon as she does so, Rex bounds back into the front seat and stands balancing himself eagerly against the dash, both ears up, on point.

Sig thinks he must have seen something on the side of the road as they passed, something low and hidden by one of the many dips and rises in the landscape, or maybe lying in one of the irrigation ditches that sporadically line the single-track to keep it clear of runoff when heavy rainstorms sheet water off the hill.

"Come on, boy," she says, crouching forward to scan the terrain. "What is it? What did you see?"

Whatever it is must be invisible. She drives a quarter mile past the point where he started barking. He continues to bark and growl at the hill itself. Sometimes at home he just pounces to the windows like this and barks at the darkness, which – as she lives alone now – she has to admit she finds a little unsettling, but this is broad daylight. She still finds this vaguely disturbing.

"Okay," she says. "We're going to be late now."

She pulls a tight U-ey in the next passing place and heads back towards the ferry. Rex is now just watching the passing hill with a low, almost subsonic growl. She reaches out to calm him.

"Easy now," she says, but she knows she's talking as much to herself as the dog. "Calm d—"

Her phone rings and she nearly jumps out of her skin. Angry at herself, she fumbles it out of her pocket and stares at the screen. The Caller ID photograph is a bearded Matt grinning out at her from some sunnier afternoon in a long-gone and much happier time.

She hasn't got time for this. She knows what he's going to say. She saw his face as he tried to tell her off at the buoy. Her buoy. Of the two men that she knows have a habit of watching her, she finds old Walter John a lot less annoying. Matt's photo may be cheery but she knows he won't be smiling in real life, not now, poised on the other end of the line, waiting for her to pick up so he can tell her what's on his mind. What's always on his mind, no matter how he finds other ways to say it. She didn't need to see his face to know what he was thinking. What he's calling her up to say. It's all they talk to each other about now, as if her freediving and his disapproval is the one topic of conversation that remains viable, but she knows it's a proxy for all the other shit they don't and can't talk about. Her thumb hovers over the answer button.

On the *An da Shealladh*, Matt is staring at the screen on his phone, waiting for her to pick up as he powers through the mile and a half of chop that lies between him and the nearest jetty he can berth alongside. He'll tie up by the fish farm and use their phone, maybe borrow the quad bike. That'll get him to his grandmother's house faster than if he goes the long way round the island and ties up in the harbour.

Trouble is that'll take valuable time his gran might not have, and the one person who can get there fastest is her nearest neighbour. And this is bigger than whatever gulf now yawns between him and Sig. But if she doesn't pick up in the next minute or so he's going to be in the patch of sea shadowed from the phone mast on the other side of the high land to his right: he knows the current and the hidden rocks around the island just as well as his father and his grandfather. On top of that, he knows where the dead zones are for cellular service, and changing course for the fish farm is about to plunge him into a big one.

"Come on," he says, as if willpower alone will make her pick up.

She doesn't.

Instead, an auto-send text blips up on his screen.

SORRY I CAN'T TAKE YOUR CALL RIGHT NOW.

Bloody Sig. He nearly throws the phone overboard in frustration. Christ. If she ends up with another death on her hands, he's going to—

No. He stops himself. He starts redialling, then decides to text her to cut through the bullshit. She may have done what she did, but she likes Kathleen. She'll go check on her. He types:

KAI HLEEN EMERGENCY PLZ CHECK ON HER
ASAP! AM ON WAY.

He hits SEND. She'll take note of that.
The message hangs. And hangs.
And now he has no bars.
He's in the dead zone.

Chapter 18

Spasm

The body of the detectorist has floated a little further away from the shore, pulled towards the open ocean by the change in the tide. It's still face down and remains hidden from normal, prying eyes by the steep sides of the narrow gulley that open seawards from the tiny scrape of sand at its point, and by the sodden Flecktarn camouflage parka it's wearing. The spots of dark green, light green, red-brown and black help it blend in with the rocks and grass and seaweed around it.

The raven does not have normal eyes. It does not know the name of the camouflage pattern, does not really register it as a disguise at all. It certainly does not know that Flecktarn is a composite word made from the German words *Fleck*, meaning stain, and *Tarnung*, meaning camouflage. If it did know, and if its corvid brain appreciated small ironies, it might gain a little amusement from this, because it clearly sees that this body is a stain. It is the source of that strand of darkness the raven noticed a day ago, the tendrils of malign possibility that it has sensed spreading across the island.

It turns away from the body and issues two urgent *kraa*s into the open sky above.

There is the sound of something stirring in the water behind it. Looking back, it sees that the shape of the body in the water has changed. Where it had lain splayed starfish-like on the surface, it is now a smaller and more humped shape. The feet have disappeared beneath the wavelets and the wand of the metal detector that had been lying flat on the corpse's back is now angling upwards, water dripping from the concentric plastic circles at the end of the telescopic arm as it comes clear of the surface and angles upwards.

The raven goes very still and watches the body right itself as its feet hit the bottom and it uncurls into a standing position, the detector wand sliding round and back down again, plopping into the water as the body snatches the handle and uses the wand as a crutch to push itself upright. Its face is water-bloated and blank, its sagging mouth and lifeless eyes leaking water as they turn towards the bird.

The eyes may be dead, but the detectorist's body stops moving, as if seeing the bird has given it pause. The corpse's neck cricks from side to side, as if stretching out a kink, and then it takes a small staggering step towards the shore.

The raven hurls itself into the air, wild warning cry echoing from the slope behind it, wings wide and angled towards the face of the body trying to get ashore. They beat in furiously powerful strokes that should loft it backwards and into the sky, but the bird seems to defy normal physics as it stays anchored four feet above the waves, beating the body backwards with each powerful wingbeat.

The figure stops and then stumbles back a pace, flat and affectless eyes angling upwards at the bird, and then it gurgles a slow watery snarl and lashes out at it with the metal detector.

The raven jinks clear of the blow and the figure lunges again, but the bird is too nimble in the air and the momentum of the swing makes the unwieldy body lose its footing and it goes down with a splash. Now it's just a head above the water staring at the bird. It pushes to its feet and as it hefts the wand again the other raven blindsides it, barrelling into the side of its head in a percussive thump of flashing talons and flailing wings. The impact turns the body, and when it tries to right itself and resume its attempt to walk ashore it finds both birds are in the air in front of it, oily-black wings forming a beating barricade that punches blocks of air into its face, forcing it back and down into the sea beyond the mouth of the narrow inlet. The body walks backwards until it disappears and all that is left are the headphones floating on the surface on the end of the coiled wire attaching them to the detector wand. The ravens keep beating and following them until the wire straightens and tautens and then pulls them below the water too.

The ravens circle the spot where they disappeared for a good twenty minutes and then return to the shore, each taking up a lookout point on either side of the gulley, eyes fixed on the seemingly innocent waters beyond as they carefully preen themselves and shake out their feathers, as if ridding themselves of some kind of contamination.

Chapter 19

Fish-farm blues

Everyone buggering off to the Modh is a good opportunity to do a deep clean of the fish processing shed and the cold store without disrupting things too much. Allie Mierson had volunteered to do it because, well, who didn't want double time for weekend work? And though she thinks she's stubbornly old-school when it comes to music, liking floor-filling bangers from the noughties, she isn't ancient-school and into all the fiddle and pipe stuff. Maybe you had to be born on the islands to have that in your blood or something. She'd only been here for twenty years, an islander by marriage but a lowlander born and bred.

Her husband Eck has gone off with his mates and is probably hitting the bar on the ferry right now, but she doesn't begrudge him that. He's a good and a funny man, and if playing the squeezebox makes him happy, well. That's at least one of them smiling, and that's what God invented earphones for anyway, as she tells him whenever he fires it up.

She'd planned to do the job with Shanna Nisbett, who is a laugh when she comes out of her shell – a bit tightly wound, but then who could blame her, given the shit her ex had put her through. Eck might murder the accordion on a regular basis, but he'd cut his hands off rather than bunch them into fists and hit a woman. And he certainly isn't a convicted bloody druggie. Allie and Shanna had planned to blitz the cleaning with the music turned up loud and cheerful since everyone else wouldn't be there to complain – turn the place into a disco, she'd said to Shanna, who'd laughed and said she'd bring a playlist. And then they'd decided to celebrate the extra wages by going to the Friday Fish Fry at the hotel and having a good old session.

She stands on the short pier by the big white and blue fish-farm processing shed and looks at the phone. She'd read Shanna's text after she'd seen Eck on his way to the ferry and had felt a jolt of disappointment, which surprised her. She hadn't until that point realised the nervy girl from Glasgow had become such a good friend. It had sort of snuck up on her, she supposed.

Still, she needs a hand and so she decides to see if the Pole from the hotel fancies some double time. She's a grafter, like Allie. She'd always been willing to come and do any hours that she could manage. They'll get the deep clean done, just without so much banter and likely no dancing. She's always so serious and a bit literal, but maybe it's just the language thing. Maybe humour doesn't translate, she thinks, as she keys the girl's number.

"Magda," she says, "it's Allie. Know it's short notice, but Shanna's had to let me down and I need a hand at the fish farm. It's double time and you'll need your wellies . . ."

She suddenly feels the strangest feeling prickle across her neck, as if there's someone behind her, watching and listening. She turns abruptly. There's no one there, the dock empty, the big doors to the shed closed tight. There is only a raven cocking its head at her from its perch on the gable end. She relaxes. But then it spreads its wings and emits a harsh *kraa-kraa* that – if you're fanciful – sounds a bit like a warning.

She barely has time to register the oddness of the moment before it lofts into the air and swoops down so low that she ducks as it overflies her and begins to circle the small black interloper that had appeared round the corner of the shed.

Walter John's dog Milly stops and rears on her back legs, barking furiously at the bird.

Allie relaxes. The dog is a harmless nutter and the raven is just mobbing it for reasons only a raven would know. She waits for Walter John to come round the corner and whistle the dog in. When he doesn't, she walks closer to the dog and peers round the corner. Her owner is nowhere to be seen.

The silly dog must have run off. And she is a silly dog, letting the raven provoke her into such energetic jumps into the air as she snarls and tries to catch it.

"What are you like?" says Allie, shaking her head. She'd better catch her and call poor old Walter John. But first she'll go and get some fishmeal pellets. The dog likes them and – being a spaniel – is never known not to be hungry.

"Milly," she shouts. "Good dog, come. D'you want a treat?"

Chapter 20

Roll on, roll off

The island shop overlooks the ferry pier and the line of cars waiting to embark once the boat easing alongside has disgorged its inbound passengers and their vehicles.

Walter John nods to the CalMac employee standing at the end of the line waiting for any last stragglers to arrive and check in. He knows him. He's called Robbie – or Robbie the Ferry to distinguish himself from the other Robbie on the island – and when not marshalling cars he's a digger driver with a responsibility for keeping the culverts and drains clear of debris that might clog them and lead to flooding in stormy weather. Walter John has heard the unkinder kids call him Robbie the Red-Nosed Drain-Clearer because of the broken veins that lattice his nose and cheeks, but he's only ever been civil to Walter John. Like most on the island, he does several things. Although people are meant to be there an hour before embarkation so Robbie can check the tickets clearing them to embark, the island is small enough that people are in the habit of arriving at the very last minute, secure in the knowledge that the CalMac guys are not sticklers for the rules.

Robbie raises his clipboard in reply. Walter John shouts across the tarmac.

"Have you seen Milly?"

Robbie shakes his head.

"Is it lost again, she is?"

Walter John nods and enters the shop. There are a few kids stocking up on sweeties and juice before they get on the ferry. He looks over their heads and meets the eyes of the red-faced woman behind the till.

"Mary-Kate. I've lost that bloody dog," he says, injecting a hearty note into his voice that he doesn't feel.

"She's a terror," says Mary-Kate.

"You haven't seen her?" he says.

"No," she says, looking at the kids. "Any of you seen Walter John's Milly?"

The kids shake their heads.

"Well, she always comes back," says Mary-Kate. She doesn't mean to be short with the poor old fool. She doesn't really think he's a fool either, truth to tell, but she just wants him to go. Like she wants these kids to go. Like she wants the passengers who will soon be driving off the ferry to come – as they always do, this being the only shop on the island – and then go. She's not antisocial. She's just very aware her rosacea is flaring badly, and she'd like to get home where she has left the cream, which is the only thing that seems to help. If she goes back into the storeroom and splashes water on her face, maybe that will soothe her a bit and stop her being so cranky, but then she remembers she has Magda back there doing inventory for her, and there's something very judgemental about the way the Polish girl looks at her sometimes. Mind you, she's likely nearly done. She just heard her talking to Allie about an extra shift at the fish farm. She might have a blunt and charmless attitude that Mary-Kate calls

120

"Germanic" – though only behind her back – but there's no doubt she's a grafter, doing bar work and housekeeping at the hotel and pulling shifts at the fish-farm processing shed when she can fit them in.

"Okay," Walter John says as he turns to go. "If anyone sees her, maybe tie her up outside and I'll get her later."

"Where are you going?" says Mary-Kate.

"I'm going to keep looking," he says.

"What about the Goodges?" she says.

"The what?" he says.

Maybe he is an old fool, she thinks.

"The new nurse," she says. "The man-nurse and his young wife, remember?"

He has forgotten. The stutter in his face gives him away. Not a man who could profit much in a world where lying was an advantage.

"Of course," he says. "Graham and Sarah."

"Was it not Sally?" she says. "You were going to show them to the Bothy."

"I know," he says. The morning's events have clearly scrambled his brain. How could he have forgotten his responsibilities?

She reaches behind herself and hefts a cardboard box on to the counter.

"I have the welcome box here."

He remembers the island council, of which he is a member, agreed that it would be neighbourly to put a box of essentials together to welcome the new health visitor to the island. He could see loo paper and milk cartons and a bottle of red wine poking above the rim of the box.

"If they've bought their own milk, tell them to drink this first," says Mary-Kate. "Mainland milk will have a longer sell-by date."

He lifts the box, surprised at the weight.

"Can you manage?" she says, suddenly seeing how to kill two birds with one stone.

"I'm fine," he says. "Thank you."

"You've your blood pressure to watch," she clucks. "Magda!"

Magda pops her head out of the storeroom, pushing the black hair out of her eyes.

"Would you be a saint and help Walter John with this box?" she says. "He's not to strain himself."

Walter John flushes, despite himself. Magda has perfect skin that always seems to run a little hotter than anyone else's, as if her endless hard work leaves her just on the point of breaking into a sweat which never quite arrives. She is the other young woman on the island who he's embarrassed to look at, but in her case he suspects she knows it. He wishes furiously that Mary-Kate had asked one of the children gathered around the sweetie shelf. They'd have done it.

They're decent, the few island children. It's something he noticed when he and his wife moved here. It was like they had retired to a place where manners hadn't died off in the way they had back in the city they had come from. His wife had always said that because people were kinder and more polite out here it felt more like the lost world of their long-past childhoods, and that was why – although they were what some of the older islanders called "incomers" – it felt to them as though they were coming home.

Magda is irritated Mary-Kate has asked her to help the uncomfortable old man. He's harmless enough, but he always smiles like he has something to apologise for and somehow that makes her not trust him. Nevertheless, she puts on a cheerful face and hefts his box for him.

She walks faster than he does, which presents him with the problem of not looking at her tight jeans as he follows her to the car, and once again he realises how disgusted with himself he has become.

When he gets to the car, she opens the boot without asking and bends to put the box inside.

"Thank you, dear," he says.

"Not a problem," she smiles, and skips off back to the shop.

He looks away and fixes his eyes on something more innocent. The children who were playing their instruments have stopped and started loading themselves back on to the minibus. He watches them, and not for the first time he regrets that he and his wife had never managed to have children of their own. It would have been nice. She had wanted to, and they had tried, and then the doctors had explained why it would never happen, and although they talked about adopting, it had never happened. Such an important – such a sad – decision, but he is damned if he can remember exactly why they had decided not to. He isn't just becoming a sad old peeper, he is losing his marbles. No question.

He closes the boot and looks around the harbour. The pier always strikes him as out of scale and too modern-looking compared with the scrabble of small houses dotted on the slopes around the small bay. It had been enlarged and re-inforced solely to accommodate the ferry and provide a small modern marina for a pleasure-cruising yacht trade that never amounted to anything. No other big boats ever dock here. It's a modest haven for precisely two fishing boats and the occasional daring pleasure yacht venturing outside the normal comfort zone of the coastal cruisers.

It was a once-pretty harbour that had been messed with, in the hope it would attract something that never came. Now it just looks like somewhere nothing of any interest or importance ever happens, he thinks.

And then he feels the stutter in his chest and the awful microsecond of cold panic begins to buckle his knees as his hand clutches reflexively at his heart and he thinks no, please no, not now, not this, not here, not this time . . .

Chapter 21

Stroke of luck

Sig crests the rise and pauses at the passing place, looking down at the harbour that has abruptly come into view on the other side. She doesn't believe in ghosts, but she knows the tug of strong memories can always be triggered by the places where traumatic things had happened, and this is the spot where she'd turned to wave at him as he waved back from the rear deck of the ferry the last time she dropped him off. It was something they always did, their version of the old highland farewell, where visitors were waved at until they were out of sight. Only this time he hadn't appeared on the rail, and though she'd been a little hurt she had not, until later, seen it as a foreshadowing.

When he'd said he'd always be there for her, she hadn't taken it literally, but it turned out there's a way in which it's true: she can't choose the moment when the thought of him comes into her mind. She doesn't want to forget him, but she always feels ambushed by the memory of him when it comes unasked, as if it's something she cannot control but wants to. Inoculated against superstition as a reaction to her parents and their fatally credulous attitude, Sig is doubly uncomfortable with the unbidden presence in her mind, not because it always comes with a faint reverberation of the original gut punch of grief – which it does – but because it blows unwelcome oxygen into the embers of guilt smoored up inside herself.

She'd wanted amniocentesis because of the brother her mother had lost at birth; he hadn't, because of the risk of miscarriage that came with it. She'd argued rationally, citing the statistical unlikelihood that the procedure would harm the pregnancy; he'd pointed out that they'd love the baby however it came out, so why jeopardise things? The argument didn't resolve, and looking back on it later she realised she'd left it vague enough that he believed she wouldn't do it without further discussion. Sometimes an omission is as good as a lie, and you can lie perfectly well without saying anything.

She didn't tell him there was one tiny part of herself that worried she might turn into a brittle mother like her own, one who would fail a challenging child despite all her determination not to.

She went alone to her check-up in Oban because he was helping Matt overhaul the boat, and she had the amnio anyway. They'd sworn to honour each other at their wedding, and he felt her doing the thing he'd argued against bent that a little. She thought him not trusting her to do what was right with her body did the same.

That was the row. Bad, stormy, but – as he said later on a crackling video call from the rig – absolutely survivable, and nothing broken. That he was on the rig was her fault because, though he'd stopped working for the oil company, they'd called and asked him to fill in for a sudden repair and he'd said yes. He told her he'd agreed because as prospective parents they could always do with the money, which would be double time since the job was an emergency. She waved him farewell, understanding that he felt they needed some cooling-off time to get over the row more than the money. By the time he got to the rig and called her, he ruefully admitted he'd actually got over it the moment he saw the helicopter waiting to whisk him away. He told her it was okay. Her body, her call. He'd been worrying too much, maybe because life was suddenly about to get out of his control. He told her he loved her.

Thirteen days after the amnio, she lost the baby and immediately knew it was a punishment for breaking her word a second time. She'd promised to protect Ebba, and hadn't. And she'd promised to honour her husband as he'd promised to honour her, but she'd snuck off and got the test without telling him, and this was her fault – her punishment, their pain. Her rational brain knew this was as irrational a belief as any her parents had held, but there was a less evolved part of her that felt it and thought the punishment far outweighed the crime. Little did she know. The doctor said it was nothing to do with the test, and that she'd likely have no problem conceiving and carrying the next baby to term. But while her head accepted that gratefully, her heart shrivelled and burned up in the flames of a different truth.

He cut short his shift, breaking his contract, and took a seat on the next helicopter back to the mainland. The chopper took off into a bright windless day and never arrived at its destination. A main rotor support strut sheared, and they found all but two bodies of the passengers floating amongst the wreckage. They didn't retrieve about a quarter of the helicopter, and they never found him. It was just a coincidence it happened on the 13th of the month, but it was sheer bad luck that the crash happened over a system of deep trenches in the otherwise quite shallow North Sea, about two hundred kilometres east of Dundee, known ominously – and in this case entirely appropriately – as The Devil's Hole, where the depth plunged from about ninety metres to more than 230 metres. Sig knows this because for a while all she could do was read about the area, as if research would give a clue to help her make sense of the void into which she found herself plummeting, shackled to a deadweight of guilt from which she now knows she'll never be able to cut herself loose. It turned out the lost baby was not the worst punishment the universe could exact for her breaking her word a second time.

She'd made an unconscious pact with herself that no one else would ever die because she broke her word. And her rigorously solitary life is, she is self-aware enough to realise, her way of guaranteeing that.

Rex bounces into the front seat and whines at someone waving up at them from outside the shop. It's Evie in her chair.

Sig waves back and pulls out into the road.

Down at the quayside, Walter John braces himself against the car roof with the hand not clutching his heart, still feeling the fluttering on the left side of his chest and feeling the relief that this is the final, fatal heart attack coming for him.

As he always does.

He swallows a sob and braces himself for the quick clean end he secretly prays for, instead of the soul-withering gauntlet of pain and indignity he'd watched his beloved suffer through.

A second later, he hears the bell ringing and reaches for the phone in the breast pocket of his shirt. He knows he should carry it in another pocket or turn off vibrate to avoid these conflicted moments of shock and hope, but he never gets around to it. Maybe it's just habit and hard to change at his age. Or maybe it's the bittersweet, lovely flood of relief when he realises the anticipated coronary is just the phone that's the other habit he's addicted to. That momentary, treacherously joyous affirmation that he is still alive.

"Hello," he says, watching the ferry slowly let the bow thrusters begin to nudge it sideways into the pierhead.

"Walter John," says the voice on the other end, "have you lost your dog again?"

"Allie," he says. "Have you got her? I'm so sorry."

"No, it's me that's sorry," says Allie. "I tried to catch her, but she ran off. Didn't even want a treat. But she's around here somewhere – I heard her barking. She's taken against a raven that's been teasing her. I thought you should know."

"No, you're a star," says Walter John, feeling his heart unclench and relax. "A star. I'll be right over, thank you."

He hangs up and turns to see Mary-Kate standing beside him, taking advantage of the momentary lull as the outbound passengers return to their vehicles and the new arrivals are a good ten minutes from disembarking.

"You can't go now," she says. "You've got to meet the Goodges, no?"

"I'll be back in fifteen," he says. "Won't take long. If they ask for me, tell them I'm on the way."

"Walter John," she says, "I'm not . . . "

He's already hurrying to his car.

"I told them to wait at the shop if I was late," he says. "It'll be fine. Sure they'll need to get some stuff. It'll be fine."

Mary-Kate sucks menthol-flavoured smoke into her lungs and then watches him drive away through the smoke as she exhales. That man and his dog. He'd been like that with Jean, his wife. Some men just needed something to love. Sweet, really.

She turns to return to the shop and sees the Swedish woman has just parked her Defender in front of it and is walking towards that troubled girl Evie in the wheelchair,

129

sitting there with a duffel bag on her knee like so much lost luggage that no one wants. Still, her grandparents will enjoy the Modh. Break will do them good. Mary-Kate is not at all offended that they had declined her offer to keep an eye on the poor wee soul while they're gone. She'd only offered out of decent Christian neighbourliness. Her two are long gone off the island and away to jobs in the south. She's used to her empty house. Likes it that way, truth to tell. She's way past the empty-nest syndrome. She has plenty of knitting to do.

Sig sketches a wave at Evie as she approaches the wheelchair. She sees the girl has had a haircut. It makes her look like a fragile boy, she thinks.

"*Hej*," she says.

"That a Swedish *hej* or a Scottish hey?" says Evie. Sig wonders if it's the newly shortened hair that makes the girl look so pale, or if she's just stuck inside too much for her own good.

"Swedish," says Sig.

"*Hej du*, then," says Evie.

This was a thing and had been ever since Evie had done a school project on the Viking mythology. She had come to Sig wanting help with her assignment on Norse words that had found their way into the British languages, specifically Scottish and English.

"New hair," says Sig.

"Katie did it," says Evie. "Said it's a pixie-cut."

"Looks good," says Sig.

"Yeah," says Evie, rolling her eyes. "Maybe if you're a pixie ..."

"No. It looks sharp," says Sig. "Sorry I'm late."

She sees Evie's grandmother waving back at her from the car window in the queue where they're waiting to embark. Sig smiles back at her and mouths an apology.

"She'll not see that," says Evie. "This far away she can probably only see your Land Rover, but she'll be happy to know you're here."

"I got held up," says Sig. "I wanted to see them before they got on the ferry."

"No worries," says Evie. "They'll be able to enjoy their break now."

"Okay," says Sig, waving at the car. "Let's get you loaded up."

She resists the impulse to wheel the girl to the passenger door; instead she stands back and watches Evie get there under her own steam. She reaches up and unlatches the door, tossing her pack up and in ahead of herself, and then brakes the chair before hoisting her whole body weight up and on to her end of the bench seat using her arms only. Sig again suppresses her urge to stand close in case she falls. She gets why this is a matter of pride for the girl. She's done her own hard miles in a wheelchair, after all. Even the excited dog knows to hold back and give the girl her space.

Evie grits her teeth as she gets her butt up and safely on to the seat, and then she reaches down to get her legs in with one hand while holding on to the grab bar with the other.

"Pretty good," says Sig.

The moment Evie is securely in the vehicle, Rex leaps up into her lap and starts licking her face, tail lashing the seat in excitement. Sig's happy to see he's behaving normally again.

"I've got to do a bit of shopping," says Sig as she collapses the chair and wheels it to the rear of the Land Rover. As she lifts it, she sees Evie and Rex are lost in their own mutual lovefest as the dog desperately tries to lick her ears, his tail thrumming like an eggbeater as the girl tries not to laugh. She's failing badly, and – just for a moment – sounds like a younger and happier version of herself as she does so. Rex doesn't know she's meant to be a tough-looking goth or emo or whatever the punk hair colour is meant to signal.

The dog just loves her, and that is why Sig, who trusts dogs more than humans these days, doesn't mind letting the girl invade her carefully tended solitude for a couple of nights.

Chapter 22

Rabbit food

The rabbit's not moving any more. And with no blur of movement to catch the eye she's almost invisible, certainly unnoticeable as she lies on the scrape of sand at the water's edge just around the headland from the fish farm, amongst the clumps of bladder-wrack left by the retreating tide. Her body lies stretched out on its left side, as if exhausted. But if she was just exhausted then her flanks would be heaving as she got her wind back, instead of lying stiff and unmoving on the sand.

Only a sharp pair of eyes would spot the body of the rabbit on this untravelled scrape of beach on the remote spur of land. The raven's eyes are sharp and honed by a hunger that has still not been satisfied since its disappointment with the swimmer and the sharks earlier in the morning, but more than that it can see the rabbit is dragging a strand of the darkness behind it, just like the dog was, weaving it into the fabric of the island like a tangled black thread.

It drops a wing and cuts a slow descending spiral through the empty vault of air above the wet sand. As it gets closer and closer its eyes remain locked on the frozen body, noting how the water lapping back and forth across its stiff legs does not trigger any reaction. The raven has never seen a rabbit lie in the water like this. It has seen many corpses stranded on the tide's edge. It knows what this is.

Still. It's a wise old bird. And something like a tiny uncomfortable vibration shivering around the base of its skull is telling it that it is being watched. It hasn't got to be an old bird without listening to that sort of thing. And this sense of being observed is only the latest addition to the growing sense of things being off balance. So it scans the surrounding water and heather for whichever pair of eyes is setting off the atavistic alarm signal at the back of its brain.

It sees nothing close by but gulls, nothing in the mid distance. In the far distance it sees Matt's boat cutting a white slash through the blue grey of the waters beyond the headland, speeding for the pier at the fish farm, but whatever has unnerved the raven is not visible.

It lands on an open piece of sand thirty metres from the rabbit and cocks its head from side to side as it hops around in a casual circle, checking out the lie of the land. It's far enough away that it does not put off a gull that drifts in and lands closer to the unmoving corpse. The raven just watches the gull as the white and grey bird hops closer, perching on a rock about a metre from the rabbit's body. It steps fretfully from one leg to the other and suddenly turns around. If anyone was watching it they might well think it looked anomalously as if it was playing a strange avian game of grandmother's footsteps. They might think it looked oddly comic in its careful approach to its meal. The raven thinks even this seabird that is not tuned into the same resonances as it is can feel something is out of the normal balance of things. The raven suddenly knows what's going to happen. It's so inevitable, so much a part of the cycle of life that it's almost not worth watching.

But then watching is what the raven does well. Watching. Waiting. And remembering.

The gull does not seem to register the raven, even though it senses something is off kilter. The raven can see both of those things too. It understands the gull is hungry and that the bird will feed if it can. It also senses its mate dropping out of the sky behind it, and shuffles sideways to give it room to land.

The other raven touches down and the two cock their heads as if in sync, watching the gull.

The gull seems satisfied that whatever is watching it is far enough away for it to be safe. It shudders and shivers its wings, as if stretching itself before the hard work of pecking and tugging at the rabbit's corpse begins in earnest. Then it launches off the top of the rock, wings flaring out to stall itself in the air as it drops to the sand at the head of the rabbit.

It looks at its options and decides that it will begin by pecking out the one visible eyeball, before beginning to eat the tongue. It knows it enjoys the eyeballs.

The ravens see the gull hop close and open the powerful hooked shears of its beak.

They see the rabbit spasm into action, see its jaws snap over the gull's head. The two buck teeth are not designed for meat, but they enter the eye socket with no resistance other than a slushy, popping noise as the rabbit rolls onto its feet, sending the bird onto its side in a disjointed flailing of wings. The ravens hear the crunch as the rabbit keeps biting down on the skull, see it savagely jerk the gull from side to side in a long, brutal – and frankly unnecessary – killing-shake that snaps its neck.

The rabbit shakes the bird back and forth until it is just a limp collection of pale feathers, and then it tosses it onto the dry sand and leaps on it, tearing at it with its two front teeth, at the same time scrabbling at it with its fore paws, as if trying to furiously dig straight through the body into the beach beyond. Feathers and gull-guts fly everywhere, and in less than a minute the gull is scarcely recognisable as a bird, reduced to shreds of bone, skin and guts and the lingering explosion of feathers that float away on the light sea breeze.

The ravens look on, unsurprised, until the rabbit stops as suddenly as she began, and lollops away, head high, white tail bobbing – once more full of life. The ravens lift off as one and split up again, one flying clockwise round the island as the other sideslips through the air in the other direction, trailing and trailing the rabbit at a safe distance, keeping in its blind spot. Instinctively it takes care that its shadow does not ever fall ahead of the rabbit to alert it to the old bird's presence.

That sort of instinct is, of course, one of the reasons it and its companion got to be such very old birds in the first place.

Chapter 23

Belly of the beast

Down in the car deck Graham Goodge is trying not to take his frustration out on the baby's car seat, but it's hard. It'd be easier if someone would help him, but Sally is sitting in the front seat with her eyes closed and a pained expression on her face, and Tom doesn't seem to have made it down the steps yet.

He loves both of them, and the baby of course. He knows why this is tricky for everyone, but it's not his fault. The heart wants what the heart wants. He heard someone say that once, and at the time he had thought the guy was a bit of a sleaze and using the words as a kind of Get Out of Jail Free card; twenty years later, he is older and wiser – well, older – and he thinks he understands the simpler truth that the words carry. If he hadn't had to do it, of course he wouldn't have done it. He's a good guy, a nurse. A care worker. In the caring profession. Of course he cares about the consequences of his actions, but they are not all his actions. Things happen in a complicated dance. In the end, you do what you have to do because all you can control is your own truth. He isn't selfish. He can see how Tom's mum had become neutral about him at best. And though she'd said it was menopause and that she was sure it would pass, she'd just got crankier and found more about him to pick at. His shoulders are broad, but at a certain point any rational person would have to stop and ask if this was the best way to spend the rest of their one life. And Tom is old enough not to take permanent harm from this. He isn't that cliched older guy falling for a younger woman. Sally's age is irrelevant. What is relevant – what had been relevant – is their connection. If things are bumpy now, it's a temporary thing, postpartum depression that will pass with time.

The baby grizzles in the seat and he tries again to fix it in place. The nurse in him registers the sweat on its face. He checks its temperature with the back of his hand, looking at his watch at the same time. Yeah. Still hot. It's just teething.

"Think she needs some more Calpol," he says. "It's about time."

Sally nods without opening her eyes. Well. Maybe it would be worse if she was overly concerned. No need to make a drama out of a crisis, he thinks. Then he corrects himself. This isn't a crisis; the baby is teething, it's not a fever. Graham is a nurse. No need to make a mountain out of a molehill, was what he had meant to think.

He looks around for his other child. There he is, sauntering sideways towards him as he edges into the narrow gap between the few cars and the lorry looming over them.

"Come on," he says. "Give me a hand with this bloody thing."

He bends forward, over the baby, feeling its heat as he tries to fit the seatbelt around the chair. It might be the last word in baby safety, this seat, and it should be for the amount it cost, but it had been designed by someone who was either a pervert or seriously double-jointed. He feels the welcoming hard contact of metal on metal and leans a little further forward to forcefully shove the buckle home into the keeper nestling in the angle of the seat below.

The pain is immediate and crippling. If he hadn't locked up in paralysis at the shocking intensity of it, he would have fallen with his full weight on the now squalling child below.

He didn't know he'd yelled, but he must have because Sally jerks round and looks at him in shock.

"My back," he chokes. "It's my fucking back . . . I can't . . . "

Tom stands and watches his father's backside sticking out of the car. Just for a moment he has to fight the sudden urge to laugh.

Inside the car, Sally bites back the urge to scream as she stares at him. He looks in real distress.

"I can't . . . I can't move," he gasps.

He looks so old. How had she never minded that before?

"You fucking idiot," she says. "You stupid fucking idiot."

Chapter 24

Bad chat

The rush of business that sometimes attends the arrival of the ferry is more of a trickle today as half a dozen vehicles come ashore, the first two of them speeding straight past her, heading home with boots full of shopping from the cheaper and more extensive supermarkets in Oban. Mary-Kate hates the Oban shops almost as much as her rosacea. They're big international chains, and they sit round the harbour strangling the livelihoods of people like her out on the islands. Tourists arrive with cars bulging with food and toilet paper and leave without buying more from her shop than postcards and the occasional can of something they'd forgotten to bring with them. And then they leave their black bags of garbage for the island to deal with.

She glances out of the window and sees Evie in the passenger seat of the Swedish woman's Land Rover. What had the poor wee soul done to her lovely hair? The Highland Telco van pulls up next to it and a good-looking boy gets out and pauses as he hitches his belt and then sees the girl. But before she can see what happens next, the Swedish woman, Sig, steps in front of her with her shopping and she has to remember to smile as she scans it into the till.

"It's a lovely day for it," she says cheerily.

"It is," says Sig, matching her smile. She has no idea what 'it' is, but this is what Mary-Kate always says as if she's on autopilot, and agreeing seems to be surest way of avoiding any further conversation without causing offence. Sig knows Mary-Kate is the biggest gossip on a pretty loose-tongued island and has always been very careful not to give her any more material than she has to.

"So you're babysitting young Evie, I hear," says Mary-Kate.

"She's a bit old for babysitting," says Sig. "But yes. She's staying for the weekend."

"That'll be nice for you both," says Mary-Kate, hitting the total button. "Bit of company."

They both wait as the printer spits out the bill.

"Brighten things up, the young, don't they?" says Mary-Kate. "Be a nice change for the pair of you."

Sig knows this game. Mary-Kate wants to press her buttons by sympathising with her for being lonely. For being alone. For being the survivor. The sad widow. She's really not going to play.

"But you're right about the babysitting," says Mary-Kate when Sig doesn't rise. "She can be very touchy. I just tried to help her with a bit of a push uphill and she rounded on me and said she wasn't a trolley."

She leans in, her expression scandalised.

"Although, what she actually said was, 'a F-word-ing trolley'."

"Well," says Sig, noncommittally tapping her payment card on the machine. "None of us like to be pushed around, do we?"

Evie makes the mistake of catching the eye of the bloke who just got out of the 4×4 next to her.

"Cheer up, doll," he says, with a grin that says he might be talking to her but the one he's really pleased with is himself. "It might never happen."

She looks away.

He doesn't get the hint.

"Bet you got a cracking smile," he says.

She can feel her face beginning to get warm. She feels embarrassed and exposed, and most of all angry that her blush is betraying her, angry that just when she needs a snappy comeback her tongue seems tied, angry that he'll see her face reddening and think he won some game she doesn't even understand the rules of.

"Ah, go on," he says, stepping closer. "Give us a wee smile, eh?"

"She doesn't owe you a smile."

Sig has emerged from the shop. Her voice cracks across the bonnet of the Land Rover like a whip.

"What?" he says, looking at her, wrongfooted.

"She doesn't owe you a smile," she says again, "so back off."

"I'm just being nice," he says.

"Be nice somewhere else," says Sig. "She's fourteen."

"I wasn't—" he begins.

"Yeah you were," says Sig. "Now go away."

It's a staredown. His eyes may be unreasonably blue, but hers in this moment have long generations of winter in them.

He breaks first, deflating as he looks at his friend for assistance. Malc keeps his mouth shut, but the shrug of his shoulders says, "You're on your own, pal."

"I, um . . . " he says.

Sig tosses the bag of groceries on to the bench seat between them as she climbs in and closes the door with a decisive thump.

"Was just trying to be nice," he says.

142

Sig backs out and pulls away.

"What a bitch," he says, watching them drive off.

"Jamie," Malc says. "Seriously, you can't talk about women like that."

"Why not?" says Jamie. "Just calling a spade a spade. She was being a bitch."

"Did you no see it?" says Malc. He wonders if Jamie knows how tiring it is being around him all day. He's on the prowl 24-7, like a dog with two dicks. As if he doesn't have a wife and two nice kids back home. And his chat is wearyingly bad.

"Did you not see in the back of the Land Rover?"

"What about it?" says Jamie.

"The girl's wheelchair."

Jamie turns back to watch the vehicle speeding away.

"A wheelchair, was it?"

"Aye," Malc says. "And you can't be talking about women like that. Especially underage ones in wheelchairs."

Jamie watches the Defender disappear round the distant curve in the road.

"Bitches, the pair of them," he grins, visibly reinflating himself. "Bitches on wheels . . ."

Malc stares at him. Christ. The arsehole actually thinks that's funny.

Chapter 25

Close

Kevo grips the steering wheel and tries to zen out the rising tide of frustration that's making him want to bumper-crunch the carload of family fannying around in front of him on the car deck. What's the hold up? The guy seems to have hurt his back, fine, but can't they push the car off to one side and let him round?

Of course, he's the last car off the fucking ferry. Why wouldn't he be? Not like he's in a hurry. Although, now he thinks about it, he really isn't.

She's not going anywhere.

He relaxes his grip a bit and exhales. Then he takes a deep breath in through the nose. Just like they told him to in the anger management classes.

That was a mistake. Just reminds him of the stink in here. He threw his mother's dangly air freshener out the window in the first half-mile, but her car still smells of some kind of minging sugary bubblegum shite. He looks in the rear-view and sees the fluffy pink arse of the soft-toy unicorn she keeps jammed on the back shelf. What's a grown woman with a mean streak to her doing with a unicorn anyway? He knows Unicorn

Carers is what she calls her precious "elderly support" business, which is four or so Polish girls who do the actual business while she stays home and bills the council, but still. What's a unicorn got to do with scrubbing some poor old soul's shit out of the shower tray? The plush little fuck just sits wedged in the back and makes googly eyes at whoever's stuck behind her in traffic. He meant to throw that out too, though out of respect for his mother – who, in fairness, didn't exactly give him permission to take the car on such a long trip – he thinks he should probably just toss it in the boot. He tells himself it's respect, but the other little voice at the back of his mind asks him if respect's not just a posh word for fear. She's probably realised he's popped out for more than a pack of fags by now, but she doesn't really need the car and she won't dob him in. She knows he's on probation. And it's not like she doesn't owe him. She might look sweet as candyfloss, his ma, but she's a hard fucking nut underneath it, and that's the truth. She'll not call the police.

Candyfloss. That's what the reek is. Not bubblegum. Car smells of plush pink unicorn farts.

"Unicorn farts," he says, and smiles despite himself.

Yeah. He's definitely losing it. Talking to himself and laughing at his own jokes.

She did this to him. Not his mum. The other one.

Well. They'll be sorting that out soon enough. Soon as Happy Fucking Families ahead of him move their bloody car.

He blips the horn.

The man who seems stuck getting into the passenger seat twists his head to look at him.

Fucking sad-eyed loser.

The bulky car deck supervisor in the yellow hi-viz walks towards him. Big, black-rimmed glasses and the wee red CalMac hard hat balanced on top of his shaved nut make him look like Mr Potato Head.

"Just give us a moment, pal. They're having a bit of a medical emergency here. We'll have you off in a jiffy."

Kevo nods. Smiles, keeping his teeth hidden behind tight lips. Watches the show in the car in front. The doll's pissed off, you can read the body language.

Happy Families. He catches a glimpse of the man's face in the side mirror. Yeah. He doesn't look so happy, the blobby-faced plook.

He looks down at the phone jammed in the cupholder. The map is back on. He thumbs the arrow and it re-centres itself. There he is. Little blue dot flashing on the shoreline. Precisely balanced on the edge of things according to whatever satellite's whirling overhead.

Happy Families drive off the ramp. Mr Potato Head waves him onwards. He feels the steel deck give way to tarmac beneath his wheels and he's on dry land. Sound as a pound. Nothing to do now but follow that blue line snaking across the bright map of the island on the wee screen in the cupholder. Helpful graphic tells him he'll be there in sixteen minutes.

Sixteen minutes to get his head straight. If he's going to do this – and he sure as guns is going to do this – he better do it right. He'll not get a second chance. Surprise is in his favour, and in a life that has done him few enough of those he's not going to waste it.

He winds down the windows and lets the clean air blow through the car. Puts on his shades, pair of knock-off Wayfarers his mum had in the glove compartment. Happily unisex, and he doesn't want to be recognised, does he? Or remembered clearly. Just in case.

He barely registers the line of cars waiting to embark, nor the activity at the front of the small shop where people seem to be going to and from the recently arrived vehicles. And then he's past the buildings clustered round the harbour and on the winding single-track road heading off into the island proper.

Fifteen minutes.

Shanna is going to make it. It'll be tight but she'll make it, and even if they've closed the car doors and won't let her on with a vehicle, she knows that the last thing they pull up is the gangplank, and they let foot passengers on at the last minute. She's seen it happen, hikers who timed their arrival wrong, running for the boat, waved on by the CalMac guys. Of course, they are not meant to let people on like that, there being an official policy about arriving at least thirty minutes early. But out here on the edge of everything is a long way from the head office in Gourock on the mainland, and lots of stuff goes by the way, official policy being one of them. It's a small island, and sticking to the rules and not letting someone get on board at the very last minute would not be forgotten or forgiven. It's live and let live that keeps things going, rather than rules. One of the reasons she likes it here. Sure, everyone has an inkling of your business, but that means they know to keep out of it if that's how you want to be.

Anyway. She looks at the time on her phone. She'll be fine. Live a life cutting things to the last minute, it gets less stressful. No point panicking. The car did start after all, so worrying about it was just a waste of her energy. She slows for a sheep and honks it out of the road, then speeds towards the long loop round the headland. Once around that corner, there's a straight and then the small quarry where they get the aggregate to mend the roads, and then she'll be in sight of the ferry.

Home free.

Though home isn't free, and if her sister doesn't make it, there's precious little left to make it home at all.

She'll make the ferry. Because she has to.

Ten minutes. Kevo checks the screen. One road ribboning ahead of him. Not much chance of getting lost here. One road round the island; you lose your way, you just turn yourself around and end up back where you began, he thinks. Bit like a parable for his own life. Or is it a metaphor? The God-botherer who did the criminal rehabilitation seminars on Thursday afternoons was always talking about parables and metaphors, and Kevo was never sure which was what. He really went along because it was a good thing for the parole and there were always good biscuits along with the tea. Usually Gingernuts. So it was never a complete waste of time.

With all the windows down, the interior of the car is his own private wind tunnel, but he doesn't mind that. He's not an outdoors kind of guy, but he's enjoying the fresh air blowing through him. Maybe because lately he's been spending twenty-three hours of every day indoors in an overcrowded facility ingrained with the smell of decades of male sweat competing with the more present funk of fear, farts and disinfectant.

Fear has its own smell. He knows that. He's smelled it on others, and he's smelled it on himself. It's another tell. Like the blinking thing. This wind bath he's taking, that feels like it's cleaning him out. Giving him a good scrubbing. She won't smell fear on him. She won't have an idea. No give away. No tell.

He's going to surprise the life out of her.

It'll be fine. He's relaxing. He's definitely relaxing.

*

148

Shanna's got her foot down. That sheep slowed her but she's making up time. She's convinced she's going to make the boat by the skin of her teeth, but still, she's got the pedal to the metal.

God helps those who help themselves.

She nearly hits the car as she takes the curve around the edge of the hill.

One minute there's nothing ahead of her, then there's a sudden Toyota that seems to leap out of the unhelpful dip in the road that has hidden it for a crucial and near-lethal instant. Her heart backflips inside her chest and she yanks the steering wheel, and the blue car hits the horn and there's a screech of rubber as it hits the brakes, but she has forgotten about the brakes and is steering for dear life, trying to bend the laws of physics and velocity by fitting her car and the blue car into a strip of tarmac that's only one car wide.

If the road builders had not put a passing place at the apex of the curve, she'd have failed badly, probably bouncing off the road and turning the car over and over until it ended up upside down in a peat hag. As it was, she barely got into the beginning of the widened scoop before the blue car was level with her and there was a splintering chunk as both cars' side mirrors pulverised themselves against each other. The blue car slewed to a halt, slanted across the roadway as she hit a small boulder on the edge of the passing place with a small percussive bump that stopped her going off the road and rebounded her back on to the tarmac.

She regained control of the car and slowed it to a halt at the other end of the passing place.

Jesus and Mary, she thought. That was close. But fuck. The ferry. She should stop and give the driver her number or something. Though it was as much their fault, and it wasn't a car she recognised from the island's residents. She really doesn't need this. She'll just give her number and get on, sort it later.

Six minutes. Kevo's in shock. He's hunched in the car at the other end of the passing place, staring at the map on his phone, like that's going to help him make sense of what just happened. What just nearly happened. Six short minutes to arrival, and he nearly didn't arrive at all.

Bits of shattered wing mirror have blown in on him through the open window. It's only by a fucking miracle he got the car stopped without plunging off the road. He wipes his cheek. Blood. Glass from the mirror. Shite. Could have lost an eye if he wasn't wearing the Wayfarers. Fuck's sake. His mind's not working right. That car came out of nowhere. This was not his fault. But if he makes something of it, he's going to get remembered, and that could be a problem.

There's a long beat as the two cars sit at either end of the passing place, no movement, no sound except their motors idling.

Kevo adjusts his rear-view mirror to look at the car. Red Corsa, with the rear offside wing painted a dull grey. Primer grey. Primer left unpainted with the red topcoat that should have matched the rest of the car, but still, primer painted on over a pretty good repair made with fibreglass and Bondo. He knows it's a pretty good job under that grey paint because he not only banjoed that car off a bollard at the bottom of Castlemilk, he did the repair himself and took a lot of trouble over it.

He feels his pulse rate begin to climb. He's not ready for this. He thought he would be fine, he thought he could control it, but this is wrong, this is bad, she nearly killed him for fuck's sake, and this is six minutes fucking early. He wrenches the door open.

And then takes a desperate calming breath before he allows himself to get out.

Shanna sees the unicorn and nearly shits herself. In an instant, she knows fine well whose car that is, and it hasn't come to clean anyone's house. What's she doing up here? How does she know where Shanna is anyway, since the point of being here is to avoid the whole lot of them? She sees the door open and a skinny leg swing out. She doesn't have to see any more. His mum's a right plumper. It's not her. It's him.

"Shanna!"

He's shouting before he knows what he's doing. His arm raises in a wave. He's not sure what he's going to do next. He's feeling about ten things at once, including the thought that this is not the simple that you're supposed to be keeping things at, stupid.

He can see that her hair is shorter, but it's that same deep copper he can't stop remembering tumbling round his face in some of the happiest moments in his life. In the before. But this is the now. The truth of that and all its implications make his voice ragged.

"Shanna!"

She burns rubber, fishtailing the car back into the road, and puts the hammer down, speeding away from him.

He stands there like a plum, one arm up in the air, smile frozen in place. Like she didn't just peel out and leave him again.

She keeps checking the rear-view. She sees him lower the arm and run back to the car. And then she drops into a dip and can't see him, and when she comes up the other side he's got the car side-on across the road, trying a fast three-point turn.

*

151

Kevo wrenches the gears. Three-point turn my arse, he thinks; I can get around in one. This passing place is just wide enough, surely.

He lurches forward and then stops abruptly as he feels the front wheel begin to drop off the metalled road. He slams the car back into reverse and gives it some gas. The wheels spin on a thin skin of gravel that's sitting on the less-travelled lip of the passing place, and the car goes just a foot too far. There's a sickening thump and scrape as the driver's side wheel drops off the road and into the ditch, bottoming out the chassis on the rim of the hardtop, tilting the car just enough that all he can see now is sky.

Now he loses it. Gunning the engine, trying to pull the car out of its predicament with only one wheel with actual drive attached to the road. The motor begins to whine and the acrid reek of overheating engine and burned rubber fills his nose. It smells like failure.

Kevo kills the engine. He's too angry to swear. Or hit anything. He tumbles out of the car and looks down the empty road. She's gone.

And him? He's only fucking crying. Like a wean.

She saw him reverse off the road. As the bonnet of his ma's car lurched upwards, she knew she was safe and her heart soared with relief. He's never been a good driver, and that had saved her. Thank God for small mercies. Mind you, she might be seeing that God in person sooner rather than later if she can't get her shit together. She's almost having one of those out-of-body experiences people talk about. Maybe her head is going to explode. Maybe she'll have a stroke – a real one, this time. What the hell is Kevo doing on the island in his ma's unicorn-mobile? She's terrified at the possibilities opening up in front of her, but she's a survivor so she clamps them down and concentrates on the road. Checks the time. She's fine; she'll squeak it, but she's fine. And maybe she should just ditch the car at the pier and go on foot anyway. Leave Kevo thinking she's still on the island so he won't follow on board. She can get the train from Oban. It always connects with the ferry, probably get her into Glasgow faster than driving anyway. She's got the money for it.

She congratulates herself for keeping her shit together enough to keep thinking, even as she keeps a watchful eye on the rear-view. Hopefully Kevo's still stuck in the ditch, but she wouldn't put it past him to start running after her. Or maybe cadge a lift. Though maybe the lift will have to move his car to get around. Yeah. She's good. She's still good.

She allows herself a thin, desperate smile.

It's like her superpower.

Skin of the teeth, always skin of the bloody teeth.

But she's still getting away with it.

Chapter 26

The get-out

"Fifteen," says Evie after they've been driving in silence for a bit.

Sig flicks a sideways look at her.

"Sorry?" she says.

"I'm fifteen now," Evie says. "Not fourteen."

"Oh," says Sig. "I know. But only just, and fourteen made him look like even more of a creep."

"You don't have to protect me," Evie says.

"I know," says Sig.

"You're not my guardian," Evie says.

"Ah," says Sig.

The silence hangs there between them, almost like a third person in the car. Sig feels desperate for the girl. Feels worse about herself, for her lack of moral courage or something. Telling Evie wouldn't have been a kind thing for her grandparents to have done, and she doubts they would have, but there was an edge to the girl's voice she didn't recognise. She looks at her.

"I'm surprised they told you that," says Sig.

"They didn't," Evie says. "But it's a small house."

"Look," says Sig. "It's, um . . . "

"It's okay," says Evie. "Really. I get it."

"We can talk about it," says Sig. "Evie. We should talk about it—"

"I don't think either of us wants that," says Evie. "Right?"

The silence reappears and solidifies between them as their eyes meet, but then Evie looks away, down at Rex, who has decided to snooze using her leg as a pillow.

"Anyway. You were pretty scary back there," says Evie. "To him. But I was okay."

"I know," says Sig. She decides she was imagining the edge in the girl's voice and puts it down to a small twinge of guilty conscience on her part. She relaxes. Maybe Evie gets it. Either way, she's grateful for the change of subject. They can talk later. She can explain. Tell her she gave her word to someone once before and that it hurts too much when you break it. "I know."

"I do kinda wish I'd been fast enough to say something," says Evie. "I know I should have, but my brain went a bit woolly. Katie would have said something snappy . . . "

"You don't have to be Katie," says Sig. "And you don't owe guys like that anything. I know you know that, but . . . "

"It's because I was in a car," says Evie. "That he said something. If I'd been in the chair, he'd have seen it and walked straight past. When you're in the chair, it's the chair they see first."

Sig wants to tell her she's beautiful in or out of the wheelchair, but she can't find a way to say it that isn't sappy. And anyway, it's not her job to protect the girl from the world, not really. The world taught its own lessons, and Evie's smart – very smart, actually – so she just concentrates on the road. She remembers the jittery feel of those awkward early teen years – not just the uncertain footing as she moved from a familiar state to a new and unfamiliar one, but also the shifting sense of betrayal as the rules changed without anyone telling you what the new ones were. But you had to learn those rules for yourself. It wasn't something people could teach you. She's pretty sure about that. That's how they stuck, the hard rules. Nailed in place by experience.

She glances sideways and sees Evie looking steadily ahead, blinking something out of her eyes. Something in the determined jut of her chin makes her look paradoxically younger and more vulnerable. And maybe a bit like Ebba. Ebba, who she hadn't really been able to help.

"Men who think you owe them a smile are going to think you owe them other more serious stuff ..." Sig says, words stumbling as she hits the sand and realises she's doing the very thing she'd just decided not to do. "Sorry. I'm not good at this."

"I know," says Evie. "I mean, not that you're not good at this ... I mean all the sketchy guy stuff."

Sig relaxes, relieved that they aren't going to have to venture any further down this particular road.

"How are the subject choices going?" she says brightly.

The last time they were together, Evie's grandmother had talked her into making sure the girl didn't give up on going to university by making the wrong subject choices for the upcoming exam years. Evie had been in the middle of a slump, and Sig had cajoled her out of it. They'd agreed they would go over Evie's options this weekend. Sig feels odd being dragooned into the role of mentor, but she is also touched by the older woman's honest bewilderment at the complicated processes that getting into university seemed to involve these days.

"It's fine," says Evie. "I mean, I know you're going to think I'm being a bit pathetic, but I'm still not sure uni's going to be the thing for me."

"Okay," says Sig. She doesn't want to say the wrong thing, so she keeps quiet as she figures out the least provocative response.

"So anyway, I was thinking," says Evie, before she can formulate the right words. "You can just take me home."

"That's the plan," says Sig, pulling into a passing place and letting the approaching car have right of way. She raises her hand in greeting. It's a tourist; they wave. "Rex has been looking forward to it."

"No," says Evie. "No, I mean my home. Gran and Grandpa's. I'll be fine. And I won't be an imposition on you."

Sig doesn't answer. A small, shameful part of her is seriously considering it. The bigger part of herself is embarrassed that she hasn't covered up her reluctance to have a guest. She had thought she was getting better, less raw with people. And then she wonders again if this is about the guardianship thing.

"Look, I'm fifteen, I've got a phone, there's food, you don't have to put yourself out," Evie says with an easy smile, like it's all no big deal.

The secret is that Evie wants to stay, but not if she isn't wanted. She wants to tell Sig something, because she knows if she doesn't say it to someone it's going to grow and grow and just do something bad to her, like burst her brain or make her too sad forever. She hasn't even told Katie. So she's made a deal with herself that if Sig says she can go home and be on her own, that's one thing. But if she makes her stay with her, that means something else, and that is that Evie can trust her, and then she'll tell her because Sig knows about accidents and loss and being private about stuff.

"Evie," says Sig, eyes on the road. "You're coming to mine. That was what was agreed."

"Yeah, but I know you don't like guests," says Evie, pushing it to be sure. "I mean, you're lovely to Gran and Grandpa and me, but you don't really like guests, right?"

The girl's bluntness cuts Sig deeper than it should.

"I'm fine with guests," she says.

"I'll be an intrusion," Evie says. "I get it. I don't take it personally. Tell me you wouldn't rather I was in my own home. Think how annoying it's going to be having me and my messy self in your perfect place."

"So, don't make a mess," says Sig, before she can stop herself.

"See?" Evie says.

"It's not perfect," says Sig. Hell, she thinks, I'm not some kind of neat freak. I just like order because order means no surprises.

She's done with surprises.

"Sig. You really don't have to have me for the weekend if you don't want to, just because Grandad asked." Evie's voice assumes a serious note it hasn't had before.

It was like this on the island. You did favours for each other because the resources were limited and people shared skills. It was one of the things that knit the community together. And Evie's right in part, because that was why Sig kept to herself as much as she could. She had nothing against the community, she just didn't want to get stitched into a fixed place by a tightening net of obligations. But she wasn't a hermit or anything.

"Evie," she says, "you're staying."

Evie steadies the dog in her lap as Sig takes the curve a little too fast.

"You don't like folk in your space," she says. "And that's cool. I get it. That's why there's only one of everything in your house: one cup, one plate, one bowl, one knife, one fork, one spoon and all that. One bedroom, no spare room."

The one-of-everything observation nettles Sig, but she bites back the words bubbling behind her teeth.

"You're staying," she says.

"But why?" says Evie. "I'll be fine at our house. I'm just a cripple, I'm not useless."

Sig pulls to the side of the road and rubs the bridge of her nose, massaging the tension away.

"Here's the deal," she says. "Cripple to cripple. You're staying because I told your grandparents I'd look after you."

"I don't really need a babysitter," says Evie.

"Suits me," says Sig, "because I've got work to do and I expect you to keep yourself occupied and not be a nuisance."

Evie looks at her.

"OK," says Evie after a beat. "You got a bit scary again there."

"Good," says Sig. "I am scary."

Evie watches the scars on the side of her lip, waiting to see them twitch into the shadow of a smile. She hopes Sig is just poker-facing it.

She takes a deep breath.

"Sig," says Evie, "can I tell you a secret?"

Sig doesn't want anyone's confidences any more. They're too heavy to carry. So she smiles and cocks her head and says, "Well, careful. It's not really a secret once you tell it . . ."

Then she sees the distress on Evie's face and realises this is not a trivial thing the girl is doing.

"But yes," she says, "of course you can. It's just that once you tell a secret to one person, it's that much easier to tell the next person and soon the secret isn't a—"

"I could have stopped it," says the girl, blurting it out with a bluntness that obliterates whatever excuse Sig was about to come out with.

"Stopped what?" she says after a beat.

Evie stares straight ahead, eyes on something in the past,

something she wants to look away from but won't let herself now that she's begun.

"The crash," she says. "I saw the car that hit us coming down the junction and I saw it wasn't slowing and my brain and my tongue must have frozen and I should have shouted, could have shouted, could have warned Dad, but I was . . ."

She takes another deep breath and holds it to keep herself from losing control. After a beat, she nods as if to thank Sig for not interrupting or asking if she was okay, and continues.

"Even just a second, even a half second – even if he'd still hit us, if I'd been able to warn Dad and he hit the brakes, maybe the car would have missed us or hit us differently. Maybe we'd have all been just injured or shaken up and not killed."

"You didn't have time," says Sig.

"I did. I was a coward. It was like slow motion, but I was too scared, too stupid, to say anything!"

"It's always like slow motion," says Sig. "Evie, I promise you. I know about stress responses. I have to when I dive. That's how the brain works. You think you've got time because you saw everything, but that's just because when you're in a dangerous moment like that the stress part of your brain kicks in and notices much more than you normally would. And because of that, you think you had more time because your brain crams more information into a second than it usually does. But you didn't. Time may have seemed to go slow, but it just didn't. You didn't have time to shout. It just feels like you did."

Evie looks at her. Sig can see how much she wants to believe.

"It's true," she says. "And you're anything but a coward. I promise. It's not your fault."

She makes herself smile at the girl. Evie swallows, nodding.

"Okay," she says. "Maybe . . ."

The fugitive quality of the small smile she allows herself as she wipes her eyes is heart-breaking.

Sig is relieved, and guilty at being relieved: the girl didn't seem to hold a grudge about her declining to be her guardian. She won't have to explain something she scarcely understands herself; instead, Evie had just been keyed up about sharing her big worry about the accident. It was just normal trauma and survivor's guilt.

She looks at the road and realises how much the weak part of her would love someone to make her believe that her own loss is not her fault.

Chapter 27

In spite

The ferry's closed up and the bow thrusters are gently backing it from the pier, and though every inch it moves puts water between her and Kevo, it seems like a painfully slow manoeuvre for Shanna. She can feel her heart still trip-hammering as she leans on the bow railing and stares alternately across at the road leading back towards her house and down at the widening strip of gunmetal water opening up between the sheer black hull of the boat and the deep green greasy sea moss covering the protective piles on the harbour wall.

She got away with it. But she knows with a sick certainty that's been hollowing out the pit of her stomach from the moment she recognised his bloody mam's car that she hasn't really got away at all. There's no such thing as coincidence, not really, not in her life. It's all cause and barely evaded effect at best.

She's stuck in slow time on the ferry now, trapped with that knowledge, and ahead of her, her sister's dying, and behind her he's on the island. So she can't go back when it's all over. She's on her own. As usual. Maybe she should call the police. Except she's only left her phone in the car down on the car deck.

Some days it feels like her life is just there to spite her.

Kevo'll have to get the car back on the road all by himself, because there are fuck-all passers-by to stop and help him. As he lies down to see what the damage to the undercarriage is, he can feel his heart thumping hard – shockingly hard – against the sharp grit and tarmac beneath his chest. Shanna. She could have stopped. Should have stopped. Would never have stopped. Not now. But. All he wants is . . . all he wants is . . . all he wants.

He needs to get his head straight and put the car back on the road. Because he knows fine well exactly why she drove away so fast and what she's running to: now she'd seen him, and because he hadn't been able to surprise her and lay it out, she's running for the ferry.

At first he thinks he's buggered everything up by grounding the chassis on the lip of the passing place, cracking the sump or bending an axle, but the one bit of luck he catches is that it's the rear wheel that has dropped, so the weight of the engine is still mainly over the front wheels. Finding somewhere to seat the jack is going to be a problem, but if he stays calm and works methodically he knows he can sort this. Two daggy sheep stand nearby like they're judging him as he gets the jack out of the boot and scrambles about in the heather looking for a large enough rock to put under the overhanging rear quarter of the car to give him something to crank against. He finds two flattish ones and manhandles them into place, and then begins to carefully wind the jack up. Once he can see daylight between the chassis and the lip of the road surface, he sticks the spare tyre on its side under the airborne wheel and then slides another rock on top of it. He lowers the jack and is relieved to see that although everything settles a bit once the weight is on the improvised wheel stand, he can still see the chassis is off the ground. He takes the jack away and actually holds his breath as he gets in the car, starts the engine and eases forward. There's a spit of rubber on gravel, a lurch, and then the car bounces forward and he's back on the road.

"Fuck yeah," he tells himself as elation floods his system with a sudden hit of warmth that he normally associated with the pills he's now sworn off forever. "Fuck yeah!"

He looks at the sheep. Whatever he is expecting, they aren't giving.

"And fuck youse," he says, hitting the accelerator.

He is halfway back to the harbour before he remembers he'd left the spare and the jack in the gully beside the parking place.

It doesn't matter. He can get them later. The ferry won't wait. He hasn't come all this way to let her get away before he can do what he'd been planning to do each and every night that he'd spent in that fucking prison.

And then he crests the rise overlooking the harbour, narrowly missing some prick in a Land Rover coming the other way, and he realises he has.

The ferry is a couple of hundred yards away from the pier, bow thrusters shredding the greasy water just as effectively as the sight of the boat tears up all his long-laid plans.

There's a figure in a red anorak on the back railing and it might just be Shanna. This far away, he can't be one hundred per cent sure.

But it would explain why it seems to be giving him the finger.

Chapter 28

Unleashed

Tom and his father sit in the car trying not to wake the baby, watching Sally walk up to the shop and disappear inside.

"Why did you have to go here?" says Tom, squinting round at the rapidly emptying harbourside.

"I thought it would be good," says Graham, wincing as he shifts to look back at his son. "When I saw the job advertised, I thought it'd be . . . fun to come here."

"Fun?" says Tom. "It looks dead. There's one shop and that hotel, about three boats and that's it."

"Granny's family came from here," says Graham.

Tom snorts.

"We're not Scottish, Dad," he says, rolling his eyes. "We really aren't."

"Two hundred years or so ago," says Graham. "She looked it up on a genealogy website. You know how she liked that stuff."

"You should have brought her, then," says Tom. "Before she died."

"I know," says Graham. "I know, I feel bad about it, but maybe—"

"It doesn't mean anything to me, Dad," says Tom. "Sorry. It's just a place that's miles from anywhere."

The baby shifts in its seat and they both go very still, as if one of them stepped on a mine that went click and they know it won't explode if no one moves.

"Hey," says Graham quietly, once it's clear she's not going to wake. "Maybe you'll find some cousins."

"That's so random," says Tom, snorting again.

"You might . . . " says Graham, trying a smile.

"We did family trees at school, Dad," says Tom. "Two hundred years is about eight generations."

"So?" says Graham.

"You double every generation and that's one hundred and twenty-eight," says Tom. "So, one out of one hundred and twenty-eight of my great-great-great whatever grandparents came from here? Why should that give me more of a connection than any of the other one hundred and twenty-seven?"

"I just thought . . . " says Graham, feeling suddenly as exhausted by his son as at the pain in his back. "I just thought, you know . . . "

The boy is bright. No doubt about that. Really good at maths in a way his father isn't, for a start. But he has that direct truth-telling thing his mother has, the thing that Graham found, in the end, too uncomfortable to live with.

"You just wanted to get away, Dad," says Tom. "Start fresh with the baby and her, and nobody blaming you for it because no one here knows you and Mum from before. I get it. But just be honest about it."

He looks round the harbour and the few remaining cars.

"We really don't have a connection with this place."

Inside the shop, Sally Goodge wonders what everyone would do if she just screamed and screamed in the way she'd like

166

to. The man who is meant to meet them is not there. Of course. Of course he bloody isn't. None of this is working for her, nothing seems to break her way any more. It's like the universe has decided not to give her any bonus points for making the hard choices she's made – the grown-up ones, the making-her-bed-and-lying-in-it ones, the choosing-Graham-and-not-Joe ones. It might have been an objective no-brainer, choosing someone with a full-time job and a pension for the father of her baby, but who ever said the heart was objective? It wants what it wants, and riding over that with common sense takes strength of will. Like dieting or giving up drink or deciding to stop smoking once the current pack is finished: do the hard work and it's not unreasonable to expect to see some results, even something as small as the universe cutting her some slack every now and then. Her eyes skate over the bottles behind the counter. She hasn't had a drink for what? Seven, eight months? That's got to be worth something in the great balance of things, surely?

The rosacea woman behind the till looks apologetically at her.

"Walter John will be here soon as he can. He had an emergency. But you're all very welcome here on the island."

She's holding something out to her. It looks like another bloody baby. That scream nearly escapes, but then Sally takes a moment to come back to earth and see what it is.

"It's a welcome basket," says the woman. "I'm Mary-Kate. I do the shop."

Sally's going to have to take the basket because the woman who is clearly a bit under the weather and not what Sally would think of as healthy is not taking it back or putting it on the counter like a normal person would.

"Thank you," she says, taking the handle. It's heavy, but then it's nearly as big as Ruby's Moses basket.

"Just some things to get you started and some island treats," Mary-Kate says, "from the island council. Some salmon and salmon pâté from the new fish farm. The pâté's lovely. Walter John should have put them in your kitchen, really, but he's having an emergency. Oh, and the phones and internet will be off for an hour at tea time. We're getting an upgrade."

She points to the notice from Highland Telco pasted above the till.

"Apparently it will be very fast," she says with a kind of shy pride that somehow puts Sally's teeth on edge. "We'll be able to stream videos and all sorts without the spinning ball of death."

"Right," says Sally. She feels she'd almost welcome the spinning ball of death right now, she's wound so tight. She puts the basket on the counter. "So. We just have to wait for this man?"

Mary-Kate nods at the customers stacked up in the narrow aisle behind Sally.

"Tell you what, if he's not back once I've served all these customers, I'll close-up and take you myself."

Sally turns and takes her own audit of the number of people and the size of the piles of things in their wire shopping baskets. At least three of them are carrying two baskets.

"It's not really good enough, is—" she begins.

"Is that your son?" says Mary-Kate, pointing out of the window. Sally follows the line of her finger and sees Tom jogging towards the door of the shop, waving to get Sally's attention.

"No," she says, and goes to meet him. She leaves the bloody basket on the counter. Let the Mary-Kate woman deal with that.

"What?" she says as she steps out into the drizzle.

Tom has his hood up and jacket clutched tightly round

him. Jesus, Sally thinks. I used to have a stomach flat as that. It makes her dislike the boy even more.

"Dad says do they have hot pads?" says Tom.

Sally stares past him as if he doesn't exist. Maybe she doesn't understand . . .

"For his bad back," Tom says. "Hot pads?"

He has to sidestep really fast to not get knocked flying as Sally lurches off the steps and launches herself towards the car like a missile.

"The fuck?" he says, nearly stumbling backwards on to the wet tarmac.

Sally can't hear him. Sally is running to the car, straight for the open back door that Tom has just got out of. She disappears inside with a loud and unintelligible shriek, and then she launches backwards with a black and white dog held by the collar. The dog yelps as she hurls it away from the car, hitting hard and scrabbling back on to its feet to stand looking as confused as Tom. It's a nice-looking spaniel. It just stands in the gathering rain and pants, tongue lolling redly out of its mouth. Doesn't seem to take the rough handling badly at all.

Sally reverses out of the back seat bum-first, and then spins towards her husband, ripping open the front door to reveal him frozen in place, face white in what is either pain or terrified anticipation of the blame about to be unleashed on him, thinks Tom.

"There was a dog in the back!" she spits.

"I can't turn around," he explains. Waving his hands with the vague weakness that Tom has only recently seen him manifest. He hates it. That's not how his dad used to behave. That's something Sally broke.

"There was a *dog* in the car, licking *Ruby*!" shouts Sally.

She turns and points at Tom. "You were meant to be watching the baby!" Yep, Tom thinks. Wicked witch has gone full beast mode. Well. He goes to a tough enough school. He's known how to handle bullies since Primary Two.

"Er," he says. "Actually, I'm not. That's the nanny's job. But oh . . . you didn't bring one."

A little red spot appears on each of Sally's cheeks. Her lips whiten.

"What?" she says.

She's not used to being talked to like that, Tom thinks. Good.

"I'm looking after Dad," he says, as calmly as he can. "I wanted to see if the shop had hot pads for his back."

Sally gapes at him.

"You left the door open," she says.

"I wasn't going to be long gone," Tom says pointing at the dog who registers the attention and wags its tail at her. "And it's a soppy old spaniel, Sally. Not a bloody wolf—"

The swearword jolts Graham out of his funk in the front seat. He cranes his head towards them, wincing at the jag of pain the movement sends through his sacroiliac nerves.

"Stop it!" he says through gritted teeth.

They both turn on him as one. Both say the same thing as one. As if they'd practised it.

"It's not me!"

It's a ridiculous moment, thinks Tom. Funny, even, if it weren't so depressingly sad. In a different world, if Sally was something other than the witch who'd broken his parents' marriage, it'd be a bonding moment.

"Jinx," he says. But under his breath.

Sally jabs that finger at him again. She looks like she's going to choke, thinks Tom.

"You are a child," says Sally. "You're only thirteen."

"And you're what? Forty, going on three," says Tom.

"I'm twenty-nine . . . " says Sally. Then, aware that she just

170

revealed a vanity, she screams at Tom, "And what does that mean? What the hell does that mean anyway?"

"I'll tell you when you grow up," says Tom.

"Is this your dog?" says a man's voice.

They turn to see a good-looking guy in a Telco rain jacket crouching by the dog and letting it lick his face enthusiastically.

Behind him, on the edge of the pier, Tom can see his colleague in a matching jacket has parked their van by a big metal cabinet and is setting up a work light and a big umbrella.

"No," Tom says.

"Oh Christ," says Sally, launching back into the car. "Oh bloody Christ! It'll have licked Ruby . . . "

"It's mine," says another man's voice.

Walter John has pulled up next to them and is smiling as he gets out of the car. He pats his knees. "Good girl, Milly."

The dog ambles towards him, tail wagging. He looks at Tom and his father.

"You must be the Goodges," he says.

"Mostly," says Tom.

"I'm Walter John, we spoke on the phone. I'm sorry to have kept you waiting for so long—"

Sally boosts herself, bottom first, out of the back seat again. She's got the baby under one arm and is swabbing its face with an antibacterial wipe. The baby is not enjoying it and making sure everyone knows about it. Half-sister or no, her crying sets Tom's teeth on edge.

"That's your dog?" says Sally.

"Yes," Walter John smiles. "She's called Milly."

"Well, you should keep it on a bloody lead!" Sally snarls, ducking back in the car, out of the rain.

"Oh," says Walter John. He flinches like he's been slapped. That was so unfair, so unbidden, so . . . unkind. Nobody behaves like that on the island. It's always been, for him, a gentle place. That's why it suited him and his wife so well. So much more pleasant than the city or the suburbs. More like their remembered childhood, really. An emptier world with better manners. He can feel his face reddening and even, God help him, a treacherous wetness springing in his eyes. He turns it into a sneeze, fumbling in his pockets for a handkerchief. What a horrible woman.

Once he's finished blowing his nose, he fishes the lead from his other pocket and looks around.

"Milly?" he says. "Milly? Where did that dog go?"

He turns to see the Goodges all looking at him.

"I've hurt my back," says Graham.

As if that explains everything.

Chapter 29

Firestarter

Robbie the ferryman finishes up the paperwork for the just departed sailing in the Portakabin that serves as the CalMac office on the edge of the jetty and hangs up his hard hat and hi-viz. He closes the door and switches the sign from OPEN to CLOSED and then sinks back into the office chair, a disreputable creaking thing patched with duct tape that squeals in muted protest as he spins it to look out of the side window and takes a can of Irn Bru from the fridge under his desk.

This is the part of the day he likes, alone in the office, door shut, no ferry, no cars waiting, just a wide expanse of tarmac separating him from the shop and the hotel and the scrabble of houses at the top of the slight slope, king of his container-sized castle. He chugs a mouthful of highly sweetened soda, making room for the hefty slug of vodka he carefully tips into the can from the flat pocket-friendly half-bottle that lives in his parka. It's a bad habit he's slid back into in the last couple of weeks – ever since his misunderstanding with Allie, really. But he's in control. He never drinks on the job. Just a bit before and sometimes a lot after at home, never in the pub.

But not enough, never enough to make an arse out of himself. He's not a moron, and he's not an islander. Islanders give each other a bit of leeway with their eccentricities.

He's only been here three years, transferred from the head office in Gourock when his predecessor retired and no one on the island wanted to take the job. Win-win really, he'd thought at the time. He'd done fine on the mainland, but his work was always coloured by the fact the head office was home to HR and HR knew his past, even though they pretended it was nothing and that his success was a testament not only to their low-key public-spiritedness but his willingness to embrace the rehabilitation offered by the penal and parole systems. And he had been a kid when he set the fires, and no one had been hurt since nobody is ever in school buildings after midnight anyway. And of course he'd been a kid. And an idiot. "The boy who put the arse in arsonist," as his mother, sharp tongued and endlessly unforgiving, had said. It was half a lifetime ago anyway, but he's happier here on the island, far from the office windows from behind which lurked eyes that knew.

He almost had a girlfriend too. He'd probably mucked that up by getting cross with her, but it was her who'd been drunk, not him, not really. He'd made the mistake of opening up to her because he thought they were close. A school? she'd said. A whole bloody school? Jings. It's always the quiet ones, eh? And then she'd done the nose trick as she laughed at him. Firestarter, she'd gurgled, waving at her friend Shanna across the bar and pointing to him. Twisted Firestarter. Like it was the funniest thing in the world. He probably shouldn't have grabbed her arms that tight, but he hadn't skelped her or anything. He's not a boy who goes about thumping birds. That'd be his dad.

He'd liked Allie. Still did, still fancied her. Even though

she was married. He thought she liked him, understood him. He'd thought she'd know he was giving her a kind of present, telling her his secret. But she'd made a joke of it. So much for being emotionally fucking available, he thought, as he bottomed out the can of Irn Bru and crushed it as flat as she'd crushed his hopes with her loud brassy laugh.

He wondered if she'd be going to the fish fry tonight.

Of course she would.

Maybe he could start again.

Chapter 30

Scar tissue

Sig goes to the rear of the Defender and pulls out Evie's bag and her wheelchair. She rolls it round to the passenger door and wrestles it open, fighting the stiff safety latches that Evie had meant to get her grandad to ease but hadn't got round to asking him about. Evie sneaks a look sideways and examines Sig's profile as she concentrates on clicking the latches in place. Her hand slips and she barks her knuckles, swearing under her breath. She instinctively puts them to her mouth and then feels the girl's eyes on her. She shakes it off and bends down to try again.

"What?" Sig says, finally clunking the latch home with a grunt and looking up.

Evie jerks her eyes away on reflex, then catches herself and looks back.

"I've been trying the oil," says Evie. "The skin stuff you gave me."

"How's it working?" says Sig after a beat.

"Don't really know," says Evie. "Hard to tell. Scars still look really angry."

"They will. Takes time," says Sig. "No harm in keeping at it, though."

176

She knows Evie had been looking at the scars on her lip. She'd given the girl some of the vitamin E oil she regularly uses when massaging her legs, which was a habit she'd got into since the physiotherapist had recommended it to stop the scar tissue becoming hard and – in her words – "snaggy". She was really talking about the internal post-operative scar tissue, but Sig, who never bothers to wear much make-up, also uses it on the scars on her lip. And it seems to work as the marks lost their livid pinkness and calmed down into less angry pale lines. Her leg feels tighter than the unbroken one, but that's what she does the stretching exercises for every morning, rain or shine.

Amazing the damage you could do falling off a rock – if you found one high enough. And Skye, several islands to the north, was full of them.

After he died, she definitely didn't try to commit suicide. She started climbing again, solo, free climbing without roping on, but she definitely wasn't trying to commit suicide. Matt, his cousin and best friend, didn't understand this, didn't believe her for an instant. But the truth – the truth she almost completely believes – was that only in the intense concentration needed to stay stuck to a vertical wall of coarse-grained gabbro high in the Black Cuillin did she find a place where, for a short but merciful passage of time, she was not haunted by the memory of him, of her guilt, and of the last and only argument they'd ever had.

She'd even told herself that solo climbing was her way of growing past the loss, of proving to herself that she could literally go onwards without him anchoring her and being her safety in case she slipped or missed a handhold.

And she really didn't climb aggressively, or out of her normal comfort zone. She took care not to overreach or make any stupid moves. She'd just fallen, bouncing her face off an outcrop as she passed it, and then shattered her leg. She hadn't been scared as she fell. She'd just had time to think "okay", register that she was calm, and then the outcrop smacked her into unconsciousness and she woke yelping in pain as a group of hillwalkers held her down and told her that she was going to be okay and a helicopter was coming.

"Not a helicopter—" she'd said, and then blacked out again. She'd fallen. She hadn't jumped.

"You've got to be tough on yourself," she says, watching Evie lower herself into the chair, fighting the urge to help her – the gesture she knows Evie would resent. "Got to really massage it in until it hurts. Only way to stop adhesions and keep the scar tissue supple."

"Supple," says Evie, settling herself with a grin. "Supple's for dancers. I'll settle for not stiff and less red. I don't think I get to be supple any more. Or a dancer . . . "

"Okay," says Sig, matter-of-factly. "Well, if it doesn't work for you, you can always use it to loosen up the latches on your chair."

Sig's flat refusal to be sentimental about her accident marks her out from everyone else on the island. Some days, especially early on, Evie almost drowned in the sea of sympathy and solicitous looks that went everywhere she did. Nevertheless, Evie feels stung by Sig's words, feeling the judgement in them, as if she's failed another test.

"Sorry," says Evie.

"It's okay," says Sig, looking at the redness on her knuckles. "Just a graze."

"I mean for being self-pitying. About the dancing," says Evie. "Was a bit whiney."

"Nothing to apologise for," says Sig. "How you feel is how you feel."

"But I shouldn't bleed it all over other people," says Evie.

Sig leads her into the house, feeling bad. The kid wants a sympathy she isn't able to give. Not because she doesn't feel for her, but because she seems to have lost the soft side of herself that allows her to express stuff like that instinctively. She'd like to take the easy way out and blame that on bereavement, but in her heart she suspects it's more to do with just living alone. That's how crazy old ladies got crazy. Maybe this is the first step on that long and lonely road. She decides to think about that later, knowing she likely wouldn't.

She gives Evie what she thinks of as the secret bedroom. It's not an actual bedroom, but the presence of a second bed in the house is not something most people know about – certainly not any friends from Sig's old life. If they knew about the box-bed in the boathouse, after all, they might ask to come and stay. And of course, when he and Sig were building the place that's exactly what it was for, friends and guests. Now it's another road not taken. But it is, despite being in the wall of a shed that opens directly on to the stone slipway and the open sea beyond it, cosy. It's like a four-poster that has sliding doors instead of curtains to keep the draughts out. There was a time, one whole long and unexpectedly hot summer, when they chose to sleep in it, abandoning the master bedroom for the joy of nights spent with the double doors of the shed thrown open to the warm sea breezes and the ocean beyond. It had been like camping indoors, and there'd always been just enough of a breeze to keep the midges away but not enough to make them cold.

As if to remind her that the warm days of summers past are not coming back, a gust of wind rattles the boathouse door and rain begins to spatter the skylight above the bed.

"I'll let you get settled in," she says to Evie, who starts unpacking her bags and making a point of showing she's brought her own cutlery and china. Sig is about to go and get her wetsuit in from the rain when she hears her phone ping and checks the screen. She stops dead.

"Shit . . ." she says as she takes in the unread message from Matt. Her gut balls with tension as she reads the timestamp and realises how long it had sat there unnoticed.

"Sig?" says Evie.

"From Matt," says Sig, grabbing the keys from the countertop. "It's Kathleen. Got to go."

"I'll come," says Evie.

"You stay," says Sig, running for the door. "I don't have time—"

Evie watches her slew the Defender around and gun the motor as she spits gravel on her way back to the road. She knows Sig means that she doesn't have time to load her and the wheelchair into the vehicle, and that stings a little, but she gets it. It's one of the things she is getting used to, always being a bit of a hindrance, even to those whom she knows care for her. She has to stop growing, and then there is an operation that just may put her back on her feet, even if she has to walk with sticks for the rest of her life. She knows she'll do it, because she's thought hard about it and has decided she's damned if she's going to let that life leave her behind without a fight. She can stand if she feels like biting back the pain and has something to hold on to, because balance turns out to be more of a bugger than she'd have thought without the fine motor skills and muscle tone needed to compensate for gravity's habit of tugging you in any direction in which you might accidentally lean. Getting conscious about the subconscious mechanisms of the body has become one of her new specialist subjects.

She cranes her head and, through the raindrops now blurring the glass on the big window, sees the Defender speeding towards Kathleen's house on the other side of the small bay on the short section where the road comes into view for a couple of yards.

Sig feels the cold knot in the pit of her stomach tightening as she speeds through the rain towards Kathleen's house. She doesn't want anything to be wrong, but the sense of foreboding is so strong her mouth has gone dry and she can feel her heart rate speeding up in anticipation of whatever it is that she's going to find when she gets there.

She desperately doesn't want any harm to have come to her elderly friend, but selfishly she also doesn't want to be the one who walks into the house and finds her still and unmoving on the kitchen floor as if she's just taken a moment to sink down on to the lino to rest. Sig's done that before with her own mother. The brute shock mixed with the treacherous ordinariness of something so heart-breaking is not something she wants to experience again. She's done those miles, and more.

Matt is on the doorstep, exiting the house as she pulls in.

"I just got your message . . ." she shouts as she jumps out of the Defender.

"She's not here," he says, all business, shaking off the implied apology as irrelevant to the urgent matter in hand.

"Probably gone for a walk," she says.

He looks right and left. Only now does she notice the quad bike still ticking over by the doorstep. He must have tied up at the fish farm and borrowed it to get here faster.

"Well, she's either done the beach walk or gone to the headland," he says.

"You check the beach, I'll do the headland," she says.

He looks at her leg.

"It's fine," she says.

And then Rex starts barking and looks at them as if they're stupid or something.

"Take the quad," he says. "I can—"

Rex whines in frustration and then turns and bolts for the headland path.

Matt looks at her.

"Go!" she says.

Suddenly there's no doubt in either of their minds about where Kathleen is.

"Jump on," he says as he straddles the bike and looks back at her.

"You'll go faster without me," she says. "I'll follow."

He looks at her for an instant, as if doing the maths, and then nods.

"Wait," she suddenly shouts and runs back to the Defender. She grabs the day pack that is always stashed on the back seat and runs back to him.

"What?" he shouts.

"Space blanket, first-aid kit," she yells, throwing it to him. He catches it and jams it under the bungee on the front cargo basket.

"OK," he says. "Good."

He wastes no more time, spinning the quad in its own length, skidding out of Kathleen's garden and then cutting hard right and back along the outside of the fence to chase Rex, who is still rocketing for the skyline along the narrow footpath leading to the seamark.

Sig grabs her stick from the back of the Defender and takes the direct route through the garden gate as she hurries along in their wake. She can't quite run, but she can walk fast if she ignores the ache in her leg.

She's ashamed of the relief she's feeling that she's not the one who walked in and found Kathleen dead on the floor, but she's worried about what's waiting for Matt over the edge of the hill.

As she pushes herself, she also thinks how familiar yet unfamiliar that exchange was, the strange way a crisis blows through the day-to-day crap that builds up between people and brings things back to something closer to normal. Or real. Or maybe honest. She can't work out which. Maybe it's all of the above, she thinks. She also knows it won't last, not just because nothing good ever does, but because the crap between them is real and honest in its own sad way. And what it's corroded will likely stay that way once this is over.

She grits her teeth and picks up the pace, pushing away the chill sense of foreboding that's still tightening that knot in her stomach.

Part 3

CUT OFF

VARANGIAN: CAPTIVITY

Gods, he would give anything to see the sea again.

The real sea, the white swan's path, the whale road, cold and merciless as the moon, not that warm sun-girt soup these desert-born scum think is one.

What a meanness of imagination to think that half-lake a sea.

What a failure of spirit to have only the one god.

Even though the northern seas have robbed him of much, he would still rather meet his end trying to avenge those losses on those cleaner waters.

Each night, as he lies alone in the darkness, he returns to the reason he'd come south all those years ago.

He does not mean to let his mind run there because those thoughts and memories are painful, almost more than he can bear, even though so many years have worn away at them.

But just as a tongue will keep returning to the sharp edge of a chipped tooth, he can't stop the thoughts coming.

He had come south to pledge his axe to the emperor because he wanted to forget, but every night reminded him he still had not been granted that mercy.

They had called her Sàga because his wife was named

for Freyja, wife of Óðr, and Sàga was a bye-name for the same goddess.

She had been the jewel of his life, a marvel of both grit and gentleness. At the very first, he had seen the unquenchable kindness in her and recognised it as a different strength to the one he possessed.

Like any small child, she loved small animals, the puppies and the chicks and the ducklings that ran around the long barn, but as she grew she was equally fierce and protective of the younger children on the farmstead or in the village. Unfairness or cruelty were the only things that kindled battle-rage in eyes that seemed to him now to have otherwise always been brim-full with laughter and warmth. The bullies amongst the older children learned to leave her alone, but if they turned their attention to other, smaller prey, she would step between them too, a fierce shield standing with a ready fist bunched tight at her side.

Like sun in the apple trees, she was both a present glory and the promise of sweetness and a full life to come.

She was all the more a glory to him because her strength seemed to come from that very sweetness, and not from the seam of cold iron that he knew his own sprang from, a hardness beaten into him by his own stern, unsmiling father.

She was the harbinger of a gentler, happier world.

And then a boat foundered, and she and her mother were swept off the face of the earth by the grey waves of the Kattegat.

That loss was what he had gone south to try and forget.

His wife, his beloved – and their daughter, the gleaming, kind, caring girl, more shielding tree than shield-maiden.

If he were not so thirsty and wool-headed, he would compose a poem about forgetting and vengeance and shout it in the faces of those who will come soon with their knives and their other sharpnesses.

He tries to spit on the floor at the thought of them, but there is not enough moisture in him now. Even his blood seems turned to sand and gravel. His heart beats so quietly he can hardly hear it, even when he puts his hands over his ears to lock himself away inside the bone-cave of his skull.

If he could just make that poem, make all the words join up, he could find some relief in conjuring the reassuring grimness of the north seas.

But this heat.

He knows he will never see them again, never feel the hoar-spray on his lips, wipe cold rime from his eyes. Only in words will he ever visit it now. He would sorely like to weave himself into a poem, for words have power – power to protect, and if not to protect, to carry what would otherwise be lost forward into the memory of the future, where understanding, if not forgiveness, might be found. And sometimes words carry the word-spinner's revenge.

He doesn't need the letter cutters to tell him that. He has known it all his life.

But his own word-hoard seems too heavy, the timber too broken to build the word-ship as he would wish.

He has the fragments of his vengeance, but they do not join up:

He would fight the stirrer of storms . . .

Brewer of waves . . .

Smite the wind's brother . . .

Battle the sea-god's wife . . .

Splinter stern seas, sunder the shield-wall screening the old ship killer . . .

He would laugh at Death, close sib of One-Eye's great enemy,

The Wolf's sister who stands alone and beckoning on the ness . . .

These are the fragments, but it is like a necklace that is broken. The string is dry and rotted away. And the brightest of the beads are lost.

Nothing joins up.

No matter.

And no remorse.

They say they will curse him for what he has done. Before they end his journey.

He still had spit to spare when they did that, and he spat at each one in turn.

They asked if he would like a quick death.

Knowing they would not give it to him, he laughed and told them no. He told them that their lonely desert-born god was a weak god and his curse would be as fleeting and meaningless as a pebble flung into the ocean.

They asked if there was anything else he wished for.

He thought for a while and then told them he wished he'd poisoned all their wells.

There will be more pain, and then, soon, he will go in search of his lost loved ones amongst the friends and family who have already found fellowship in Folkvangr or the lord of spears' great hall. That is a thought to hold on to when the sandmen come and the cutting begins.

Chapter 31

Good dogs go to heaven

There are dogs in heaven.

That's the first thing Kathleen thinks as she opens her eyes, because there is definitely a dog and it is aggressively licking her face and neck.

The second thing she thinks is that this dog angel has vile breath that stinks like the rotting corpse of the whale that beached itself one summer when she was ten and kept everyone from that end of the bay until the following January washed it clean again. And then Kathleen realises she isn't dead at all and the dog is no angel but the goofy spaniel that sad Walter John owns, Milly.

"Get off," she says gruffly, and pushes the dog away. The movement makes her head split with pain and she lies back and gets her breath. She closes her eyes because the rain is driving into them, and as she does so she realises she's very cold and soaking wet. If she's not dead, she needs to get up and get moving, but even as she thinks that she can't remember why she thought she was dead in the first place.

"Stupid," she says. She rolls on to her side and wedges herself upright on one elbow. The immediate all-round assault of competing aches and pains that accompany this movement reminds her that though she is not dead, she is old, too old to be lying out here on the heather. She's so wet she wonders if she has shamefully pissed herself. The thought makes her irrationally angry, and she draws her knees up in preparation for struggling stiffly to her feet.

Milly snarls at her.

It's almost as shocking as the rubble from the seamark behind the dog. She'd forgotten about it. Who'd do a thing like this, and why is that stupid dog behaving like that?

"Ach, away with you," she says, waving a hand at the dog. She hasn't got time for this. Milly snaps at the hand. Kathleen feels the teeth graze her as she snatches it back just in time.

She goes very still, eyes now locked on the normally docile spaniel whose barks she cannot hear but whose bared teeth she can see as it moves closer. She shouldn't be scared of a soppy dog like that, but she's down on the ground and her head is on the same level as the dog, which means she can see its eyes. They're locked on hers as it moves closer. Dogs don't normally like eye contact. Milly is suddenly anything but normal, and the shiver that runs through Kathleen's body is not caused by the cold she's feeling. She's not scared so much as angry about this too. She wouldn't have imagined the dog had so many teeth, nor such big ones.

"Don't you ... dare," she says, fingers closing round one of the cairn stones scattered beside her. She'll dash its bloody brains out if it goes for her. She'll smash and pulp its—

Milly springs at her and, in the flash when she realises she will not be fast or strong enough to do any of those things, a blur of black and tan fires into view, rocketing out of her blind spot.

Rex slams into Milly like an express train, T-boning the heavier dog broadside-on with a velocity that knocks her off her feet and sends them both tumbling down the heathered slope below Kathleen in an untidy snapping ball of angry snarls and fur.

They bounce off a rock and the impact sends them flying apart. By the time Milly gets up, Rex has braced himself between her and Kathleen. Milly snarls and shows her teeth, hackles raised, going low to the ground and creeping towards him. Rex barks a warning at her. She stops and looks at him, as if sizing him up. Then she bares her teeth and snarls louder. Her raised fur makes her look even larger. Rex streaks forward without any more warning signs, leaping for her throat. As the bigger dog snaps at him, he curves in the air and switches target, going up and round her jaws, his teeth biting into the bristling ruff at the back of her neck and holding tight as his momentum jerks her off her feet again and then flips her over his own rolling body so that she tumbles away with a sharp yelp of pain. Rex is on his feet in an instant, his warning growl so deep it's almost subsonic. This time she whimpers as if she is the aggrieved party and slinks away.

Kathleen is so shocked by the speed and aggression of what has just happened that she didn't register the vibrations of the quad bike until she sees Matt leap off it and drop to his knees beside her.

His arrival does not make sense to her. Why is he here?

"What happened?" he signs.

She looks at him as if he's a fool.

"I don't ..."

"Take it easy," he signs, putting a hand on her shoulder to keep her still.

She shrugs his hand off and sits up.

"Stupid dog attacked me," she says. "I should have thought that was obvious."

"Let me help," he signs, reaching for her.

She allows him to pull her to her feet and hold her until she feels steady on her legs. She can feel his eyes checking her out all over. The scrutiny makes her feel a wave of irrational anger like a physical thing spiking behind the bridge of her nose. She shrugs him off.

"Don't fuss at me," she says.

"Fine," he says, signing as he talks, though she's perfectly able to read his lips. "I'll not fuss at you, but let's get you on the quad and we'll head for home. You're soaking."

"I'm all right," she lies. She doesn't think she'll be able to swing a leg up and over the saddle of the quad bike and she's always hated the thing anyway. "I'll walk."

He reaches for her again and she bats his hand away.

"You've had a fall," he says. "You called me."

"I did not," she says.

"Gran, you called me out on the boat . . ."

"Stuff and nonsense," she says. She does not know what he's talking about.

"What are you so angry about?" he signs. "Gran, what is it?"

His brow is wrinkled in concern. Such a good-looking boy. Man now, really. Such a shame.

"What?" he says. "Did you bump your head, maybe?"

Kathleen doesn't want to tell him she woke thinking she was dead, though the reasons for that are muzzy in her head. She certainly doesn't want to tell him about the thing she saw herself doing, attacking him with the poker, the hatred she felt still a bilious aftertaste in her mouth. He'll only worry more and fuss, and truth is she decided a long time ago that there were worse things than a weakening heart as an exit door she was close to anyway. She'd been offered surgery but couldn't have faced the hospital, not after the many visits with her husband. If she was going to go – and she was – she would go clean, not in some overheated and impersonal space where you weren't anyone except a name in a bed.

"I just . . . " she says. But the muzziness is spreading. She sees the ruin of the cairn.

"Look," she says. "Look what someone has done."

Matt sees the desecration for the first time. For a moment he can't see what she's pointing at because it's gone, and then the shocking absence and incongruity hits him with the same intensity that she felt.

"The fuck . . . ?" he says.

"Language," she says automatically.

The shock galvanises him.

"Come on," he says. "We need to get you seen to and then we need to report this."

"I'm not going on that thing," she says and then feels the outrage of being lifted off her feet, albeit gently enough, as he walks her towards the quad.

"No," she shouts and slaps him. He stops dead.

"No," she says, getting control of herself. She didn't mean to do that. "No. Stupid boy."

The spark of anger is not aimed at him. It's at the flashing forward, the sight. Those glimpses of the future have always made her angry and impotent, not because they come unbidden but because they make her feel powerless in the face of the inevitable. That's the true curse of the sight. It's not the partial visions of the future but the preview of the thing you can't change or avoid – the seeing of the inevitable.

He gingerly puts her down. She's never hit him before. He'd bet money she'd never hit anyone before. But wet as she is, he can feel the hot rage coming off her in waves.

She looks at him in horror, somehow as if he is responsible for making her hit him, as if he is the one who has crossed a boundary. And then she turns and sets off down the hill.

He feels the raw slap-mark on his face and looks down to see Rex cocking his head at him as if asking what just happened.

"I don't know, boy," he says, and then jogs after Kathleen.

He catches up and walks beside her. Allowing her as much distance as he can while staying close enough to catch her if she stumbles.

"You should get that stupid quad bike," she says, eyes fixed on the track in front of her.

"I'll get it later," he signs. "I'm not having you slip and fall."

They walk on in dogged silence. All she can hear is the rain drumming on her waterproof and the plasticky swish-swish of his oilskin dungarees on the heather beside them.

She says nothing until they top the sloped rise on the side of the hill and see Sig striding towards them.

"What's she doing here?" says Kathleen.

"She came to look for you too," he signs.

Kathleen snorts.

"I'm not a baby," she says. All this concern, all those connective strands that weave the web of the community she's spent her life in are now somehow insupportable. Even Sig's smile of relief as she stops to let them approach nettles her.

"Kathleen!" she says.

"I'm fine," Kathleen says.

"You're soaking," says Sig.

"Well," Kathleen says. "Out of my way and let me get home and into something dry."

Sig is surprised by her briskness. This is not a side of Kathleen that she's ever seen. She starts to say something and then steps aside.

"Thank you," says Kathleen.

She pushes past.

"Wait," says Sig, looking a question at Matt, who stops next to her. She reaches for her shoulder. "Take my stick—"

She holds it out as an offering. Kathleen snorts.

"We're not all cripples," she says.

Sig stares at her back.

"She doesn't mean it," says Matt. "Not like that."

"Sounded like that," says Sig. "What happened?"

"Says the dog attacked her," he says.

"What dog?" she says, looking over his shoulder to see where Rex is.

"Walter John's spaniel."

Now it's Sig's turn to snort.

"Only thing that dog would attack is its dinner."

He scowls.

"I know. But it was growling at her and Rex saw it off as I got there."

"Rex?"

"Attacked the dog and then stood over Kathleen. Like he was protecting her."

"Rex doesn't fight bitches," she says.

"Fought this one," he says.

"Doesn't make sense. Did Kathleen hit her head, d'you think?"

"I don't know," he says. "But something's not right. I better crack on. She might fall again. You mind getting the quad?"

She looks at him.

"She refused to get on it. I've never seen her this . . . mean."

"She could have had a small stroke," she says.

"Great," he says, jogging after Kathleen.

"See if you can get her in a warm bath," she shouts. "And then call the nurse. The new one. Arrived today, I think."

He waves over his shoulder. Sig turns and hauls herself onwards. As she goes, she sticks two fingers between her lips and whistles ahead for Rex.

He always comes when she whistles.

Except today. Today he doesn't come. And alone on the hill, with no sign of life except a distant black bird riding the wind high overhead and a desecrated monument in bits at her feet, she feels uncharacteristically unnerved and abandoned.

Chapter 32

Left behind

Kevo had stayed a long time watching the ferry get smaller and smaller as it powered back towards the mainland. He had watched until a squall swept over the intervening expanse of water and hid it behind grey curtains of rain that dropped from the overhanging gloom like falling shadows.

To start with, he'd just sat gripping the steering wheel, paralysed by frustration and something sharp that sparked back and forth between rage and disappointment, like there was a loose connection in his wiring. All he could hear was the blood pounding in his ears and the dull buffeting the car was taking from the occasional gusts of wind that came off the water and swept up the slope to the ridge on which he'd parked. The ridge from which he was now watching the frustration of all his carefully made plans sailing way back to bloody Oban. He'd thought he might snap the wheel in anger. But by the time the squall blew in, he found he'd achieved an unexpected calmness.

He had tried to let go of the hard plastic rim and found it unexpectedly difficult to unclaw hands which had been clenched much too tight for way too long. As he'd worked some flexibility back into them, he'd taken stock, the first observation being surprise at the fact he wasn't out there kicking or breaking something. It helped that he wasn't trolleyed or on anything, he supposed. Sobriety was a choice and he'd decided to give it a go, at least for now. He'd necked, smoked, and jagged himself with enough of the substances laid out on the mind-altering smorgasbord that stretched invitingly from Categories A to C to suspect they weren't always helping him make the wisest of choices. He wasn't a complete numpty. That's why he was laying off any of that gear. He had plans. And plans needed a life to make them happen in. Basic stuff.

He had to give the rehabilitation programme that: they'd kept it simple enough to make it seem doable. He'd thought it would be airy-fairy bullshit and gone once, thinking he'd stick his nose in and swing the lead, just sit there and keep mum at the back because word was it helped with the prospects of early release, parole and shit. But there were enough hard men in that room to make it seem like something maybe worth sticking at. So he'd gone again. And again. Until it became a habit. The habit that got him off the other habit.

So maybe what he was addicted to was habits.

He'd said that in a session and nobody had laughed as he had expected them to. Instead, the group leader had just nodded and grinned a bit and said maybe so, but choosing a habit that wasn't going to kill you or make you hurt other people was a good and possible choice. And making good choices was what it was all about from now on.

He'd taken a deep breath and admitted to himself that maybe coming to the island hadn't been the best choice, but then, what the hell, he was here now. He was fucked right enough, but to be fair this wasn't exactly a novel sensation. Or situation. Fucked was where he lived most of the time. SNAFU City, his dad used to call it. He ran the likely fallout scenario on this particular iteration of fuckedness and felt a familiar sense of tired resignation: Shanna might dob him in for breaching the control order that was meant to keep him away from her, or maybe just get him lifted by the polis for leaving his agreed parole area. Or maybe she'd do nothing. Fuck no; when she found out about her sister, she'd go nuclear. What was he thinking?

That was fairy stories. She'd sure as fuck do something. One way or the other, he was stuffed.

He didn't care about that, not much.

He cared about not getting in the same room with her. Not doing what he'd come to do. Best laid plans of mice and men, eh? Though what the hell mice had to do with making plans he didn't know. Bad choices were bad choices, even if he'd made them from a good place.

Mice. They could fuck off and all.

Though maybe he was getting ahead of himself, he'd thought. Maybe that hadn't been her in the red anorak, giving him the finger. Maybe he was seeing what he thought was there and not what actually was. Maybe Shanna hadn't got on the ferry. Maybe she'd missed it after all. He'd known she hadn't bloody missed it, not really, but he should make sure. It was a small island. He'd seen the map, done his reconnaissance like a grown-up, like someone who meant business. He knew there was one road that ran in a loop. He should check. He definitely should check. Even though he knew for a fact she was on the boat because that was the way his particular cookie always crumbled, he knew the itch in the back of his head would grow and grow until it made him nuts if he didn't scratch it. He should check the car wasn't

201

on the island. Make sure she hadn't gone and bunkered up with some new teuchter friend he didn't know about. Maybe a boyfriend.

The thought of a boyfriend made him restart the car and chunk it into gear.

Chapter 33

Void

Sig stands over the ruin of the seamark, whistling for Rex. She can't stop glancing back at it. It's quietly shocking, the seemingly random violation of something so very old. Despite herself, she kneels and runs her finger gently along the long lichen beard stretching off the edge of one of the stones.

"*Faan*," she breathes, stretching out the Swedish swearword. This is not good, and, taken in tandem with Kathleen's uncharacteristic behaviour, it's distinctly unsettling. She wonders if Kathleen had a turn up here on her own, and if she lashed out at the cairn herself. Somehow that makes more sense than some stranger indulging in a random act of vandalism. It's disturbing, and the last thing Kathleen would ever do in normal circumstances, but her ferocious ill humour on the path was hardly normal Kathleen either.

Her eye is caught by something flashing at the foot of the remains of the cairn. It's the screen on Kathleen's mobile phone, lying where she must have dropped it. She bends to pick it up, and as she does so she stops and looks closer at the hole in the ground into which it had fallen.

"*Helvete*," she swears, reaching in and feeling the

squared-off sides of the space. It's too regular to be a mistake. The roots of the grass and the heather have grown round it in the peat over the centuries, so it had not lost its definition. It's a perfect rectangular void, and it had been directly beneath the seamark – and been there for a long time from the way the heather roots had grown around it and thickened with age. It isn't big, maybe the shape and size of an old VHS tape, but it is just too perfect a squared-off thing to be an accident.

Sig stares at it, trying not to believe what her eyes are telling her, which is that something has been unearthed here. Someone has disturbed the cairn while digging for loot. And as the thought hits her, she looks at the hole again and sees the white ends of roots that have been cut through, and she immediately thinks of the serrated teeth on the knife-like trowel she'd found earlier.

"*Faan*," she swears again, and she takes her phone out and takes a picture. She's read about this happening on other islands, people euphemistically called "amateur archaeologists" by the papers – men who are in her mind closer kin to grave robbers than actual archaeologists – who go into Iron Age brochs in the night with their metal detectors and dig out anything of value they can find and sell on.

Sig is self-aware enough to know her jaundiced view of humanity is largely a by-product of personal grief and guilt and all-round not coping very well, but people who would do something like this? In her mind, they're lower than whale shit.

She stands, ignoring the twinge in her leg, and whistles again for Rex as she heads back downhill towards Kathleen's house.

As she walks, she finds herself thinking of him again, caught by the old familiar ambush, as she imagines how outraged he would have been by this. He'd loved the ancient things on the island, taking a real pleasure in showing them to people and telling the old stories he'd grown up with. He'd always had a quality of belonging that she envied. Matt has it too, as does Kathleen. She, on the other hand, doesn't have that sense of roots. What keeps her on the island is the emptiness, the lack of people to whom she has to explain herself. As good here as anywhere else, she thinks, wincing as her ankle turns on a tussock of heather, making her knee twinge.

And in her deepest moments of self-reflection, she admits that it's not exactly a penance, staying on in a place where there are so many things to remind her of him, but it is a kind of debt. Him dying and her quitting the stage would be too brutal for those that knew him. It would trivialise his parting. The least she can do is endure for a while, live half of the future they'd planned together. It isn't really a debt to him because he is gone for good. He'll never know. Won't ever be back to call it in. But she will know. And it is a debt of sorts, twisted and inexplicable maybe, but one that some days makes sense to her. Or maybe it's just good manners. If she'd trusted him, and not done the amnio—

She shakes her head. No profit in unwrapping that bundle of guilt. She doesn't believe in karma any more than ghosts or gods. Things are as they are, and she is what she is: a left-behind – an uncollected debt, maybe, but one that fate has decided is so small and insignificant that it's not worth pursuing. The cosmic auditors just decided there's no profit to be made in throwing pounds after pennies and moved on, leaving Sig as a small oversight in the overall scheme of things. Nothing more than a rounding error, stuck on the wrong side of the balance sheet.

She turns and whistles for Rex, eyes scanning the slope behind her, and then turns back to find him already at her feet, wagging his tail.

"Idiot," she says, scratching his ears. "Where'd you get to?"

He stiffens and barks at something behind her. She turns, but all she can see is sea and heather.

"What is it?" she says.

Whatever it is, he seems happy not to go and chase it.

She scans the horizon again and sees nothing else unfamiliar, only a raven circling in the mid-distance. She watches it as it drifts closer, then turns to the dog and points back downhill.

"Come on," she says. "There's nothing there."

He trots alongside her, but she notices he keeps stopping to look backwards, as if he too can feel a prickle on the back of the neck. As if whatever isn't really there is watching them go.

"Rex, it's okay," she says.

He looks back and whines, a high-pitched nicker of unease.

"Don't be silly," she says. "Come on. It's all good."

She is pretty sure she's talking to the dog.

Chapter 34

Torn out

Kevo drives round the loop twice, slowing at each driveway to check her car isn't parked beside any of the houses that dot the landscape. Truth is, most of the landscape is unpeopled and the houses tend to cluster in small bunches as if for company, but he drives the loop clockwise and then anticlockwise in case he'd missed something going in the other direction. He sees more sheep than people, though he imagines curious eyes watching him from behind the blank double-glazed windows as he passes. He knows about these small communities, everyone seeming sweet as pie but watching each other like hawks. Much easier to stay hidden in a crowd. He likes crowds.

He stops at Shanna's cottage and checks the house number twice before pulling in. There is another house about a quarter of a mile down the road, but it only has one window facing in his direction and that one is frosted, as if for a bathroom, so he feels safe enough as he gets out of the car and walks up to the front door. Shanna's hideaway is a squat pebble-dashed box with a pitched roof out of which jut two dormer windows. He'd seen several twins of the building as he'd circled the island. It's one of the kit houses the Highlands and Islands Development Board had approved in the seventies, spartan but reasonably practical and weatherproof.

He puts a hand in his pocket and finds the Stanley knife, the reassuring heft of the chequered metal handle familiar against his fingertips. He won't use it, but it's good to know it's there.

The door just opens as he pushes at it. That surprises him enough to make him pause on the threshold.

"Shanna?"

He doesn't expect a reply, and gets none. Still, he hears himself call out for her again. Maybe there's someone else in the house.

"Shanna? It's me. I don't mean any bother, eh?"

Again, he is greeted by silence, so he steps in and closes the door behind him.

The house is still, except for a dripping noise from the kitchen and the sound of his heart racing.

Fuck. The house smells of her. He'd forgot how she filled a room even if she wasn't in it. That soap she used. Lemons. Shanna loved a lemon smell. Shampoo, soap, washing-up liquid, cleaning spray. She always went for the yellow stuff. And the house smells of that, of her, though the clean smell is at odds with the chaos he finds as he does a fast check of all the rooms, a sort of controlled untidiness upstairs and downstairs. Chaos, but no Shanna, no boyfriend, no anyone hiding in a cupboard or under a bed. The stillness is no lie. He has the house to himself.

He lets go of the Stanley knife and walks slowly around the house again, letting his eyes make sense of what she had left behind. First thing he sees was the absence of anything male – no men's clothes, only one toothbrush, no shaving kit. All the shoes are Shanna sized. So no bidey-in, he thinks.

Doesn't mean there isn't one elsewhere on the island. Just because there's no sign here doesn't mean she hasn't been playing away.

Still. It's something.

He searches the kitchen, opening cupboards and drawers, finding there's bugger-all to eat, just fruit and vegetables and not even any milk in the fridge, just a carton of some kind of oat drink and an unopened litre bottle of that alcoholic creamy muck she drank when she did drink. Baileys. So sweet it puts your teeth on edge. He'd never had any use for it. But there is a hammer in one of the drawers.

He takes it, and as he turns back to leave the room he stops dead. The wall by the door had been behind him as he entered, so he'd missed all the photographs stuck on it.

The photos are heavily outnumbered by the drawings, and none, he immediately noted, are of him. Shanna and her sister and her sister's kids feature. Photos he hasn't seen before. And then he finds a picture he does recognise, one of the rare ones she'd liked of herself: she is smiling at the camera and the warm light that brings out the colour of her hair, and he knows the scatter of freckles across her nose and cheeks came from a sunset on the Clyde a long time ago. He knows that because he'd once been in the same photo, though all that remains of him now is his hand on her knee, next to the ragged edge where she'd torn him out of the photo.

The fruit bowl smithereens in all directions as the hammer finds something to do.

Bitch.

He sits down on the floor. Shocked.

He hadn't expected to find himself crying.

Chapter 35

Spilt milk

Sig has come off the hill to find Matt standing outside Kathleen's kitchen door waiting for her. She asks how she is, and he shrugs and looks unsettled as he tells her she seems fine but crotchety. As if to underline this, Kathleen taps on the kitchen window and waves a hand at them, rolling her eyes as if they are stupid children and she is shooing them away for making a fuss about nothing.

"Think she gave herself a shock and now's embarrassed about it," he says.

"Maybe," Sig says. "There's a new nurse on the island now. You want me to call him?"

"Him?" he says. "I forgot. No. Think that'll just make her more pissed off. I'm going to stick around and then get her a carry-out from the fish-fry thing. You going?"

It's the first almost-nice thing he's said to her since it happened. Sig figures he's thanking her for coming after his grandmother with him.

"Not my scene," she says. "I've got Evie for the weekend."

"I heard," he says with a hint of a grin that she realises she's

210

missed more than she's allowed herself to admit. "Look at you. Babysitting."

It suddenly feels like a delicate moment, this unexpected hint of a thaw between them – fragile with a hint of vertigo.

"I know," she says. "Her grandparents must have run out of reliable people to ask."

"You'll do fine," he says.

"Maybe, maybe not," she says, matching his grin. "Rex likes her, but you're right. It's not exactly my normal speed. Looking after kids."

"Auntie Sig," he says.

"I'm not an aunt," she says. It's a reflex. The words are out before she knows she's going to say them. Before she can qualify them. "I'm not her aunt. Not a real one. Not an auntie aunt."

"That right?" he says, and there's a barb in his voice that catches at her.

"Matt," she says. "I'm not. We both know I'm just someone who was with her uncle . . . "

He shakes his head as if offended by something and looks away, back towards the house.

"You know why he left?" he says.

"That's an old road," she says, instantly regretting letting her guard down for a moment. "Let's not go down it."

"You know why he needed space?" he says.

She exhales, already exhausted by the turn in the conversation.

"Because I had the amnio," she says. "Matt, I don't—"

"No," he says.

"Oh," she says, bristling despite herself. "You know better, do you?"

"Because you didn't trust yourself," he says. "You didn't

211

bloody trust him when he told you you'd be a great mum, whatever fate threw at you."

"I always trusted him," she says. "But I knew myself, Matt. Christ. I had a sister I was meant to look out for. I didn't. I grew up with it. I'm sure I wasn't good enough to manage that, so I had to know—"

"He was," Matt says. "Even if you're right about you, he was."

"He was what?" she says.

"Good enough to manage it," he says. "You'd have been fine. You know you'd have been fine. He'd have made sure you were good enough together."

"You don't know that," she says. "I've got to go."

She begins to turn away, but he reaches out and gently puts a hand on her shoulder.

"Of course I bloody do," he says. "Sig. When I was 15, I told him how I am. Not an easy thing back then on a small island like this, but I didn't want it coming between us. Being gay. And you know what he said?"

"No," she says.

"He laughed and asked if I was going to try and get with him, and I said no and he said then why would it make any difference? And it never did," he says. "Or rather, only a difference in a good way. Grandad used to call people like me all sorts of names. He didn't mean anything by it, really. Thought it was funny, just the way his generation spoke."

Matt lets go of her shoulder and jerks his thumb towards the open door behind him.

"John went into that bloody kitchen there and had a quiet word with Gran, and she must have spoken to Grandad because he never, ever used any of those words again, not in front of me. And in a funny way, because

John was so matter-of-fact about it, everyone else was too. He was only bloody thirteen when he did that. He had a great heart, Sig."

"Yeah," she says, not meeting his eyes. "Know what?"

"What?" he says.

"That doesn't make me feel one damned bit better."

"And that's why you're playing Russian roulette every time you dive alone," he says. "Because you feel bad, because you feel responsible."

"I am," she says.

"You're not, Sig," he says. "Christ, it's not all about you. You didn't fail to service a helicopter so it crashed. That was other people. Not you. It was an accident. And it's certainly not your fault you survived."

"Thanks. But I really don't need the amateur shrink stuff," she says. "I'm not freediving because I have survivor's guilt. I'm doing it to exercise self-control. Because it calms me."

He stares at her. Shakes his head.

"Yeah," he says. "Yeah. OK. Whatever."

She turns toward the Defender.

"You know what?" he says.

She turns back, knowing this is a mistake, knowing she should keep on walking because turning like this is like leading with your chin. His eyes are level and hard. Not unkind. Just truthful, which is worse.

"You can't have survivor's guilt if you haven't survived. And I'm not sure you have survived, Sig, not yet."

"That's deep, Matt," she says after a beat has taken the sting out of the blow. "Very deep. Thanks for your input."

She really wants to tell him to go fuck himself, but she just turns and heads for the Defender. She can feel him watching her go, and when she pulls up into the driving seat he just nods at her and heads back inside. She can hear Kathleen begin to scold him for making such a fuss as she turns the ignition and heads out of the drive and on to the road, picking up speed as a vicious rain squall suddenly starts spattering down all round her.

She drives home still carrying that foggy sense of foreboding she'd been hit with out on the headland by the ruined cairn, and she walks in to find Evie sitting at the table, on her computer, headphones on and oblivious to Sig's arrival.

She's about to touch her on the shoulder, to let her know she's home and that Kathleen has been found, when she catches sight of the lead-sealed metal box in the plastic bag and the leather booklet in the Tupperware tray. She reaches for the box and runs her thumb over its buckled right angles. It's the size of a thick paperback.

And in a jolt of certainty that bounces her out of that earlier fogginess and into a very hard-edged present, she knows it's exactly the same shape as the void she'd seen beneath the ruined seamark, the one the grass and heather roots had grown around over the long years, making it retain its shape even after this box had been taken away.

Her eyes snap to the Tupperware. The leather looks different than she remembered it being. Paler, revealing some kind of design, swirling curves intertwined or overlaid with sharper shapes. And when she puts her fingers on it, it's no longer bone dry, but wet.

Sig stares at the table. At the leather folder, then at the dry crocosmia vase with thirsty stems she last saw deep in water – water she clearly remembers filling it with this morning. She realises what must have happened. She takes a deep calming breath and then taps Evie on the shoulder. The girl looks round and unplugs one earpiece.

"Is Kathleen—?" she begins.

"She's fine. Had a turn out on her walk," says Sig. "Matt's with her. Did you knock over the vase?"

"No," says Evie. "What—?"

"Well, someone knocked this over," Sig says.

"It wasn't me," says Evie, cheeks pinking as she held her gaze.

Sig can't tell if she's lying or just embarrassed. She gingerly picks up the sodden square of folded leather from the Tupperware and feels it.

"What?" says Evie, rolling closer.

"Did you spill water on this?" Sig says, taking a deep breath. "It's okay. Accidents happen, but—"

"Sig," Evie says.

Sig takes another calming breath. Everything today is too much.

"Please," she says. "Don't lie—"

"I'm not lying," Evie insists, voice raised suddenly. "I'm not! I don't lie!"

Sig looks around the room for other clues to what happened here. That crack in Evie's voice stabbed at her. She feels very old. When did she turn into a grown-up shouting at a kid?

"Sorry," she says. "But it doesn't make sense."

Evie follows her gaze and twirls her wheelchair in a slow 360.

"You think someone's been in here?"

Sig doesn't answer. She's looking slowly round the room for more clues.

"No one comes in here," Evie says.

"Exactly," Sig says.

Evie chin-points at the book.

"What is that?"

"It's a thing. A book," says Sig. She points to the backpack. "I found it in that pack, which was on the beach."

215

"And it matters that it got wet because ...?" says Evie carefully.

"Because it's evidence," says Sig. "Police might have been able to get fingerprints off it or something."

"Fingerprints?" says Evie. "Why'd they want—"

"The cairn on the north headland, where we found Kathleen, was pushed over," says Sig. "Someone had been digging under it."

"Treasure hunters?" says Evie. "You think it's treasure hunters?"

"Don't know," says Sig. "Yes. It's like the ones in North Uist who dug up the dun."

It had been all over the papers about a year back, a well-known but remote ruin of a small Iron Age fort that had been found pocked with hastily dug holes that had appeared overnight. There was strong speculation that valuable archaeological finds had been stolen and spirited away off the more northerly island.

"That was so bad," says Evie. "Granpa said every idiot who can spend thirty quid on a metal detector thinks they're Indiana Jones."

"Your granpa's not wrong," says Sig, looking closely at the folded leather. "If this is as old as I think, then it should be in a museum."

"You called the police?" says Evie.

"Not yet," says Sig. "Been a lot of other stuff going on, you know."

"I know," says Evie. "But the robbers could still be on the island. There's a chance of catching them!"

Sig smiles tightly.

"I'll do it," says Sig. "But I don't expect they're going to take my say-so as a reason to fly a crack team of detectives out to the arse end of nowhere."

"Is that where we are?" says Evie, bristling despite herself. "I always wondered."

"It's what John always called it," Sig says, realising Evie is island born and is upset by an incomer speaking ill of her home. "No offence intended."

Evie starts to give her a strange look and then covers it up, but it's there just long enough to register.

"Hey, I'm only here by mistake too," she says brightly. "Mum and Dad were moving us off the island, remember?"

"Yeah," Sig says. They had got exactly six and a half miles on to the mainland when that plan was brutally cut short by the speeding car that misjudged overtaking a caravan and hit them head on. "I'm sorry."

"Me too," says Evie.

"One of those days," says Sig.

"One of those lives," says Evie.

And – neither knowing quite why – they both find themselves smiling ruefully. They look back at the book thing as if it holds a key that might break the uncomfortable silence that hangs in the air between them.

"You said his name," says Evie carefully.

"So what?" says Sig.

"You don't do that," says Evie. "I mean, I don't remember actually hearing you say it before."

"Let's get some soup on," says Sig. "And I need to feed the dog. And then call Matt to see how Kathleen is doing and tell him about the treasure hunters."

Evie is looking at the leather cover and the metal box.

"This is cool," she says.

"Maybe you could study Archaeology," says Sig.

"No," says Evie. "I mean the treasure hunters, the police." Sig looks at her. Evie shrugs.

"I get it," says Evie. "They're thieves and vandals and

all that. But it's exciting. And nothing exciting ever happens here."

"And that's why I like it so much," says Sig, taking out her phone and dialling Matt's number.

This'll be more conversation in a day than they've had all year, but he's co-chair of the island council and is the right person to tell about the treasure hunters. It's not really her problem, and he'll know what to do and who to call.

Chapter 36

Pat the dog

Of course it starts raining the moment they back the Telco 4×4 up to the squat, grey, weather-proofed cabinet that is the island's phone exchange and start a brew up. Beyond the cabinet is the sea wall, and below the water beyond that is the undersea cable that connects the islanders with the rest of the world, their landlines, their internet and even their mobile phones, since the two cell towers on the island are too far from mainland cells to communicate without being relayed back through the cable that connects to the cabinet.

Because it's the single node that all communication goes through, it's vulnerable, and so it's protected from accidents by two heavy steel bollards, just in case some idiot backs into it. Malc has used the flat top of one of the bollards to rest his small camping stove on. Highland Telco is what it says on the tin, and the reason they drive around in a 4×4 is that they're often working on phone poles sat at the far end of wild tracks, places where there are no convenient cafes or pubs. And Malc runs on sweet tea, or that's what his wife says.

He hasn't even got it lit before big fat raindrops start pelting down on them. He looks up and round. Sky's clamped down like a lead vice all the way to the horizon. It's not going to be a short spattering.

"Tent," he says. "Fuck it."

"On it," says Jamie, already pulling the red and white striped awning from the back of the vehicle.

Malc helps him unfold the articulated frame and snap the stretcher bars in place, swiftly forming a rigid tent with a curved roof that overhangs the cabinet and the bollards. The rain hits the taut plastic canvas above them so hard it's like being inside a snare drum.

"We could sit it out," Jamie says.

"Nah," says Malc. "Whole bloody island has been told they're offline for an hour starting at four o'clock, so let's get a brew on and get on with it."

He turns and unlocks the cabinet while Jamie powers up the work light on a stand behind him. He's faced with the familiar mare's nest of brightly coloured wires and junction boards, and off to one side the old filter box they've come to replace. He and Jamie work silently in a cramped and strangely workmanlike ballet within the dry confines of the tent. This is a standard job they've done a hundred times before. Jamie unpacks the stools, Malc sits and reaches over his shoulder for the ruggedized laptop. While he brings up the schematics of this particular cabinet, Jamie lights the camping stove and puts the big brew-mug on it, full of water.

"I'll get the new box," he says, ducking back out into the rain.

"Don't get it wet," says Malc without turning.

"I'm not a fucking idiot," says Jamie.

Malc doesn't reply. Maybe he's not an idiot but he did bollocks up a job in Achiltibuie by leaving a component on

220

the ground close enough to the tent door to soak the thing by the time they turned to get it.

Jamie jogs to the passenger side of the 4×4 and gets in, leaving it a bit ajar as he reaches into the rear of the vehicle. Malc gets on his tits sometimes, but mostly he's okay, even if he looks like a pint-sized Hagrid and pulls rank a bit too often for Jamie's liking.

"Fucking Malc," he says as he lifts out the packaging containing the new filter. Something moves behind him, and for a moment he thinks it's Malc and it's going to be embarrassing being overheard swearing at him, but then he looks and it's that black spaniel that's jumped up into the cockpit.

The dog wags its tail wetly at him.

"Hey, pal," Jamie says. "Coming out of the rain?"

He's always considered himself a dog person.

"You're no fool," he says and reaches down to scratch the dog energetically behind the ears.

Milly yelps and snaps at him like a snake striking, catching his thumb in a painful nip.

"Shit!" he says, and reflexively lashes out with his boot, backheeling the dog back out into the rain. "Shit."

He watches it pad off into the downpour as he sticks his thumb in his mouth.

"Fucking dog."

He sticks the filter under his hi-viz and heads back to the tent.

He still has his thumb in his mouth as he hands the box to Malc.

"What?" says the older man.

"That dog, the one the woman was spazzing about earlier," he says.

"What about it?"

"Bit me," says Jamie.

221

"Let's see," says Malc. Inwardly, he sighs. Jamie attracts this kind of unnecessary shit like jam attracts wasps. They both look at the wet thumb.

"No blood," he says.

"Nips like fuck," says Jamie.

"What you do to it?" says Malc.

"Nothing," Jamie says. "I just scritched it."

"Fuck is 'scritched'?" says Malc.

"You know. Scratched it behind the ears. Dogs love that shit."

"Not this one," says Malc.

Jamie looks at his thumb.

"It's sore," he says.

"Well, I've told you before about watching where you put your hands," says Malc, turning back to the cabinet with the new filter box on his knees.

"And what d'you mean by that?" says Jamie.

Malc sighs.

"I mean she's an old dog and old dogs get sore places, and if you poke at them they'll likely snap at you."

Jamie watches his back as he hunches forward and unscrews the plate holding the old filter box in place. Malc's an old dog too, he thinks. Gets humpty when Jamie gets friendly with a doll, but it's just jealousy, he reckons. Old dog slowing down and not liking it. He checks the water: nearly boiling. He sticks a teabag in each of the tin cups they travel with.

"Oh, for Christ's sake," says Malc, sitting back.

"What?" says Jamie.

"Can't fit this thing," says Malc, his voice tight with disbelief.

"It's plug-and-play," says Jamie.

"It's plug-and-bloody-play if the fitting's standard," says

222

Malc. "But some idiot's done a relay repair and put in a non-standard fucking link. Who was on it last?"

Jamie kneels and scrolls through the repair log on the laptop.

"That lazy prick Johnson," he says.

"I'm gonna call him," Malc says, reaching for his phone.

"He retired," says Jamie.

Malc re-pockets his phone.

"Well, he got bloody sloppy before he did," he says. "He should have written it up."

He stares at the cabinet.

"We can work around it, I guess."

"If we have the parts on the truck," says Jamie.

"We've got a soldering iron," says Malc. "It's not rocket science. Just going to take the service offline for a wee bit longer than advertised."

Jamie rolls his eyes.

"Who's going to tell the natives?" he says. "They won't be happy."

"You're the charmer," Malc says.

Jamie snorts.

"Sod off. We'll toss for it."

"Nah," says Malc. "You'll do it."

Jamie laughs. He really doesn't want to go out in that rain right now.

"And you're the boss of me, are you?"

Malc looks at the botched-up job of wiring he's going to be wrestling with for the next couple of hours and suddenly feels very tired.

"Well James, yeah, I suppose I am."

He's never pulled rank before but technically he is the gaffer. Jamie laughs again, but with less conviction.

"You serious? We'll toss a coin."

"I am," says Malc. "And we won't."

Jamie stares at his back. This shouldn't piss him off this much, but it does.

"Fine," he says and pushes his way back into the downpour, which has doubled down and is now hammering the ground so hard raindrops are bouncing a foot back up in the air.

"But you're getting the first round in."

Malc hears him start the engine.

"Fucksake," he says. "Would it kill you to walk! It's not more than thirty metres!"

He knows Jamie can't hear him. He listens to the vehicle drive up the slope to the island shop.

"Fucking showboat," he tells the assembled circuit boards. "Laziest prick on the planet."

Chapter 37

Vellum

Sig keeps daylight hours, which means she has supper early this time of year, as the evenings draw in. The soup's been eaten, Rex is fed and sleeping beside her seat, and Evie's doing the washing up, which is minimal and a little awkward for her since the sink is not wheelchair friendly, but Sig isn't going to patronise her by pointing out she could do it in half the time. She's still feeling jangled by the sight of the fallen seamark and the evidence of it having been done by amateur treasure hunters. She'd had a short conversation with Matt about it and had sent him photos of the bag, the box and the weird leather booklet. He'd been as shocked as she was and said he'd pass it straight on to the island's police liaison officer who was, of course, based in Oban on the mainland. He'd also said he'd put the word out at the community Friday Fish Fry at the hotel pub. With half the island away at the Modh, the word would spread fast amongst the thirty or so islanders who remained. It would also make any visitors very easy to spot and keep an eye on. He'd asked her to keep hold of the evidence until the police got back to him. She looks at the booklet on the table and wishes he'd come and pick it up. It has a wrongness to it, no doubt because it's been dug up illegally and after such a long time, but the thing that hangs in her mind like a sticky, dark cloud she can't get free of is Kathleen's odd behaviour. She's normally such a warm and loving woman.

"Old people get cranky," says Evie. "I mean, they just do. I live with two of them: I know what I'm talking about. And I couldn't love them more, but they do get sort of crabby and snappy for no reason, and then I realise they're moving stiffly or spending too long in the loo and I get it. Their bodies are basically betraying them and it makes them worry."

"Your grandparents are great," says Sig, rolling an apple across the table to her.

"Of course they are," says Evie, fielding it. "What makes it worse for them is they think when they go I'll be helpless and on my own in the world because of, you know . . . "

She takes a bite out of the apple.

"You'll be fine," says Sig.

"I know," says Evie. "I mean, I know you don't believe in that stuff, and some of the time I don't either, but most of the time I kind of feel I've still got Mum and Dad standing just behind me, pushing me on. So I tell Granny and Granpa they'll be still there with me too anyway."

Her eyes flick at Sig then slide away quickly.

"That's how I see it. But you think that's wishful thinking, right?"

Sig shrugs. Being so young can be as painful for the one observing it as the one it's happening to, she thinks.

"You think when we're gone, we're just gone," says Evie.

"Yes," says Sig after a beat. "Sorry. I do."

She gets up and puts the kettle on. She knows her views are spartan and lacking in comfort, but they suit her. On the other hand, Evie's optimism and humour seem too valuable to stamp down on.

"But," says Sig. "I mean, whatever works is good for you. Doesn't have to work for me."

"Seems stupid to you, though," says Evie. "Sentimental."

"No," says Sig. "It's a story. I don't have to believe it. What matters is if it helps you. No reason you shouldn't believe it."

Evie looks away.

Sig boosts herself up and sits on the countertop by the stove, looking back at the girl staring up at her with a defiant tilt to her chin. She feels bad. Kid's already weighed down, trapped in that chair. She shouldn't pop any balloons she might need to keep her spirits buoyed up.

"You know what an *umwelt* is?" she says.

"No," says Evie. "Is it animal, vegetable or mineral?"

"It's each individual creature's experience of the world," says Sig. "We all live in our own *umwelt* – Rex lives in a world of smells that's so complex and full of . . . useful information that we can't begin to understand it. And some insects see parts of the light spectrum we're blind to. But Rex's world isn't any less valid than yours. Or a butterfly's: it's just different. Not wrong or right."

"So we share the same planet, but each inhabit our own private *umwelt*," says Evie. "Like I sometimes believe in ghosts and you never do."

"There you go," says Sig. "And because we each inhabit our own *umwelt*, neither of us has to be right or wrong by each other's criteria."

"Cool concept."

"That's why you'll enjoy university," says Sig. "It's full of cool concepts."

Evie rolls her eyes at her.

"Okay, thanks, Mum," she says.

It's clearly an uncharacteristically sarcastic dig and meant with humour, but Sig feels herself caught somewhere between a flinch and a smile as if, given her loss, Evie shouldn't be joking about that word, and Sig shouldn't be so aware of it despite hers. It's just one more slightly unsettling thing in a day of off-kilter moments.

"Just saying," she grunts. "Don't be in such a hurry to close any doors you might want to go through later."

"Fine," says Evie. She also wants to divert the talk's focus away from herself, so she points at the small leather booklet in the Tupperware.

"So, what do you think that is?" she says, nodding at it.

"It's a book, or a binding of some sort. A cover to protect whatever's inside," Sig says, grateful to the girl for moving the conversation on. She hands her the big magnifying glass and nudges the tray towards her.

Evie wheels up to the table edge and has a closer look.

"It's not paper," she says, squinting through the lens. "Or it is very thick paper? Or is it thin leather?"

"Could be vellum," Sig says.

Evie raises her head and looks a question at her.

"Vellum is an old writing surface," Sig explains, "made from cow skin. Or goat. Or sheep, in fact. They split it, scrape it and then dry it. Then they wash it with lime. Quicklime. It's what the monks used. Before there was paper."

"It's thicker than paper," Evie says.

Sig leans in next to her, picks a pencil off the table and uses the rubber end to point.

"It didn't have those marks on it," she says. "Not this morning."

"The writing?" says Evie.

"Whatever it is," Sig says. She nods at the dry vase. "I think someone spilt that vase, soaked the book by mistake and tried to mop it up, but the water must have, I don't know, cleaned up the book. It used to have a dark sort of bloom on it that made it hard to see the markings."

"Aren't these runes?" Evie says.

"They look like them," Sig admits.

"That's a letter T," says Evie, jabbing a finger.

"Maybe," says Sig.

"Or Thor's hammer!" says Evie, voice rising in excitement. "Not very Christian ... "

Sig looks sideways at her.

"I mean, I don't think a monk made it," says Evie.

Sig pulls the Anglepoise work-lamp closer and switches it on. With their heads together in the cone of light at the centre of the dark room, with the night sea thumping against the jetty beyond, they are joined in a moment that is simultaneously companionable and conspiratorial.

Sig realises how long it has been since she did something with someone else. She's surprised to find it's not unpleasant.

She pulls the lamp closer. She traces the more sinuous lines that contrast with the sharp jags of the runic writing.

"And that looks sort of like Arabic," she says.

"So weird," says Evie.

Sig watches the girl take another picture of the reverse. The truth is, it's been a while since she's seen Evie look so enthusiastic about anything, and it's infectious.

"It doesn't make much sense," Sig says. "Arabic and runic writing on the same document. We might be seeing something that isn't really there."

"Maybe. But it'll keep me busy. Be like *CSI*," says Evie, sounding excited. "I'll run the picture through Photoshop and extract the lettering, then we can put it through OCR to see if we can generate some more text that Google can recognise ... "

She notices the look Sig is giving her. She shrugs.

"Hey. If I could still be sporty, I would be. But I'm a geek now – and forensics? Maybe forensics is something I could do at uni. That could be fun. I could be a forensics person in a wheelchair ... "

"You could be walking by then," says Sig.

Evie turns away.

Sig bites her lip. She shouldn't have said that. She of all people knows how treacherous hope is. Evie waves her phone over her shoulder.

"This'll take me a bit," she says, adding a note of jollity to her voice that doesn't quite fool Sig. "Think of all the time I'll be occupied and quiet and out of your hair."

"You're not in my hair," says Sig. "Stay there."

Evie watches her disappear through the door into the boat-house end of the cottage.

Alone in the darkened room, Evie goes over to the window to get the laptop out of her bag. She likes puzzles and she was only half joking about *CSI* and forensics and university. It was a thin, fragile strand, but it felt like a lifeline to the future, something she could haul herself along. It had been a while since she'd been able to think of that future as anything other than a bleak landscape of potential operations and physiotherapists that might just mean more discomfort and no improvement. And she knows everyone wants her to go to uni, and she's been sketchy about it partly out of fear and embarrassment but mainly from a kind of fatalism, a sense of "what's-the-point?" But this little flicker of an idea is something, maybe the thing she's been waiting for.

Sig returns and hands Evie a purple lightbulb in a corrugated cardboard sleeve.

"What is it?" says Evie.

"You're the geek," she says, taking the bulb back from Evie. She snags the oven glove from the cooker and uses it to switch out the hot lightbulb in the lamp. Now the booklet looks different.

"Ultraviolet," says Evie.

"It can help isolate different inks," says Sig.

They lean in over the magnifying lens.

"How do you know this stuff?" says Evie.

"I studied materials science at university," says Sig.

"That's why you've got an ultraviolet lightbulb?" says Evie.

"No," says Sig. "John used it to cure polymer sheets when he was mending the kayaks." Evie looks at her.

"It makes things glue faster."

"Wow," says Evie, looking back at the magnifying glass. "It's like two layers, isn't it?"

Sig cranes in close over her head and nods.

"As if the Arabic has been written over the runes in some places; in others, the opposite way around."

"Like it's crossing it out," says Evie. "So cool."

"It is," says Sig. And she's not sure whether she means the booklet and the writing or this experience of just sharing something – that and the fact the girl is looking more alive and engaged with the world than she's seen her for a long while.

She looks closer at the shapes on the hide.

"It's not really … lettering. It's more like, I don't know, tattoos."

"I wouldn't like ink like that," Evie says. "Mind you, I wouldn't like a tattoo at all."

"Really?" says Sig. Evie shakes her head.

"Too permanent. I mean, how do you know you're going to like what you like now in five years? I change my mind all the time. When Katie and I dyed our hair pink, I almost got a panic attack, and that was dye you can wash out in the shower."

"Looked sharp, though," says Sig. "I remember that."

"I looked like a peeled prawn," grins Evie. "Katie looked cool cos she's got dark eyebrows. I just disappeared."

231

Sig grins back.

"You didn't look like a prawn, Evie. And your face is much too strong to ever disappear."

She sees Evie blush and looks away. She hadn't meant to unsettle her, so she leans over the book and examines it to spare her the embarrassment.

"It's not really a tattoo," she says after a moment. "It's a sort of book cover. But maybe the technique is like tattooing. Putting the ink into the hide for permanence, instead of writing on the surface."

"We can translate it," says Evie, taking another picture with her phone.

"You speak Arabic?" Sig says.

Evie shakes her head with a grin.

"No," she says. "But like I said, we have Google."

Sig shakes her head and turns away, reaching for her own phone.

"No," she says. "We've got better than that."

"What's better than Google Translate?" says Evie.

"Baba," says Sig turning back. She leans in front of Evie and takes her own picture of the text writhing across the leather rectangle.

"What's Baba?" says Evie.

"She owns the gallery that sells my jewellery in Stockholm," says Sig with a smile. "She's a friend. Her family's from Syria. Let's send her a picture and then FaceTime her and see if she can read it."

Chapter 38

Disconnect

Jamie's got a bad habit. He doesn't always put the parking brake on when he leaves the vehicle. He believes it's just as effective to leave it in gear, because that means it can't roll back and there's no chance of driving off with the handbrake on, which is something he is in fear of, having done it in the past, only noticing his error when his nose caught the smell of burning brake shoes.

He sees the red-faced woman who runs the village shop is turning the OPEN sign in the window to CLOSED as he stops the 4×4 outside the door.

"Hang on!" he says, waving as he ducks out of the driver's-side door. "Just a sec!"

She watches him jog towards her and then starts waving back energetically.

"Hi . . ." he says as she wrenches the door open and points behind him.

"The truck!" she yells.

He spins in time to see the 4×4 trundling backwards down the slope towards the harbour's edge.

In a horrible flash he realises three things simultaneously:

he forgot to put the car in gear; there is nothing in the empty swathe of wet tarmac to stop the truck from careening all the way over the abrupt drop into the sea at the harbour's edge; and Malc's going to kill him.

He sprints for the vehicle, feet kicking against the wet hardtop, heart bumping in his chest. He tells himself if he can just get to the passenger door and get it open, he'll have enough time to yank the damned handbrake and all will be well, saved by the bell, victory snatched from the jaws of defeat, an anecdote for the ages . . .

He pulls level and his hand finds the door handle and yanks it open, and for an instant everything is going to be good. And then something unexpected messes him up, something in the physics of the door opening towards him as he runs to catch up with the moving vehicle, and he stumbles and slips and falls, hitting the tarmac chest first.

His eyes follow the 4×4 at ground level, and now he can see through the rain bouncing off the pavement that he was wrong – there actually is one obstruction that is going to stop it plopping ignominiously into the harbour water.

It's hard to miss it because it's garishly striped in red and white. The tent.

He tries to shout a warning, but he's winded. He scrambles to his feet gasping for air.

"Malc," he rasps.

The shopkeeper is yelling a warning as she runs past him.

Malc can't hear anything except the rain thrumming on the plasticised canvas above him. He has his back to the slope and is still hunched on his stool halfway into the exchange box, so he doesn't see the tent behind him suddenly concertina as the 4×4 hits.

He does hear the massive thump as those safety bollards take the full impact of the loaded vehicle and mercifully stop it dead, the crash sending the primus stove flying past his head and slamming his toolbox into the back of his leg, knocking him off the stool. He feels the dispiriting crunch as he falls sideways on to the laptop, snapping the screen off the keyboard.

Malc lies there in the ruin of the tent, gasping with shock, staring at the back of the 4×4 which is dripping rainwater a couple of feet from his nose.

Because the mind does strange things in moments of shock, his first thought is that they might have a hard time opening the back door now, because the bollards have bent the rear bumper brutally upwards.

Then he sees Jamie appear round the side of the vehicle, gasping for breath, blood leaking from a graze on his chin.

"You okay?" he shouts.

Malc needs a moment.

"Malc?" Jamie scrambles over the mess of the tent and the strewn tools.

Malc looks at him.

"You're a fucking idiot," he says. "You didn't put the hand-brake on, right?"

Jamie hasn't got the words for that one.

"How many times ..." says Malc. "How many bloody times ...?"

Jamie waves at the 4×4 as if it's a witness for the defence.

"I left it in gear, I swear ... Must have jumped out ..."

Malc gets to his feet. Looks at the wonky laptop.

"Thank God for safety bollards, eh?" says Jamie, trying to lighten the moment.

"You could have killed me," says Malc.

The truth of this hangs between them for a long beat.

"Sorry," says Jamie.

Malc stares at him. The shop woman is hovering behind his shoulder.

"Should I call someone?" she says.

"No. Thanks," Malc says. "It's okay. I'm okay."

She shakes her head at them. Points to Jamie.

"You hurt yourself."

He notices the graze on his chin for the first time, feels it, winces and looks at the blood on his hand.

"I've got a first aid box," she says, and walks back up to the shop, shaking her head.

"You banjoed the back end to buggery," says Malc, pointing to the damage.

"Malc," says Jamie. "I'm really sorry."

Malc picks up the broken laptop.

"Ruggedized my ass," he says.

He stares at it, letting the adrenaline flush out of his system. He feels shaky. And he knows one new thing: he's going to tell his supervisor that he's not going to work with Jamie any more. Not after this. The certainty allows him to feel a calmness that steadies the shake in his leg almost instantly.

"Come on, let's get this straight," he says. "Then you can go and get patched up by Florence Nightingale up there."

Jamie feels a flush of relief. Malc's going to take this well. He'll buy him a few pints later. The truck's a bit buggered but nothing terrible. It's going to be fine.

He steps into the wreckage of the tent and starts seeing if it's possible to bend the struts back into something like a shelter.

"Jamie," says Malc. "Where's the Primus?"

"Yeah," says Jamie, misunderstanding. "Let's have a brew—"

"No—" says Malc.

There's a hissing noise behind them. They both turn and look at the cabinet in one perfectly synchronised moment, as if they'd rehearsed this.

"Ah fuck—" says Malc.

The lit stove is on its side in the guts of the exchange cabinet. It's already started a small fire. The thin wires sprouting from the circuit board it's come to rest against have begun to melt as the plastic sheathing goes up.

Jamie instinctively lunges forward to yank it out.

Malc, equally instinctively, grabs him and wrenches him sideways.

"No!" he shouts as they tangle and fall together.

The explosion is not a big one in the grand scheme of things. The gas canister is small and only half full. But the space it happens in is confined and sturdily built, so the force of the explosion shreds the plastic and thin metal of the exchanger racks and blows them up and out of the narrow door opening that shapes the blast and peppers the already abused back of the 4×4 with circuit-board shrapnel.

Jamie and Malc are untouched by anything but the sudden heat of the flash as it passes over them. They lie there, too stunned to mind the rain that's still pounding on to their upturned faces.

"Malc," says Jamie after a bit.

"Better use the first-aid kit in the truck for your chin," says Malc, slowly getting to his feet and heading to the vehicle to get the fire extinguisher. He feels a little bumped and bruised from where he'd landed. But most of all he's exhausted by all this and what it will now take to clear it all up. He wipes the rain out of his eyes and shakes his head at Jamie.

"Mind you, you pole up to the shop and tell them you just severed the island's phone and internet for the foreseeable, they'll probably rip the rest of your face off."

Chapter 39

Black mark

Sig's friend Baba grins out of the FaceTime window on her laptop. She's got thick, dark hair cut in a Louise Brooks bob and a wide, engaging smile, and Evie immediately likes her as much for that as her immediate agreement to look at the photo Sig sent her, as if it's the most normal thing in the world to get such a request on what must be, given the time difference, a late hour on a Friday night. She also looks cool and urban and exotic all at the same time, an effect enhanced by the lights of the city skyline behind her, visible from her penthouse window, as well as a crackling fire in a glass fireplace that looks like a piece of modern sculpture. Evie had never thought about what Sig's friends might be like. Hadn't really thought of her as having friends, really. She was so solitary.

"Okay," Baba says. "I'm game."

She looks down at what must be the photo on her screen, then back at the camera. Evie begins to feel excited again, though she's not sure why. Something in Baba's eyes looks mischievous. Or interested. Or interesting.

"What's the joke?" says Baba.

"Joke?" says Sig.

"Well, Sigrid, it's a little early for Halloween, but—"

"What does it say?" says Evie, wheeling herself into frame.

Baba raises a perfectly arced eyebrow at the camera.

"Baba, this is Evie," says Sig. "She's a—she's staying with me for the weekend."

"Hi," says Evie. "Is it something weird?"

Baba laughs and shakes her head, then nods.

"Well, it's old Arabic, so I'm a little sketchy about the precise wording, but—"

She takes a deep breath and widens her eyes at them, shrugging as she does so.

"But?" says Evie.

"It's a curse," she says. "It's a curse, Sig."

The bubble of impatience that Evie had felt rising in her chest feels as if it just popped, releasing cold air inside it, making her shiver. She looks up at Sig, who says, "What kind of curse?"

"A curse is a curse, Sig," snorts Baba. "I mean, I don't think they come in different flavours. Like, I don't think there are good ones. They're all bad."

"What does it say?" says Evie, watching the muscles tighten on the side of Sig's jaw.

"Roughly," says Baba, leaning in to the camera and crinkling her eyes in concentration as she reads the words on the picture on her screen, "To the oath breaker and poisoner of wells: may any who give water – I think that's clean water, actually – may any who give clean water meet the well's, um ... I don't know—"

"What don't you know?" says Evie.

"This word," says Baba, stabbing a finger at her screen. "Revenge? Vengeance. Okay, may they meet the well's vengeance and the walking water."

"Walking water?" says Sig. "Water can't walk."

"Water that walks," says Baba. "It's what it says. It's an old curse. It doesn't have to make sense."

"It doesn't," says Sig.

"Creepy AF, though," says Evie.

"It's just words," says Sig.

"Well, darling, I know you think I'm a bit New Agey," says Baba, "but I wouldn't want it in my house."

"No?" says Sig.

"No," says Baba, grinning again as she begins to chuckle. "That shit would *definitely* mess up my Feng Shu—"

Her image freezes, caught in a horribly distorted version of herself, eyes half closed, mouth stuck open as if caught in a silent shriek of anger.

Both Sig and Evie are unnerved by the sudden interruption and stare at the screen, hoping it will reanimate into comforting normality, turning the stillborn scream into a comforting peal of laughter, but it stays frozen and then the connection goes down and kills the window.

Sig hears Evie quietly say, "Seriously?"

She tries to reconnect but gets the "Cannot connect to the internet" message.

"What happened to the net?" says Evie. "That was proper spooky."

"Yeah," says Sig, and checks her watch. "It was scheduled to be off for an hour so the engineers could do the upgrade," she says. "We all got a note, remember? It's going to be much faster, so that's going to be worth waiting a bit for—"

"But it's so frustrating," says Evie. "It was just getting good!"

"You've got a funny idea about what makes something good," says Sig.

"I know," says Evie.

She takes the tongs and turns the book over in the Tupperware tray.

"Evie," says Sig. "Careful."

"It's okay," Evie says. "Promise I'm not going to break it."

"I'll go check the router," says Sig. "But I'm pretty sure it's the upgrade cut us off."

She checks her watch as she walks towards the boathouse door.

"Though if it's off for an hour it'll be too late to call her back. We can talk in the morning."

"I might pop with frustration by the morning," says Evie. "That's so messed up."

She looks across the table. The floor-to-ceiling glass is all that's between her and an increasingly wild night. She can see the silvered waves stacking up in the moonlight, relentlessly marching in from the wild Atlantic sea wastes beyond the horizon to break in small explosions of windblown spray against the dark stone breakwater that protects the house. It's an exhilarating view, she thinks, maybe even more so by night than by day, perhaps because the dark heightens the outer wildness as your mind fills in the unseen parts of the nightscape with its own imagined dangers.

As she spins away from the view, something catches the tail of her eye and she sees a figure standing in the dark, moving towards the boathouse. Her heart jolts and she gasps until she cranes back to see it's Sig's wetsuit blowing in the wind.

"What is it?" says Sig, closing the boathouse door behind her, alarmed at the sound of surprise from the girl.

"Me being a numpty," says Evie, pointing. "I thought there was something out there watching us. It's just your wetsuit, blowing in the wind."

Sig smiles.

"You thought it was the Water's Vengeance coming to get you."

"The Well's Vengeance," says Evie, watching Sig slide the

241

door open and step out into the wind. The gusts catch her blonde hair and thrash it around her head as she unhooks the suit and brings it back inside. She closes the window and drops the wetsuit over the chair. "It was the Well's Vengeance and the Walking Water, coming to get oath breakers. No. I just thought it was someone watching us."

"Yes, happens to me all the time," says Sig. "But good you saw it and reminded me. Nothing nastier than putting on a cold, clammy wetsuit in the morning."

While she lowers the drying rack from the ceiling and hooks the suit to it before hoisting it back up to its place on the ceiling over the Aga, Evie has another look at the tattooed leather in the tray in front of her. She uses the camera screen to zoom in on it like a magnifying glass.

"I'm going to make a camomile tea," says Sig. "You want one?"

She grins as she reaches for the tin canister.

"Very calming for the nerves."

"Sig?" says Evie, her tone changing enough for Sig to stop and turn.

"Yes?" she says, looking at Evie enlarging the image on her phone and squinting at it. She holds the screen towards her.

"What kind of vellum has one of those on it?"

"One of what?" says Sig, taking the phone and trying to see what Evie's talking about.

"That," says Evie, pointing. "A nipple."

Sig looks up at her. She then peers at the screen that Evie's holding out.

"A human nipple?"

Sig feels something brackish rise in the back of her throat. She has to concentrate hard on swallowing it back down.

"Sig," says Evie, "I think that really is a tattoo. I think the curse is written on human skin."

Sig puts the phone down on the table. Even the image on the screen is enough to make the whole device seem somehow unclean. She instinctively pushes the tray holding the booklet away from them both, trying to control the involuntary shudder that touching it triggers.

"I think I really don't like that in my house," she says.

"Now who's being superstitious?" says Evie.

Sig doesn't rise to this – but it takes an effort she's not proud of having to make.

"Maybe the curse is like the mummy's tomb," says Evie, grinning nervously. "Maybe the treasure hunter made a terrible mistake . . ."

"Evie," says Sig sharply. "It's just a nasty thing. There's no such thing as a curse. Not like that."

They look at each other. Outside the window, a large wave smashes against the jetty, sending spray spattering against the windows, just for an instant making them both think someone is out there trying to get their attention.

Each decides not to tell the other about their overactive imagination.

Chapter 40

No service

Tom Goodge isn't planning to run away from home, although the Bothy – the windblown house that the sad, smiling man (Walter something, with the dog) had brought them to – is not actually going to be his home, any more than he is really running away from it. He's not escaping, never to return; he's just going to try and find a place where he can get cell coverage on his phone. If he can't find some service, he's pretty certain he'll burst. It has been a crazy day and he needs to let off steam by having a good rant and a debrief with his mates. It's not that he's addicted to his phone, it's just that he misses the virtual umbilical that keeps him tethered to the tight group of friends that have represented normal during the last couple of erratic years. It hadn't been a pretty sight watching his parents decoupling and then reforming into something ugly that he couldn't really understand. He just needs to touch base with his non-family fam, to ground himself.

Once Walter Something had left them alone with their welcome basket of groceries and helpful list of things like the wi-fi password and the weekly refuse collection timetable, it had got worse. His father had taken painkillers and diazepam and decided the stairs were out of the question, taking a long time to park himself gingerly on the sofa in front of the electric fire. Tom had shuttled all the luggage into the house and put it in the rooms the witch indicated. There had been a period of respite as he made them all a cup of tea and they sat awkwardly in front of the electric fire not saying how crap and depressing the little house was. It was painted and wallpapered in muted pastel shades that were so dilute that the overall effect was of a house composed entirely of different greys and barely contrasting putty colours. It was, however, almost aggressively clean, which you could tell from the clinging powdery scent of the floral carpet shampoo, a smell that hung so thickly in the air that you could almost see it.

It triggered the witch's allergies, and once she began sneezing the baby woke and started crying and the arguing began again.

Tom had gone to his bedroom, notionally to unpack, actually to avoid losing the game of pass-the-parcel into which the baby's care routine seemed to default at moments like this. He stuck on his earphones and tried messaging his friends.

The messages just hung, the annoying red exclamation mark telling him he'd been unsuccessful. He refreshed the connection and tried with the wi-fi and then with the data package via the cell coverage. He got nothing either way and sat there looking at the absence of bars at the top of his screen. The old guy Walter? had said something about cell coverage being patchy and made a joke about sometimes going outside and standing on one leg to catch what coverage there was. Tom unplugged his earphones and sat on the end of the bed, listening to the rest of the house. The baby was quiet. He could hear the distant thunder of the bath being filled above his head, so that was the witch. He got to his feet, thinking to ask his dad if his phone had coverage.

When he got to the sitting room, he saw his father was asleep, head cocked back awkwardly, snoring. He watched him for a bit, even though it felt like he was spying on an unguarded moment. He tried to force his mind back to a place where he hadn't felt the way he did now about his dad. It was almost easy, but just not possible, like there was a strong magnetic pull that drew him close, only to be met by a closer field that pushed at him and maintained a distance that would never be crossable. His mum had told him to forgive his dad because not forgiving would leave him with an anger that would fester into all sorts of unhealthiness in future years. She'd told him that whatever had happened and would happen between his father and her was their business and not Tom's, neither to take any blame for nor to sort out. It was why she'd pushed him to come to the island with them. And her words had made sense in the cold light of their new, smaller kitchen in their new, smaller flat that would, she assured him, eventually feel like home, despite not being the old, bigger house he'd grown up in. And the thing he couldn't forgive his father for had never actually happened, it was true: his dad hadn't hit his mum, but Tom had stood in the doorway of their old bedroom and watched his father pull back his hand to slap her. And maybe Tom had misread the gesture, maybe his dad would have pulled the blow, maybe that wasn't what he was going to do at all, maybe he was just going to stand there and take the listing of all his many failings being shouted into his face. But he'd seen Tom and just turned the gesture into a wave of disgusted surrender and walked out of the room. And his mum, later, had said his dad wasn't going to hit her, never had shown a sign of it, never would. But Tom had seen what he'd seen in his dad's hot eyes and, worse than that, he'd been frozen as he watched his parents tearing emotional chunks out of each other, so stuck and unmoving that he realised he wouldn't have called out in time to stop his dad from lashing out. And in the end maybe this is the unbridgeable gap, his failure, not his dad's. Maybe he was weak too. He should have stepped in to protect his mum, just in case.

Then again, as one of his friends had put it, he was a kid. They were meant to be the grown-ups. So, not his grief, really. Except it was.

He'd decided to leave all the sleeping dogs lying, snagged his anorak from the hook and set out into the night to find better coverage.

The wind is fitful and worries at him as he leans into it and walks up the driveway on to the road. It blows occasional spits of drizzle into his face, but he ignores it, keeping his focus on the small screen in his right hand. He tries holding the phone high above his head as he squints at it, eyes searching for the elusive bars that will plug him back in to the real world. He keeps walking in the direction of the distant glow of lights that outline the rise in the land obscuring the harbour and the hotel beyond. He has the vague thought that if he can't get any service he might get some wi-fi at the hotel, but he doesn't really expect to have to walk the mile to get it. He's sure that once he gets out of the dip in which the new, ugly house squats he'll get some bars.

Part 4

THE WALKING WATER

VARANGIAN: THE WELLS' VENGEANCE

They have not killed him.

Each step he takes on the long road North to the Bosphorus hurts so much he curses them for that.

But that is their vengeance.

Making him bear the pain and shoulder his shame at still breathing after what they have done to him.

Making him carry his own curse.

Not the many that spill from his lips with each step he takes on the long, sun-baked road to the Bosphorus.

The one they have carved and inked into his own skin. The skin they have flayed from his chest and folded into a square for him to show his shield-brethren and the ruler they serve.

He does not think that he will survive the journey, even though they have done him the cruel compassion of binding his flayed torso with honey and silk and some sharp-smelling unguent.

They told him it would heal.

That he would not die.

That the strength of the curse and the art of their medicine would keep him walking.

That is what they carved on the now-folded square of his skin.

A true curse.

He asked if what they have written across his face is also a curse.

They told him no. That was a blessing.

It told any who met him to help him, on pain of death.

It said he was who he was now.

Poisoner of wells? he said. Lower than vermin?

No, they said.

He is now The Well's Vengeance.

To be fed and watered. But only to be given water that animals had fouled.

Carrying a dark curse that would blight the life and lands of any that gave him clean water ever again.

A curse that would first poison the oath breakers and the liars like him, they said, and which would then turn those deceivers into an even more terrible vengeance against the innocent amongst his own people. The deaths he had brought to their kin would be repaid tenfold as the walking water itself would rise up against them.

Chapter 41

Arrive late, leave early

The one hotel on the island is really more of a bar with rooms than a hotel, and it's not big enough to turn much of a profit. The summer season has expanded over the years as weather has got warmer, and as foreign travel's got more complicated and uncomfortable due to the patchily enforced public health requirements following the successive virus scares and lockdowns over the past few years. The hotel has benefited somewhat from more people deciding to take holidays closer to home, though the first lockdown and the second wave that followed it bankrupted the optimistic couple who'd owned it at the time. Now it's technically owned by the small island council as a co-operative venture, and though it barely washes its face financially the pub does provide one focal point for the island beyond the two churches and the shop. The fish farm's parent company subsidises it further by paying for the electricity and the water and provides the fish for Fish Fry Fridays. It's good PR, cheap social outreach, and ongoing corporate balm for any mild irritation the expanding fish farm might cause now or in the future.

With half the island away at the Modh, it's not as packed as normal and there's a good choice of places to sit. Malc and Jamie had decided, without consultation, not to take any of the ones at the bar. Instead, they sit side by side on a padded bench behind a table already showing several deadmen as well as their current pints. The unspoken understanding was that this was not the night to draw the islanders' attention to themselves. Cutting everyone off from their phones was one thing, but no internet was going to make them even less popular. There was a limit to the number of times Malc could face saying sorry – though Jamie, he noted, seemed happy enough to do so, which wouldn't have rankled so much if every time he did so he hadn't somehow managed to weasel-word his way round to make it seem like the blame was on both of them, rather than his own undisciplined self.

Jamie's temperament – pretty much unsinkable at any time – had regained its normal buoyancy with each pint drunk. Clearly he'd decided Malc had forgiven him. Well, Malc thinks, no point in disabusing him of that until they're back at the depot. And even then, might as well let the supervisors deliver the bad news. It's what they're paid for, sitting on their dry arses behind a desk all day.

Jamie keeps looking at the barmaid who has just arrived, replacing the sad old boy with the dog. She sees him looking, squints across the hall, and shakes her head with a half-smile, before waving at him.

Fucksakes, thinks Malc. Everything really is back to normal.

"Malc," Jamie says. "Malc, you've got to do me a favour."

"Is that right?" Malc says.

"The doll at the bar," Jamie says. "The barmaid."

Malc looks across the room.

"What about her?" he says.

"I've forgotten her name," Jamie says.

"Search me," says Malc, finishing his pint. "I lose count."

"I'll buy the next round if you ask her," says Jamie.

"Thought the drinks were on you anyway," says Malc. "Given you nearly killed me, and all."

Jamie grins, thinking he doesn't mean it. Punches him on the arm and leans in.

"Go on, big man," he says. "Ask her, eh?"

"You ask her," says Malc.

"I can't," Jamie says.

"Yeah, you can," says Malc. "You just go up and say, 'Hi, sorry, I'm a jerk, but I've forgotten your name'."

"I can't," Jamie says. "We, you know . . . "

"You didn't," says Malc. "You haven't been here before."

"She's Latvian or Lithuanian, you know. Some kind of thing like that. They move around these summer jobs, right? Think she was working in that hotel in Ballachulish."

"Jamie," says Malc.

"Go on, man," says Jamie. "I don't want to be ungentlemanly."

Malc looks at him. And for the hundredth time, he realises Jamie's superpower, the thing that makes him kind of bullet-proof, is that he actually believes his own bullshit. Thinks he is a nice guy, every girl's dream date. Each time Malc realises this, it surprises him in a way it shouldn't: he told his wife about it and she said it's because Jamie's a bit of a sociopath. He discounted it at the time. She was taking some courses to upgrade her job as a nurse, and he figured she was just throwing big words around because that was what she was studying, but over the last year he'd talked more to her about

255

his irritation, and he has to admit she might know what she's talking about.

She'd told him it was hard for people who were wired normally to remember that other people – like sociopaths – weren't. We're designed to trust, she'd said. Liars rely on that. Liars, politicians, con men and Jamie.

"Go on," says Jamie. "You'll be making it easier on her too. I'll be embarrassed but she'll be humiliated if she thinks I've forgotten her name, after we've done the—"

"OK," says Malc, cutting him off by standing up. He really doesn't want to know what Jamie and the barmaid did. Jamie would tell you details if you let him, and frankly that's the thing about him that Malc likes least. Who told other people personal shit like that, the whole who-did-what-to-whom-and-how-many-times stuff? And why? Were you meant to nod along, say "well done", maybe high-five the more athletic parts of the story? Malc knows there's a thing where men were supposed to indulge in locker room talk, but in his experience they don't – not the normal ones, anyway. Jamie, on the other hand, would – at the drop of a hat – spill stuff that made you feel mildly revolted and unclean for the rest of the day. Christ, if he was going through a fallow patch he'd even give you a play-by-play on whatever porn he'd watched most recently.

Because of Jamie, there are things in Malc's head that he would much rather weren't, things that people did to each other and what those things were called. It's like Jamie enjoys sowing little seeds of corruption wherever he goes, making Malc complicit in the long saga of his conquests, the real and the imagined. No. Malc is done with him.

"I'll get them in," he says, walking to the bar.

"You're a doll," says Jamie.

Doll.

In some parallel universe, Malc turns and punches him

right in the smiling face. But in this world, Malc is a patient man who swallows the flash of anger and barely breaks step as he keeps going for the bar.

There are other ways to deal with pretty boy.

Chapter 42

Baby love

She hates the baby. She hates the baby. She hates the dull throb in her head and she hates the nasty smoked fishy taste in her mouth that won't go away even though she's brushed her teeth twice and it keeps repeating on her like it's got into her guts and her lungs at the same time, but most of all she hates the squalling baby. She hates the pain lodged just behind her brow-line too, and she hates the repetitive sound it makes as she smacks her forehead against the tiles, and somewhere inside she hates the jolt that comes with each smack too, like she's knocking her brain off its moorings. But most of all, she hates the baby.

She hates the man downstairs, and she hates the baby.

The bab—

She hates the b—

She hates the—

She hates—

Sally can't now remember the word for what she hates, but she still knows she hates it, the squalling thing, the thing, the screaming angry raw thing in the room next door. The little thing in the bed-cage thing, the little wood bed ... what's it

258

called? Bed thing. She hates the thing in the bed thing and she hates it doubly for not having a word for it any more.

She's losing words.

Maybe it's because of this banging her head against the wall. Maybe she's knocking the big words loose inside her head thing so they can shatter into small pieces and the broken fragments can just tinkle out into the world outside so she can be all alone and quiet in a nice empty space, an inside place without the squealing thing in the small mattress-cage thing next door. Where she won't have to think of the heavy meat-bellied man downstairs, the hurty-back one who can't get up and stop the squealing red-mouthed thing making that noise, the meat-man who likes to lie on top of her and rub himself outside and inside her trying to make more squealy red holes to shriek want at her like the one next door, the thing that is hers that she hates and can't remember the word for.

And then she vomits.

The water that sprays the wall in front of her dilutes the mark her repeated banging has been making on the floral tiles, blurring the pink outline her bloodied forehead has left on the wall. She stares, transfixed by the rosy streaks that flow downwards from it. Pretty, maybe, she thinks. How did she make the pretty maybe?

One of the last thoughts she has is that she should maybe worry more about forgetting things like this. The other is that the meat-man is downstairs, and she should share this with him.

Chapter 43

Drinkers and non-drinkers

Kevo doesn't know why he's in the pub. He came back to the harbour to buy something from the shop before it closed and the woman who ran it had been locking up and a bit arsey about letting him in, but he'd got it, and it sat in his pocket like a small spark of redemption, making him feel calmer, calm enough to enter the pub and have a look around. Now here he is at the bar, watching the locals and nursing a pint of rum and coke – without the rum. He silently toasts himself. Glory days, he thinks. Rum would be nice, but he's made a promise to himself, not the higher power he couldn't quite get a handle on, no matter how much his sponsor wanged on about it. He's jonesing for the bite of the alcohol, but he knows it's a serpent, the forbidden fruit, pure poison to him now. More's the pity.

Matt doesn't miss the drink. Not with his rational mind. His body has other opinions, of course, because he's an alcoholic – but sod it, he tells himself, that's just biology. His choice not to drink again came with the realisation that he didn't have to let himself be limited by the genetic accident that had wired the dopamine receptors in his brain in such a self-destructive way. The sharp loss that severed his friendship with Sig taught him that life's short enough as it is without checking out early or missing what there is left of it in an undisciplined blur of booze and bad behaviour. So it took him a few missteps along the way, but he likes his mind clear these days, and he's comfortable enough in his own head that he's happy to spend time in rather than out of it. Because of this, he knows he's got a reputation as being a bit of a fun-sponge when the bevvy starts flowing in the island pub, prone to leave early and go home to a book or to tinker with something complicated in his workshop.

He nods at Robbie the red-nosed ferryman, who's propping up the bar on his own, hunched over a beer. His eyes have a sad, hungry look that Matt suspects is as much to do with the drink that Robbie thinks no one knows he sips in his Irn Bru cans as anything else. Although he's clearly trying to catch an uncomfortable-looking Allie's eye on the other side of the room. Well. There's a lot of drink on the island and many long nights in the winter to fill. Nobody judges. In fact, they're more likely to judge an avowed non-drinker like Matt, which is why he tries to keep a low profile on his teetotalism.

He sometimes thinks he's not given enough credit for showing up in the first place and nursing the lime cordial and soda that is his preferred poison these days. He drops in to the pub because it's a good place to catch up with folk and see what's new on the island. And he's a sociable man who likes the craic when its sharp and good, but after everybody else has had a couple of pints the noise level rises, the talk becomes more and more circular or less and less interesting with each successive drink. It wasn't something he'd noticed when he was happily drinking with both fists, but now he feels a sharp twinge of shame at what a garrulous bore he in turn must have been. So Matt always leaves early, partly self-ishly – to avoid boredom – and partly magnanimously – to continue to think well of his fellows.

And, absent other distractions not normally available to him on the sparsely populated and closely watched island, most nights he's happier to be at home with a good book. Right now, he's standing in line, waiting for the food with one of the older island couples. They've known him all his life, and he them, but this is the third time she's asked him about the soup.

"Is there soup?" she says. "What kind?"

The husband smiles at Matt.

"She's got her hearing aids in, but she forgets the batteries," he explains as he leans in to talk into her ear. Matt nods as if he believes him, but the truth is everyone on the island knows she's getting dementia and the husband's been in a cheerful funk of protective denial for a while now.

He tunes out of the man's circular conversation with his wife, distracted by Magda, the Polish girl who worked as seasonal cleaner and waitress at the hotel, who was getting into a semi-public argument with a good-looking guy Matt didn't recognise.

The gist of it seems to be that they knew each other from before, but the guy got her name wrong, and since she's so pissed off Matt assumes that the knowing was in the biblical sense rather than just a passing acquaintance. He watches closely, wondering if he'll have to step in and cool off the guy, who is drunk and way less charming than he clearly believes himself to be, but he doesn't because Magda is dealing with it well, and he doesn't want to take that away from her by sweeping up and making it a guy thing, as if she doesn't have the power she clearly does. Good Looker is also pissed off at the bearded guy he's drinking with, who seemed to have told him the wrong name for the girl as a joke. Doesn't seem funny to Matt, but also not dangerous for Magda, so he turns back into the old folks, only to see they've moved on and are now being served. He looks at the catering table in front of them and decides he'll grab two slices of cake for Kathleen as well as a carry-out supper.

Allie has been trying to avoid catching Robbie's eye and watching Magda and the good-looking guy have their stooshie, so hasn't noticed the wiry stranger in the hoodie taking the bar stool next to her until she turns back and sees him leaning a little too close to her.

"You're Shanna's friend," he says.

Allie leans back to take a better look at the guy. He's wiry and pale and unshaven, and though he's smiling he's got his lips closed tight like he's hiding bad teeth or something, and the tautness it gives his waxy face makes him look like a junkie. Maybe he is a junkie, she thinks. His eyes flutter when he speaks.

"Am I?" she says.

He nods.

"Seen pictures of you together," he says. "In her house."

"And who are you?" she says.

"Name's Sean," he says, eyes flickering sideways before re-centring on her. It's not much of a lie, he thinks. His dad had been a Sean, and since he'd vamoosed and given him fuck-all he figures there's no harm in borrowing his name for a bit.

"Is it?" she says. And everything in the sharp look she nails him with says: the fuck it is.

"Aye," he says. "I'm an old pal. Shanna and me, we go way back."

"All right, Allie?" says Magda, walking past on the other side of the counter.

"Friend of Shanna's," she says. Magda raises an eyebrow. She knows exactly who he is too. They both like Shanna and know her sad story. And given the nature of that story, Allie's glad to have Magda hovering in the background, providing air cover.

Kevo's oblivious to this. He tries a wider smile and catches himself, but not quickly enough that she doesn't spot a missing tooth, front and just off-centre.

"Right," she says. She looks over his shoulder and sees Matt the fisherman. Holds his smile long enough to get his attention. Her eyes flick to the runty guy and back to Matt. His brow crinkles in a question she doesn't have time to answer.

"Buy you a drink?" the runty guy says.

"I'm good," she says. "I was just leaving."

"You see her around?" he says.

"No," she says. "She didn't come in today. Family emergency."

"So, she made the ferry," he says. At first, she thinks he's drunk, but on closer inspection she sees he isn't. It's something else: the flickering eyes when he speaks give him a kind of blurry edge, making him hard to pin down, like a guy who's never quite there even when he's right in front of you, she thinks.

"Yes, Kevo," she says. "She went on the ferry."

He nods, waits a beat as his mind catches up with itself.

"It's Sean," he says.

"OK," she says. "My mistake."

She steps round away but stops as a hand snakes out and takes her arm. She turns angrily and finds it's not the runty guy but Robbie, who's clearly drunk enough courage to come over. The realisation doesn't dissipate her anger.

"I just wanted to talk," Robbie says, the sharp whine

in his voice matched by a more dangerous sharpness in his eyes.

"Aye well, I'd say you've burned your boats on that one," she says, twisting her arm free.

"You what?" he says, shaking his head at her.

"You've burned your bloody boats," she says. "Just leave me alone."

He grabs her arm again, but before he can say anything Matt's hand grips his shoulder. He spins to see the big fisherman smiling at him.

"Allie's going to go now, so why don't you let go of her arm."

It's not an entirely friendly smile. And the grip on his shoulder is like a steel trap. He lets go of her arm.

Matt lets go of Robbie's shoulder, pats him on the back, turns up the candlepower on the smile.

"Robbie, pal. Sure you didn't mean to grab on like that. Probably the booze, eh? But nobody wants to see stuff like that in the pub. I was you, I'd keep my head down, have one for the road if you must, then think about hitting, eh?"

He slaps him on the back again, like they're the best of pals, and then scoops his styrofoam carry-outs under one arm and walks Allie to the door.

As they step out, the rain hits them and they pause in the relative shelter of the porch while Allie fumbles for her keys. They step aside as Kevo walks out, nods awkwardly at them and gets into his car. Allie watches his taillights disappear into the rain. Matt looks at her, then at the disappearing car.

"You all right," he says.

"That was Shanna's ex," she says.

"I meant about Robbie," he says.

"Yeah. He's a bit ... I dunno. I thought he was OK, but there's an angry streak in there I don't want any part of," she says. "But thanks."

"Nah," he says. "I was doing him the favour. You could take him with one hand tied behind your back. You sure you're good?"

"I'm good," she says nodding at her car.

"You're right, y'know. It's the drink sort of curdles him," she says. "Brings out the nasty."

"Right," he says.

Back inside the bar, Robbie is hunched back over the countertop feeling like everyone is looking at his back. Fuck 'em, he thinks. It's a free country and he hasn't done anything wrong. Not here. He'll have another drink. Not because the big man told him to.

He rubs his shoulder with his left hand, still feeling the man's grip. His other hand finds the familiar comfort of the dimpled glass pint mug. When he was a kid, he'd thought they looked like tortoise shells when they were full of dark amber beer. Should have glassed the fucker, he thinks, gripping the handle tighter. That's going to be a bruise.

And that Allie. Telling him he's burned his boats. Fuck does she think she is? He's got a job here. He's got every bloody right to be here.

He waves at the barman. He's going to have a double.

Chapter 44

Busybody

By the time he stands on the crest of the road looking down on the lights themselves, Tom realises he's not going to get any bars at all. He pockets his phone and looks back over the road he'd walked. It loops and ribbons away into the night behind him, wet and silvery until it disappears beyond another slight rise in the moor. He shivers, partly at the cold, partly at the thought of having to walk home without a beckoning light to pull him across the lonely darkness he'd not really noticed as he'd trudged along, focusing on the disappointment manifesting on his phone's screen.

Turning to look at the cheerier prospect of the hotel and the bright lights on the pier, he decides to carry on and try the wi-fi there. He is more than three quarters of the way there anyway, and it's a more hopeful thing to do than plod home without anything to show for it. And the renegade thought that adds a kick to his step is that his dad and the witch might actually notice he's gone and actually worry a little.

Not a noble thought, really, and kind of immature, but then he doesn't see why the adults on this trip should have a monopoly on immaturity.

There are two people walking across the parking lot as he trudges into it. A guy is following a woman. He's laughing and saying something to her. She doesn't seem to be in on the joke. He keeps on walking.

"You can't even remember my name!" she says. "Jesus. Piss off."

"Don't be like that ... " the guy says.

Tom recognises him as one of the Telco engineers from the ferry canteen.

"Come on," the guy says, with a frustrated wheedling note to his voice.

"Go away," the woman says. "Seriously, go away."

She gets into her car and closes the door. Tom sees her fumbling in her bag, looking for the car keys.

The man slaps his hand on the side window. His face is smiling, but the smack on the glass is hard enough to make her jump a little.

"Sorry," he says. "But come on. I do remember your name!"

Maybe it's because the woman has hair the same colour as his mum, but Tom finds himself speaking without knowing he was going to.

"Hey," says Tom. The man turns to look at him. Sways a little.

"Help you, son?" he says. He seems more confused than hostile.

"I think she wants you to leave her alone," says Tom.

"Sorry?" says the man. He appears genuinely confused. "You talking to me?"

"I'm just saying you shouldn't pester her," says Tom. "Maybe ... "

The guy keeps looking at him, and for a moment Tom regrets getting into this. Then the man snorts a laugh and grins.

"Nah, that's not what this is," he says.

"It's exactly what this is," says the woman through the crack in the window.

"It's not," says the man. "We're friends."

"We're not," says the woman. She sounded Eastern European. Polish, maybe.

"We were friends," says the man, as if his conceding the point but being very exact about the detail is going to make everything better. Tom realises he's pretty drunk.

"No," says the woman. "You were a mistake."

The man notices the phone in Tom's hand.

"What are you filming this for?" he says. "Hoi—"

"I'm not," says Tom, immediately wondering if he should have been. "I'm just saying she just wants you to leave her alone."

"Give it here," says the man, and he suddenly lunges at Tom. Tom steps back and would easily have been able to outrun the drunk, except his heel catches on the lip of the pavement and he goes sprawling and lands hard on his bum, his phone skittering off into the darkness to one side.

Even as he lands and then scrambles to his feet, he's not worried, not really, because the woman is there, another adult, and adults don't let other adults beat up kids.

That's when he hears the engine spark, and the woman backs up and drives off without a backward look.

The man stumbles out of her way and stares at the taillights disappearing into the distance.

"You see what you did?" he says.

He's not smiling when he turns back to look at Tom. He walks towards him and picks his phone off the ground.

"Jamie."

The voice comes from behind Tom. He turns to see the other engineer, the one with the beard, and the sad old man with the dog standing in the doorway.

"What?" says Jamie.

"Leave the kid alone," says the bearded one.

"Fuck off, Malc," says Jamie. "You tell him to leave me alone, fucking little busybody. Filming me with his fucking camera ..."

"I wasn't," says Tom.

"Give him his phone," says Malc. He sounds tired.

"Or what?" says Jamie, his chin rising petulantly.

Malc exhales and shakes his head at him.

"I've had enough of your shit, Jamie," he says. "Give him the phone now, and then piss off to your room and see if you can sleep it off."

"I'm not bevvied," says Jamie.

"Yeah, you are," says Malc. "You're also a prick. Was going to let someone else tell you that, but what the hell, if the kid can do it, so can I."

The jut of Jamie's jaw becomes even more stubborn, but just as he's about to speak the door behind Malc and the old man opens and more people spill out into the car park, buttoning and zipping themselves tight against the night. Jamie shakes his head at Malc, throws the phone at Tom, who snatches it out of the air, and walks off unsteadily.

The old man with the sad eyes – Walter Something – comes over to Tom.

"Are you okay?" he says. "Tom, isn't it? I'm afraid you're too late for the fish."

"It's all right," says Tom, checking his phone for damage and happily finding none. "I just tripped. I was just trying to get a signal, maybe use the hotel's wi-fi—"

Malc appears over Walter's shoulder.

"I'm afraid the bad news is the phones are all screwed, internet too."

Tom looks at the Telco logo on his hi-viz.

"Are you going to mend it?" he says.

"We were going to upgrade it," says Malc. He nods in the direction Jamie had gone. "Genius there broke it instead. Likely be out for a couple of days."

"A couple of days!"

"I know," Malc says, "but without the phone we can't get in touch with head office and have them put the right spares on the ferry tomorrow."

"There'll be no ferry tomorrow if the weather forecast holds," says Walter.

"Right," says Malc. "Maybe three days, then."

"Would you like me to drive you home, young man?" says Walter John, turning to Tom. "It's on my way."

Maybe his smile's too needy. Maybe there's something in his eyes hiding behind the sadness. Maybe Tom's had too many stranger-danger lessons. Or, most likely, Tom thinks he's getting creeped out by this whole island thing and wishing his mate's older brother hadn't made them watch that film. Still . . .

"No thanks," says Tom. "I'm good. I need the exercise. Been sitting in a car for two days. My dad knows I'm out here. I'll be fine."

Chapter 45

Always the same dream

Sig jerks awake on a sudden inrush of breath and lies there, listening to her heart, momentarily wondering what woke her, straining for any outside noise of disturbance before she remembers it's not real. She's sleeping badly because there's a guest in the house, that's all. Sig goes to bed early these days, part of the disciplined routine she hangs her life on; in bed at 9 o'clock, up at 5.30. Evie's probably sitting up reading or watching something on her laptop. Most likely, she made a noise that woke Sig. She looks towards the boathouse door but sees no light spilling out from under it.

She closes her eyes and realises it's not real waking she just did. It's the false wake. She knows this feeling. It's just a dream. It's the shape her dreams have, like Russian dolls, nesting in each other, waking then waking then waking again, every wake but the last one a betrayal and a trick. But the first dream is usually a variation on this one, the one that has been lying in wait behind her eyelids to snare her the moment she closes them.

She somehow knows it's just a dream each time it comes, every time she dreams it, while she dreams it. That doesn't make it any less genuine to her each time she finds herself in the familiar grip of the thing. In fact, this dual sense – of knowing that what seems so pungently real actually isn't – is as much a part of it as the floating. She's always both in the dream and watching herself in the dream. Like she's two people.

And she's always floating.

Or at least the figure at the centre of the space is floating – it's not always definitely her. That's one of the uneasy things about the otherwise deceptively calm dream. Sometimes she does feels like she is the floating one; other times it's different, like she's seeing it all happen to someone else. But, even when it's probably not her, the tight connection she feels to the figure is so close that maybe it's more like an out-of-body experience, one where she is observing the dream happening to herself.

The fact that sometimes the naked body is a male one doesn't lessen that sense of connection.

She is pretty sure she remembers the dreams exactly and often finds herself picking at them when she is awake, trying to dig out a meaning. Not that she believes dreams have meanings, not really, any more than she thinks they can be harbingers or warnings. Sig's a rationalist. But she's also smart enough to know the mind thinks magically if you let it stray and don't keep a firm grip on it. And she knows that just because it tends to wander off and hunt for hidden meanings, it doesn't mean that what it comes back with is the truth. There are just as many lies as there are facts roaming free in the less-trodden wilderness of the subconscious.

And the wild truth, even when you do catch it, is rarely pure and never simple. That used to be one of his favourite quotations. She can picture the arch of his eyebrow and the smiling shake of his head as he would say it.

And, of course, it is memories like that which lurk in the darker wastes of her mind waiting to ambush her, which is why she disciplines her mind against visiting them.

The brain loves making patterns to map the world so it can find a way through the uncharted territories of the present and the future. Superstitious thinking's just a by-product of that tendency. She knows that. But still.

She's not particularly haunted by the dream. Nor is it sharply painful any more. It's no real obstacle to a good night's sleep on the nights when she has it. It has become familiar. If it jolts her out of her slumbers, she is not disturbed enough by it to lie awake unsettled by the afterglow any more.

And in some ways, it's a happy dream. That's what she always knows at the beginning, at least. The floating is good. In fact, she welcomes it – not so much the dream but the floating figure, the her/not-her at the centre of it all. The her/not-her is what she looks forward to, the sense of connection, of familiarity, the deep comfort of a known person mixed with the excitement of someone new to be discovered. So it may eventually be dark, but it's not really a bad dream, not a nightmare, because if it was, why would she wait for it?

The floating figure tumbles naked and slow in the centre of the space, like an object in zero gravity. Long hair always floats in a cloud around the head, whether the body is male or female, and that head is always tantalisingly bowed in on itself so that she can never really see the features, though she knows the eyes are closed. The hands are gently twisted together beneath the nose, hiding half the face, mirroring the way the whole body is comfortably curled in rest. It's the position she sleeps in, though when she observes the spinning self/not-self the dream logic makes her think it looks like the slow whorl of a galaxy spinning in space.

Except what the body is spinning in is not space but a space. She knows this because although she cannot see any walls in the pale gloom around the body, she can hear noises, and they are noises that are muffled as if coming from a different place altogether. Somewhere outside.

One noise seems like a regular but indistinct voice repeatedly saying something that might just be "one-two" but might also be a wordless pair of contrapuntal grunts. The other noise is actual words, a lot of them all jumbled together in fragments, the kind of noise you might hear if there was a party next door and you put your ear to the wall trying to eavesdrop on what was being said. It is an indistinguishable tumbling slurry of words punctuated by sharp spikes of laughter, but unquestionably it is evidence of a world beyond whatever walls contain the space and the body slowly spiralling at its centre.

It is not an intrusive noise, this hubbub. It does not disturb the stillness at the centre of this gentle, turning world. This is her favourite part of the dream, and when she dreams it she also dreams that knowledge, that she loves this peace but knows it will never go on long enough for her not to mourn its passing. She watches the body, sometimes looking down its length as if it is her own, sometimes seeing it as other/not-other, and as she does so there is always an ache in the throat, a herald of as-yet-unshed tears. She does not cry on waking, though. Not any more. The tears remain unshed, and the ache fades by morning.

When the music begins, the voices ebb away into the background, and though she knows that she knows the music she can never remember what it is when she wakes. The tune is also muffled, as if coming from another room.

She sees the intruder as a ball. She never sees it appear but instead realises it is there, as if it had always been there and she had just forgotten to notice it. When she sees it, she tries to swim closer to the body. It is not a sudden thing, rather a sense she must get to the body before the ball does. Because the ball is growing larger; not quickly, but relentlessly. There is no sense of urgency, not yet. She always thinks she has plenty of time to reach out and touch the body.

She knows if she can touch the body everything will be all right. She knows the ball will go away and she can return to just watching the body, which is what she likes doing. It's calming and it seems important, though in the dream she cannot remember why this is so.

As she swims towards the body, her movement seems to unbalance the whole space and it tilts alarmingly. In a sudden lurch, she sees the ball is not a ball at all but the tip of a grey line or maybe a pipe extending towards them, seen head on. The change in perspective seems to jolt things. The music fades back and the indistinct "one-twos" increase their tempo, getting faster as if matching her movements as she begins to thrash her arms through whatever it is that fills the space, supporting her and the body. She never knows if it's air or fluid.

The faster and more furiously she thrashes, the slower she progresses towards the body. The sad ache in her throat grows and becomes more like the familiar lactic-acid burn of overstrained muscles. Her desperate efforts get her no closer to her target, but they do change her perspective again as the space continues to tilt. It is almost as if her flailing hands are scooping at the fluid air and rotating everything. And then, as she moves over the grey strip, she sees it is not in fact a line or a pipe moving towards the tantalisingly unreachable figure – it is a wall.

This is the bad part of the dream as she freezes in terror, unable to stop this wall dividing the space with all the awful finality of a guillotine, leaving her with her hands splayed against a blank slab of scratched grey metal, forever separated from the her/not-her on the other side.

When the blood begins to sheet down from the top of the wall, she tries to get her hands clear before it reaches them, but she is stuck to it, and always, just as the slick redness hits her fingertips and begins to pool in the V's between her fingers, she wakes.

Sometimes it's not red.

Sometimes it's blue.

Like the bleach she uses to clean her toilet bowl.

But even then, she knows it's blood.

Awake now, Sig holds her fingers out in the darkness above her. She can only just make them out because she sleeps with the sides of the box-bed closed. She likes the private space it creates.

So does Rex, who shifts on the mattress, making a sleepy grunt of protest as she moves her thigh, which he was leaning against. She knows people say you shouldn't sleep with dogs on the bed, but even when there were two of them they always let Rex in. Some of her happiest moments were spent in the middle of winter, with the curtains drawn and the wall lamp on over the pillows throwing a golden glow, both of them reading, with Rex as a puppy lying splayed on his back deeply asleep in the narrow trough of bedclothes between them.

That was happiness, she thinks. I remember that. I had it. I'm not sad. I'm lucky.

She reaches down and scratches the now-grown dog between the ears.

"Good dog," she mumbles. "Sorry to wake you. Just a dream."

Sig closes her eyes, her hand resting lightly on Rex's rough fur, keeping herself connected to all the good that remains in the world as she waits for the undertow to drag her back to sleep, listening to the rain on the roof and the lap and slap of the water on the stone jetty outside.

It's a peaceful sound, and she lets it begin to wash the sad ache of the dream out of her mind and away from her throat.

She's lucky. She's happy. Everything is fine.

Chapter 46

Kiss

The co-codamol, the Diclofenac and the one emergency diazepam have taken the edge off the pain, enough for Graham Goodge to have dozed a little. He jerks awake as the door to the living room smacks open and has a momentary flash of irritation, sure that his coming to so quickly means he has twitched his back into another agonising spasm, but then he relaxes and realises he hasn't moved and the pain is still low and ignorable. He turns slowly, carefully, towards the door.

"Hey," he says. "Is the baby okay?"

The baby's not okay, not from the wailing noise coming into the room behind her.

"My love?" he says.

She's walking oddly. He can't see her face clearly because he's not wearing his glasses and she's looking down at her hands and her hair is hanging in front of her in a wet and unruly tangle, but he can see something's wrong.

"Sally?" he says, pushing himself gently upright and pulling his spectacles off the coffee table. "Are you okay?"

He slides the glasses on and can immediately see she isn't anything like okay.

"Fuck, Sal ... how'd you get so wet?" he says. "Have you been outside?"

Her face comes up. He has a sudden and involuntary urge to piss, and then the warmth spreading across his thigh tells him he's done it. The spasm of revulsion that twinges his back is not at himself, however. And it's not the sharp pain that feels like it's bisecting his spine that makes him gasp.

It's not even the bloody bruise on her head, leaking red and pink rivulets down her face, over her eyes and across her cheeks. It's the water welling from those eyes, the water speeding the rivulets on their way. It's spilling gently out of her mouth too, unending water, water that can't possibly keep coming, any more than he can push himself backwards through the sofa as she clamps her hands on to his shoulders and clamps her mouth over his rising scream and drowns it.

She drowns it with the water that pulses out of her and he chokes, and the gag reflex fails him and he feels it filling him, flushing deep into his lungs, but he can't unclamp their mouths and he can't fight her off, and all he can do is scream silently and suffocate, and keep suffocating, waiting for an end that won't come to drop him into a merciful oblivion. As he feels the water now welling freely from his own eyes, with the last bit of him that is himself and not whatever is entering his body, he wonders if this is all it will now be for him, the what-remains-of-him crowded out, squashed back into a tiny portion of his mind, voiceless and agonised and drowning forever.

Chapter 47

Carry-out

Matt looks sideways at the styrofoam takeaway boxes on the passenger seat of his truck, one loaded with a generous portion of fish and vegetables balanced on another one with a couple of slices of cake. Kathleen has a sweet tooth. He'll drop them round at her house. He knows she'll have eaten her supper by now, but she sits up late because she doesn't sleep much or well. She's lost the zest for cooking she once had when she was cooking for a family or just his grandfather, and now she swears by her microwave and reheated food. This fish will do her for a couple of meals, and more than that it'll give him an excuse to check up on her. He's still concerned about her fall, and in truth he's not going to get a good night's sleep unless he can figure out the cause of her earlier sharp-tongued unpleasantness. It must be that she gave herself a scare out on the hill and then bit his head off for fussing while she was keeping the fear in check. His worry must have undermined her already shaken self-confidence, triggering a kind of aggressive denial about it all.

That makes sense, he thinks, as he drives through the sheeting rain. She was rattled, that's all. Rattled and too damn proud and independent to want to be seen in a vulnerable moment. Of all people, he could relate to that, he decides. Must be a family trait. Blood will out.

A strengthening gale out of the north gusts sheets of rain sideways through the cone of light his high-beams punch through the darkness ahead of him as he crosses the first saddle of moorland. That low-pressure system is moving in fast, deteriorating the wet night into something wilder and wind blasted. There are no friendly house lights in the distance to offer any cheer on this stretch of road. He always thinks of it as no man's land, not so much because you can't see any sign of human habitation here, but because the phones don't work. Crossing it alone on nights like this, the child inside him wishes he hadn't given it such an unlucky name. The wind roughly buffets the truck and he has to grip the wheel hard to keep it on the thin ribbon of waterlogged tarmac. He sees three pairs of eyes glint in the reflection of his headlights as he passes a trio of sheep crowded in the lee of a boulder on the side of the road.

He shivers a little. The truth is he's less unnerved by his grandmother's uncharacteristic snappiness than he was by her earlier phone call when he was out on the boat, the one calling him in, the one telling him it was an unchancy day to be on the water and that something malevolent was inbound. That had been her true voice, the one he'd trusted since childhood.

"It's bad," she had croaked. "Oh, Matty, son. It's bad. And worse is coming . . ."

She might easily have been talking about the weather. But she wasn't. He shivers again and then chops out a small half-laugh at what a fool he is for spooking himself.

"Stupid," he says and thumbs on the music player. The last song playing kicks in mid-track, and as Cornershop tells him repeatedly that everybody needs a bosom for a pillow his spirits lift and he grins and finds his foot tapping along.

Dancing. He does miss dancing.

It is likely just coincidence that this thought occurs as he swings down off the lonely moorland stretch across the saddle and turns along the shore where the road sweeps him past the hidden entrance to Sig's house.

Sig's house. Somewhere he no longer goes, but once a place he'd danced, happily, freely, danced both drunk and sober, dancing in a warm kitchen full of laughter and hope and thinking happiness was a possible thing, easy as breathing, easy as dancing, easy as friendship – just loosen up, listen to the beat and let it carry you. Matt, who spends most of the time in stiff oilskins and heavy rubber boots, loves the lithe freedom of dancing. He'd danced in plenty of clubs, in crowded cities and on far-flung island beaches in warmer seas, tripped out, blissed and Balearic, going with the flow, allowing the beat to tell the body what to do. Not a world any of his island friends had ever seen him in, but a real thing, a passage of unexpected grace, not a secret, just a thing not shared. Or rather, not shared by anyone still living, or anyone still willing to talk to him. Only he knows that in some ways nothing had been as good as dancing in that kitchen, dancing in a warmth so close to home that it had indeed felt like homecoming. Nothing. Not really.

Another life.

Chapter 48

Something in the dark

S ig lies in the dark, controlling her breathing and medi-
tating herself back into a state of calm. She sees a set of
headlights sweep round the headland and somehow knows
it's Matt, her one-time friend, and she feels her face relax as
a tension she hadn't realised was there slowly disappears and
is replaced by a gentle sleepy smile.

Everything is really fine.

Rex goes batshit, jerking to his feet and barking aggressively
at something beyond the box bed.

Sig's heart bumps hard and nearly stops in shock. She
scrambles into a sitting position, brain woozy with the jolt
the dog has given her.

Just for an instant, she is frozen by the hardwired fear
always triggered by a dog barking at an unseen threat it senses
out in the darkness.

And then she reaches for Rex, feeling the barely controlled
tension like a held bowstring shaking through the muscles of
his wiry little body. She can feel his hackles have risen and
are bristling.

"Hey," she whispers. "What?"

He snarls and bounds off the bed. She hears him hit the ground in a thump and then hears the skitter of his claws as he charges across the wooden floor. As she scissors off the bed, she hears him stop in front of the wall of glass facing the sea and stand there snarling.

She hits the lights and sees him braced four-square against the outer darkness, again ready to fight whatever he knows is out there, whatever it is that she can't see.

The growling is a low, rumbling noise that unmistakably says, "Don't fuck with me or mine", and the sound of it triggers some atavistic mainline to her older, reptilian brain where the fight-or-flight reflex lives and everything speeds up as her heart begins to race and she flushes with adrenaline and she realises she can't see what he is growling at because she put the inside lights on and has turned the night beyond to a wall of impenetrable blackness blinding her and so she picks up a hatchet and turns to put the light off again and then twists back towards the window and she does not falter now as the fear has turned to rage as pure and elemental as the flash of lightning that outlines the sea-slick silhouette standing in the sleeting rain beyond the window peering in at her private space as she sleeps and then Rex uncoils and launches at the hooded man and the force of his attack would have shattered the window except Sig has sprinted across the room and has leapt over the dog her face snarling in an outraged shout of defiance and the adrenaline must make everything around her seem like it's in slow motion as she sees the thick tattoos coiling around her left arm flex as the side of her hand punches out and towards the window and just for an instant she catches sight of herself jumping at herself in the reflection of the unbroken glass a wild-eyed berserker snarling white teeth bared in battle-fury long braids whipping behind her head a face that seems to glitch disconcertingly between male and female a bearded one and then hers again and the axe the axe is cocked and ready and then her forearm smithereens the window and at the last moment it's definitely her face as the force of her leap makes her seem like a shield-maiden floating through a snowstorm of powdered glass as her right hand clenches on the leather-wrapped haft of the hawk-billed axe that she scythes down towards the head of the watcher in the dark and he cannot move fast enough to avoid the blade and only has enough time to raise his face his face his child's face the face of him as a child the happy laughing trusting toddler in the faded pictures she cannot bear to look at and she cannot stop the blow, and though she screws her eyes shut she feels the inarguable solid chunk of the impact jar death through her wrist and up her arm as iron splits skull . . . and she wakes.

Rex grunts as she moves her leg under the covers, mildly protesting because he was using it as a pillow as he slept.

Sig clicks on the light above her head and looks down at him in the golden light. He huffs and curls into a ball, then raises his head a bit and looks a dozy-eyed question at her. She smiles and reaches down to pat him with an arm that is once more tattoo-free.

"It's okay," she says. "Good dog. Sorry. Sorry, boy. It's only a dream."

The dog drops his head and closes his eyes. This is a familiar routine for him. She leaves her hand resting on him for comfort – hers and his – and allows her breathing to calm down, staring at the roof of the box-bed, listening to the storm. She likes the sound of the weather outside. Somehow it makes her bed and the house it stands in feel safer. Which doesn't make much sense, she knows, but then she is still half asleep. She smiles and turns out the light.

"Good dog," she says again.

All is quiet except the comforting white noise of rain on the wriggly-tin roof and the lap and slap of the tide against the stone jetty.

And now the spark of light within the house is once again extinguished, there is nothing to see, nor any illumination in the storm-dark night to see it by.

Then there's a flash of lightning; a flickering, short moment of blue white in the night.

Just enough to see the pale outline that might only be a waterlogged figure in a hooded Flecktarn parka standing outside the wall of glass.

Looking in.

It's trailing a pair of headphones on the ground behind it. They hang by a curve of coiled wire attached to something in its hand. It might be a broken crutch. Or a metal detector wand.

And then it's dark again as thunder rumbles in from the westering darkness beyond the sleeping island.

Chapter 49

Nobody goes home

Tom ducks his head and lets the hood of his jacket take the brunt of the weather as he pushes against the wind and jogs homewards. Half a mile hadn't seemed so far when the drizzle was light and what breeze there was had been gently pushing him onwards from behind. Now the storm has developed into something less amiable and it's he who is having to push as he forces his way against the wind.

This bloody island. No trees, no buildings, no walls to stop the weather getting at you. It feels like it's hurling itself at him, trying to sweep his legs out from under him as he runs. The thought makes him slow a bit to be sure of his footing. The wind might have blown anything across the road in the dark ahead of him. He doesn't want to trip on something he can't see. That would be about the only thing he could think of that would make this evening worse. He feels his useless phone bumping against his thigh as he goes and takes it out. It does have one application that he could still use even if he was cut off from the real world. He stops, turns his back to the wind and thumbs up the torch.

Out in the darkness on the slope of the hill, something

raises its head and sees the small spark of illumination flick on, on what it had thought was the deserted road below.

It's a meagre light, but it gives Tom some confidence as he runs onwards towards the house. He sees the lighted windows suddenly appear to lift out of the ground as he crests a small rise and looks down on them. The sight gives his spirits a small boost and he speeds down the final slope a little faster, careless of his footing, almost giddy. He knows there will be angry words when he gets in, lots of "where-have-you-beens", but he feels ready for it. He now doesn't mind how wet he is or how bedraggled he's going to look. It's a plus, really. They'll see it, and even if they tell him off they'll be feeling bad: somewhere deep down they'll see how upset he must be to get into such a state. He won't even have to tell them about the leery guy in the pub to make them feel sorry for him. Though he will tell, because why not? Misery loves company, so the more the merrier.

The door is on the windward side of the house, and as Tom runs round the building he slows a little, deciding whether the thing to do would be to get caught (on purpose) sneaking back in or to fling open the door and make an entrance.

The wind is at his back again, seeming to push him towards the door: it's a constant blow now, blowing the white clothes-line into a taut curve that arcs away until it escapes the throw of the porch light, losing itself in the night. The wind might have lost its early gustiness and smoothed out into a consistent flow, but with it behind him again he feels a sudden chill, as if the blackness that anchored the clothesline behind him was getting closer.

He thinks he hears someone call his name, and he turns back and looks into the unbroken dark.

"Yeah?" he says. Then, "Hello?"

And when no answer comes, he figures it was probably

just a trick of the wind humming through the clothesline. That and his imagination working overtime. Still. It must just be the cold, but he feels the hairs on the back of his neck rise, and he finds himself turned around and stumbling quickly forward again over that last few feet, pushing hurriedly through the door and forcing it back into place. The wind resists, but the lock clicks decisively as he shoves the door home against the seals on the frame. The sound deadens considerably, becoming a safely outside sound. He pushes his hood off his head and listens. All he can hear is the bloody baby squalling upstairs. Well, that isn't his problem. No doubt the witch is up there being useless at dealing with it.

He watches the water splash on to the lino as it drips off his waterproof. He should probably take his boots off, but the floor seems wet and messy already. No doubt they'd decided there was some bit of baby-kit they needed in the car and had braved the downpour to rescue it. He can't imagine any other reason they'd brave the weather.

Tom walks out and along the short length of carpet that leads to the living room. His boots squish as he steps. The door opposite the living room opens into a white-painted room with white cabinets and a sink. This is the dispensary, the nearest thing the island has to a surgery, where his dad would be doing the nursing. It has a cool hi-tech light that swings on an arm fixed to the ceiling, like in a dentist's. He flicks it on. Nothing but white surfaces look blankly back at him. He flicks it back off.

The door to the living room is half open, and he pushes in and looks to see if his dad is still flat out on the ugly velour sofa. This room is also empty but much, much messier. And the impromptu bed set up on the sofa is thrown untidily aside, hanging half on the floor like a discarded shroud.

Obviously, the pills had cured his back and he'd gone upstairs. Tom feels a twinge of irritation at the lack of an immediate audience to greet and berate him as he makes his dramatic return as the rain-lashed prodigal.

He picks his dad's specs off the floor and puts them on the coffee table. It's an automatic gesture, putting them somewhere safe. It doesn't mean he's forgiven him.

As he straightens up, Tom sees the black rectangle of the window, and for a moment imagines how he would look if the darkness was really looking back at him. A sad, wet boy in a lightbox, a peep-show for the passing viewer. Standing there like a figure in a toy theatre makes him feel exposed and vulnerable. He squishes across the carpet and pulls the curtains shut.

He feels like a child for doing it, but the dark and the constant sound of the wind does make it feel like something's rubbing against the windows and watching.

He redirects his unease back into a sense of aggrievement at the lack of a welcoming committee. No doubt they're both trying to calm the wailing baby upstairs and doing their usual useless job of it, but—

The thought that they might simply have not bloody noticed he had gone out into the wild night and been gone for such a long time sends a sudden blaze of anger through him. He takes the stairs three at a time, strides past the open door to the bathroom and the next door showing the emptiness of their bedroom and barges into the baby's room.

"You didn't even notice I was—" he begins and then stops.

Only one pair of eyes looks back at him from behind the pale wood bars of the cot.

"Where the fuck are they?" he asks. "Jesus!"

The baby starts crying again.

Tom leaves the room and shouts.

"Hey," he says. And when that doesn't get an answer, he adds: "Your baby needs changing! Where are you?"

There is no answer. He starts to go down the stairs to check if they are, for some bizarre reason, holed up in his tiny bedroom, but the noise of the baby makes him pause.

"Christ," he says and turns back. This isn't the baby's fault. He reaches in and lifts it. Immediately, it stops making the noise and stares at him, fascinated.

"Stop that," he says. "I know what you're doing."

He smells the nappy.

Changing the little monster is easy. He doesn't know why people make a fuss. The baby lies there and looks at him with those dark blue eyes and doesn't seem to mind as he unfastens and wipes and dries and then straps on a new pad.

Damn baby smiles at him sleepily as he poppers it back into the onesie. He lets it hold his finger in its tiny hand.

"Okay. I'm not going to like you," he says quietly. "I mean, I will, obviously, in the end, but right now? You and me? Mortal enemies."

Tom lifts it into his arms and goes back through the house. The only place they could be is in his room. Maybe they had sat there, worried, on his bed, feeling bad about how they'd treated him, and then fallen asleep.

It has been a long day. That's possible.

His room is as empty as the rest of the house. He looks at the baby. The baby looks at him and maybe smiles.

"Where have they gone?" he asks it.

It doesn't seem to know. He peers out of the window and sees the red rear reflectors on the car glitter back at him, so he knows they haven't driven off to look for him.

Maybe they're out in that garage by the shore. Maybe they're playing a trick on him, teaching him a lesson.

Fine, he thinks. Fine. That's all that makes sense.

He grabs his sleeping bag and a dry T-shirt and goes back upstairs.

He lays the baby back in the cot and lays down on the floor next to it.

Let them play their game, he thinks. He'll be discovered loyally sleeping like a guard dog next to the tiny monster. That'll make them feel pretty sheepish.

The little monster sticks a soft pink hand out of the cot, reaching for him.

"No," he says. "Shhh. Sleepy time, okay."

But in the end, he moves closer and lets it hold his finger.

And then silence takes over the inside of the house while the thing that had been alerted by the light of Tom's phone's flashlight and followed him home watches the wind and the rain lash at the windows and doors, trying to find a way in as a brief, merciful sleep washes over the boy and the baby.

Chapter 50

The drowning chair

Matt sees the light on in the porch of Kathleen's house, and a slit in the curtains shows she is still awake and downstairs in the living room. Her driveway is blocked by another clump of dripping sheep sheltering from the storm. He nudges the truck forward and has to blip the horn to move a particularly mulish ram who just stands looking at him blank-eyed as the wind ribbons a thin stream of water off its horns.

He figures Kathleen will hear him and twitch the curtains to see who's visiting at this latish hour, but the slash of warm reddish light in the drawing room curtains remains thin and unmoving. He parks up and scoops the takeaway boxes under his arm before stepping down into the full force of the storm.

Rain stings his face as he jogs to the front porch, ducks beneath it and knocks. When there is no reply, he steps sideways and raps on the window. When that produces no result, he tries the front door. Locked. He decides Kathleen must be in the kitchen at the rear of the house and goes back out into the full force of the weather, which slaps at him as he turns the corner and hurries to the side door, now entirely unprotected from the gale. The scaffolding against the gable end clanks with the force of it, and the orange buoy he had tied on to the pipes so that Kathleen would always see it and not bang her head is bouncing and twisting on the end of its short tether of blue rope. He ducks under the scaffolding and turns the handle. The door is unlocked, and it opens so easily that the wet handle slips out of his fingertips as the wind blows it in. It smacks into the side of the kitchen unit with a loud crash.

"It's just me," he calls, stepping inside.

No answering call from Kathleen, but he hears a sudden movement within the house and then a scrabble of claws on linoleum and blur of black and white fur as Bobby barrels into the room, running faster than Matt has ever seen him move.

"Hey—" he begins.

He sees a flash of wide-eyed terror in the dog's face as it missiles straight at him. He doesn't have time or room in the narrow doorway to step aside. The dog is beelining for the darkness beyond the open door like his life depends on it. He hits Matt's right leg and cannons off him into the night without breaking pace, half knocking him over so he stumbles and lands painfully on one knee, dropping food and cake all over the kitchen floor.

"Jesus!" he grunts. "Bobby, what the—?"

He instinctively cranes round to look after the dog, of which now nothing is visible in the outer darkness. He thinks he hears a panicked yelping, but it might be the wind.

He gets to his feet, shaky and unsettled by the sheepdog's behaviour, and steps over the debris now strewn across the neat, well-polished squares on Kathleen's kitchen floor.

"Gran?" he calls, moving faster as he begins to wonder what had frightened the old dog into such a panicked escape.

The living room door is closed, so the dog had not come from there. Matt turns the handle to enter. It doesn't move.

"Gran?" he says loudly. "Are you okay?"

He'd never known the living room door locked. Hadn't any idea it could be locked, in fact. And no clue as to why Kathleen would have locked it in the first place. But as he processes this, a rising dread washes the thought away as it occurs to him that, since the old dog hadn't run out of the drawing room, it must have come from upstairs. He takes the steps two at a time, his heart dropping as he ascends towards what he now knows will be the lonely, sad horror of discovering his grandmother dead and alone on the floor above. He skates across the small landing and looks in the bathroom on his way to check her bedroom. Nothing. He bursts on and in, flicking on the lights and scanning the bed and carpet. Exhaling in relief to see both bare and neat and empty.

He ducks back out and checks the spare room, which holds no terrors, only her sewing machine and the quilts she works on to keep her hands busy and her mind sharp.

He hurtles down the stairs and tries the living room door again.

"Gran!" he shouts. "I'm going to kick the door in."

He boots the lock, which splinters and bursts out of the thin, softwood lintel, and runs into the room.

And stops dead.

In a way, the room looks like an inferno in a cheap stage melodrama, the only light coming from low down at knee level, thrown by the electric fire in the hearth. Kathleen sits beside it in her favourite wing chair, unmoving, head cocked back so her open mouth points at the ceiling. One hand rests in her lap, holding a black book. The other hangs at her side, holding the poker that had once been used in the real fire that once had filled the hearth but was now a sentimental ornament, a kind of set-dressing to sell the authenticity of the new electric fire's flame-effect lighting, which is the only thing moving in the still room. He watches it glister red and orange light across the wetness soaking her legs for a moment.

Matt had always known one day it would very likely be him who found her if she got to go as she had wanted to go – suddenly, at home – rather than dwindling to an increasingly undignified nothing in an anonymous hospital on the mainland. That knowledge has not prepared him for the choking ball of ice that seems to have just formed behind his breastbone.

"Gran?" he croaks as he makes himself break the spell and step forward to touch her. He feels his feet squelch on the wet carpet. "Oh, my lovely Gran—"

He feels the tears prick as he reaches for her pulse.

And then he freezes.

She is soaking. The wetness on her legs isn't due to her muscles relaxing, post-mortem. She's wet from head to toe, as drenched as if someone had stood behind the chair and emptied several buckets of water over her.

Any hope she might still be alive is destroyed by the sight of her upturned, open mouth. It is full of water. In fact, it is so full he can see the meniscus as it stands proud of her gaping lips, dribbling a little out of each side. Her eyes are open and leaking more water, as if she is still weeping and cannot stop.

Matt's mind can't make sense of what he is seeing. Of what she has become. But whatever that is, the still water standing in her mouth means she definitely isn't breathing any more.

The ball of ice in his chest is growing, squashing the air out of his lungs as he finds it harder and harder to breathe.

"No," he says, fighting to keep a grip on himself. "No."

He doesn't have time to panic. He needs to check her pulse. He reaches for her wrist, holds his breath and feels the slip of water flowing down it but no pulse fluttering beneath the papery skin.

"Oh, Gran . . ." he says.

The poker comes out of nowhere and hits him in the ribs, winding him with shock more than the power of the blow. He staggers back a half-pace, uncomprehending. Her face is still pointed at the ceiling but the hand with the poker comes slowly back, and even more slowly finds his chest, pushing against it – gently at first, then more forcefully, and then, as if with a superhuman effort, jabbing him away from her. His legs tangle in the coffee table, and he sprawls back to squelch wetly on to the carpet.

"Gran," he says, scrambling to his feet. "Gran?"

Kathleen's body stays rigid, the only change being the hand with the poker is now at full stretch pointing at him.

And then the hand spasms and the poker drops, and the other hand that holds on to the black book rises to meet it, making shapes. Matt realises she is using sign language. Saying something. It is horrible and deliberate and he can't quite get what she is trying to say . . .

"Gran?" he says. His voice sounds reedy and choked.

The left hand comes up again, held palm-down at a slight angle to the floor, while the right hand points its index finger and jabs out from under it, making an unmistakable word in sign language before darting back to grip the black book.

He stops breathing again.

"Run . . . run away?" he says. "Gran, what the—"

He seems to hear bones crack as she forces her head away from its position staring at the ceiling and cranks it ninety painful degrees back to normal. Her expression is frozen in an open-mouthed rictus of shock, water welling out of it as the angle changes and spilling down her front. Her eyes don't blink; they just keep spilling water.

Her right hand rises slowly to the side of her forehead, shaking with the effort, but clearly: palm out, a fist with the ring and index fingers extended to make horns.

"Evil?" Matt breathes, watching the ring finger on the right hand now change words, folding in to curl alongside the others, leaving the lone index finger sticking out as Kathleen reverses the position of the out-turned hand and points it decisively at the floor.

"Evil . . . here?"

Her eyes stare blankly at him, their lack of affect disconcerting next to the urgency of the hand gestures. And then her head snaps back as if on a spring and a fresh gout of water glugs out of her mouth and keeps on pouring – pouring and pouring without let-up as her legs begin to straighten while her hands fight them by clamping tightly on the black book that Matt now recognises as his grandfather's Bible, as if she could pin her body to the chair by pulling it hard against her stomach to weigh her down.

Then the water must have soaked the electrics because the fire gives a sharp click and the lights go out.

Matt runs. He yanks the door shut behind him and crashes through the kitchen, feet skidding on the ruins of the takeaway supper as he hurtles into the night. He tears into the dark heart of the storm, has a microsecond to see the fluorescent orange coming at him like a bowling ball, and then a brutal force drops a mountain on him. The scaff pipe poleaxes into his temple with an impact so brutally hard and sudden that the false black of night smash-cuts to the true black of oblivion as he makes contact with the hard metal, out like a light before he hits the gravel.

Chapter 51

Boats for the burning

Robbie hadn't drunk enough to feel this bad. That's the thought that comes to him the moment he opens his eyes and realises that he must've passed out in his car because all he can see is the boats in the harbour but no sign of anyone left awake. He checks his watch. It's late. The only people likely to be awake at this hour are elderly men using their bladders. He feels strangely betrayed by the fact that everyone has left and no one thought to do anything about him passed out in the front seat of his car. He should—

Then the thought goes away and is replaced by a kind of woolly emptiness, his head simultaneously feeling stuffed and lacking something. He realises it's not just the old men who need to relieve their bladders. He staggers out of the car and walks unsteadily to the edge of the stone pier. The wind blows heavy splats of rain into the side of his face as he stands staring out beyond the harbour at the waves stacking up in the outer channel. He braces himself and unzips, watching the wind winnow the stream of piss as it arcs down into the darkness. He hears it spattering on the deck of one of the two fishing boats below. Maybe because something seems to pop in his head as he feels the release, he doesn't worry about that any more than he notices the wind buffet some of the urine back across the knees of his trousers, wetting them thoroughly.

Instead, he listens to the thrum of his urine stream on the plastic coaming below. A good noise. Strong flow. He's still got it. Piss like a firehose. He's resilient. Buoyant. Unsinkable, even if he is lost. He can't quite remember why he is lost, though.

Boats, he thinks. Something about boats.

Boats to be burned. If there are boats to be burned, he is the man. He is the firestarter. He is the man who gets the job done. The twisted firestarter.

He shuffles back to his car and takes the petrol can from the boot. He looks at it hanging from his hand, trying to remember why he's holding it.

He is lost. Allie-less. Unless he something. Unless he. Unless he burns. He can take the pain, he is the man, the painstaking man. The new pain in his head is his to take, his to ride, even if it stops him thinking right, right? Even if it leaves a hole where more thinking should really be, he will, can, should take the pain. His job. He will take it. Same as he will burn the boats.

He listens to the heavier drumming of falling liquid as he upends the petrol can over the wet stone edge of the harbour. Good noise. Strong. A doing noise. And doing is better than thinking because doing has no holes in it; doing is the thing complete.

He feels the wind on his gums and realises he is smiling. And then the smile finds a voice that he dimly recognises as his own and he wonders why he is laughing, and then he forgets the thought. He is too busy.

Boats to burn. Things to do.

Chapter 52

Foreseen

The night is wild now. On this stretch of road, there are no comforting lights to be seen, only the weakest of rain-blurred glows that dimly silhouettes the hump of moorland hiding the single light on the distant fish-farm jetty beyond it. It's no fit weather for man nor beast. And yet the eyes that are hidden in the dark see the rain-soaked figure of Kathleen stumbling painfully along the lonely single-track.

The ever-dwindling part of her that is still Kathleen makes the worn-out body stagger forward, leaning into the relentless curtains of rain marching across the island in the opposite direction. They buffet against her as if trying to knock her off her feet and wash her back to the house she now knows she'll never see again.

It's not just the storm outside fighting her. What remains of the tough old woman inside is taken up with pushing back the treacly darkness that has entered her, like a malevolent cuckoo trying to barge her out of the familiar nest of her own self. She's struggling against it as it tries to drown the last bit of her willpower and stop her doing what she knows she must do. She doesn't have the energy or the time to think of why this is happening, or even how. She just knows what must happen. It must happen because she saw it, and so what has to be done has to be done, no matter how painful it is to walk this old and nearly broken body through the storm while simultaneously fighting the thing trying to wrest control of her limbs for itself. The darkness has arms, she thinks. Or rather, it wants hers.

She feels it spiking behind her nose, a kind of banked-up rage that will, if she lets it, hollow out the core of her like a fire set to burn out a stump, immolating the last vestige of her free will. She is sure of this without knowing how she knows it, just as surely as she knows it means harm – not just to her, but through her. To all the islanders.

Well. She's not having that. Not after spending a life watching out for them. Not that they ever really knew that's what she and her mother and her mother's mother and God only knows how many before them did. And that's not why they stood their watches anyway. Not for thanks. And it wasn't all they did. Mostly they had normal and happy and comfortingly uneventful lives, with the same loves and laughter and disappointments and sadness as any of their neighbours and kinfolk. But there was also this duty passed on, sometimes forgotten for years, but always there – like a box of rat poison kept unseen at the back of the top shelf that you had to remember to warn the young ones about, just in case. They hadn't carried the weight of the watching for thanks, that long line of women she came from, but just because they had to. It wasn't really spoken of, so the why of it was long forgotten.

Maybe this was why, she thinks, as she comes to the dip leading down to the fish farm walking into the sleeting rain; maybe they'd always been preparing for this moment, the seamark toppled, something freed that should have stayed penned beneath it, some malice unbound, something that has turned into the malign thing now lodged inside her, pushing at her, making it hard to walk properly—

She stumbles badly, going down hard on her knees. It feels like she's landed on shards of glass. She hangs there on all fours, mouth stretched in a soundless sob of pain, her tears indistinguishable from the hard rain sheeting off her humped back.

She doesn't know how she will get up now. It makes no sense. She is on her own. She can foresee what will happen, but she can't see how she'll get to it. She will fail. Maybe the unnatural thing inside her has changed things, cuckooing her off into a different future that ends here on the unforgiving storm-lashed tarmac, knee-smashed and shaking, dying of exposure before the light comes up. She hasn't been able to bear the weight on her own. She lowers her forehead to the road and feels the hard coldness against her skull as she rocks it from side to side in a silent gesture of despair. There isn't enough of her left to fight this, she thinks. Between the darkness pushing her out and the despair, there is no room for her now.

Something nudges her arm. She cranes her head round, fighting the blackness that is somehow suddenly fighting her harder, as if it really doesn't want her to see what's there.

Two eyes at her level glint in the darkness. She hears a snuffling and a whine and smells wet dog.

Bobby, she thinks. Good dog.

The dog whines louder, looking at her as if making sure of something, then walks round her, as if assessing a threat. Then it darts in to lick her face, then prances back, eyes locked on hers.

Well, she thinks. If he thinks I'm still in here, maybe I am. She decides her knees are just pain, nothing more, and parks that sensation elsewhere in the narrow bit of herself that persists as she levers shakily back on to her feet. The dog steps in and licks her hand.

Kathleen pats his head, and then takes the first step towards the glow of light at the bottom of the track. One step, then another. That's all she has to keep doing. Walk downhill into the rain. Walk with the dog. Get to the boat. Take whatever's in her off the island to where it can't hurt any of her folk. Her and Bobby. Two old wrecks against the storm. But not alone.

Not yet.

Chapter 53

Woke

Tom is asleep. And then he isn't.

He props himself up on his elbows.

The house is quiet. The only sounds are the rain spattering the window and the blood drumming in his ears. But he knows something woke him. His subconscious heard whatever it was while he was sleeping and has kicked him awake to deal with it. His brain may be slow catching up, but his heart's way ahead of it, booted into action, motor running fast, cranked because it knows something's up.

The baby's quiet. It heard nothing, sleeping happily. Tom stays still, looking at the door, ears reaching out into the dark beyond, waiting for it to happen again. It doesn't.

Must have been his dad and Sally coming back from wherever they went, he thinks. Probably looked in, saw them both asleep, left them to it. Well. They can be on baby duty now if she wakes. He's bursting for a pee too. He'll hit the bathroom and then he's going to go and sleep in his bed now.

As he stands, he feels something at his back. Not quite a noise, not quite a presence, just something like ... an attention.

Like he's being noticed. Or watched. It's like an itch. He turns to see the black square of the window in the wall behind him. He steps quietly across the carpet and looks out. Nothing to see but wet heather moving in the wind beyond the barbed-wire fence. Nothing but the rain-slick slates on the angle of roof below the window, nothing but the nothing-to-see, and nothing seeing him. Nobody's watching him.

It was just a feeling. Probably the tail-end of a bad dream that he can't remember waking up out of. The kind of uncomfortable dream you get if you're sleeping on a hard floor instead of a soft mattress. Well, he can solve that problem, he thinks as he turns for the door.

RUN.

He almost says, "What?" but stops himself. Because although the voice telling him to run is urgent, it's not in the room with him, nor in the house beyond the door, and it isn't coming from outside. The voice is inside his head.

RUN.

But it's not his voice. It's not his dad's voice. It's a voice he doesn't recognise. But it's insistent.

RUN.

He realises he stopped breathing two "runs" ago and takes a breath that's more than half a shiver.

"Fuck off," he says quietly. He grins and shakes his head at himself. He's just freaked by being in a strange house in the middle of nowhere. He's tired too. And because he's tired, he suddenly doesn't want to have the row with his dad that he knows is coming – not now, not here in the middle of the night. So he eases across the room and quietly opens the door. The house is still. The door to their bedroom is open, but then they would leave it open because Sally would always want to hear if the baby wakes. He walks quietly past it on the landing, wincing and pausing at the telltale creak of a floorboard as he steps on it. Nobody challenges him, so he tiptoes past and slips into the bathroom. He doesn't turn the light on until the door is closed. Let sleeping parents lie, he thinks. Not that she's a real parent.

He lifts the lid and pisses groggily, eyes unfocused on the wallpaper. He feels the tug of sleep reasserting its pull as the pressure on his bladder mercifully eases.

It's only when he bends to flush the cistern that he sees the blood.

At first he thinks it's just a patch of damp, but it's not. It's damp, because he reaches out to touch it, but when he looks at his finger it's red. It's like a bruise on the wall, about head height, and if there was any doubt there are two partial, bloodied handprints on either side of it, as if someone was leaning against the wall and—

. . . he really doesn't want to know.

RUN.

"Dad!"

He hears the word ripping raw from his throat, sounding like a scared little boy which is what, in this moment, he knows he is.

"Dad!"

He yanks open the door and runs into the bedroom. In the slash of light coming from the bathroom behind him, he can see the bed is vacant and has not been slept in.

He twists and runs for the stairs and clatters down them, panic rising in his throat like it's going to choke him.

RUN.

"Dad!" he's still trying to shout, but now it comes out as a strangled thing.

He makes it to the door into the living room before he stops dead and slowly turns to see what he can feel, standing in the hallway between him and the kitchen.

And because the mind protects itself, this is the moment that later he can never quite remember, never quite explain, never talk about. This is the split in time where the words begin to go, leaking into it, through it, draining away to nothing.

He knows he stands staring for a long beat because he has a memory of his leg twitching in horror, trying to take him away from it. From him. From them. He has a sense of the horror being like a magnet, pulling him towards it, wanting him to be part of it.

But he knows he must run, because although his words are going, leaking away into the void, that one remains and keeps repeating itself.

RUN.

He knows he could still get to the front door behind him and escape, except he can't turn.

He will never remember the next bit. The noise that comes down the stairs and breaks the spell.

It snaps him out of the paralysis and spins him towards the safety beyond the front door, only ten feet away. As he runs for it, the animal in him surges exultantly, knowing it's going to be safe, that he can make it out into the night, out to where he can run and run and keep going and escape what lies behind him.

The baby wails again as he grabs the front door and tears it open.

He will never remember leaping into the night, nor how the sound of his half-sister makes him slide to a stop on the gravel and take a fast look over his shoulder.

They haven't moved.

The baby cries.

He could just leave it.

He could. He is halfway to safe now.

Maybe the horror will leave her alone.

RUN. RUN NOW.

"No," he says.

Nobody hears. Nobody, not even he, will ever remember him saying it.

Not all bravery is explainable. Not all bravery is marked. Some bravery just happens.

Tom runs back into the house, straight for the waiting horror, and then jinks, doglegging on to the stairs, legs pistoning him upwards towards the baby's room.

He crashes in and slams the door behind him. There is no lock, so he grabs the chest of drawers and crashes it over in front of it.

He hears nothing, but he knows it's coming slowly up the stairs behind him. They are coming. His—

He grabs the baby, wraps it in the little comforter, and as he runs for the window he must realise he'll need his hands free, so his mind must have been working a bit, because the next memories he has are pain in his knee and right hip, as he lands on the grass below the sloping roof under the open bedroom window, and rolling with his arms in a protective cage around a squalling thing stuffed into a changing bag.

He stumbles to his feet, checks over his shoulder, and whatever he sees in the window, whatever the thing that he has no words for was, who it is, what it is, it makes him gasp and turn and run blindly right into the barbed-wire fence. He never notices, not then, the gashes and tears on his leg as he just scrambles over the wire and hurls himself into the outer darkness.

GOOD. RUN.

He does run. He runs and runs and he slips and stumbles but there are two things he does not do: he does not drop the baby, and he does not stop.

He runs until he can't hear the voice telling him to run any more. He runs so far and so fast that he is not only out of breath but out of words. Like they just kept leaking out of him as he went, like petrol leaking out of a punctured fuel tank.

He runs until he is nowhere, with no houses and no lights. He only stops when he stumbles round a hummock and trips on a length of rope tethering an upturned rowboat that is stowed at the top of the beach and goes down hard on one knee, gasping as the full force of the wind and the roar of the Atlantic breakers hits him like a slap in the face.

He clutches the baby.

He looks behind him.

The horror has not followed.

The voice is silent.

There is just him and his sister and the night and the wind and the ocean and the rain. And nowhere to go.

He crawls in under the boat and places her next to him on the heather.

They'll be dry and out of the wind while he figures out what to do.

He should definitely figure out what to do.

But they should stay here for a short while. Just a short while. Try not to think of what he saw. The thing with no words for it. The darkness in the darkness behind them.

It's dark in here. Different dark. He can't see her face. She can't see his. But he knows she is looking at him. He knows he should say something. But all his words are gone and blown away in the storm behind them. He's lost them all. He scrabbles around and finds her hand. She holds his finger again. This time, it feels like she's the one holding him up. Stopping him falling.

Darkness comes. But it's the normal darkness of sleep.

311

Chapter 54

Point of departure

By the time Kathleen gets down the long track to where the *An da Shealladh* is moored at the fish-farm jetty, she's in more pain but strangely stronger because of it, as if getting to the old boat with its new coat of paint has given her a small second wind. Despite Matt's choice of red, this is still the boat she and her Donald spent so many days on. It's as much home to her as the house she knows she'll never see again. Bobby stands on the edge of the jetty, rain ribboning off his coat as Kathleen forces hands clawed by arthritis to work well enough to cast off the heavy wet ropes from the stanchions. She drops them into the boat and then half-scrambles, half-tumbles down after them, holding on to the cold metal rungs of the ladder bolted on to the jetty wall. Her hands can't bear her weight and she falls the last couple of feet. The impact bounces that momentary surge of strength out of her and the predatory darkness instantly fills the vacated space, squatting malignantly in her chest, pinning her. It feels like an anvil crushing her to the deck, squeezing the last remnants of her resolve out of her. Toothpaste, she thinks. I'm no more than an old dried-out tube of toothpaste.

That's me. Useless. Nothing left. Nothing left to squeeze out of me. Just this thought and then I'm gone.

A second lump of darkness drops out of the sky and jolts Kathleen back into the world as it pecks at her ear. As she turns to see what it is, it hops into view: a raven, cocking its head at her. She sees a third pair of eyes glinting down at her from the lip of the jetty and sees, rather than hears, the dog barking at her.

"Bobby," she croaks. "Bobby."

The old dog whimpers and wags its tail encouragingly.

The dark thing that is trying to oust her from her own body spikes anger behind her nose and she grits her teeth, fighting its urgent attempt to make her stay down. And she knows she so easily could. Maybe she should just lie there, face to the rain, and let it win. But since the dwindling part of herself still is who she is and has always been, she turns herself over in a long, awkward series of jerks and tugs, and then crawls herself to the wheel, where she leans, one hand on a heavy drum of green lead-line and the other hand on the spare anchor clipped to the taffrail. She hauls herself painfully to her feet, slumping back on the stool, water still pouring out of her mouth and eyes. Everything is blurry but she can still see things for what they are. It's only her inside that isn't normal any more.

Kathleen looks at the reel of lead-weighted rope and then tugs at the free end. As she sits there getting her breath back, she starts looping the rope round and round her waist, like a heavy belt. The darkness in her rebels and she stops, no longer the mistress of her own body. Maybe she's exhausted herself now. Maybe she should have stayed down. She doesn't know where she's going to get the energy to carry on. She drops her head, beginning to fall into the beckoning dark pool.

She feels the weight of the bird and the dig of its talons as it settles on her shoulder and bites her ear, hard.

She spasms, the sharp pain lifting her back into herself. Her head comes up. She's more or less eye-level with the dog on the jetty. She reaches over and holds its paw.

"Been a very good dog," she thinks, words choked by the water in her throat. "Thank you."

She sees him bark. Feels him lick her hand. Gives him one last shaky-handed pat, then fumbles the key out of her pocket and into the ignition and wearily tugs and pushes the primer-pump lever. The raven shifts position but stays on her shoulder. Okay, she thinks. Maybe I'm a pirate now.

It's no stranger than anything else that's happening.

The engine fires on the first go. With a last nod at the old dog on the edge of the jetty, Kathleen eases the lever forward, feeling the screws vibrate beneath the deck as they bite into the dark sea below and push the boat out into the curtains of rain that stand between the last feeble light thrown by the single security light on the jetty and the outer darkness waiting in the channel beyond.

She catches sight of her face in the windshield lit up by the green glow from the instrument panel and gives herself such a shock she nearly slips off the stool. Head cocked to one side, mouth clenched in a thin razor cut across a white face with grey hairs rat-tailed across it by the rain – she looks like a madwoman. Or a corpse. The razor slash curves into a grim smile. Who cares? She has this one last thing to do, and nobody will see her again anyway.

The blackness inside her lurches nauseously as it lets her know she must not do what she is doing. She retches a little and shakes her head to get the water out of her eyes.

Harm for harm. Blood for blood. Water will walk. Vengeance will be taken. You must be the means.

It's as if the darkness has now stolen so much of herself that it has found her inner voice, the one she hears inside her head, and is using it against her.

Kathleen feels the raven on her shoulder, somehow holding her upright, keeping enough of herself within her to do what must be done. She takes strength from the heavy weight pressing against her. One last thing to do, she thinks.

Yes, yes! Vengeance must be taken, says the dark voice.

"Over my dead body," she says.

The raven *kraa*s in agreement as she turns the boat out of the sheltered mooring, skirting the outer skerries and heading into the thickening rain-squalls coming in from the wilder waters of the open ocean lurking in the west.

Chapter 55

Bloody Shanna

Kevo's back sitting on the floor in Shanna's house. He'd really like that drink, that proper drink, right now. But he's on a plan, on a promise; not that kind of on a promise, but a deeper more life-and-death one, and he's blown part of keeping it simple – stupidly – already. He shouldn't have gone to the pub and opened his mouth. Now he'd left a footprint, now tongues would wag. Now word would, inevitably, get back and his plan is broken. As bust up as this bloody fruit bowl, he thinks, and then he remembers the tube of redemption he'd bought in the shop before his stupid pub visit.

He reaches into his pocket and pulls out the small tube of superglue and looks at it. Once upon a time, the only use he'd had for glue was huffing it. Once it got him out of himself for a bit, leaving nothing but a shit headache and the reality of hours passed in an unknowing haze of giggles and general torpor. Now, as he looks at the shards of fruit bowl, he hopes it might just get him back into himself, back on track, eye of the tiger, least said, soonest mended. Christ, he thinks, he might as well have had a drink because his mind is running too fast right now, jumbling thoughts and emotions and stuff he has neither time nor wish to examine.

It's the lemon smell in the house. It's everywhere, it's all her, all here even though she isn't. He gets to his knees and collects the fruit and the fragments of china. An hour later, he's mended the bowl and put the fruit back in it. Not a bad job, he thinks, yawning. Noticeable, but then he might get points for owning up about breaking it and then trying to make it better. His sponsor used to talk about a redemptive arc, and Kevo always imagined it as a big boat he could float away to forgiveness on, until the guy explained it wasn't that kind of ark. But showing willing, mending the bowl, surely that's kind of showing a redemptive arc. A little thing that means a bigger one.

Maybe Shanna won't see it like that.

Maybe she will.

He tidies the house before crawling into her bed, where he wraps the duvet over his head and goes to sleep surrounded by the heady smell of her, both sides, the soap and the sweat, the ghost of everything he had loved without knowing it and lost without meaning to.

No wonder he has bad dreams.

Chapter 56

Bloody Jamie

Malc wakes groggily and is instantly pissed off. It's definitely the deep in the dead watch of the night, and he knows without looking that it's bloody Jamie who's woken him because that's what the strutting little prick always does when an overnight means they have to share a twin room. He stays up drinking and trying to get his end away with anyone sad or pissed enough to sit up with him until chucking-out time, and then he either strikes out and crashes noisily into the room without a thought for normal folk who might be asleep, or he gets lucky and crawls in with the dawn, eyes like bloody piss-holes in the snow and a shit-eating grin on his face. Once he even tried to bring a woman into the room, but Malc read him the riot act and he sulked for the next two days without let-up.

But when Malc turns over he sees the bed on the other side of the room has not been slept in. The noise that woke him is coming from outside. He can hear feet shuffling and what sounds like the white noise of the rain lashing down on the roofs of the cars outside. He swears under his breath, cursing the hotel for giving them a room on the ground floor by the car parking area. It's likely nothing, this noise – just some

318

drunk locals having a scuffle, fighting or fucking, though they'd have to be pretty bevvied to be fucking in the rain. Either way, he decides it's none of his business and turns away from the curtains. He is about to jam a pillow over his ear to muffle the noise when he swears he hears Jamie shrieking his name.

His voice sounds panicked and muffled, as if someone is trying to gag him. Malc sits bolt upright and reaches for the bedside light but then freezes as he sees the struggling shadows on the net curtains, outlined by the sour orange of the sodium street light on the edge of the car park. Two people are wrestling with each other, faces locked together as they bang against the window.

He scissors out of bed and rips the curtain aside to find himself looking at a couple writhing together, the back of a woman smashed against the glass, face glued to Jamie's, her hands splayed on the window, and Malc has a flash of irritation on seeing Jamie locked in yet another embrace with a strange woman, but it quickly changes to something else entirely. The dynamics are all wrong – Jamie's hands are white with the force with which he is trying to wrestle free of the woman, and then Malc looks at his eyes and sees with a shock that they are terrified, panicked and lost. Jamie wrenches his mouth free of the woman's and shouts something at Malc, but no discernible word emerges, just a gurgling shriek of despair that escapes his mouth in a thunderous gout of water splattering against the glass and obscuring Malc's vision before the woman clamps on again and jerks him away from the building, wrestling him across the tarmac towards the harbour. Malc can see that there are other figures moving across the sodium-washed monochrome of the harbour tarmac. He has time to register that none of them are taking any notice of Jamie and the woman, not even when Jamie's efforts to break free topple them on to the ground in a sprawl of thrashing limbs. The other figures just walk past as if blind to them, like sleepwalkers.

By the time Malc crashes out of the fire door and into the parking lot, running barefoot in the rain, the woman has got up and is actually dragging Jamie in the same direction as the other walkers, heading for the water's edge. She pulls him by the cuff of his jeans with what looks like superhuman strength. Jamie's fingers are scraping themselves raw and bloody as they claw at the tarmac trying to find something, anything, to hold on to, to halt his progress.

It's Jamie's face, and it isn't. It looks like him on the exterior, but it doesn't look like he is inside it – not fully, certainly not safely. His mouth is gagging as a scream tries to fight its way past the unending spew of water retching out of it. Malc is hit with a strong and sudden conviction that the reason Jamie is no longer fully present in his own eyes is because he is falling away inwards, somehow drowning inside himself.

He looks round for help from the other people crossing the metalled apron flanking the harbour. No one meets his eyes; everyone keeps shambling away from him. It's like a dream, he thinks, except they're all the ones locked in a nightmare and he is just watching. The orange light is not coming from the sodium glare from the street lights, which are in fact blue white; it's coming from a broken line of flames at the harbour's edge. The few boats that normally line it are ablaze at their moorings, except for one, the orange lifeboat that is drifting off in the middle of the bay – its plastic superstructure a blaze like a small and toxic Viking funeral. But none of the people are hurrying to put these fires out. They're not hurrying at all. They just keep walking towards the water and – he sees as the first and then the second one falls over the edge – just letting themselves drop into the sea beyond.

Malc shouts but no one turns. On the angled slipway, he recognises the woman from the village shop in a T-shirt and nothing else, just walking into the water without any reaction, disappearing without any fuss at all. It's the worst thing he's ever seen, a small slice of a very specific hell, lit by the guttering fires of the few boats in the mooring burning down to their waterlines.

Jamie has grabbed hold of the wheel arch of the Telco van and is clinging on so hard that his jeans – cuffs firmly gripped in the woman's hands – just slide off. She trips forward as the resistance abruptly ceases, and her momentum takes her over the edge of the jetty straight into one of the burning boats. The only noise is her body thumping into the fibreglass hull. No scream or anything, and Malc is running before he knows why or what he is doing, and he gets to Jamie and tries to help him up. But as soon as he gets on to his feet, the prick stares at him blankly, vomits water down his front and then shoves him away brutally.

"Jamie, fuck's sake!" Malc shouts, grabbing him. "Come on!"

Jamie – what used to be Jamie – starts walking towards the lip of the harbour. And for reasons that he spends the rest of the long terrifying night trying to figure out, Malc gets too angry to be scared or confused, grabs him by the collar and yanks him backwards so hard that he falls on his arse and sits there stunned as Malc drags him back along the side of the van. Only when Malc tries to help him up again does he show any sign of life, suddenly grabbing him in a clinch and trying to bite his face or fucking kiss him or something, but Malc's blood is up, and maybe he's only now remembered to be scared by this whole hell-on-sea nightmare he's walked into because he chins him and then spins and kicks his knee sideways. The crunch of it sounds like he broke it, and Jamie loses balance, and that's good because Malc uses the moment to slam him against the back of the truck, feeling a sharp jag of pain as he barks his knuckles on the sharp hasp of the padlock latch on the rear doors. The hinged steel is there for extra protection when they leave the vehicle because there's often a lot of expensive equipment in there, so it's belt and braces with the regular lock. The chunk of sharp steel has cut up his knuckles, and now he is more than pissed and scared; he's hurting and he doesn't know what he's going to do about it, about this fucking Jamie who has now gone violently bloody nuts. And as Jamie squirms and pushes back, trying to attack him, Malc hits him hard – three brutal punches to the side of the head that he prays hurt Jamie more than they hurt him because his fist now throbs like a bastard and then he rips the back of the truck open and hurls the momentarily stunned Jamie inside.

He knows without having to look that his tool belt is hooked on the back of the door; he grabs it and slams the door closed. He can hear Jamie scramble to his feet and fumble at the door handle inside, but before he can get it open Malc smacks the padlock latch to, snatches a screwdriver from his belt, and jams it into the hasp, locking it tight.

He then grabs the hammer and spins, ready to protect himself against the next sleepwalker.

One woman in a nightdress stands on the edge of the jetty, and she looks so normal and calm that he almost calls out to save her, but he remembers the face of Jamie's attacker and pauses, and then it's too late and she's gone and – as suddenly as it all began – there is no one there. They're all gone.

Malc staggers to the edge of the water and looks down to see the last woman's face looking calmly up at him as she disappears into the depths below. He steps back from the edge and listens.

The only sounds are the constant rain and the crackle and occasional pop of the dwindling fires on the quayside, and the furious bass thuds of Jamie slamming around inside the van.

Malc spins in a slow 360, checking. But he didn't miss anyone. He was right. He is alone. The scene is suddenly so eerily empty he might as well have imagined what he saw.

The thumps and growls of Jamie thrashing about is the only fly in that particular ointment denying his bruised psyche the soothing balm of denial.

"Fuck," he hears himself say. "What was that?"

He shivers – and not just because he's soaked by the driving rain. He needs to get inside. He needs to find someone. He needs to tell someone what just happened. There is no one in sight but he feels like he's being watched. He starts to run for the hotel, picking up speed as he goes.

There will be people there. There will have to be people there – some people, safe people – and if not people, there are doors and locks and safety. Suddenly the only thing that matters is sunrise. He needs to get out of the wet and cold and these shorts because fuck it, he's pissed himself in fright and only now notices it, and he needs most of all to get out of the dark away from the water and wait for the light.

Because the light will come, he tells himself as he runs for the safety of the hotel.

The light always comes.

It'll be better in the daylight.

Chapter 57

Into my arms

The beleaguered remnant of Kathleen has taken the *An da Shealladh* as far from her island as she can, forging a lumpy passage through the relentless succession of rain-battened combers rolling in from the deep Atlantic. She's soaked and shaking with cold, as much from the water welling out through the gaps in her tightly clenched teeth as from the endless series of squalls that have assaulted her since turning the boat's stern to the last lights on the headland.

She feels like an interloper in her own body now. The grip of the raven's claws on her shoulder may be the only thing keeping her upright, because the treacly darkness has taken over almost all the space within her. She has all her remaining concentration focused on two things: the hand steering the boat, making sure the darkness doesn't make it turn back to land; and the vibrations of the engine driving the screws cutting her passage through the troughs and up the slopes of the incoming waves.

She must go as far as she can, as far as the fuel will take her, and then and only then will she submit to the water and drown – drown on her own terms, not according to whatever this thing wants. She will not be its subject; she will not let it turn her back to harm the islanders, her friends, her loved ones.

She will go as she has seen herself go. It will be like falling gently back into a bath, as like a warm bath as anything, for she is now so cold that she will not notice the punch of bone-cracking cold when she hits the water.

Kathleen hopes the fuel will last her until she gets to the edge of the sloping continental shelf and is somewhere over the unfathomed fastness of the Rockall Trough. One last long breath and the sea, the familiar sea that has girded her whole long life, will welcome her with arms she hopes will be gentle as she buries the malicious darkness her body carries deep beyond harm, far from the island on which it wants to exercise its implacable curse.

Because she knows that it's a curse now, knows it's more than a hostile darkness, knows it has a kind of predatory will, knows it has a sort of unchallengeable belief in its own inevitability, an ancient malign entitlement. It has no words, it does not speak to her, but she can feel the shape of its sense of itself butting up against her: it is a curse, and what is cursed will be, for what can stand against a curse?

A promise, she thinks. I have promised to keep them safe.

Something nips her ear. Gentle, but firm.

The engine has stopped, she realises.

The raven clacks its beak and hops off her shoulder into the protection of the cowling above the wheel.

The boat loses its way and begins to slew side-on to the waves. Kathleen does not have much time or strength, and yet it must be done. She slides off the stool and staggers to the taffrail and the waiting anchor. The lead line she looped round her waist had been fine when she was supported on the stool, but now it is almost too heavy to carry and she feels her joints and muscles shriek in protest.

One last thing, she thinks, coughing out a huge gout of water, as if the curse within is rebelling against this last remnant of her will. One last thing.

She has almost no strength or energy left in her. But what she has she will use, for after this she will have no use for it. She grasps the anchor in both hands and lifts it to her chest, hugging it in her arms. And then as the boat begins to roll dangerously, she catches the raven's eye. Now, at this final moment, she recognises it, and she realises the ravens have always been there watching over her and hers, as she watched over the islanders, and that they have always been the unannounced allies, invisible in their ubiquity.

"Oh," she says quietly, voice whipped away in the wind. "Oh."

She smiles at it. Recognising an old friend for the first time. It clacks its beak.

A heavy sea is now rolling beam-on against the sides of the boat, threatening to capsize it as it rocks back and forth. Kathleen takes the next roll as the action of the heavy sea brings the wave surface up against her shoulders like the back of a chair, and she doesn't fight gravity by bending forward but leans back. And as the roll reverses, she looks up at the sky, seeing the first farewell blush of her last dawn, and smiles and says:

"Matty. It's all right."

And then, as the counter-roll continues, she just gently stays with the sea.

It's not cold, she thinks. It's warm. It feels like her Donald has been biding there for her all the time, and she leans back into the forgotten warmth of his waiting arms.

The darkness within her shrieks in protest, but her smile

only deepens as her feet come gently off the deck; and as the boat rights itself, she is gone.

The raven lofts into the rain, circles the wallowing *An da Shealladh* twice, and, seeing nothing else on the surface of the ocean, lets the wind take its wings and heads homewards.

Part 5

RED SKY AT MORNING

VARANGIAN: CONSTANTINOPLE

He sits under the great dome, waiting for the emperor.

Above him, the stones arc across the vault of air like a second sky.

He does not know how they do not fall down. His own people have no more knowledge of this way of building than do the smiling tent-dwellers who have mutilated and shamed him.

He knows he must wait for the emperor to finish the ritual with his god on the cross.

He knows he must wait, but after all the miles he has come, sitting is a great pleasure. So is the cool grey stone beneath his hands. He spreads both of them across it and turns his face to the underside of the dome, as if basking in the sun beyond it.

He does not care if he never sees the southern sun again. He will deliver the message and then he will ask to be released from his oath and go north. Home to die under richer skies and stronger winds, going happily into the welcoming cold, the cold he has dreamed of every night.

He will go to the temple grove at Uppsala and talk to the priests. He will tell them of the broken oath that has doomed him, and the curse, and he will make himself an offering, and if they accept he will ask that when they cut him down they leave his bones in the same seas that hold his wife and daughter.

He scratches his ear, wincing as the scarring across his chest pulls taut. It is part healed, though he doubts it will ever heal fully. And even if it does, he will never swing an axe as freely as he did, though he may still pull an oar on the way north.

No matter. If he dies of it, he will have died in a kind of battle with his enemies, and that may yet gain him admission to the hall of the slain – and if not that, then Folkvangr, the field of the host. Maybe waiting for the last battle will be sweeter under Freyja's care than old One-Eye's anyway. He smiles at himself.

He misses the ruby as he misses his arm rings.

They took the rings but never found the gemstone.

He thumbed it deep into the sand with the last of his strength when he felt their hoofbeats coming closer.

So he has left his mark in their lands.

No satisfaction in that, not really. Though he cursed it as he did so. Tit for tat.

Child's fancies.

He looks around.

Everyone has their back to him, looking at the emperor. Their emperor, bowing before the man nailed to the tree. Wrong man, wrong tree, he thinks.

Even the friend standing beside him, the shield-brother, is looking at the ceremony. He reaches up and taps his friend's leg.

"A loan of your knife, brother," he says quietly.

The ceremony is long, and as the incense is swung and the candles are lit he sits and carves. Stone is harder than skin, but a rune needs no curves.

It is, after all, a writing made for blades and not ink.

By the time the ceremony ends, he has left his mark here too. He hands the knife back and apologises for dulling the edge.

He offers to sharpen it when this is over. His friend smiles and shakes his head.

"I sharpen my own blade, brother," he says. "What did you write?"

He stands aside, letting the other see. His friend smiles.

"Good job the emperor doesn't read our script, Halvdan Korpensson," he says. "Otherwise he might have your head."

He shrugs.

"No," he says. "I will go north to die."

"Your wounds will heal," the other says. "You have years in you yet."

"No," he says. "I have decided to offer myself at the ash grove."

His friend looks at him, scanning his face to see if this is a joke. He sees it is not and shakes his head slowly.

"You are old for an offering, brother."

"I am strong for an offering," he says. "And besides, I think it may be the only way to draw the poison of this curse. I will ask the keepers of the grove."

His shield-brother shrugs and looks away, back down at the newly carved runes.

"Still," he says. "They will think the words a sacrilege: they think their god is all powerful because he does not die and has this, the biggest hall in the world."

"And I have just reminded them that the hall of the slain is to this place as this place is to a tent in the desert," he says, wincing as he straightens. "And if they take offence, I have left them my name. They can come after me."

He swoons a little. Maybe he stood too fast. He leans against the stone columns, soaking in the coolness stored within.

"Halvdan," says his companion. "Are you all right? Should I bring you water?"

He shakes his head. Finds a smile.

"Never water, brother. I told you. I am cursed, as are mine and any who give me clean water."

"And you believe this curse?" the other says, watching the emperor slowly make his way through the throng of courtiers and supplicants, heading towards them.

"I believe ale and wine are not clean water," he says. "So it's not much of a curse, is it?"

They laugh. Later they will drink. First, he has to deliver a message. The folded square of skin he carries in the bag at his side has dried and stiffened like uncured goat-skin, but it too is part of that message.

It is also what will take him home. Real home, heart's home.

He will tell the emperor he will take the curse carved on his skin north and bury it where it will never be found, far from this centre of empire. His last service will be to continue to protect according to the oath he swore when he entered the guard. And then, if he does not die of this great unhealing scar on his chest, he will stay; and if not, he and the vileness the smiling men have sent with him like a plague will remain bound and hidden forever.

And the counter-curse he has carved into the stone here, that may have power. For he has sworn that if the sand-slaves' curse is ever visited on those he loves or the children of those he loves, then he will leave the fellowship and feasting in the last mead hall and return to do whatever the gods allow to protect them.

That is his word.

He is a man of the North, and though his gods will one day die just as men do, they are many. And when they do die on that last day?

They die fighting.

Chapter 58

Early riser

Cheated out of a proper sleep by the nightmare, Sig wakes feeling exhausted and vaguely bitter.

She can tell she never reached the recuperative depths of actual rest but had merely been dragged through the thin shallows of unconsciousness, a night spent never relaxed and always on the point of waking. Her eyes feel gritty and her mouth tastes dry and sour. She turns on her side and finds that Rex had been doing his unsettling thing of patiently waiting for her, chin on the mattress, eyes eight inches from hers.

"Hey," she murmurs, arching her back.

His tail thumps.

"Shh," she says, levering herself into an upright position and stretching the stiffness out of her leg. "Don't wake her."

She doesn't feel like talking yet, and really hopes Evie will stay asleep until she gets out the door. She knows from experience that the only thing that will wash the memory of the bad night out of her head and reset her system is a swim. That's the real reason why it's her routine – the swim every morning, no matter how good or bad the night had been – because the shock of the cold and the half hour of exertion gives the body something else to react to, a flush of endorphins and a way of breaking out of the cycle of negativity that a bad night always threatens to plunge her into.

She writes Evie a note before getting her wetsuit. A minute later, she's in the Defender and pulling out on to the main road, Rex standing beside her with his paws up on the dashboard, already panting and whining in excitement.

The road is empty and dawn is still only halfway broken, so she doesn't expect to see any traffic, but as she turns the headland and passes the junction point where she takes the turnoff to the bay and can see down the shallow valley that leads back to the harbour, she is hit by a strange sense of desolation, strong enough to make her stop the Defender and look around her.

Rex whines.

Everything looks as it normally does at this time of year: the road still slick with the night's rain, the low clouds still nailed in overhead like a lead roof. Even the two ravens perched on the road sign are familiar enough not to get her attention.

Rex pushes off the dashboard, corkscrewing ninety degrees to the right so his front paws bounce on her thigh, as if prodding her before bouncing right back up into his original lookout position, peering through the windshield, tail quivering.

"It's okay," she says.

One of the ravens turns its head sharply, fixing her with a black, bead-bright eye.

"It's the lights," she says, somehow relieved that she's able to put her finger on the subtle detail that had triggered the sense of abnormality. Normally, she sees three or four tiny lights down the valley, lights from her neighbours' kitchen windows and bedrooms as they go through whatever regular rituals that mark their own morning routines. An ageing population means a lot of light sleepers and early risers, but today the lights are not lit yet.

"It's just the lights," she repeats.

She checks her watch.

"Everyone's sleeping in."

That's all it is. Nothing sinister, just a coincidence; a few dropped stitches in the fabric of the island's day-to-day life.

She chunks back into gear and heads towards the bay.

As she passes Kathleen's house, she sees the lights are on and notes that Matt's truck is parked outside. He'd obviously dropped in for breakfast. The sight of the warm lights in the windows is a relief that lifts the unease that had come on her at the junction.

"See?" she says to Rex as they pass. "Everything's okay."

Chapter 59

Sea walkers

Tom opens his eyes. The sound of the sea has calmed to a distant roar and the percussive rattle of the night's rain on the hull above has stopped completely. From where he is lying beneath the upturned boat, he can see no sky, only a sliver of pale sand and a dark tussock of breeze-tossed heather bobbing in the thin grey light of the pre-dawn. Cold has stiffened his body, and he finds it hard to move as he shifts to ease the ache in his hip from having spent the night in a foetal hunch wrapped around the changing bag. There is a sucking noise from the bag. He looks down to see Ruby happily asleep, well wrapped in the down jacket with her thumb in her mouth.

He stops moving. Better to lie with the ache for a bit longer. If he wakes her, she'll cry and be hungry and he doesn't know what he will do then. He knows there is something he shouldn't do, even though it is the obvious thing to do, but he can't quite focus on what it is. It isn't just his body that has become stiff: his mind has curled in on itself with a defensive rigidity all of its own, clenched in a kind of protective cringe that is all about not looking backwards and definitely not remembering something. He wonders with a distant lack of concern if the something he is being very careful not to look back at is so devastating in its unthinkability that it has actually broken something in his head. As he lies there trying to ignore the growing ache in his hip, his mind trundles along like a computer running a very simple, recursive sub-routine that successively loops back on itself, executing up a kind of dynamic stasis that confirms his decision to stay still:

He knows it's odd to be under a boat on the edge of a beach. But it is safe.

He sees it is unusual to be lying here with the baby. But it is safe.

He feels it is strange not to want to remember what has happened. But it is safe.

He has other pains than the ache in his hip. But it is safe.

He can feel from the breeze on his right leg that his jeans are ripped. But it is safe.

There are no other people here. But it is safe.

It is safe. Safe is good. Maybe he should turn off and sleep some more.

Tom closes his eyes.

He misses the first slow-moving set of feet walking past the boat, heading for the beach. But the light crunch they make as they drop down on to the sand jerks open his eyes in time to see the second pair of legs passing in their wake.

He hears his voice croak out an involuntary cry for help that he definitely hadn't intended to make, and he slaps his hand over his own mouth, trapping the banked-up torrent of words that wants to follow. His eyes stretch wide as he stares out from under the boat to see what damage he'd just done. It hadn't been a loud cry, and the owners of the legs are out in the weather so they must not have heard it over the sound of the wind and the waves because they plod away seawards, without a break in their sluggish cadence. Ruby, however, did hear him and begins to grizzle in a way that he knows is going to build into a wail of protest that the whole world will hear, weather or no weather. He reaches out and urgently pulls her close, burying her face tight against his chest. He crushes her to him and lies there listening and watching, tense as a held bowstring. Forgetting that though she is small, she still needs to breathe a little.

A third pair of legs passes the slit of the world that Tom can see, and then the bit of his brain that is working reminds him of what he had forgotten, and he pushes the baby away from him and stares at her in horror.

Her face is creased and shmushed into a mask of shrivelled outrage, eyes clenched shut, mouth wide and horribly unbreathing.

"Ruby," he says, feeling the world dropping away from under him.

And then the eyes open and stare at him as she takes a deep breath, and he's never seen eyes so blue, so outraged, so welcome. The falling world stops and returns and plants itself solidly back under his feet as he rolls with her out from under the boat and staggers rustily to his feet in the wakening morning light.

"Ruby," he says again. "Ruby."

He can't take his eyes from her face, and even as she scrunches her eyes shut again and begins to scream furiously at the outrage the young day has already begun to heap on her, he smiles. He hadn't broken her. He nearly had. But he hadn't. He hadn't broken Ruby. These are the simple things his mind could cope with.

They are safe.

An old woman brushes past them and walks down on to the sand.

She doesn't stop and doesn't notice the squalling baby.

It takes Tom a moment to realise this is unusual. He raises his head from Ruby's glorious, life-affirming indignation and looks at the beach for the first time.

Five figures are walking away from him; dark and different-sized silhouettes against the flat, silvery light coming off the wet sand. Two younger men, a young woman, a stooped old man in pyjamas and the old woman. The old woman is in a nightie, whipped by the wind, her feet as bare as the bent man's she walks beside.

The sight is too complicated for him to process. None of the figures turns to see what the noise honking out of the baby is about. They just trudge doggedly onwards and away, towards the sea. The tide is going out, so it takes a minute or so for Tom to realise they are not stopping once they get to the water.

One of the men is wearing a hoodie.

And even in outline, there is something familiar about it, something about the shape of the man wearing it, something so known that it makes Tom stumble off the heather and on to the sand and start jogging towards him, the shrieking baby in the changing bag bouncing in his arms, running instinctively even though he can't (won't) think why he is doing so, even though he won't (can't) acknowledge the danger of what his body has decided to do.

He overtakes the old couple, who pay him no mind at all, and catches up with the man in the shallow water. He tries to shout but can't think of his name – knows it but can't get it out – so he grabs at his sleeve.

The man keeps walking, knee-deep, then thigh deep.

The words still won't come out of Tom's mouth, trapped as they are behind teeth clenched tight.

He wades after the man into the slap of waves hitting him waist high and grabs the back of the hood, yanking back with all his strength.

The man topples off balance and falls into the water. His face turns to Tom, looks at him as if he is a memory the man is trying to grasp, and reaches out a hand. Tom reaches back and pulls the man to his feet, tugging him shorewards.

The man won't come. He stands his ground, holding Tom's hand, just dripping and staring at Tom more flatly now, with no real affect to his expression, as if the memory he had been straining at is eluding him. Then – as if he had just managed to snatch the last fugitive, trailing wisp of recollection as it slipped through his fingertips into the ether – a pale shimmer of something akin to a smile washes over his face and he tugs encouragingly at Tom's hand and turns back out to the sea, dragging the boy and the baby after him.

Tom won't (can't) let go, pulling shorewards but being dragged deeper and deeper into the surf. He can't tear his eyes off the familiar back as it begins to disappear into the waves.

Then he feels a tugging at his shoulder and realises the woman is trying to yank the changing bag off his shoulders.

He looks at her face in shock. She does not look back, her eyes locked dully but determinedly on the baby whose screams Tom has somehow stopped hearing.

His ears seem to snap back online: the shriek cuts through everything and severs whatever the connection was that had him glued to the man's hand.

He drops it and bunches his fist as it whistles through the air and catches the woman hard on the side of the head. She goes down sideways with a splash, landing on one knee and looking back at him in a kind of dull incomprehension, almost as if he has saddened and offended more than actually hurt her with the blow.

She reaches for the baby again.

Tom runs.

Spray kicks up as he sprints for the shore. He sees the old couple in front of him and doglegs sideways to avoid them, but they don't even follow him with their eyes. His pace picks up the shallower the water gets, and then he is on the sand and allows himself a fast look over his shoulder, and then he stops, panting for breath. No one is following. The two men are already gone, and then the woman, the familiar woman whom he had hit, turns away and follows them into the water, walking stolidly forward until all he can see is her hair, for a moment washing like seaweed on the face of a wave, and then she too is gone.

The baby screams its throat raw and then finds its thumb.

He watches the old couple walk into the sea too, side by side, the crouched man going first, then the old lady is there for a moment longer and then gone in the flash of the following wave. And the sea is again a regular pattern of waves whose surface is untroubled by their presence – as if everything is normal and the five sea walkers had never been there.

Tom's thinking is still not right, but he takes a deep breath and watches the surface for as long as he can hold his breath, as long as anyone can hold their breath, hoping for something so long that his lungs ache and burn and feel like acid pulsing within his ribcage, and then they choke and gasp and refill his chest with air. And he does it again, his eyes now streaming with silent tears; and then, when he takes the next breath and sees the sky and the sea still hold no trace of them, he tightens his grip on Ruby and turns and runs.

He runs with the thought that the only thing that can save

him from the hunger of the sea at his back is the solid land ahead of him, and the higher he can go, the safer he will be, and then even that thought disappears as he begins to plunge upwards through the waist-high heather, heading for the top of the hill rising ahead of him.

Chapter 60

Peeper

Walter John is out on the hill early, not otter-watching, not even waiting for Sig to cut her clear line across the bay as she swims from buoy to buoy, but instead hoping to exorcise the growing sense of dread he's wrestled with through a largely sleepless night by finding Milly.

The dog has never run off and left him for so long, and never overnight. He has a horror of her lying twisted by the side of the road somewhere, hit by a car, and as soon as light began to bleed back into the sky he'd got dressed and began driving round the island, dreading what he might see at every turn or when he crested a sudden rise in the road as it dipped and twisted across the moor.

He doesn't encounter anyone else as he drives, which is unusual, but he doesn't think much on it as all of his focus is on scouring the landscape and roadsides for the black and white bundle that he knows will break his heart.

The one thing that does occur to him as he passes the unlit exteriors of the few houses sprinkled across the island is that Milly had been acting strange since about this time yesterday. He remembers the flush of relief when, after what had seemed like an age of calling and whistling, he'd finally seen her bounding up the slope from a little hidden inlet at the back of the bay, just round the northern headland. He'd almost given up calling for her then, and he takes his past perseverance as a kind of totem for what will work now: he should not give up looking. Of course, it's a needle in what is – given the night's rain and the incoming clouds he can see out to sea – a very wet haystack. But if he stops looking, then bad things will have happened to her; if he keeps looking, then his diligence will be rewarded. He knows that this kind of thinking is a childish attempt to influence a reality that is entirely indifferent to whatever he does or does not do, and he'd certainly done enough of that trying to bargain away his wife's cancer with a deaf universe to know it didn't really mean anything, but he sticks to the idea. In fact, remembering that moment of relief as Milly had appeared bounding up the slope, gives him an idea of where to look next.

Whenever they ran across something particularly noxious on their walks – a rotting seal, a gull's carcase – Milly's memory would always make her beeline for the spot where they'd seen it the next time they passed. Based on that behaviour, Walter John realises he should go and see if she'd returned to that inlet at the back of the bay. She had smelled pretty foul when she came back, and there was every chance there was something lying in there that was acting like catnip. When that whale carcase had wedged into a similar narrow slit in the rocks many years ago, all the dogs had loved the stink so much they'd kept going back to roll in it for days.

Walter John parks up and takes her lead with him as he hurries across the saddle of moorland above the bay. He notes that Sig is not there yet, and he wonders if she's going to give it a miss because of the incoming wave of bad weather he can see bellying in from the west. She's pretty hardy, never seems to mind swimming in the rain and only takes a day off if the sea in the bay is too big, which happens rarely since the two horns of land at either end shield it nearly as effectively as a reef. He can see whitecaps beyond the protection of the land, but within the bay itself the water is only mildly choppy.

He ignores the thumping of his heart and presses on into the strengthening breeze as he hits the downslope, quickly losing sight of the bay as he passes the point where he'd seen Milly bouncing into view. He feels the going harder as he descends, his knees sending increasingly sharp messages of protest that make him wince and ignore the tingling in his left arm. It gets quite steep as he comes to the final few yards and the slope divides on each side of a pair of rocky ledges with a narrow pie-slice of sea between them. At the sharp end there is definitely something, but though he shouts for Milly and whistles in case she's hidden by the lip of heather, she doesn't come. He slides the last part and gasps as his walking boots crunch down on the tapering scrape of sand and shells at the sharp end of the inlet.

At first, Walter John thinks it's a man lying half in, half out of the water, but then he sees it's just a red anorak with something metallic snagged beneath it. He looks round and calls for Milly, unconsciously rubbing the numbness out of his left hand with his right hand. Then he reaches down and twitches the anorak off the thing that is hooking it up.

He steps back in surprise, staring at it.

It is a metal detector, and it looks both new and expensive. He's seen them on TV shows about treasure hunters. "Detectorists", they like to call themselves. And that's what it looks like to him, a kind of space-age mine detector. And it hasn't been in the water long enough to become tarnished or bashed about by the waves and the rocks around it.

It certainly looks salvageable. Walter John flexes his

tingling fingertips and reaches for it with his left hand, scowling as he has to step into the water to do so and the wave slaps up over his boots and soaks his socks.

He takes another step and manages to reach it, though his foot slips on a slab of seaweed covering a slick rock beneath it and he goes down on one knee.

"Bugger!" he says and gets back to his feet, standing shakily, now calf-deep in the water. He pulls the handle, but it won't come free. Maybe the other end is jammed under something. He gives it another tug, beginning to wonder if it's really worth getting his trousers soaked for. The electrics will probably be shot even if he dries it out properly.

"Come on," he says, pulling at it. "Come on—"

He feels it move, and he begins to smile. And then it pulls back hard, tugging him off his feet so he splashes down on all fours, facing the sea, as shocked by the sense that someone has done this malicious thing to him as by the pain on his scraped hands as he hits. He stays there, winded and gaping as the next wave slaps him insolently in the face, filling his mouth and eyes and making him splutter and blink hard.

It feels like he is fighting tears at the nasty prank someone has played on him. It feels like he is again the child he once had been. It feels like he is very alone, and he begins to worry that no one will know where he is.

And then Walter John sees them. Reaching for him. Out of the water, out of the heaving sea where no people should be. Hands and heads with dulled, drowned faces coming to drag him under, drowned men and women walking up out of the waves to bring him home, except it is no home he wants to visit.

"Please, God," he says. "Please, God, no—"

He is frozen, unable to escape as the strength to lift himself from his hands and knees has drained from him in shock.

And then a large bird swoops in between him and the drowned and flaps the iridescent black feathers of its wings in an untidy stalling motion. It seems to hover in front of them, suspended in time for just long enough to break the spell of horror freezing him in place.

Walter John lurches to his feet and runs blind uphill, away from the horrors from the sea, his body shrieking in protest as terror puts long neglected muscles to work, the forgotten feeling of running pounding fragile joints he's been babying for twenty years or more. He doesn't notice any of it, not enough to stop. He just runs and runs until he crests the low ridge and pelts helter-skelter downhill, running hard just to stay upright now, his legs thrashing to keep up with the rest of him, breath coming in jagged shrieks, eyes only barely noticing the road in the distance. And then he finally gets away from himself as the frantic beat of his overtaxed heart outpaces the pounding rhythm of his feet on the ground and he trips and topples and falls hard, brutally slamming into the heather and a welcoming darkness.

Chapter 61

Kiss of life

It's Kathleen's face and it's lashed by the wind and rain, grey strands of hair plastered diagonally across it like scratch marks, like someone's trying to erase a photograph, and her eyes are closed with the effort and it's all happening at once and she's concentrating hard, winding loops of heavy green lead line around her, and the boat is beam-on to the sea and in danger of capsizing with each roll and the deck is tilting beneath her and she catches her balance on the taffrail as she bends and lifts the heavy bow anchor, straining to lift the impossible weight of it, the sinews in her neck standing out like whipcords, grimacing like a skull as she clutches it to her chest like a knight on an old gravestone holding his sword, and then her eyes open and all the wind catches the rat-tails of hair and blows them off her face and for a moment it's as if it blows all the years and the pain and the fear and the worry away, smoothing her skin as she opens her eyes and relaxes into a smile that reaches deep into him and hooks him out of the darkness of sleep as she says:

"Matty. It's all right."

And then before he can wake properly and reach out to

stop her, she leans back over the taffrail and meets the heaving swell of the night sea rising to meet her. She stays with it as the boat rolls back – and is gone without trace.

Matt wakes and sits upright, shouting, "No!"

But he is not at sea. He is on the wet gravel outside Kathleen's kitchen door. He sits there for a couple of minutes, stunned and shivering, trying to gather the strands of himself back into a viable enough shape to stand up. He doesn't know why he isn't dead.

He's certainly never felt worse. The physical stuff is bad enough. When he comes out of the dream – it was a dream, he tells himself, knowing he's lying but needing the lie to hold on to for now – he can hardly move, he's so wet and cold. He is shivering so badly that getting up seems like an impossibility, like lying on the gravel all night in the rain has rusted him in place, and the pain in his head feels like a spike has been hammered through it, tent-pegging him to the ground for good measure. He smells terrible and realises he must have just vomited himself awake. But it is when he focuses on the open door to Kathleen's kitchen that it gets really bad as he starts replaying the shattered fragments of memory from the night before – her face, the terrible fixed grin with water welling endlessly out of it, the sense her spirit was fighting what her body was doing to her, the spasming hands signing a warning . . .

Matt staggers to his feet and retches again. His vision is off because one eye is not working and his head is pulsing with pain. He catches sight of himself in the kitchen window, a distorted reflection in the rain-lashed glass, one side of his head swollen and bloody, one eye just a slit in a burst and purpling fruit. It looks like a chunk of skin is hanging off the side of his head, and when he puts his hand up to feel it he finds it is, and the unnatural sensation of his fingers touching it makes him stagger so he has to hold himself up by the wall.

Everything in him wants to run away from the black doorway beckoning so wickedly just in front of him. All he has to do is turn and run to his car.

"Kathleen?" he says. Then he cleared his throat and shouted, "Kathleen!"

He listens, hears no sound, sees no grandmother, rouses no fat old dog. He straightens up and walks carefully inside.

The house is empty. He goes from room to room, finding nothing. He picks up the phone to call for help, but doesn't even get a dial tone. His mobile phone is just as useless. He sees himself shaking in a mirror and realises he must be in shock or hypothermia. He decides that if he moves fast he won't have time to think too much about what he saw the night before, and what needed doing needed doing quickly. Matt strips stiffly out of his wet clothes and gets in the hot shower, yelling in pain as the water hits the raw wound on the side of his head.

He tapes it back in place as best he can, dry-swallows some ibuprofen from Kathleen's medicine cabinet, puts on his grandfather's clothes three sweaters deep, and finds his way back to the kitchen where he waits for the kettle to boil and then scorches his palate drinking hot instant coffee with too much sugar to warm himself from the inside.

While he waits impatiently for the water to heat, grudging the minute that it takes, he focuses on the keyboard by the door. It is a jaunty bit of tourist bait from the island shop, a piece of wood cut in the shape of a fishing boat and painted in bright colours. His grandparents had bought it to support Mary-Kate, who had made them in a burst of unexpected crafty-ness one winter.

What's missing from the keyboard is the second set of keys for his boat, which Matt keeps there for emergencies. It's easy to see that it's gone because both of his sets of boat keys are attached to small flotation devices in case he drops them in the water. The long yellow fob is not there.

Now he has coffee in him, he finally looks at the lie he'd told himself about the vision that had woken him being a dream.

"Shit," he says, chugging the last of the coffee and staggering out to his car.

Chapter 62

Last straws

Allie wakes as the first buffeting of the coming storm rattles her windows and hooks her abruptly out of the thin, shallow sleep she has been fitfully drifting in and out of all night. On reflex, she reaches out for Eck's comforting warmth and feels a pang of disappointment as she finds only cold flat bedsheet. Of course. He's off in accordion heaven at the Modh, and she's still got half the deep clean to finish. No rest for the wicked. She swings out of bed, swipes her phone off the bedside table and pads gritty-eyed towards the bathroom, checking to see if it has any bars yet. It doesn't. She swears wearily under her breath and turns it off and on again, just in case. No service. Her face stares back at her from the mirror over the sink, confirming the bad news: like the phone, she's awake but looking pretty useless. She sticks a toothbrush in her mouth and twists the shower on. She decides to get going and have coffee at work with Magda. She wants to find the full story about the stooshie with the good-looking guy, for a start. And then she's got her own news about Shanna's runty ex poling up out of nowhere. Allie grabs a pack of biscuits on her way through the kitchen. The wicked might not get any rest, but only a sadist would deny them a chocolate Hobnob.

It's just a five-minute drive to the fish farm. The road is empty, and the only vehicle she sees is the red one that seems to have been sitting in the passing place on the curve below the north headland for a few days. She checks her watch to see if it's earlier than she thinks, but it isn't. She's surprised at the clean run into work. None of the four houses she passes on the way have lights on, even though it's a dark morning due to the incoming storm. Maybe they're all off-island at the Modh, she thinks. She passes a small inaccessible inlet, and out of the corner of her eye she thinks she sees a man standing waist-deep in the water, but before she can turn and confirm what she's seeing the car's moved on and the sea is hidden from view. She decides it was probably a seal. It's too cold for anyone not in a wetsuit to be bathing, and that little inlet has no track going to it. She's never seen anyone there before.

Allie pulls up outside the offices and sees Magda's not arrived yet. She checks her watch, realises she's early and decides she does want that coffee she thought she didn't need. She flicks the switch on the coffee machine and stretches. While the machine squeezes her out an Americano, she decides to call Shanna and tell her the weird boyfriend is on the island. She'd have done it last night, but the phones weren't working.

She takes the cup of steaming coffee out into the freshness of the morning. She likes the contrast between cold mornings and hot coffee and takes a first sip, enjoying the bitter kick of it as it goes down. She walks to the edge of the jetty and balances the cup on a mooring bollard and dials the number. The phone still doesn't want to connect, and so she holds it up to the sky, feeling instantly stupid as she does it, as if the extra couple of feet will make it more visible to the network.

She gets nothing except the first fat raindrops falling out of the sky right into her eyes. Allie ducks her head and wipes her face, deciding to head inside before this gets heavier.

She's reaching for the coffee cup when she hears a foot scrape on the concrete behind her and turns to see Walter John lurching towards her. There's something wrong with his face, something she instinctively misreads as anger. She holds up a calming hand.

"Hey," she says. "Walter John. Hey, hold on, it's OK. What's happened, love?"

Love. That tears it.

Literally.

Something small rips inside Walter John's head. It's not a big thing, it doesn't hurt; and maybe it's his imagination, but it feels physical, this last straw. But it doesn't feel like it is his back that is broken by it: it feels more like a membrane tearing. And it's a little thing, like the membrane was delicate and tissue-thin anyway. It does, however, make him feel momentarily sick, and he has a sharp spiking sensation at the top of his nose. And then he's on the other side of it, or maybe the membrane was a dam that has broken, a gossamer barrier just thick enough to stop him hearing the other voice in his head. Because he can hear that voice now and it's arguing with him. (Or maybe he's arguing with himself, it says.) Or perhaps they're both arguing about who he's going to be. He's never heard the voices and yet he's always heard them. Always known they've been there. Maybe they were just whispering before, talking behind his back. Betraying him. Hiding. No wonder he feels sick. (He doesn't. It was just a moment.)

The woman is still holding up a hand as if she's the boss of him.

"Seriously," she says. "Walter John, I'm just—"

She never gets to say what she is just saying or doing or asking, because that's when he hits her.

She makes a very surprised noise as she falls over. And his hand hurts.

She stares at him in disbelief. Stupid mouth open, gasping for air. Stupid mouth. Surprised he's not a weak old man.

He watches her pick herself off the concrete, pushing herself unsteadily to her knees.

He hears a distant horn blaring at him from somewhere he can't see and feels that spike behind his nose again. He doesn't need this hassle. He hears the warning blast again, a little louder this time, and ignores it. He really doesn't need this interruption. (Yes. He really does.) He should kick her right off the jetty. (He definitely shouldn't.)

But.

He sees the phone. Calling someone. Calling for help, most like. As if he's a bad man. Women like that, always misunderstanding him. What he's doing. What he wants to do. He just wanted . . .

His foot is in motion before he can think of stopping it, and when he does think of stopping it before it hits her in the small of the back, he decides not to. (Serve her right.)

The woman grunts in shock as the force of the kick knocks her off balance again. She hits hard. Something cracks. Her phone goes skittering across the rain-slick slabs on the top of the jetty as she splays her hands to stop herself falling further. The bright screen maps a slow arc as it sails out over the dark water and then hits with a small plop. He watches the brightness tumble away into the depths and disappear. (Pretty.)

"What the fuck . . . ?"

He looks down. The woman, the problem, the bossy cow, has scrabbled herself around so she's sitting in a puddle staring at him with a funny expression on her face. What is that expression? (Shock.) Why is she shocked? (She's a woman. You don't kick women.) What's a woman? (A woman is a . . . A woman is a . . .)

He feels sick again. Really sick. Sick like he wants to bend over and heave. It's a physical sensation and he knows that in a minute or so he's going have to do so, but it's not caused by anything physical. He knows it's not something he ate, because he's eaten nothing since forever. He knows it's not because he's ill. It's a need to vomit that comes from a suddenly noticed abyss inside himself and the terror that void has hit him with. He can't remember the name of the woman staring at him with an expression he is sure he knew the word for a moment ago but now also cannot name.

It's that small tear and the fragile membrane. It kept going.

That small tear has slowly ripped a widening hole in his head and things are falling through it. Things have been falling through it fast while the two voices have been talking to himself. He wants to cry at the loss and then he can't think why tears are rolling down his face. What are tears? (Wet. Tears are wet. Wet is . . .) Wet is what? (What?)

The woman gets slowly to her feet. She's getting her breath back. Her hands are grazed and bloody. Her eyes are very something. (Angry. Her eyeholes are angry.) When she speaks, spittle flies from her mouth. Why is she speaking a noise big like that? (Shouting? She's shouting.)

"What the hell's your problem, you mad bastard?"

He knows he's expected to do something. (Answer. He should answer.) He doesn't know how. (Speak.) What's speak? (He doesn't know how.) Open the mouth. Speaking is open mouthing. (Then what?) Noise comes. (Can't hear it. Is it coming?) Is what coming?

"Who the fuck do you think you are?"

He doesn't remember. (What's remember?)

358

And then, what was Walter John just is, and the "is" steps swiftly towards the woman, who shouts "No" and tries to block the swinging boot with flailing hands that are slapped aside as his foot pile-drives into her with a nasty final-sounding crack, and she makes her own arc off the edge of the jetty.

She flies through the air, as limp and unresisting as a flung rag doll, and hits the water below with a much messier splash than the neat plop the phone made.

That "No" must have taken all the wind out of her because she sinks like an anvil. The water closes over her and the next wave smooths out the momentary disturbance, and Walter John is left staring down at the surface with no memory of why he is doing so or what is now beneath the water. He's just watching the swell, mesmerised by the regular back and forth. It somehow soothes the spikes of anger still prickling behind his nose, almost the last thing of him left hanging on, tenacious as a cocklebur. Almost everything else has dropped into the void beyond the torn membrane.

"W-w-wet," he says, his finger making a small twitch towards it, like a vestigial stab of muscle memory trying to point. His voice is slow and becoming slurred and unintelligible, but it doesn't really matter as he is talking to someone screaming as they fall away from him (No, wait, wait just a m—!), someone who has also now fallen away through that tear in his head.

His finger twitches again, an even smaller movement towards the water.

"Wet is ... wet is ... that."

If he could say more, he might say that he remains standing there, staring at the surface of the sea slapping against the jetty, because there's nothing left to be angry at. There's nothing much left inside now. Just the anger and no one to let it feed on.

He jackknifes reflexively and does the vomiting he knew was coming, back in the long-ago forgotten time when he was a person that knew stuff. It's thin, watery stuff but there is a lot of it.

A raven circles overhead, crying as if in distress. He looks up. Fires an arm skywards, clawing the air. His fingers close on nothing, thirty feet below the bird. It soars away inland.

He's so focused on the bird that he barely notices the car slide to a stop beside him, doesn't hear the man shouting at him as he runs for the edge of the jetty. Doesn't register any of it.

He just huffs in annoyance and begins to follow it, slowly at first, then in a loping run that picks up speed as he tries not to lose sight of the vexing flash of black that barely stands out against the louring gunmetal clouds crowding in above it as it streams away ahead of him through the thickening rain.

Chapter 63

Negative buoyancy

Today is different.

It started the same way as every day's swim, but by the time she locks the dog in the Defender and hobbles into the water Sig feels the divergence from the norm like an unsettling wrong note in the morning air. Probably the nightmare, she thinks. Though it's more intense than normal, this discordant vibration isn't an especially unusual feeling for her: she senses it, when it happens, as a kind of hangover from a broken and dream-torn night's sleep. It's an atmosphere of mind, really, a nocturnal remembrance that remains wrapped around her like a clingy shroud, and she knows on a normal day she would soon slough it off in the cold morning water. But this is a different difference. It's more like an actual itch in her back-brain.

Knee-deep in the water, she turns and looks back. The vehicle. Rex. The hill and then the louring sky beyond. No sign of the old man and his spaniel, but their non-presence isn't it. They weren't there every morning, and she would not register their absence as such a powerfully off-kilter feeling.

No, she tells herself. It's just the lingering funk of a particularly pungent nightmare. It had been more intense than normal, so it's quite understandable that the resonance of it should persist a little longer into the waking day than normal. She hates dreams, she thinks as she turns and wades deeper, pulling her goggles on and attaching her nose clip. She hates them because they are the one thing whose comings and goings she cannot control in what is her otherwise rigorously ordered and carefully protected life. They are the wildcards, the landmines, the slow knives that can sneak in below the armour and wound her and make her feel the way she felt now. Defenceless. As if all her carefully curated strategies for never feeling vulnerable again are and always have been a futile waste of time.

It is that waste that makes Sig angry, not the revelation of vulnerability. She knows she is vulnerable. That's why she'd worked out the strategies, after all. She just doesn't like feeling it. Wallowing in self-pity, sinking under its weight. Fuck it. There are better ways not to drown.

Keeping on swimming, for one.

She reaches back, hits PLAY on her ancient iPod in its waterproof case and dives through the face of the next wave, churning rhythmically towards the buoy on the southern tip of the bay, determined to get her day back on track.

By the time she gets to the buoy she's hit her groove, the familiar kick and pull of the stroke calming her mind with its comforting regularity. One of the things she enjoys about the stroke is the way it pulls her body straight and free of kinks, each powerful sweep her arms make through the water towing the rest of her body forward as she twists her core from side to side as if strung on invisible wire that enters through the top of her head. No matter how hard she kicks, the raw power of her arms always provides much more forward momentum. Some days she imagines her feet are churning just to keep up.

Sig touches the buoy and turns, heading for the other buoy, her buoy. This passage of her swim takes her over the deepest water as she crosses the open mouth of the bay where the protection of the southern cape gives way to the heavier oceanic heave of the unobstructed Atlantic. It's almost the most challenging part of the triangular swim as she travels at a rough right angle to whatever waves are rolling in to broadside her. Sometimes the difference is only a mild swell compared to the millpond calm of the sheltered legs. Today the sea is querulous and choppy, the rhythm of the lateral waves hard to figure out and anticipate. Sometimes the sea catches her careful rolling motion and tips her further over so she has to claw her hand deeper and push back harder to regain her equilibrium; other times, she compensates for a wave that doesn't arrive and finds herself getting out of whack on the other side of the stroke. It all breaks her sense of flow, messing up the rhythm of her inhales and exhales, adding a fretful quality to the swim and making her feel she is floundering breathlessly towards the protected waters marked by the northern buoy instead of cutting a neat groove through the water. It irritates her, and when she hits the buoy she holds on, feeling fractious and dissatisfied with herself.

As Sig clings to the buoy and gets her breathing sorted out, she lets herself again become one with the swell and ebb of the sea, letting the measured heave of the deep rock her back into better spirits. A shadow passes overhead and she squints up at the raven once again floating across the sky on the updraught of coastal air. She doesn't know why she always thinks of it as "the raven" rather than "a raven". Since all ravens look the same she doesn't suppose it matters, though there's something comforting in the thought that it's the same one, keeping a mildly disinterested eye on her seaborne exertions.

She wasn't going to freedive this morning, not when she

planned her session, but now she's here and has regained her calm, she decides there's no harm in it – although, despite herself, she does scan the horizon for Matt's boat. The absence of his baleful glare confirms her change of plan. She's going to have to share the rest of her day with Evie, and even if that takes place in the companionable silence that it usually does, it's still not her preferred solitude. She decides a short dive is a private indulgence she can allow herself. The calm she has to achieve in order to transgress safely will wash away the last of that odd vibration she's been carrying around since she woke.

The familiar preparations Sig goes through are their own kind of self-levelling ritual, so that when she inverts and begins to swim down the buoy rope she is already feeling relaxed and correctly unflustered. She automatically adjusts pressure as she sounds, feeling the comforting squeeze of compression on her chest as the deeper water takes her into its embrace. It's this feeling that makes her solo freediving habit seem like a drug, this hidden watery hug and the sense of coming home that it brings, not the clandestine nature of the deed. She's not doing anything illegal, and she's not putting anyone else in harm's way. Even if it were a crime, it would fall into the grey moral area of a consensual crime, and back in the days when Sig was more of a firebrand about justice and what went on in the bigger, outer world, she had believed behaviours that hurt no one else were not things lawmakers should deal with. What people did in the privacy of their own homes or bedrooms by themselves or with other consenting adults was not anyone else's business. But this far down the rope, the memory of her earlier political engagement seems superfluous and silly when weighed against the abyssal tug of the ocean's beckoning depths.

The mammal swimming towards the bottom is not the same one who had gone on demonstrations and signed petitions. She feels her mouth twitch in a smile at the thought of that self-important other past Sig who thought she could save the world by adding her name to things and going on marches, the long-gone girl who felt the world was bright and worth saving in the first place. The present Sig drifts downwards, finning slowly, super-calm as she has to be, hardly noticing she's reached the point where she begins to experience negative buoyancy.

And then she hears the voices.

They are distant enough that she can't hear what they're saying but close enough to feel like they are possibly familiar and definitely talking to her.

It's all in her head, of course, since the only sound coming in via her ears is the systolic wash and thump of blood pumping around her body, but it's enough to make her miss a kick with her feet and just hang in there, head down, paused but still gliding downwards.

It's all in her head – of course it is – the friendly voices tantalisingly there but just beyond the reach of comprehension. Beckoning her like a magnet. And though most of her knows it's irrational, a renegade piece of her feels that if she just carries on a little deeper she'll get close enough to the noise to hear what they're saying.

In fact, she has to.

It is suddenly very important to keep going downwards, otherwise she'll never clearly hear the message the friendly – and surely known – voices are trying to give her, and she starts kicking again.

Sig sees the kelp emerge from the gloom below, like figures materialising out of the mist. It must be kelp, but when is kelp white, reaching for her long before the point where the bottom should be in sight? It's not any kelp she's seen before, and then she notices it isn't quite kelp, but more like fingers, more like hands, and she sees that she is reaching for the waiting hands without meaning to, and the rational remnant of her brain suddenly realises something is wrong, more than wrong, maybe fatally wrong.

She'd never dived deep enough to get this close to the kelp. If she is in touching distance, she must have lost discipline, lost track of her depth, lost it to hypoxia; she must be depth-happy and rapturing badly, seeing kelp as hands, lethally imagining a friendly hubbub of voices calling her deeper.

She is a dead woman swimming. Too far from the surface to do anything but drown on the way up.

And as Sig thinks this, in the precious second it takes her to come to what remains of her senses, her hand still out-stretched towards their waiting grasp, she imagines seeing eyes and mouths upturned beyond them as one hand lunges higher than the others, and she feels sharp fingernails rake the back of her hand. Instinctively, she flinches back as their friendly clamour instantly changes into a snarl of hate and frustration, and she sees the kelp is not kelp but a crowd, an angry crowd gaping up at her, and the reality of the impossible vision gut-punches her, almost making her gasp in a lungful of seawater, but a new, louder, single voice hits her with the blunt force of a swung sledgehammer.

GO.

And because that voice is clean and safe and almost her own, it drowns the cacophony beckoning her downwards and she reacts on instinct, jackknifing in her own length and kicking wildly for the suddenly-too-distant surface.

GO. SLOW.

SLOW!

BUT GO.

She overrides the panic and slows herself down. Hypoxia. She'd done something wrong, she'd starved her brain of oxygen or something, begun to hallucinate. And hallucinating at depth will lead to dying at depth if she doesn't get her shit together and follow procedures right now.

Calm and slow will let her travel further on whatever unwasted oxygen remains. She needs to cruise back up to the air. If she thrashes, she'll move faster but burn oxygen faster too.

Move faster, drown quicker, she thinks.

Sig forces her mind into a tight cone of concentration. She desperately wants to look down and make sure those grasping hands are not even now about to coil round her ankle and flippers and pull her back down, but she doesn't, telling herself it's a waste of energy that she cannot afford. Especially because the hands are kelp, just a hallucination. She notes that the clamour of beckoning voices has stopped and takes that as a further good sign, a proof that whatever had produced the glitch in her brain is gone for the moment, and if she can just acknowledge the searing burn of oxygen starvation in her lungs as something unthreatening that she has trained herself to push through if she embraces it and keeps rhythmically finning for the waves above, she will be safe.

GO.

I'm going, she tells herself. Slow and steady does the trick. Slow and steady. Her legs begin to feel heavy and waterlogged, each stroke costing more and more of the energy that she no longer has. Each increasingly leaden kick makes her feel more and more stupid. Stupid to be here. Stupid to be alone. Stupid to mistake a hallucination for something real. Stupid to panic at an illusion. Stupid to have wasted the valuable energy she now needs in that initial frenzied getaway – energy that might have got her the last few metres to the unreachable air she can now see above the wave-deckled surface overhead.

Stupid to die like this.

Now, though, it is happening. Now her legs are slowing to a stop. Now she can admit to herself the thing she's always hidden, the thing she has known will always happen: she's known it will end like this, and maybe she tempted this particular fate because she was in the end too much the coward to seek death directly and cleanly. Maybe she has been edging up to this point for a long time. Maybe this is okay, the quiet and unheralded end. Unlamented and alone. Maybe this is the logical extension of all the accidents that have led her to this moment. She always claimed, even to herself, that she had fallen from the rockface by mistake, the accident that had maimed her leg and nearly killed her. Actually, it doesn't matter, she thinks; now it's all over, nothing really matters. There is one destination so absolute that how you arrive becomes immediately and eternally irrelevant.

This isn't a terrible thing.

She feels her body begin to convulse, her throat twitching and contracting, her body about to open her mouth on its own say-so, no matter what she tries to tell it, her autonomic system overriding rational thought so it can convulsively breathe in, even if all there is to breathe is ocean. A thought flies in and out of her mind like a passing gull catching the flash of the sun on its white belly – there, then not there but making her smile: she'd come to life in her mother's belly breathing liquid, and it is fitting and symmetrical that she should exit with her lungs similarly full of brine.

This isn't a terrible thing at all.

NO.

That sledgehammer voice in her head slams her into a final paroxysm, a kick of unlooked-for energy. It hits her so hard that for a moment she feels gripped by another momentary hallucination, a palpable sense of being grabbed by the scruff of the neck and yanked to the surface by main force and then slapped against the side of the buoy, which she grabs and holds on to on reflex.

DON'T LET GO.

She holds on, coughing and spluttering, and then she concentrates on not passing out. She focuses on not squandering this unexpected salvation, the last spark that has plucked her from a death she now realises she absolutely does not want. She has promises to keep. The wind brings the sound of a dog barking urgently. She turns to the shore and raises a hand weakly.

"It's okay, Rex," she croaks. "I'm okay."

IDIOT.

"I'm an idiot," she agrees. "I'm definitely an idiot, but I am okay."

Chapter 64

Addicted to the shindig

Tom has run himself out of everything. He's standing, shaking with exhaustion as he gulps for air on the top of the hill in the centre of the island. He's stopped because he's reached the watershed of this small sea-girt world, and his legs are screaming for a moment's rest. The wind has been in his face all the way to the top, but now he's on the ridgeline he's no longer protected from the full force of it and he doesn't have the strength to plough onwards. Besides, he's reached the high ground. High ground is safe.

Once more, he's forgotten something, something he mustn't try to remember because it'll likely break his thinking even more. The baby is crying. He doesn't remember why he's up here, only that he was running from something that is behind him. He turns to look. Just the long, hummocked downslope of heather, a few rocks, and in the far distance the rain-slick single-track road reflecting the light like a silver ribbon that runs protectively along the edge of the land, on the other side of which is a scrape of beach and the sea beyond that.

He doesn't want to look at that sea, so he turns away. He

looks down at his legs. They're wet and shaking and they hurt, and not just from the running up the hill that had felt like it would never end. One side of his jeans is ripped from thigh to knee, and there are cuts and blood.

He is soaked and cold, and if he could make a noise it would be very like the one the baby is making. Instead, his mouth gapes as wide as his eyes but is echoingly silent. Maybe because there's nothing left inside him. Maybe he's hollow. Maybe if he turns his mouth cavern to the wind it'll fill him until he swells like a balloon and is blown away to somewhere else, somewhere where he doesn't hurt, where he's safe.

His thinking is broken. That's almost all he knows. That's all there is room in his head for. That and the fact the baby needs something he can't give it.

His hands seem to have a mind of their own because they are feeling in the pockets of the changing bag.

They find a bottle.

It's empty and unwashed, the insides opaque with dried formula.

Formula. How does he know that word?

He puts the teat in the baby's mouth. She locks on immediately. When she is unable to suck anything from it, she spits it out and shrieks.

He sits with her in his lap, using his back to protect her from the freshening wind.

He knows they are alone up here. But it's safe.

He knows she wants to eat. But it's safe.

Maybe if they both sleep a bit it will be safer. He closes his eyes.

One great thing about a barely inhabited island is that you can really crank the stereo because there are no neighbours or grandparents to complain. And since Sig has abandoned her,

Evie has no qualms about turning things up to eleven. And since the phone service died, her phone's only real use is as a music player anyway. She Bluetooths to Sig's fancy speaker and hits PLAY.

Normally when she works out this playlist is on her headphones, but she enjoys the bigger sound that begins pumping, filling the room as she eyes the weights she is going to start with. Since the odds are she's going to have to propel her way into whatever future lies ahead of her with her arms and not her legs, it makes sense to work her upper body into the best shape possible. It's a routine she's private about. Her grandparents know about it, of course, but they can't hear the tunes in her headphones and they'd hate the pounding sound blast – not because of the music per se, but because it's not the kind of music the little girl they are still somehow invested in her being would like. It'd be like rubbing their noses in the fact she will outgrow them but always need them, and it's a complicated thing that's snarled up in too much poignancy for her. And it's also private because she'd hate for her few island friends to see her doing it, maybe because it feels a little too nakedly like hope or something.

She stretches as the music intros with a heavy stringed guitar playing a red-hot lick in a funked-out counterpoint to a rising crescendo of drums, and then the singer arrives on the track and explains he can't stop, because he's addicted to the shindig and that Chop Top (whoever that is) says he's going to win big. The next line, exhorting her not to choose a life of imitation, is the starting pistol she always begins her sessions with. She frowns, picks up the first weight and launches into a series of punishing arm curls. This is her own invented routine, frankensteined from exercises recommended by her physio and other things she picked up online, and she has each set of repetitions painstakingly timed to the tracks of her workout playlist. It makes the sessions go quicker and helps pump enough adrenaline to keep her powering through it. It's an old band playing, but they keep pretty fresh, and it was one of her dad's favourites. It's probably silly, the sentimental thinking involved in this, but Evie figures if life crashes into you and smashes the lucky things you thought you had, there's no shame in making your own totems out of the broken things that remain.

Tom opens his eyes and stops breathing. He strains his ears, tilting his head gently from side to side to keep the thundering of the wind out of both his ears at the same time, wondering if he dozed off for a moment and dreamed that he heard a familiar voice gusting up at him from somewhere below. He decides he imagined it, and then, just before Ruby starts chuntering again, he catches another familiar sound and half stands, crouched and quivering like a dog on point. He has his back to the way he came, and the slope ahead of him is shorter. He can see the distant roof of a house by a stone jetty. He listens some more, hearing something familiar that shouldn't be here. He hears himself say two words he forgot he knew.

"Chili Peppers."

Ruby is unimpressed – a view she makes vocally apparent all the stumbling way down the other side of the hill.

Chapter 65

Rex at bay

Sig clings on to the buoy until she is sure she isn't going to black out and then swims back to the beach at a steady clip. She doesn't swim the longer leg across the bay to where she had started, but cheats, heading for the much closer headland end and then walking back to the Land Rover. To her right, she can see darkness beyond the low hills, which means much heavier rain is sweeping in from the landward side of the island. She realises Rex is still barking, so she whistles and waves, but he just ricochets around from window to window inside the vehicle, his eyes locked on her, tail erect and on alert. There is still no one on the slope above to see her hobble lopsidedly on the soft sand.

When she unlatches the rear door, she braces herself for Rex to bounce at her and dance around her in his usual happy greeting dance, but the moment the door opens just wide enough for his head he slips through the narrow gap like quicksilver and tears across the beach towards the water, his furiously churning back legs spitting divots of sand into the air behind him like afterburners. He hits the edge of the water and stops, stiff as a statue, hackles risen, growling low and menacingly.

She tries to whistle him in, but he ignores her.

"Fine," she says, reaching back to rip the Velcro and free the zipper-pull at the back of her neck. "You do you."

Sig unpeels the wetsuit and steps out of it with her back to the water. She rubs the towel over her body with even less attention than normal and dresses equally quickly. She pulls on the sweatshirt and grabs the jeans and her leg brace and then chucks the wetsuit and towel and fins into the back of the Defender and slams the door closed. She wants to get off the beach fast.

It's only when she turns to whistle for the dog again, and finds to her surprise that she can't seem to purse her lips properly because she is shaking, that she admits to herself that she's rattled. She blows out her cheeks and stretches her mouth out to limber up, and tries again. It's better, but still a weedy half-whistle, not the normal shrill note she once prided herself on – the abrupt business-like sharpness that cut through the air, beckoning distant taxis in cities she no longer wants to visit. Rex doesn't react to it, so she calls for him, her voice hoarser and more urgent than she'd expected. The dog just stays put, as if on guard, threatening the sea. Sig straps on the leg brace with a grimace and pegs lopsidedly over the sand towards him as she buttons her Levis. She's irritated by his deafness. She wants to get going so she can have a hot drink and an even hotter shower. She has every reason to feel this rattled, she tells herself – rattled and stupid: if she hadn't almost died by her own hand exactly, the blame of the near miss still lay at the feet of her own foolishness.

It's only when she tries to pull Rex away from the water's edge and he shrugs away from her hand and keeps on growling that Sig acknowledges to herself that it isn't just because she nearly died that she's shaken. It's the white kelp, the hallucination, the thing she has carefully not thought about since she resurfaced. She'd turned her mind away from it to keep calm and make sure she did not trigger hypoxia as she regained her discipline and went through the post-dive safety routine. It was the reason she'd swum the short leg to shore rather than spend any longer than strictly needed passing over the deeper water with who-knows-what reaching up for her from below.

It doesn't help that the dog's growling is recognisably a warning, as if there is something out there that needs to be prevented from coming ashore. It's as unsettling as a dog barking at night, a noise that kindles an atavistic fear of some unseen malevolence. It rips a small hole in her rational backdrop of the world and makes her shiver despite herself.

"Hoi," she says, grabbing Rex's tail and tugging him back so she can scoop him into her arms. "Enough of that."

His rough fur beneath her hands and the thrumming of his small heart against her breastbone soothes her as he lets her carry him back to the Land Rover. They get in just as the heavy rain hits the beach, drumming noisily on the roof overhead. He sits close to her on the bench seat as she cranks on the windscreen wipers and turns for home, sharing his warmth, as if he instinctively knows she needs it.

It's companionable, but she'd have been happier if he hadn't kept his head craned backwards until the choppy waters of the bay were lost to sight in the rear-view mirror.

Chapter 66

Van opener

The incoming storm kicks up a gear as Magda reverses out of the driveway. She's in a foul morning mood, having spent the night sleeping fitfully, angry that her internet and phone were down so she couldn't play video games or stream anything when she got in, angry at herself for having shown the pretty boy she was upset he'd forgotten her name. It hadn't been a meaningful one-night stand in the first place, though meaning was not what she'd been after at the time anyway. She'd just felt like sex and was uncomplicated about things like that. He was obviously interested and so they'd gone to bed together. It had not been particularly good sex, which was only surprising in retrospect because she'd forgotten a rule she'd formulated a couple of years earlier when she'd worked at a gym: the guys who spent time watching themselves in the mirrors often had great bodies but were equally self-obsessed in bed, which didn't make for mutual fun.

Heavier raindrops begin to hit and bounce off the bonnet ahead of her as she clears the windscreen and accelerates towards the harbour. There's a scrabble of four houses close to the road around the next bend, and she is used to seeing the welcoming lights in their windows come into view as she drives to work in the morning. Today, there are no lights and no signs of life. And without their warmth, the small houses seem ominously blinded as they crouch defensively back into the dark heather, as if beaten into submission by the rain hammering viciously down on them. Magda shivers and doesn't slow down as she passes through. The whole hamlet feels like an aftermath, a place where something bad had happened. Maybe they were all at the Modh.

Once she's gone another mile, she realises that two of the houses had seemed particularly deserted because their front doors were hanging mutely open. She decides she'd imagined that. Or that there was a perfectly good explanation for it.

Her spirits are not lifted by the raven that lofts off a fence-post and flaps alongside her for a while like an escort. It seems like a bad-luck bird, not least because it's ploughing effortlessly through rain that's coming down like stair rods, and she is suddenly not sure she's ever seen a bird fly in such a brutal downpour.

"Go away," she says.

The raven seems to cock a disappointed eye at her before it sheers off and flies ahead, winding along the roadway until it's lost to view. And as soon as she can't see it any more, she regrets sending it away because she suddenly feels more alone than she had before the bird had appeared.

Ten minutes later, Magda crests the last rise before the harbour and feels her heart lift as she sees a warmly lit window in the hotel and the familiar lights along the jetty.

She parks in front of the island shop. It should be open but the lights there are still off. That isn't like Mary-Kate, she thinks. And then she notices it too has the front door ajar, and she stops dead.

Something is off. It's too like the lifeless hamlet she'd sped

378

through for comfort. She spins in a slow 360, adding up all the unfamiliar things she is and isn't seeing. All the surrounding buildings are unlit, except the hotel further up the slope, where there are lights but no sign of anyone inside.

Outside, there is nobody moving around, but then the storm is hitting and anyone sensible would be indoors anyway. Though it's so dark they surely would have the lights on. But again, there is no sign of life.

Only once she stops turning does she hear the knocking and thumping.

The noise is coming from behind her, towards the sea. It's a frantic sound, as if someone or something is in a frenzy, trying to get her – or anybody's – attention. Despite wanting to get out of the rain, she steps towards it.

It seems to be coming from inside the Highland Telco van that's jammed up against the protective bollards on the very edge of the jetty. Magda walks up to the back door and listens for a beat. There is definitely someone in there. And they're not happy about it.

"Hello?" she says, then clears her throat and says it again, louder. "Hello?"

There is a sudden silence from inside the van.

"Are you okay?" she says.

There is no reply, but she thinks she can hear a kind of low moaning. She leans gingerly forward and puts her ear to the door.

The moaning stops, like someone on the other side is holding their breath, listening right back at her. She knocks on the door.

"Hello?" she says.

The moaning begins again.

"Hang on," she says. "I'm going to open the door, okay?"

The moaning continues.

"Okay," she says, taking a deep breath and reaching for the latch, which had been secured with a screwdriver through the hasp. She pulls it clear and flips the metal hinge.

She hears a voice screaming "NO" just as she cracks the doors open.

Water gushes out of the interior and sprays her thighs as if they had been damming a shallow pool, and she sees the man who had been trapped inside – half naked, bloodied, on his knees on the soaked floor, surrounded by a chaotic jumble of tools and wires, as if he'd ripped everything loose in his frenzy to escape.

But what gets Magda's horrified attention is not that it's Jamie, the once-pretty boy – it's the grotesque way he's staring at her with water welling out of his mouth in a continual flow, water that is also streaming from his eyes, so much water that he's wearing the wetness as a sort of second flickering skin that jumps and fritzes and seems to make him go in and out of focus. She stares at him, frozen in terror.

He lurches to one knee and suddenly launches himself at her.

And then something grabs her from behind, and a man in a hi-viz jacket yanks her backwards as he throws himself against the doors, slamming them shut, just in time. Even as she falls backwards she hears the man inside hit the door and start banging and roaring in wordless frustration.

Magda sprawls painfully back on her tailbone as the big guy in the hi-viz leans back on the door, making sure it's latched shut. He looks at her as he scrabbles on the ground and retrieves the dropped screwdriver, which he jams back in the hasp.

"You all right?" he says.

She nods and gets back on her feet.

"You didn't hear me shouting?" he says.

She shakes her head, then points at the van that's now

rocking back and forth on its springs as the man inside throws himself at the door again and again.

"The fuck was that?"

"Bloody Jamie," the man says. "You okay?"

"Not even close," she says.

He nods.

"Aye," he says. "Me neither."

"Where is everyone?" she says.

He frowns again, and she sees the deep bruises beneath his eyes and the whiteness of his skin against the darker beard and realises how shockingly exhausted he looks.

"Um," he says.

"Um?" she says. "Mister. Where did they go?"

He tilts his chin towards the water beyond the harbour edge.

"They all walked into the water."

Magda follows his gaze.

"I know. I've spent all night hoping I've gone mad," he says, voice cracking. "Sorry."

She angles her head towards the lights of the hotel.

"Who's in there?"

"Just me," he says. "After the boats caught fire and everyone . . ."

He shrugged.

"I barricaded myself in," he says. "You know. In case I had to make a last stand. If they came back. Me against all of them. John fucking Wayne."

He snorts and looks disgusted with himself.

"What a plum, eh?" he says, beginning to deflate. "Look, I tried to save Jamie, managed to lock him in . . . you know . . . but then . . ."

He exhales and shakes his head.

"I was scared shitless. I ran. And then all I could think of doing was waiting until the ferry gets in."

She looks out at the building fury of the waves beginning to stack up beyond the breakwater.

"I don't think they'll run the ferry today," she says. Her mind feels queasy, rebelling against the vision of Jamie and the water pouring out of him.

"Would be easier if I was going doolally," says the man, eyes locked on the rocking van. "Then none of this would be real."

"Yes," she says. "But it is real, and it won't get better if we stand out here in the rain, will it?"

She turns and walks towards the hotel. She needs to make sure he's not also crazy. She needs to see other people. She suddenly, desperately, needs for there to be other people inside.

"You can tell me what happened when we're in the dry." She turns and sees him looking at her.

"I'm Magda," she says.

"Malc," he replies. He is hovering listlessly, as if in rescuing her he'd used up the last drop of energy in his body and can't decide to move away from the harbour's edge and the rocking van and the horror he'd just penned inside it.

"Come on then, Malc," she says. "I'll get us a cup of tea on."

"Tea," he says.

"And a Tunnocks. They have them behind the bar," she says, encouragingly.

He gives her a wintery smile.

"Tea and a Tunnocks?" he says.

"Least I can do," she says. "You just saving my life there, and all. And then maybe you tell me what you mean about the boats catching fire."

They don't say anything else until they get up to the hotel, and then once they are inside she stands waiting as he locks the doors behind them and shoots the bolt.

It makes her a little uneasy, so she turns and shouts, "Hello?"

"You lock the pub doors and the kitchen?" she says.

"You bet," he says, shucking out of his hi-viz.

"I'm going to do a quick check around," she says. "Meet you in the kitchen."

Three minutes later, Magda has checked all the rooms and found them empty and some in disarray. Malc had not been lying. There should have been at least four guests and Morag, who made the breakfasts.

Somehow, the fact that he had not been lying didn't make things better.

Chapter 67

Be sharp, say nowt

Evie is on to the bit of her routine she likes least. She's finished the seated push-ups and is doing her first set of crunches, sitting tall with her back held straight as she can manage, arms across her chest like a pharaoh. She sucks her belly button close to her spine while at the same time pressing the lower part of her back against the seat, and bends her head, shoulders and chest towards her thighs, folding herself like a pocketknife, pushing herself as far as she can manage. Then she straightens back to her starting position and does it again. And again. And again. When she was first shown the exercise, she could do it for about twenty seconds before needing to stop. Now she can sustain it for the full three minutes and forty-eight seconds of the bouncing house track that she uses to time this part of the set. She knows she should do a series of reps, with pauses, but it's the last part of her daily workout, the point where she goes into what she has come to call "beast mode", and she just keeps doing the crunches until the music cuts. Sometimes she deals with the burn by tuning in to the deep thump of the bass line that powers under the kick drum as the hooky synth groove builds over them; other times, she finds herself swooping and soaring with the raw power of the diva's voice that alternately growls and wails a call-and-response with the answering gospel choir.

The singer has just asked how in the world a brown cow can eat green grass and then turn around and give up some white milk when Evie feels the door behind her open, the sudden blast of air from behind her cooling the sweat on her neck. Sig's back early, she thinks, and digs in, keeping on going. She knows there's only about half a minute to go and Sig is one of the very few people she's not embarrassed to be seen by while doing her workout. She knows Sig did the same hard miles when she was in rehab for her leg.

"Nearly . . . done," she puffs in between reps. "Sorry about the music—"

It's the screaming that stops her.

The new and unexpected noise is shrill and loud enough to be heard over the speaker. She stops mid-crunch, breathing hard with the exertion, and kills the sound as she swivels her chair to look behind her.

The sudden silence is almost as shocking as the shaking figure standing in the open door. It's a bedraggled young boy she's never seen before in her life – twelve, maybe thirteen, maybe older – clutching a bright bag that's looped over his shoulder. His jeans are spotted with blood, half torn off one leg so she can see the nasty gashes that the blood came from. He is breathing hard, like he's run here from a long way off, and wet through with rain and sweat. His eyes are locked on hers, and his mouth keeps opening as if to say something, but he is entirely silent. The screaming is coming from the bag. Evie can see the hand that isn't clutching it tight to his heaving chest is cupped protectively around the back of something. A baby's head.

They stare at each other. Evie tries to think straight and stop breathing so hard.

"What happened?" she says. It seems the obvious thing to say.

The boy doesn't react.

"Come in" she says, rolling forward. "Sorry, come in, my name's Evie. It's okay, you're okay. It's going to be okay . . . "

He takes a step back. He must be in shock, she thinks. And then her mind puts things together and she realises there has obviously been an accident.

"Was there a crash?" she says, rolling towards him. "Are you okay?"

He flinches away from her, stepping back out into the rain.

"It's okay," she says. "Get inside. I'll be back, I just need to see—"

He watches her speed the chair down the drive. As she powers through the driving rain over the treacherously uneven surface, she has to admit she's scared about seeing another car crash, car crashes being the one thing she spends a lot of time training herself not to think about or remember in any detail, but she tells herself to get a grip and have the post-traumatic freak-out later. Right now, there is a limit to how useful she can be in a wheelchair and with no phone service to call for help, but maybe she can do something.

She gets to the end of the drive and skitters to a stop in a puddle, turning both ways, straining her eyes to the horizon. She sees no one else, no sign of life – or death – no buckled metal or broken cars. She allows herself a sigh of relief, and then spins and hurries back to the boy. He is standing exactly where she'd left him.

"What happened?" she says.

He just stares at her. Shock. He is having his own PTSD freak-out.

"Come in," she says. "Hey, come on in. It's okay."

He stares at her.

"It's wet out here," she says. "And look, the phones are broken and I can't drive and there's no car anyway, but Sig, my friend, she'll be back soon," Evie says.

The baby keeps up its wailing.

"Can I see the baby?" she says. "Is it hurt?"

The boy stares at her and says nothing, his mouth still moving like he is trying to remember how words work but keeps forgetting.

"Please," she says, pointing at the baby. "It's cold and she's just getting wetter the longer we stand out here."

He looks down at the baby. And then at Evie.

"Come on," she says. "Follow me. It's warm and dry in here."

He flinches back a little as she passes him, but she decides he's like a spooked animal, so just carries on as if everything is normal, making herself not look back as she re-enters the room, goes to the kettle and turns it on.

"Hot, sweet tea," she says without looking round, trying to sound calm while her mind races around figuring what to do.

Shock. He's in shock. Poor kid. Get something warm in him. On him. On the baby.

She heads for the box-bed. By the time she returns with one of Sig's blankets in her lap, he's edged inside, into the narrow bit of hall that leads into the main room.

"Here," she says. "Get your wet shirt off, wrap up in this."

He looks over her head, into the room.

"Baby's wet too," she says, deciding that if she adopts a cheerful matter-of-fact tone it will help. "We need to get her dry. Or is she a he?"

The boy just won't talk. She spins and grabs a warm tea towel off the rail in front of the stove.

"You want to dry her?" she says. Anything to get him to

engage. Anything to stop that screaming. The state of him popping up like that freaked her enough, but the volume of the noise coming from the baby's small mouth is filling her head and stopping her thinking straight.

She goes up to him again and holds out the towel. No movement, like he's a statue staring across the room. She reaches for the baby, just to stroke it, but the contact breaks the spell. He shudders and shucks the strap of what she can now see is a changing bag and dumps it, baby and all, in her lap.

"OK," she says, scrambling to stop the bag and its squalling contents slipping off her knees and on to the hard kitchen floor. "Okay. That's good."

"Not," says the boy. "Not. Not good."

His voice is cracked and raw and intermittently deeper than she expected, like he's at the treacherous bit of boyhood where it's breaking but not yet broken.

"No," she says, and then sees the stiffly pointing arm he has jabbed out towards the window that he's just come in sight of.

"Not good," he says.

She follows his eyeline.

"It's just the sea," she says. "There's nothing there—"

He's spooking her a bit. Then he stumbles away, back to the doorway, back into the shadowed hall where he cannot see the sea. He slumps down the wall and sits in a half-crouch and begins rocking back and forth.

Fuck. She doesn't know how to help him. But he's not bleeding out or anything, so she should look after this thing squealing in her lap. She heads for Sig's box-bed. She can get it out of the wet onesie and wrap it in the towel.

It's soaked, and pale with cold. She can see it's not hurt as she gently peels its clothes off, worrying about breaking its tiny fingers as she awkwardly gets its arms free from the tubes of wet cotton. The good news is balanced by the bad news her nose tells her, which is that its nappy is full.

"OK," says Evie. "First time for everything."

She finds wipes, a pot of Sudocrem, two nappies and the empty feeding bottle on a quick rummage through the changing bag. She slips the kitchen towel under the baby and holds her breath, unsticking the side tabs on the wadded blue paper clamped round its middle.

The baby's red and chapped like she's needed changing since yesterday.

"Jesus," says Evie. "I'd be bawling my head off too with a raw old bum like that. You poor wee thing. Let's get you cleaned up and then Sig should be back and she'll know what to do.

"At least you haven't crapped yourself," she says. "I was worried this might have been a bigger job than it is."

She's wadding the old nappy to throw in the bin when the baby stops crying for a moment. Evie looks up to see the baby gazing at her with a look of intense contemplation. For a moment, the quiet hangs there, and then the baby almost smiles in a shudder of relief.

"Ah," says Evie. "Spoke too soon. And all over Sig's nice duvet."

Chapter 68

Deadweight

Matt only thinks of driving to Sig's for help when he's gone more than halfway in the wrong direction, heading to the jetty at the fish farm where he'd tied up the *An da Shealladh*, so he keeps going. He can ask the guys there for help if they're in already. The pills haven't taken away the pain in his head but it has changed from sharp pain to a more pervasive dull bruising throb that hammers in time with his pulse. Driving with one eye is more challenging than he'd imagined since it messes up his depth perception and he's driving fast, but he is pleased that the one break he seems to be getting is that no one is up and on the roads yet.

He fishtails the car turning hard into the approach to the jetty, and as he corrects he sees something that shocks him more than the thing that isn't there.

At the other end of the straight half-mile of track he distinctly sees Walter John kick Allie on to her knees. Walter John, who wouldn't say boo to a fucking goose. But he sees it and hits the horn in shocked reflex, but Walter John doesn't seem to hear it.

Matt stamps down on the accelerator and just keeps hitting

the horn. The old man seems oblivious to his incoming presence. He just waits calmly until the woman is almost back on her feet and then – before Matt is close enough to do anything other than yell and impotently mash the horn again – with a calmness that makes the act all the more brutal, boots Allie off the edge of the jetty.

Matt skids the car to a halt and bolts out of it, running through the downpour to the edge of the water. He shouts something angry at Walter John as he runs, but it's really just noise and rage. He hits the stone lip and brakes himself against the rain-slick bollard. Horrified, he sees the woman floating below the surface, already beginning to fade from view as she goes deeper. He dives in without thinking.

The cold sea tears at his face as he spears through the chop and claws himself towards Allie. It's clear water, but it stings his eye as he looks for the blurry outline of her jacket ahead of him. He kicks and pulls himself downwards, fingers reaching for her lifeless body. His fingertips graze her head but close on nothing as she continues to drop. The pressure on his ears is pounding at him and he feels the treacherous buoyancy of the lungful of air he'd managed to gasp as he dived beginning to pull him up and away from her. In a strange moment of clarity, he realises air in his lungs is keeping him alive but condemning her to drown. He exhales and pulls himself deeper, kicking through the ascending bubbles of his last breath.

He swipes at her head again, and misses, but his fingers brush her ponytail, and he grabs one last time with the other hand and feels his fist close on the thick hank of hair. He holds on and jackknifes his body, now kicking and dragging himself towards the surface.

His face breaks water, and he sucks air as he yanks her up after him. He grabs her collar and shouts her name, but she just lolls in the water, her own sodden, deadweight trying to pull her back down. He throws an arm round her neck, pulling her close, and swims on his back to the slimy steps that lead up to the top of the jetty.

Dragging an adult out of the water single-handed is a tough enough business, but pulling the deadweight up sixteen seaweed-slippery steps almost kills Matt as he slides and falls his way upwards. Once he has her on the flat, he goes into autopilot, performing the first aid that had been drilled into him by his grandfather and his father, neither of whom had subscribed to the old superstition about fisherman not learning how to swim. Save yourself, then save others, is what they'd believed, and he chokes in relief when he sees that belief paying off as Allie suddenly spasms and throws up great sputtering gouts of seawater.

He holds her steady as she coughs and hacks and watches as her eyes swim back into focus.

"It's okay," he says. "Allie? You're okay. It's me. It's Matt."

She stares at his face, fishmouthing for breaths that come painfully hard.

"What—" she rasps, and then she jerks her head, looking right and left, eyes suddenly feral with fear.

"The mad old bastard," she says. "Where . . . ?"

Matt looks round. Walter John is gone.

"Walter bloody John. Where's Walter John?" she says.

He scans the immediate area.

"Forget Walter John," he says, finally addressing the first thing he'd seen missing from the jetty. "Where's my bloody boat?"

His voice sounds raw, and it's because he knows the answer – the what of it, if not the why of it: Kathleen had taken keys to the boat off the key rack in her kitchen, which means she had taken the boat, and with a nasty lurch he realises he doesn't know if the impulse to do so had come from the part of her that had clung on and signed the warning to him or the destructive impulse fighting to control her.

He looks at Allie.

"Is there a first-aid kit in your office?"

He has to half carry, half drag her there, but by the time he's gotten her inside out of the rain she is walking more surely, and her eyes regain more of their normal sharpness as she watches him find a parka and some foul-weather dungarees on the rack where the day workers hang their kit.

"We need to get dry," he says. "Out of the wet clothes."

She nods.

"Towels in the restroom," she says, pointing to the door at the top of the stairs.

He turns away as they strip and dry off, each moving as fast as they can.

"I can't," she says, and he turns to see her standing in padded dungarees that swamp her, trying to adjust the braces one-handed – her right held away from her body as if to protect it.

"Sorry," she says. "I think he broke my finger when he kicked me."

She sounds so matter-of-fact about it that Matt just nods calmly.

"Yeah," he says. "Yeah. Oh, Allie, love, I saw it. Why did he do that . . . ?"

"I think he's gone mad," she says.

"Not mad enough to stick around," he says, as he gently helps her fasten the braces and adjust them.

"Hang on," he says, kneeling at her feet. There was about a foot of extra length on each dungaree leg, so he turns them up as best he can. She looks down at the wound on his head, seeing it clearly for the first time.

"Matt, your head. Jesus."

"Worse than it looks," he says, trying for a smile. "Nah. It's fine. Hold still."

"You're a shit liar," she says. "You need to get that head cleaned up and stitched by the nurse."

He concentrates on turning up the thick cuffs on the dungarees. It's a way of meeting Allie's eyes. And she's right. The side of his head is throbbing like a bastard. Two bastards, in fact.

"Who took your boat?" she says.

"Kathleen," he says.

"Why?"

He finishes adjusting her dungarees and pulls a space blanket from the first-aid kit.

"Wrap yourself in that and I'll see if I can't rustle up a hot drink. We need to get warmth inside you, then let's go see if the new nurse has arrived."

"Why did Kathleen take your boat?" she says.

He grimaces.

"Matty?" she says.

"I don't want to say," he says. "You don't want to know."

"Because you think I'll be scared?" she says.

"No," he says. "No. Because you'll think the dunt on my head knocked all the sense out of me too. You'll think I've gone dafter than Walter John."

"You are daft," she says, finding a grin. "Always have been. One of your most endearing qualities. Why would she take your boat?"

"To protect me. To protect all of us," he says. "Let's go find this new nurse. See if they've got any fancy painkillers."

Chapter 69

Chocolate, no bars

When Magda re-enters the hotel kitchen after a fruitless search of the other rooms, Malc seems to have powered down and is standing looking as vacant as the rest of the building, like he's gone into standby mode. She decides the best way to get him going again is to give him something hot and sweet for shock and so she sets about quickly making mugs of tea. Once she raids the store cupboards and finds the chocolate wafer bars he's looking a bit more lifelike, and they decide to go and sit in the upper lounge, where there's a good view of the ferry terminal and the jetty.

They don't sit once they get there; they stand, looking out of the windows, each aware they're now on guard, acting as lookouts. And after a bit, he begins to tell her what had happened to him since he arrived on the island.

She lets him talk without interruption because he seems to loosen up the more he talks, and that has to be a good thing. If she's going to be holed up here for a while, much better not to be holed up with a nutter, she thinks.

"So your pal Jamie screwed up the phones," she says, staring down at the Telco van below them.

"Yeah," he says, sipping from his mug. "Christ. To think I thought that was the low point of the day . . . "

"And then after the fish fry, nothing happened until you woke up and saw the boats on fire on the jetty?" she says.

He dips his head and lifts his shoulders.

"I'd have missed it if I hadn't heard the banging on the window," he says. "I thought it was him, too pissed to care about waking me up as long as he was getting his end away. And then when I saw it wasn't . . . wasn't him on the shag – wasn't really him at all but was her, trying to do something to Jamie and he wasn't horny, he was shitting himself in terror really, and she was so strong . . . "

He rubs his face violently, like he's trying to scrub the memory away. Then takes a deep breath and lets it out long and slow, staring at the ceiling.

"When I got outside, it was so quiet. Apart from Jamie kind of sobbing. I think it happening without any noise made it worse. I'd seen the shadows of . . . of the flames, I guess, moving on the other side of the curtains before I opened them, but when I got out it was . . . I don't know . . . it was like a war zone, or a painting or something. The three boats on the harbour wall were on fire and there was a sort of drizzle misting down so that the droplets kind of caught the reflection of the flames, and it looked like sparks were showering out of the night instead of raindrops, like you get in a steelworks, you know?"

Magda nods. It seems like a dam has burst inside the man because the words begin to come faster and faster, like he has to share this as fast as he can.

"And then there are all these people moving across that open parking area down there, towards the van, towards the water, and the fires are throwing long shadows behind them as they walk towards the water, which makes it look like

396

there are more people than there are, and for a moment – I mean, I was kind of groggy – but for a moment it looked kinda beautiful even, and maybe it being so quiet and no one talking or shouting or hurrying, just moving slowly, maybe that was why it seemed like that, but I did think, Why aren't they in a hurry? Because they should have been – because of the boats, you see, on fire. Why weren't they trying to put them out? And then I saw half of them at least were in, like, bed clothes, you know? T-shirts and pants and nighties and stuff – and barefoot, a lot of them, too. And I recognised them, faces from the fish fry, the shop and all. And then I saw Jamie being dragged by some woman, and then I saw the first few folk just walk off the edge of the jetty – just walk calmly and drop and disappear into the blackness – and I saw what she wanted to do with him, and I ran down there. And by the time I get there, most have followed them because there's maybe ten folk left shuffling towards the sea, and they've no interest in the fires – it's like the fires are a beacon that's drawn them there, but they don't care about the boats really, just like moths or something, moths on a lightbulb maybe, and they're dropping into the harbour like bloody lemmings, you know? Have you seen lemmings? That's what they're like, and they're dropping, not swimming or bobbing about on the water, they're just gone, wiped clean off the face of the earth—"

He takes a deep breath, and she thinks he's done, but he shakes his head and plunges on.

"And all I can see moving on the water is the orange life-boat drifting away with the plastic on one side ... on the side away from the wind, on fire a bit, you know, the flames blown flat by the wind, and the mooring rope whipping behind it like a sort of fiery snake until it goes out. And then I see there's only about maybe eight or so folk still left on dry land, and of course one's that prick Jamie being dragged by the lassie, who has water pouring out of her mouth like she's got a fucking pump inside her, and there's real panic in his eyes as she tugs him, and his jeans slide off his skinny arse and save him as she birls right over the edge holding on to them and falls into one of the burning boats without a sound except a thump as she hits it. And I manage to grab him, and we fall on the ground and then I'm on top of him and he starts fighting me like what was in her is now in him, thrashing at me – who was trying to save him – like a crazy man, and then of course I saw he was leaking water too, but I got lucky and kicked his knee sideways, think I broke it, and got him in a headlock from behind. I managed to drag him over to the back of the van and throw him in. I didn't know what else to do. Once you're in the back you can't open it from the inside and . . . "

He looks down from the ceiling and meets her eyes.

"And here we are," he says, trying for a smile and fumbling it.

If Magda hadn't seen Jamie in the van she knows she'd have been running for her life to escape this man and his mad story. But she had seen it. He looks up at her. In his own way, he's drowning in the horror of what he's seen. And if he's telling the truth, she doesn't need him going off his head too. She's a practical woman, and that's just a practical reality. There's safety in numbers.

"It's okay," she lies, handing him another chocolate bar. "It's all okay. Have another Tunnocks."

He stares at the little red-and-gold-wrapped brick in her hand.

"Sugar," she says. "It's good for shock."

"It's not," he says.

But he takes it anyway and unwraps the bar.

"Maybe not," she admits. "Maybe it's just good."

He bites off an inch and chews it, looking out through the heavy curtains of rain sweeping across the expanse of tarmac between them and the distant Telco van.

"I looked over the edge after one of the last went over. A woman, youngish, maybe thirty. She just dropped away from me and sank like a stone," he says. "Sea just swallowed her up. White face – pretty face, really – just fell away and faded out of sight as she went down. Her expression was just blank. Like she didn't care, or wasn't there any more. It was horrible. I mean, I was bricking myself by then, and I came back here and tried to get help but there was no one left, and then I ran round the houses and that was no good. I think everyone went into the sea. So I came back here and locked and bolted all the doors and ... well, I just decided to wait. For the ferry ... "

He sits down suddenly, as if he's just relieved himself of a heavy burden and isn't sure what happens next.

" ... the ferry you say won't come."

Magda sits next to him. They both stare out at the sea.

"It might come," she says. "Not due till later. The weather might clear by then."

"This weather isn't clearing," he says, finishing the chocolate bar. "It's getting worse."

She takes her phone out. No bars. He catches her eye.

"I wanted to call my friend Allie, but ... "

He nods.

"I know. Sorry."

Maybe she should drive to Allie and Eck's house. Maybe see if she's at the fish farm. She suddenly really doesn't want to go driving through this storm on her own.

She puts the phone away.

"Bloody Jamie."

Chapter 70

Full house

By the time Sig pulls round the long curve in the road that gives her first sight of her own white gatepost in the distance, she's slowed her pulse back to normal and wrestled her mind securely back into its rational groove. She knows that the reaching fingers and the voice in her head were hallucinations, no doubt caused by nitrogen narcosis. She hadn't thought she'd dived deep enough to trigger it, but then all the commenters on the online freediving forums agree it's a notoriously inexact boundary, and the only proof that matters is that she clearly had become disoriented, lethargic and, above all, subject to both visual and aural delusions. Until today, she'd always felt that any mental boost she got from diving was strictly limited, short and bracing, like a single strong cocktail at the end of a day – enough to re-invigorate the mind and sharpen the senses, not enough to dull the mind. But freedivers often talked about the Martini Effect, claiming that the first ten metres of depth acted like drinking a martini and each subsequent ten metres is like drinking another one, but until this morning's dive she'd always discounted that as something that happened to other people who didn't prepare correctly. She'd been wrong: today there was no question that she'd got herself dangerously drunk way too far underwater for it to be funny, or indeed excusable.

Sig had given herself a very bad fright, probably the fright Matt had been trying and failing to give her for months, and she has to admit that the solitary freediving is probably something she should ease back on. She'd messed up in precisely the way she had sworn she never would. If she and Matt were still friends, she'd tell him he'd been right. She won't give up freediving, because she does really like the bodily control and discipline it takes. But in a happier world, one where she had not burned her bridges, she would probably have asked him to come out with her and act as safety. Since he thinks she was responsible for John's death, that's never going to happen.

There is a pair of ravens sitting on her gate as she pulls past it, but she's so used to the birds that she scarcely notices them until they push off into the air and precede her down the track, landing on her roof and watching her get out of the Land Rover. Rex bounces out and runs around the outside of the house barking up at them, which is something he tends to do when they come too close to the house. It's never clear to her whether he's barking in excitement or outrage, but there is something about the stern old birds that always gets his attention.

She grins at him, enjoying the return to the familiar routines of their day.

"Rex," she says indulgently. "Don't be such a doofus."

She gets to the door and reaches for the handle, but her hand closes on thin air as it's yanked violently inwards to reveal Evie, white faced, with what looks in the glimpse she catches of it to be – impossibly – a baby in her lap. The girl is already spinning her chair in its own length and powering back into the kitchen.

"Sig," she says. "Thank God. Come on—"

"Evie," Sig says. "Wait, slow down, what's happened?"

There's a boy she doesn't recognise sitting on her kitchen floor, leaning up against the kitchen island, back to the sea view, eyes shut, rocking back and forth. He's scratched and bleeding, and he's soaking wet.

"He just came to the door," says Evie. "I thought there'd been an accident out on the road, but I went and couldn't see one and the phones don't work and—"

"Slow down," says Sig, kneeling by the boy.

"He's in shock," says Evie. "I mean, he's in a bad way, really traumatised, but he was protecting the baby. Like protecting her was all he seemed worried about, and then he went like that."

"Her?" says Sig.

"I changed a nappy," says Evie. "So that was a first."

"OK," says Sig, reaching gently for the boy's arm. "You know who he is?"

"No. And he doesn't really speak," says Evie. "Did a lot of moaning at first, poor wee bugger, but I couldn't get a name out of him."

"Must be a visitor," says Sig. "Phone's still not working, you say?"

"Dead as a dodo," says Evie.

"Right. Let's get him into dry clothes and then go to the new nurse," says Sig. "See if he's okay, see if we pass an accident, and then we'll go to the ferry, see if anyone at the hotel or the shop knows where his people are."

"Don't think you'll get him to change," says Evie. "He's been clenched up like a fist since he got in here. Doesn't much like your view either . . . "

She points at the big window and the sea beyond.

"He was fine coming in but then he saw that and went a

bit mental. Dropped down there, sitting against the kitchen island with his back to it, sort of flinching away, like looking at it hurts."

"Maybe it's his eyes. The brightness," says Sig, touching the boy's arm very gently. "Maybe he's had a bang on the head—"

"Hi," she says. "Hi, I'm Sig. What's your name?"

"Good luck with that," says Evie. The baby begins to wail.

"Ruby," says the boy.

"He doesn't look like a Ruby," says Evie.

"He means the baby," says Sig.

The boy closes his eyes again.

"Can you tell me what happened?" says Sig.

He shakes his head so slightly she almost misses the gesture. She looks at Evie.

"Shock," says Evie.

"Okay. We'll get you a blanket and then we're going to get help," says Sig, standing decisively and looking at Evie. "We'll take them to Mhairi."

"Mhairi's gone away on her year," says Evie, "remember?"

The island nurse had taken a well-deserved year off to take some holiday and then do some mainland training to raise her skills to Nurse Practitioner.

"Right, well we'll take them to whoever's the new Mhairi," she says. "They'll check these guys out and we can find out from them if there's been an accident somewhere on the island. I should think their parents are beside themselves."

Getting the boy off the floor and into the Land Rover is easier than she'd feared, largely because about the only thing he seems to care about is the baby, and when Evie wheels backwards towards the door with her, he gets up and follows her.

He accepts the blanket Sig wraps him in and sits behind Sig in the middle seat next to Evie, who gives him the baby to hold as they drive. It seems to calm him. Rex sits on the other side of him, also watching the baby.

"Keep your eyes peeled," says Sig quietly. "For, you know—"

"Yeah," says Evie. "He might have walked a long way."

The pair of them scan the roadside as they drive, looking for any signs of a crashed vehicle. The boy remains hunched over the baby, and the only sounds are the hiss of the car's wheels on the soaked roadway and the thump-squeak-thump of the windscreen wipers doggedly trying to keep up with the ever-increasing volume of rain now hurling down on them.

"Sig," says Evie after a while, "none of the houses we've passed have the lights on."

"They're at the Modh," says Sig. "Stop with the imagination."

"Just saying," says Evie.

"Would have thought all this was quite enough excitement for one day," says Sig, nodding back at the boy and the baby.

"Not excited, Sig," says Evie. "I'm worried."

"Sorry," says Sig. "I'm crabby. Did something stupid this morning. Then all this . . . "

They speed past another collection of houses. Evie wipes the condensation off the side window and squints at them.

"That's the third house we've passed with the front door open," says Evie. "I mean, that's weird, right? And the last two were the Macleans' and the Innes's houses. They haven't gone to the Modh."

"So what are you saying?" says Sig. "You think everyone's hiding?"

"Not with the doors open, no," says Evie.

"So what? They've been abducted?" Sig laughs shortly and shakes her head. "You think aliens came down and took them?"

"I think we haven't passed any cars on the road," says Evie.

"It's raining stair rods," says Sig. "No one would be out in this if they didn't have to be. Besides," she points to distant red brake lights and a familiar vehicle pulled up in front of a house in the dip ahead of them, "look. It's Matt. At the Bothy. Probably saying hi to the new nurse's family."

Evie leans back. The boy opens his eyes and peers ahead through the windscreen at the approaching house, eyes widening.

"Okay," Evie says. "OK. Maybe I was getting a bit over-dramatic. Sorry."

"No worries," says Sig. "It's going to be fine."

Tom begins to scream.

Chapter 71

Empty house

The storm is pelting the roof of Matt's car with what sounds like gravel as they drive through a heavy squall. Allie is leaning against the passenger door, hunched in on herself, trying to keep warm. She's processing what Matt has told her and trying to make it add up. From her expression and her body language, he can see it's a struggle she isn't necessarily winning.

"You really think Kathleen took your boat out to sea . . . to protect you?" she says.

"To protect everyone," says Matt, turning to look at her again, before returning his attention to the rain-lashed road unwinding slowly ahead of them. He shrugs.

"I know. Told you you'd think I'm mad."

She watches the beaded drops streaming diagonally across the side window.

"I think she may have had an . . . episode," she says. "Some kind of psychotic incident. Like Walter John did."

"It wasn't a psychotic episode," he says, trying not to replay the scene from last night's horror show, the one starring the thing that both was and – most disturbingly – was not his beloved grandmother.

"I told you: she was, there was . . . something in her, and it wasn't a good thing, and she was fighting it as hard as she knew how. Like she was trying to be in charge of her own body."

"You ever see anyone else in the grip of a psychotic thingy?" Allie says.

"No," he says. "You?"

"No," she admits. "So we don't know enough to know that what you're describing isn't actually a big fucking example of one—"

Allie brings herself up short. She isn't normally a big swearer.

"Sorry," she says.

"I saw what I saw," Matt says. "Allie, I was there. It was horrible and it was unnatural, and it scared the living shit out of me. I ran like a bastard, because I knew that whatever she was fighting was going to kill me if she let it. Or worse."

"Or worse?" she says.

"Yep," he says, slowing for a gaggle of sheep that had decided to weather the storm by lying down in a clump that spilled over the road in the lee of a big boulder. "She was covered in water. It was coming out of her eyes and mouth, like it was never going to stop. More water than a person could have inside them. It's impossible. But I saw it."

"Maybe you had an episode," she says, pointing at the wound on the side of his head. "And you've taken a big old dunt to the head and all. I mean, don't take it bad, but that is possible, right? And it's way more likely than some weird supernatural explanation."

"All in my mind?" he says.

"No," she says. "I mean, not like you're lying or making it up, just . . . I mean I'm sure you *think* you saw what you saw, but . . ."

Matt stops the truck and looks at her.

"Allie," he says. "You think I was having a psychotic episode too? And Gran? And Walter John? How likely is it that three people have them at the same time? Come on!"

She looks at him.

"What?" he says.

"Come on, Matty," she says. "Keep driving. You need to get that head stitched by the nurse."

He chunks back into gear and pulls away.

"If you imagined Kathleen's behaviour – I mean, if you had an episode and believed she did something – it's not necessary that she did do it, is it? Not if you went . . . a bit odd?" she says very carefully.

"She did it," he says.

"OK," she says.

"Am I being odd now?" he says.

"No," she says. "You saved me, Matty. But it's a rational explanation. And the simplest explanation is usually the most likely."

"Yeah," he says, sounding entirely unconvinced as he slows and turns into the driveway of the Bothy and stops his pick-up next to an unfamiliar estate car. "Sounds very rational. But rational's not the right way to describe a world as warped and twisted as the one I saw last night."

"That doesn't make sense," she says.

"I know," he says, getting out into the rain. "And for what it's worth, I'm still scared shitless by that."

She watches him jog round the front of the vehicle and lets him open her door and help her out, and then they both hurry through the rain and into the house.

They shelter under the meagre protection of the porch as he knocks on the open door.

"Hello?" he shouts. "Anyone home? The door was open . . ."

There is no reply from within, so they look at each other, shrug and enter. They stand on the bare boards of the hallway, dripping and listening.

"Hello?" Allie calls.

"You know what they're called?" Matt says quietly.

She shakes her head.

He walks down the hall and knocks on the kitchen door before opening it.

"Nope," he says, backing out. She walks ahead of him into the drawing room.

"Okay," she says slowly.

"Not really," he says, taking in the mess strewn across the room: the upturned chairs, the broken coffee table, the blanket crumpled on the floor, the smashed crockery.

"This doesn't look good," she says quietly.

"Maybe they're just messy?" he says, backing out into the hall and looking up the stairs.

"I think they just moved in yesterday," says Allie, following him.

"Hello?" he shouts up the stairs.

There is no reply. He looks at her. She nods.

They climb the stairs slowly.

"Someone's left a window open," Matt says.

"Yes," she says.

He calls out again on the landing, and then they quickly check out the bedrooms and the bathroom.

"Marie Celeste," he says.

Allie stands on the landing and has such a bad feeling it almost stops her breathing. She wishes her Eck was with her. She has a worse pang at the thought that she is never going to see him again. She knows that's probably just her coming down off the adrenaline and takes a deep breath to get a grip on herself.

"Where have they gone?" she says. "There's a baby cot in that room, the one with the window open. They wouldn't be outside with a baby in this weather."

"Maybe they went to the shop?" he says.

"Car's still here," she says.

"Maybe they have two cars," he says.

"Maybe," she says, shaking her head. "Feels like something happened."

"Feels?" he says, raising an eyebrow. "Now you're doing 'feels'?"

"There's plenty of evidence for that to be a rational response," she says. "You saying I'm wrong?"

"No," he says. "I'm saying welcome to *my* world."

There's a crunch of gravel from outside.

Allie relaxes.

"Okay," she says. "Want to bet that's them coming back?"

They hear a car door open and close.

And then they hear the scream.

Chapter 72

You can never go home

The man who has almost forgotten his name is Walter John also can't quite think why he's here, in the middle of the island, knee-deep in a bog and surrounded by rain-lashed heather. His head is pounding and his mouth is so dry that his tongue is glued to the roof of his mouth. He tries to open his mouth and discovers his lips are stuck together. He stretches wider and feels their chapped surfaces crack as he pulls them apart.

How can he feel so parched inside when he is so wet on the outside? (It doesn't make sense.) He knows it doesn't make sense. (Being in this bog is what doesn't make sense.)

He notices he is hearing the voices in his head again, and feels a kind of unexpected relief, almost as if he has found something he'd forgotten he had lost. Which is stupid, because how could you lose the way you think? (Through the hole in your head.) There is no hole in his head. (There is.)

"No."

His voice sounds thick and gummy as he rebels against himself. He staggers out of the bog and drops to his knees, breathing hard.

It's the worst hangover he's ever had. That ache at the base of his skull is getting substantially worse, and he's so thirsty that he seriously considers drinking the peat-brown water from the bog, lapping like an animal at a waterhole. Maybe if he hadn't seen the tangle of weathered sheep bones on the other side, he would have done it.

He shudders to his feet and tries to get his bearings. He reckons he should head back to the road by walking away from the small hill on the other side of the bog, and he stumbles into motion. He walks with his head tilted back, mouth open to the sky, enjoying the rain falling directly on to his tongue as he goes. One of the voices in his head tells him he must look stupid. Like a daftie. But no one is looking, so who cares?

He does. He needs to get home. Get a warm shower. Drink some water. And a lot of coffee. He must have been blackout drunk. It's happened once before, when he was much, much younger, and it's the only thing that could explain the blank in his memory. But back then – on his stag night, in fact – he had woken knowing he'd been drinking. He could remember how the night began, the pub, the few friends gathered, the pints and the shorts. That blank in his memories was a one-off, anchored in space and time; it had a beginning and an end, which started when he woke up. This is different because he can't remember drinking too much. He'd been at the fish fry, yes, but he'd drunk modestly. Always modest, these days; always quiet and well behaved. A looker, not a doer.

Walter John trips out of the heather's edge and jolts untidily on to the narrow ribbon of metalled road. He scowls at the added pain this brings to his head and looks around to see if there's a car coming. Maybe he can get a lift. He's cold and soaked to the skin. But there's no one in sight, and only a trio of scabby sheep looking at him from the other verge.

He tells them to go to hell and pulls his dripping shirt tight around his shivering frame as he begins the long walk back to his house. He walks lopsided. His right foot hurts. Feels like he stubbed his toes badly, or maybe kicked something by mistake. (How much did he drink?) He can't remember. He can't remember drinking anything at all. He doesn't quite remember where his house is.

His teeth are tightly clenched once he finally makes it to the house door thirty minutes later – partly in anger at himself for getting himself into this state, partly to stop them chattering together at the cold that he now feels to his core. He stumbles in and bounces off the walls on the way to the bathroom, moving with such determination that he doesn't remember to close the door behind him. He can feel the marvellous heat from the radiator as he passes it, and he stops for a moment to rest his hand on it. Thank God. He made it. It's going to be okay. He peels off his shirt as he walks on. He barges into the bathroom and turns the shower that hangs over the bathtub on. He bends over the sink to drink directly from the tap. He chugs cool water until he can take no more, and belches uncomfortably as he stands up to unbuckle his corduroys. His legs are blue with cold and he should have taken his shoes off first because now he's hobbled, but that cold water sloshing around inside him was not a good idea, so he levers himself awkwardly into the bath before trying to take them off and then forgets and stands in the merciful stream of hot water, shirt still on, hands braced on the tiles, head bowed in gratitude at the warmth cascading over his cold body.

He stands there for ten minutes, scarcely moving. He's not even really thinking. He's just watching the water sheet down his legs and pool in the wrinkles of heavy corduroy round his ankles until the water level rises and drowns them. Then the hot water begins to run cooler and he turns it off before it gets cold. Walter John hears himself say, "Gosh", and then bends to untangle his trousers from his boots, untying the laces with some difficulty. He kicks them out of the bath and turns the water on again. Half a minute of lukewarm water gives way to cold and he gives up, staring vacantly round the steam-filled bathroom.

The back of his head still feels like the pressure inside has popped a couple of rivets and the whole thing might just blow clean off at any minute. He tries not to move it too much.

He hears himself say, "Gosh" again. He must really have been dicing with hypothermia.

His brow crinkles and he shakes his head, forgetting it's going to hurt. It throbs nastily, but he does it again. Nothing makes sense.

Maybe he has a fever. (It's not a fever.) Maybe it is. (Maybe. But it's not.)

He's so cold again. The bath isn't helping. And he's hearing the dark chasm inside him again. He sits down in the water, still half-clothed. Tells himself to shut up. Looks across the bathroom and sees himself in the mirror. His mouth twists.

"Please."

He doesn't know why he's scared, but he is. (Terrified.) Maybe he should take his temperature or something. (No. He should get dry and warm himself.) No harm in taking his temperature too. (There might be.) Where's he going to find a thermometer. This isn't his house. (Is he going to get in trouble for being here?)

He sinks deeper into the bathwater.

"I'm okay," he tells himself.

(No.)

"I'm ..." Walter John knows he wants to finish the sentence, but it gets away from him.

(I'm what?)

" . . . me?" he says, staring across the room at a face that is his, but which is now sheeted with so much water flowing from his eyes and nose and trickling out of the sides of his mouth as to make it something else entirely. "I'm me."

And he is. For one moment more, he is, and what remains of Walter John thinks he is crying even though he can't see his tears – he will never be able to see his tears again because they will be lost in the other wetness. For a moment, just for a moment, he remembers spilling clean water on to the book on Sig's table. Such a strange thing to remember at a time like th—

And then he convulses and spews dark water into the bath, and then he hears a sound he has heard once before – a small sound, tiny and terminal, the ghost sound of the thinnest of membranes tearing a last small hole in itself, maybe a hole pricked by the jag of anger behind his nose – and then he falls through the abyssal darkness behind the hole and he's gone.

And all that remains to look back at him from the flickering eyes in the face in the mirror is a blank, banked-up fury that seems to be making his reflection flicker and judder as if he's suddenly out of phase with the world itself. And then he jerks away from the mirror as he slides beneath the brimming bathwater. And everything is still and silent for more than an hour, except for the water gently overflowing and spattering on the linoleum floor.

Chapter 73

Least said

In the Defender, the screaming has stopped, and Tom is now gently rocking backward and forward, shaking his head, while Evie is rubbing his back in slow circles, trying to calm him with one hand while holding the baby with the other. She watches Sig return from the house. She has a bag of nappies swinging from one hand and a can of baby formula in the other. She opens the door and puts them on the seat beside Evie.

"What?" says Evie.

She keeps her hand moving, soothing Tom, feeling the tension in his back as she listens to Sig explain that Matt and Allie are inside, and that she's going to go back in and help them get fixed up in the dispensary since the nurse is not there and there's been an "incident" at the fish farm. She raises her eyebrows as she says "incident", nodding at Tom. Evie gets that whatever the "incident" is, it's not something the shocked boy needs to know about, in case it makes him worse.

Sig then gently puts her hand on Tom's shoulder.

"Hey . . . is this your house?" she says.

Tom doesn't react.

"Did something happen here?" she says. "It's okay. We're

here with you. It's safe. But is this your house? Did you just arrive on the island?"

Tom might as well be deaf for all the reaction he gives. Evie looks a question at Sig over his head. Sig nods at the bag of nappies.

"There's a travelling baby cot in there and . . ."

She shakes her head.

"And?" says Evie.

"It's a mess inside," says Sig quietly. "Like there was a fight or something."

Tom looks out of the window, away from the house. Like the last thing he wants to do is be part of this conversation.

"What are we going to do?" says Evie.

"You're going to stay here for a couple of minutes, maybe change that nappy," says Sig.

"Lucky me," says Evie.

"I'm going to go back and patch up Matt's head. He and Allie have had a bit of a morning. Keep the doors locked."

Evie's eyes widen.

"What do you mean, keep the doors locked?"

Sig scowls and watches Rex running round the house, nose to the ground like he's on the trail of a rat.

"Walter John," she says. "You know Walter John? He attacked Allie. We don't know where he's got to. So keep the door locked and hit the horn if you see him."

"Sig," says Evie, her eyes flicking to Tom and the baby. "You think he . . . you know. Attacked them, in there?"

Sig shrugs.

"No idea."

"Not a good day, is it?" says Evie.

"Not so far," says Sig. "I'll be back as soon as I can."

"Wait," Evie says. "You don't think—"

"No," says Sig. "Not more of this Evie. I've got Matt in

there with a bad bang on his head, and he's spouting some weird story about Kathleen that's clearly delusional, and right now I only have the bandwidth to deal with the real-world problems, not the fantasy ones, okay? Thinking like that it's just . . . squid ink: you squirt dark stuff all over the place and things just get harder to see and deal with."

"Just saying. It feels really unlucky," says Evie.

"You read too much," says Sig, exhaling in frustration. "Curses aren't a thing."

"Right," says Evie. "And there's no such thing as ghosts."

"Only in books and comics," says Sig. "I've got to go."

"Thing is, Sig," says Evie, "you cut me off before I could finish what I was going to say. I didn't say anything about the curse."

Sig falters for a moment.

"I'm sure you did."

"Nope," says Evie. "I thought it, but didn't say it, because I knew what you'd say. So you're the one thinks it's the curse."

"That's rubbish," snaps Sig. "And Walter John is not a curse, he's an old guy who's gone senile. Lock the doors."

The raven perched on the roof watches Rex circle the house as Sig goes back inside. Part of its mind is hoping the dog finds the rabbit that has gone to ground beneath the propane tank. The terrier kills every rabbit it can find, on principle, but it leaves the bodies for the carrion birds. Another part of its mind wonders if its mate is seeing the same things it has seen today as it patrols the other side of the island, the disturbance in the normal pattern of things. It sees the girl in the Defender moving around, but she doesn't look up or see that she is being watched. The raven is old enough to remember when people would have looked up and taken note of who watched them. And why.

*

In the house beneath the raven's current perch, Allie watches Sig strapping her pinkie finger to the one next to it.

"That feels better," she says, wincing. "No, really. I think it was just staved. I don't think it's broken or dislocated."

She makes a fist, gingerly at first, then again with more confidence. The two fingers stay straight, but she grins.

"That's super," she says. "I could totally hold a steering wheel. I was worried I was going to be stuck needing lifts everywhere."

"I can't tell if anything's broken," Sig says. "We still need to find the nurse. I'm going to patch Matt's head up."

He sits stiffly as she pulls supplies from the medicine cabinet and lines them up on the nurse's table.

"This is ugly," she says, looking closely at the wound. "It's going to hurt when I clean it."

"Try not to enjoy it too much, then," says Matt. "Just get on with it."

"I'll do my best and Steri-Strip it for now," she says, soaking a cotton wool pad in disinfectant. "But it needs proper stitches."

"Sig," he says, wincing as she starts cleaning the wound, reaching up and catching her wrist. "I wasn't lying about Kathleen."

She looks at Allie.

"I don't think you're lying," she says carefully.

"But—" he says.

"But I think Allie's right. I think maybe you had an episode. I don't know."

"Forget it," he says, pushing her away.

"Matt," she says, standing there with Betadine dripping on to the floor from the cotton wool swab in her hand.

"No," he says, voice choked and angry. "Just because it doesn't make sense doesn't mean it isn't true."

"Let me do this," she says, reaching for his head. He shakes it and moves out of reach.

"Just stick a big plaster on it and we'll go find this bloody nurse," he says.

Sig grips his chin, steadying his head. She can feel the tension as he holds himself rigid, really wanting to rip free.

"That really needs to be taken care of, Matt," Allie says.

Sig keeps a grip until she feels the resistance in Matt's head ease a fraction. She nods. The look in both their eyes says, truce, not peace. She carefully finishes cleaning up and then starts applying the Steri-Strips, repositioning the flap of skin as best as she can. He growls and grinds his teeth, not wanting to cry out.

"Everything doesn't have to be a fight, Matt," she says quietly, as she smooths a waterproof dressing over the whole area.

He stands the moment she steps back to look at her handiwork.

"Apparently it does," he says.

"Matt—" she says.

He looks at Allie.

"You want to ride with Sig, that's fine with me," he says, and walks out.

Chapter 74

Not the time

Matt sits in his truck, listening to the rain beating on the roof of the cab. His eyes are closed. He's just going to sit here holding on to the steering wheel and keep doing the breathing exercises he picked up from an online yoga class to calm himself until Sig and Allie get in the Land Rover and unblock him.

He hears the front door of the house shut and then feet crunch up and past. He feels the cold blast of weather as the passenger door opens, and he senses Allie get in. The door clunks shut.

He exhales, still gripping the steering wheel.

"Sorry," he says. "It wasn't you. It's me and her. Too much bad blood."

She says nothing. He feels the question in it anyway.

"She did a thing," he says. "I can't, I don't seem to be able to forgive her—"

"What makes you think she forgives herself?" Sig replies.

His eyes snap open and he turns to see her sitting there looking out of the window.

"I thought you were Allie," he says.

"No," she says. "She's going to drive the Defender."

"Why?" he says.

"Because I think you've had a really bad whack on your head and I'm going to keep an eye on you in case you start getting crazier than normal," she says.

"It happened," he says, his mouth feeling dry and sticky. He licks his lips and swallows. "With Kathleen. It happened like I said it did."

She turns and meets his eyes.

"Supernatural shit is just that, Matt: shit. It's all ... woo and it's all not real—"

He opens his mouth, but she shakes her head and talks right over him, so he starts the truck and waits for Allie to pull out and make way.

"—doesn't mean something bad isn't happening. But it's not evil spirits or ghosts or the wee folk or aliens or zombies. If you've been keeping up with what's going on in the world, you'll have noticed people are perfectly good enough at finding new and unpleasant ways to abuse each other in real life – we don't need to believe in old made-up shit to torture ourselves even more."

Matt swings out on to the road and follows the Land Rover towards the harbour. There it is, he thinks: her intolerable certainty about everything.

"You don't have to watch me," he says.

"Actually, I do," she says. "You took a blow to the head powerful enough to half-scalp you. You could seem fine and dandy, and then just drop. So you're going to tell me if you start getting headaches or blurred vision."

"Do I sound like I've got brain damage," he says.

"Not more than usual, no," she replies.

"So," he says. "You could have gone with Allie."

"But just because you sound okay doesn't mean you might

not have a brain bleed," she says. "Subdural haematoma. It's called Talk and Die Syndrome."

He lets that one hang there for a long beat, concentrating on keeping the truck steady as it ploughs through a deep puddle at the bottom of a dip, sending wings of water spraying out on either side.

"You've got a really shit bedside manner," he says.

"I do," she says. "But I'm what you've got, until we find the nurse."

"We don't even like each other any more, Sig," he says. "I'm definitely not your responsibility."

"I'm not doing it for you," she says.

The pick-up shudders as it pulls clear of the water and powers up the slope ahead.

"Right," he says. "I thought you didn't believe in ghosts."

"It's not about John either," she says. "I don't want to fight. Let's just find the nurse and see if the phones work in the hotel and call the police on the mainland."

They crest the next rise and see the distant harbour and the scrabble of buildings around it spread out below them.

"He loved you, Sig. He didn't blame you for the miscarriage," he says. "He was pissed at you for a bit about doing the test without talking him through it, but he got over it—"

"We've got a storm, a violent man on the loose and a couple of kids who need to find their parents. You've got a really nasty head injury and Allic's been attacked," she says. "I don't think this is the time to finally have this conversation."

"I don't remember my life without him in it," Matt says. "More like brothers than cousins. You know that. I knew him as well as you. You didn't drive him away."

"Matt," Sig says, "really. Let's not do family therapy now."

He chunks out a bitter half-laugh.

"I'm fresh out of family, Sig."

"You've got Kathleen."

"Gran's gone," he says.

There's something in the way he says it that makes the words land with more than just their normal weight. There's a finality to it that compels her to take her eyes off the road and stare at him.

"How do you know?" she says.

"I just do," he says, looking away.

"Matt," she says.

He takes a deep breath.

"She thought there was something evil inside her and tried to warn me away from it. From her," he says.

"Evil?" she says, punching his arm and making him look at her. "What kind of evil? Matt. It doesn't make sense . . . "

"I know," he says. "But she protected me, and now she's protected the whole island by taking the boat out to sea."

"We must call the coastguard!" she says urgently.

Matt shakes his head. He's suddenly even more tired.

"Sig. Can't call anyone if the phones are down."

"But she's too old to be out there. She—"

"She's dead," he says. It hurts saying it out loud. It rips something loose inside him and whatever it is now feels lodged behind his breastbone, like a bubble he can't swallow. "She took herself and whatever's inside her where it could do no harm. She wrapped herself in the lead line and took it over the side with the stern anchor. She wanted to make sure she stayed down."

"You can't know that!" she says, wishing she wasn't convinced by the certainty in his voice.

"I know," he says and he's crying as he says it and he doesn't care enough to hide it or even wipe the tears away. He finds a smile and taps his head. "But I saw it. She was

424

okay. She smiled. Maybe she knew I'd see it. See her. It was her goodbye."

Sig stares at the road ahead.

"You always said you didn't have the sight," she says. "Said it was old wives' tales. You always joked about it. We joked about it and how the others were nutty for believing in stuff like that . . . "

"I know," he says.

"So you're saying you've got it now?" she says. "Christ, Matt, how hard did you hit your head?"

He looks at her sharply, as if the question's a betrayal.

"It's always been a feeling. This was different."

"Okay," she says carefully.

"Not really," he says. "It's a bit shit, actually. It was Kathleen who held the sight. And apart from seeing her like I was there, that's how I know she's gone."

"Because . . . ?" she says.

"Because she's not using it any more," he says, feeling that unswallowable thing behind his breastbone again.

She shakes her head.

"You're saying she passed on her 'gift'?" she says carefully.

"Not a gift," he says. "It's a life sentence."

"You know this is nuts?" she says.

"Yeah," Matt sighs. "Again. Doesn't mean it's not real."

There's a loaded pause as the harbour comes into sight and he slows the vehicle.

"Yes it does," she says. "Sorry. But it does."

He pulls up next door to the Defender, which has parked outside the shop. Allie winds down the side window. Sig does the same.

"Looks deserted," she says.

Allie nods. Sig turns to Matt.

"You go to the hotel, see if they know where this nurse has

got to. I'll go and see why Mary-Kate's left the shop open. She'll know where the guy is if anyone does. Okay?"

Matt stares at her. Then he just shrugs, nods, and opens his door and sets off up the hill towards the hotel at a jog. She watches him go, then gets out of her side of the truck.

"Okay?" says Evie.

"Not even close," says Sig, climbing the steps to the shop.

The door is open, but the lights aren't on. She pushes in and looks around the unlit shelves. It's clean and orderly as always, but there's no movement that she can see. She flicks the light-switches and waits as the neon tubes in the overheads hum for a moment and then punch into life.

"Mary-Kate?" she says. "Hello?"

The door to the storeroom at the back is ajar, and so she pushes further on into the darkness beyond it.

Outside, the rain lightens and Allie lets herself out of the Defender. She pauses and cocks her head. Tom and Evie look at her.

"What?" says Evie.

"You hear that?" says Allie.

"No," says Evie.

"There's a banging coming from . . . I think it's coming from that van," says Allie. "There. I think someone's shouting."

"Wait for the others," says Evie.

"I'm just going to see," says Allie. "I'll be fine."

Chapter 75

Over the edge

Matt stands dripping rainwater off his jacket on to the patterned carpet in the upper lounge of the hotel, overlooking the jetty. Magda and Malc stare at him.

"Your grandmother?" says Magda. "But she's lovely—"

"She's something else now," says Matt. "Jesus. You've no idea what a relief it is to talk to someone who doesn't think I'm a nutter."

"Where's she going?" says Malc.

They follow the direction of his gaze and see Allie walking round the Telco van in the distance.

"No," he says. "No, fuck no, not again, she shouldn't be doing that!"

He bangs the window and then runs from the room.

"Oh shit," says Magda, and takes over banging on the window, which is a big sheet of double-glazed glass.

"What's happening?" says Matt.

"She's trying to open the bloody van!" says Magda. "Jesus!"

"What?" says Matt.

*

The rain's picked up again, but Allie doesn't notice. She's got her ear pressed against the back door of the van.

"It's okay!" she shouts. "I can't hear what you're saying, but it's okay. I'll get you out!"

The noise inside changes from a moaning to a scrabbling against the thin skin of metal that separates them.

"Hang on," she says, reaching for the screwdriver in the hasp. "Nearly there!"

Evie and Tom see Malc burst out of the hotel and careen down the slope towards them, his yellow hi-viz jacket flapping in the slipstream as he passes.

"What's his problem?" says Evie.

Allie pockets the screwdriver from the hasp and unlatches it, then she yanks at the door handle. The doors are locked.

"Hang on!" she shouts. "They're still—"

Whoever is inside kicks them – hard. The metal doors buckle but hold. A second kick – harder – breaks the lock with a sharp crack and bursts them wide with such force that Allie is knocked over, sprawling untidily backwards on to the wet tarmac.

Jamie staggers to the lip of the van and gurgles something between a wet scream and a shout of rage as he glares down with streaming, water-filled eyes. He looks like a drowned man. His hands claw towards her as if they have a life of their own.

Two things seem to happen at once.

He leaps.

And a blur in a hi-viz jacket flies in from the edge of her vision and tackles him in mid-air, knocking him sideways.

They both hit the puddled ground in a thumping impact that sends up a wall of spray as they start to wrestle untidily with each other, clawing and tugging as they roll towards the edge of the jetty.

Allie staggers to her feet and sees the older, bearded man wrench himself free of her attacker, who seems to flicker somehow, as if the water he's sheeted in is reflecting a distant lightning storm she can't see. Then the attacker stands and pauses and swivels his head towards her, and she is suddenly frozen in terror.

And then the man in the hi-viz steps in and kicks him squarely in the chest, and the drowned man flies backwards off the edge of the jetty and drops into the sea beyond, sending up a splash like a depth charge.

"And good riddance, you stupid bastard!" shouts hi-viz, pumped with adrenaline. He steps to the edge. "You stupid, stupid—"

Hands, not the attacker's – two or three other people's hands – come up over the edge of the jetty and grab his ankles and brutally yank his feet out from under him. It happens too fast for him to protect himself, and he falls straight backwards like a tall tree going down. The back of his head smacks the stone top of the jetty with a sickening finality, and then the many hands scrabble on his trouser legs and drag the body towards the edge. Allie is too shocked to think straight, but she sees her rescuer about to be dragged over and stumbles forward, grabbing his shoulders, trying to pull him back, but gravity and the people pulling him are too strong. By the time the thought "What people?" has formed in her head, she's regretting her impulse because she's scared at a deeper level than she knew existed and this makes no sense and he's more than halfway over and she's in danger of being dragged under with him. And then a head appears over the edge as one of the attackers reaches up and grabs his belt for a better purchase, and Allie says:

"Mary-Kate?"

The familiar and unfamiliar face looks at her, and Allie can see the redness of the rosacea still pulsing below the wet skin. Mary-Kate's teeth flash whitely as she roars and yanks herself forward by the belt and grabs Allie's hair. She screams, and that seems to pause the world for one gut-churning beat of echoing silence – and then there's a sudden, terrible lurching forward momentum as the three bodies slide abruptly back over the edge, slick as otters. Allie is too shocked and too horribly falling to take a breath as the freezing water below slams up to smack her in the face. And then other hands are grabbing her, and something seems to latch on to her mouth and she drops away from the world in a thrashing maelstrom of bubbles as she is pulled deeper and deeper into the cold, waiting depths.

Sig comes out of the shop at speed, drawn by the screaming, and sees Matt running past her towards the threshing bodies on the edge of the jetty. Rex barrels out from behind her, nearly knocking her over as he arrows on a converging course across the sloping expanse of tarmac, overtaking Matt and arriving just as the bodies slide over the edge with a terrifying finality.

Matt catches up with the dog and they both stand on the edge, looking down. All Sig can hear is the rain and the uneven slap of her boots as she sprint-hobbles towards them.

"What are you waiting for?" she shouts. "Get her out of the water!"

Matt steps back, white faced, and tackles her, pushing her backwards.

"No," he says. "No. Sig, we've got to go."

"What?" says Sig. "I'll do it!"

He shoves her backwards.

430

"No! She's gone. They're down there. Under the water," Matt says, trying to keep the shake out of his voice. "Looking at us."

Sig wrenches out of his grasp to push past him and peers over the edge. She doesn't move. Now all she can hear is the rain hissing on the sea below and Rex's deep warning growl getting louder and louder.

"See?" says Matt. "Sig, we really have to go!"

She can't believe her eyes, but she can't tear them away.

It's like she's been gut-punched, sideswiped by a planetary force that has sent her whole rational world lurching off-axis, uncoupling itself from anything she recognises as real.

What she is seeing makes her woozy and deeply unsteady, like her feet suddenly can't trust the familiar ground beneath them.

The distant white faces staring up at her from deep below the surface are so impossible and yet so horrifically familiar to her that one part of her wants to throw up while another feels the siren pull of a rising vertigo that would make it so easy just to let go and drop into the beckoning water. She feels sickeningly unmoored, with no purchase on a tilting world she, until this very moment, had thought was tethered and ordered. Then, something nips her sharply in the calf and grabs the bottom of her Levis and yanks, hard. Wrenching her away from the sea. She looks down. Rex is pulling her clear of the edge, backing up in a series of powerful tugs.

"Okay," she says. "Yes, yes, good dog. Let's go!"

"We need to get away from the jetty," shouts Matt, running beside her as they sprint for the vehicles.

She smacks into the driving seat of the Defender and starts the engine, waits a beat for Rex to leap in after her, then slams the door and swerves backwards at an angle that sends Evie and Tom bouncing to one side of the cab. She peels out, heading away from the harbour for the higher ground behind the village. She checks her rear-view and sees Matt start to follow her, but then he hits the brakes and jinks his truck sideways up the approach to the hotel.

"Hell's he doing?" she says.

Evie is looking back, white faced.

"What happened there?" she says. "Sig. Are they dead?"

"Yes," says Sig tightly.

"Just 'yes'?" says Evie. "What the hell's going on?"

Sig slews to a halt in the passing place overlooking the harbour half a mile below. She sits there, breathing hard, staring at her hands on the wheel.

"You're asking the wrong person," she says. "What the hell is Matt playing at?"

For a long beat, there is no sign of any movement below. Sig holds her breath and listens to her heart thumping – and then Matt's truck punches backwards out of the hotel turn-off, skids to an untidy halt and then guns the motor towards them. Sig exhales and sucks in a deep lungful of air.

"He picked someone up," says Evie, watching the pick-up barrel up the hill towards them.

"It's the Polish girl," says Sig.

"Magda," says Evie. "He went back for her."

Matt hits the brakes and slides to a halt, level with Sig. He's breathing hard like she is.

"Christ," he says.

"Yep," says Sig. She looks at her white knuckles and realises she's got her hands clenched too tight on the steering wheel. She's holding on because she still feels she might fall off this newly tilting world. She tells herself to relax and think calmly, but even as she makes herself let go of the wheel she feels like she's watching somebody else's hands from a distance. She closes her eyes.

432

BREATHE.

The voice in her head she uses to keep calm when free-diving feels strangely comforting, and instinctively she takes a moment to get herself more centred. And, just like when diving, she knows panic is the worst thing she can do right now.

"I guess that explains where everyone is," she says, opening her eyes again.

"No shit," says Matt.

She looks at her watch.

"What?" he says.

"Ferry is due in half an hour," she says.

Magda leans across Matt.

"Malc, the Telco guy, said all the phones are screwed. We were waiting to get on the ferry when it gets here and call for help."

"You really think the ferry will run today?" Matt says, gesturing at the weather.

"Maybe," Sig says.

"Maybe not," he says. "Weather like this, wind coming from the north this heavy, tide low at this time of year, they'll likely scratch the sailing as not."

"Damn," says Magda.

"Exactly," he says.

"We should wait here until we're sure," says Sig.

"And if it doesn't come?" he says.

"It'll come," says Magda. "Malc was sure they'd come."

"He's a phone engineer, not a sailor," says Matt. "Was, I mean. Christ ... "

"We'll wait," says Sig.

"And if they do scratch the sailing?" says Matt.

"Well, I don't think we should hang around here for-ever," says Sig.

"You think they're going to come out of the water and attack us?" Matt says.

"They?" says Evie. "Sig, who are they?"

"If the ferry doesn't come, we need to know how many of us are still here," Sig says. Making rational choices seems a good way of building a ladder back to normal. "I think we need to find out who's left on the island."

"You want to check all the houses?" Matt says.

"You'd think someone on the island would have a gun," says Magda.

They stare at her.

"Come on," she says. "You know how this goes: zombies, shotgun, chainsaw, axe?"

Matt looks over his shoulder at the back seats in his cab.

"Got my bait shovel," he says.

"Bait shovel?" says Magda. "Oh well, we've got nothing to worry about."

"Sig," says Evie. "Sig! Seriously, you need to fill some of us in here."

Sig looks at Matt. He shrugs.

"Tell her."

"Drowned people, Evie," Sig says. "It's like . . . people we know, waiting under the water. They pulled Allie and the Telco man in."

"His name was Malc," says Magda.

Evie looks at Sig, then at Tom, who has his eyes closed but has his hands in Rex's fur, like he's holding on to a security blanket.

"So," she says quietly to Sig. "Walking water. The Well's Vengeance. Oath-breakers. It wasn't all squid ink."

"No," says Sig. She still feels like she might throw up at any moment. The thought of swearing to Evie's grandparents that she would keep her safe. "I wish it was."

"But that's ... " Evie begins and then stops. "What do we do?"

"Wait," says Matt, pulling binoculars from his glove-box and aiming them at the grey sea on the far side of the breakwater.

"And pray."

Part 6

LAST LAND

VARANGIAN: UPPSALA

He picks his way slowly home from Constantinople by land, travelling with different groups of merchants who trade the long and winding river route north up the Dnepr.

All are happy to have a battle-scarred Varangian to add to the security of their party, especially as they ascend the seven rapids that take them through the dangerous sun-baked khaganate of the Pecheneg horse tribes before slowly moving on up into the fertile, birch-girt lands of the Rus.

He travels slow and steady, never quite believing he will heal properly, wondering if an infection will grow and carry him off before he sees the cold seas he so hungers for.

He had certainly never thought to make this return journey, and even as he sets out he finds it hard to believe he will, but once he passes through the growing city of Kœnugarðr he begins to believe he might actually make it to the end of his journey.

Partly it is the wound healing on his chest, enough so he can pull an oar properly, and partly it is the laugh of a merchant's widow, two years older than he, who is also returning home. Her husband has died, and she is going back to find her kin, who she claims have settled a farmstead in the furthest of the Southern Isles, far out on the whale-roads in the West.

She has a straight-backed, severe manner and grey-green eyes that he had first taken for cold, but one night he heard her laugh across the campfire and saw the warm, pink curve of her neck as her head tilted back and had been reminded of something so strongly that he had kept looking and had then been caught as she finished laughing and dropped her chin.

Their eyes had met, and she had not looked away. It had been a straight look — direct, unhurried, unsurprised — and, from the tiny good-natured shake of her head that ended it, entirely uninterested.

There had been no heat in it, but in the innermost chamber of his heart where he had thought nothing but cold ashes remained, something had kindled.

He feels it as an unwelcome thing, as if he has been challenged to fight in a battle he had forsworn long ago, and because of that he has decided not to pursue her. Especially as he is, in his mind, now pledged to offer himself as a sacrifice at the sacred grove.

She laughs again when he tells her that, the first time he finds himself not alone in his bed-roll. She ran a gentle hand over the ugly scar on his chest and asked him why in Freyja's name did he think it was his choice anyway.

He first feels the chill sting of salt on his cheeks standing beside her in the prow as they make the last easy sea-passage across the Austmarr to the great trading centre at Birca, where they part.

She had been unable to persuade him to change his plans, and he had been clear from the start that he travelled as a man with a broken oath to redress, and a curse he had sworn to bind or break with his own blood sacrifice.

She had taken it surprisingly well, understanding that living under a broken oath would eventually have made him not himself any more. She thanks him for his friendship. He thanks her for the unexpected last happiness she had brought him.

They part as friends, and she even gives him her own offering for the priests at the temple grove, making him swear not to forget to give them the heavy package and the letter the first moment he arrives. She does not want him to forget it as he faces the reality of his own doom.

By the time he arrives in Uppsala, the warm promise of summer has waxed and is now waning away into the sharp wolf's bite of winter.

Chapter 76

Overspill

Kevo's headache is viciously persistent, which is making him all the more unforgiving about the island's failure to deliver a passing Samaritan in a warm dry car with the offer of a lift.

He woke after a bad night's sleep and got in the car, intending to drive into town and find out when the next ferry leaves. He hadn't expected to run out of petrol and realised he must have dislodged a fuel line when he grounded the car. He's not stupid enough to run out of gas without knowing it; he's sure he had a good half tank in there, but here he is on a cold, grey rainy morning in the middle of bloody nowhere and not having had a proper breakfast or even a coffee. Hellish, he thinks. No wonder the island seems deserted. Who'd want to live here?

The only sign of life remains the lit window in the distant house. By the time the punishing rain has eased to a patchy drizzle, the frustrating boredom of waiting has become as unbearable as the ache behind his eyes and he decides to risk a run for it before the weather closes in again. Truth is, he's so parched he would almost welcome a drenching.

Which is lucky, because he gets about a third of the way there before the sky opens again and dumps on him. He gets a stitch from trying to outrun the inevitable and trudges the last half-mile in a defensive crouch, accepting the fact that he's going to get soaked through to his underwear.

The house is built on the edge of an inlet that probes deep into the island like a narrow dagger. The back of the building has a deck that overhangs the low cliff edge it's built on. It's a posher house than Shanna's, he thinks, as he ducks under the porch, out of the rain.

The lights are on, but no one is home – or if they are, they're not answering as he knocks. The front door is, however, open wide. The porch doesn't really protect him from the sideways rain, and so he knocks again on the door frame and steps inside, pausing just within the threshold.

"Hello?" he says for the second time, louder. "Hello?"

At first, he thinks there is still no reply, but then he's pretty sure he hears someone moving around inside the house, maybe someone upstairs.

"Hiya?" he says, stepping carefully further into the hall. "Sorry to bother you but I've had a bit of an accident on the road ... "

Again, nobody replies, but now he definitely hears someone upstairs; it sounds like a bathroom noise, like somebody shifting their weight in a plastic bath.

"No hurry!" he says. "I'll just wait down here if that's OK, out of the rain!"

He perches on the radiator on the side of the hall at the bottom of the stairs and watches water drip on to the carpet at his feet. He wonders who's in the bath. From the time it's taking, he begins to think it's maybe an old dear who's having a spot of bother in the bath. Or maybe someone so old they're too deaf to hear him in the first place.

At least it's dry and the radiator he's leaning against is warm. He doesn't mind waiting, and his headache actually seems to be easing after the brisk walk in the rain.

Things could be worse.

Chapter 77

Plan B

Matt knows the ferry isn't coming. The wind that hits him as he gets out of his truck is too strong and it's coming from exactly the wrong direction. Nevertheless, he walks to the crest of the rise leading down to the harbour and raises his binoculars again. The view isn't much better than he was getting from the cab of his pick-up, but he needs to be on his own for a moment because Magda is coping with her shock by firing words and questions at him, as if he has a clue as to what's happening. As a coping mechanism, it might be helping her, but it's making his head hurt and his heart race. Maybe that's what a panic attack is, he thinks.

The view through the binoculars is just as depressing as it has been for the past forty minutes since the ferry should have docked. There's a heaving cross-sea at the mouth of the harbour, and beyond the skerries the waves are white capped and mountainous. The only colour is the orange flash of the lifeboat – sole survivor of the harbour fire – which has got snarled up on the inner skerries, too far to reach. From the awkward, static buck-and-weave of the unsinkable boat as it sidewinds against the waves, he figures either the mooring linc or an anchor has got jammed in the snaggle-toothed rocks below, but apart from that there's nothing but grey and white out there, a monochrome vision of hopelessness.

"They're dead," says Sig.

He looks sideways to see she's come to stand next to him.

"Allie and the phone engineer," she says. "One minute they were there, next yanked off the dock and just . . . gone. I was trying to make sense of it, but I can't."

"There's no sense to it," he says. "I mean, you were right. It's all impossible. But it's still happening."

"So, my old working theory was I've gone mad," she says. "Except the cruellest twist is I know I haven't."

"What's your new working theory," he says, handing her the binoculars.

She takes them and scans the distant seascape.

"My new working theory is that working theories are a luxury we don't need," she says. "We just need to survive until the ferry does arrive."

"It's not coming today," he says.

"No," she says, "No, you were right about that. So tomorrow."

"If Kathleen hadn't taken my boat, we could have run for it," he says.

"Maybe you're wrong about her being dead," she says.

"No," he says. "No, I saw it."

"Yeah," she says.

"I know," he says. "You don't believe in all that—"

"No," she says. "No. After today, all bets are off. You say you saw it, you saw it."

She hands him back the binoculars.

"You see the lifeboat too?" she says.

"Of course," he says. "Looks like someone cut it loose. Probably whichever maniac set fire to the other boats."

"You think it was them?" she says. "The . . . I don't know what to call them."

"The drowned," he says.

"Yes," she says. "I mean, they don't make sense, so why should the boats being wrecked make sense?"

"I know," he says. "Pity, though, because we could have used them for a getaway."

"Maybe," she says. "But I don't think I want to go near that harbour until there's a big ferry full of a lot of normal people alongside."

She turns and looks at the Land Rover and his pick-up. Three pairs of eyes look back at them.

"Right," she says. "Let's tell the others the cavalry's not coming and make a bloody plan."

The two ravens have reunited and are now flying in a wide circle, each at opposite ends of a diameter that kisses the edge of the harbour at one extreme and the passing place where the Defender and Matt's pick-up are parked at the other. They see no change in the violence of the sea beating the burned-out shells of the boats against the slab's concrete at the mooring; but though they see no sign of what lies beneath the water, they each sense it.

They see the people at the passing place all congregate in the Land Rover. One of the ravens dips a wing and swings closer to the ground, watching them listening to the blonde swimmer talking intently. It lofts back up into the sky, fighting the increased strength of the wind, and resumes its station as the two birds continue their patrol.

It's fuggy with everyone crammed inside the Defender, even though it's meant to seat twelve at a pinch. Matt has climbed in the back while Magda has got into the passenger seat next

447

to Sig. Evie and Tom and the baby sit in the middle seats, looking back and forth as the discussion flows across them.

"You want us to check all the houses for survivors?" says Matt.

"I think there's safety in numbers, yes," says Sig. "Seems logical."

"I'm with you," says Magda.

"Fine," says Matt.

"It'll go faster if we split up," says Evie. "Drive the loop in different directions, meet back at Sig's. I mean, that's about halfway in both directions, right?"

Sig looks at Matt.

"Given what's in the water over here, I'd rather wait on the other side of the island," he says.

"Me too," says Magda. "Oh fuck. Sorry. I can't believe Allie has just . . . gone."

"It's okay," says Sig, checking her watch. "Then we bring everyone back here tomorrow morning when the ferry comes . . ."

The ravens see the people get back into the other vehicle and then watch them split apart and drive away from each other. No one in the vehicles notices the birds break their patrol and veer off in similarly opposite directions, as if they are acting as outriders to each party.

Evie leans forward and rests her elbows on the back of the seat in front.

"You scared as I am?" she says.

"Terrified," says Sig. "But that isn't going to help."

"But I'm stuck," Evie says. "Really stuck. I mean, like if this was a videogame, I'm the one gets left behind. I can't run, can't drive the car. I saw what happened back there. I can't do anything. I'm the one they get while everyone else runs away. I'm the sacrifice that buys you all time to escape."

"It's not a game and I won't leave you behind," says Sig. "Ever."

Evie snorts and shakes her head.

"Sig, if you get attacked, you aren't going to have the time to help me out of this seat and assemble my wheelchair and get me in it. Be realistic."

"I am being realistic," says Sig, turning to look her squarely in the eye. "The reality is, I don't leave you."

"Or the baby," says a voice from behind them. Evie cranes round to see Tom looking at Sig.

"Or the baby," he says. "Don't leave Ruby."

"Okay," says Evie, carefully. "OK, we won't leave Ruby."

"Or you," says Sig, and then gently: "What's your name?"

"Scared too," Tom says. "I'm scared too."

He wipes something out of his eye and looks away out of the side window.

He should tell them there's a voice in his head telling him they have to get on the boat, they must get in a boat, that the boat is the only safe place on the island. But he can't find enough words to do it.

Chapter 78

Bathtime

Kevo reckons he's waited for a polite five minutes, but it feels kind of rude to shout up the stairs again, as if he's chivvying the person in the bath along. So he bites his tongue for another few minutes, by which time he's decided fuck it, they can't have heard him the first time. He cranes his neck and shouts up the stairwell.

"Hello?" he shouts.

This time, he definitely hears an answering noise. He makes out the unmistakable sound of a body slipping and sliding on a bathtub, the slap of water spilling on to a hard floor and then a voice – or rather, a kind of strangled moaning.

"You OK?" he shouts. "Hello? Are you OK up there?"

The noises pause this time, as if listening, and then resume with more intensity.

Just his bloody luck, he thinks. He was right. Some old soul's having a stroke or something and now he's going to have to go up there and help, and Christ knows what he's going to have to see, old-naked-person-wise – nobody wants to see that – and of course, great, there's no phone so he won't be able to call a bloody ambulance . . .

Kevo goes upstairs, gingerly stepping over a soaked jacket that's been thrown on to the steps.

He looks round the upper hall and there's only one door closed, and the others are obviously bedrooms, so he's pretty sure he's knocking on the bathroom door. The hesitation that hits him just a beat too late, after he's knocked, is not about that. It's about the horrible possibility that crystalises into a near certainty the moment it drops into his mind, the realisation that the animal noises might be people having sex in the bath. The grunting and moaning that punctuate the splashing have a suitably hungry and intense quality to them, but now it's too late. The die is cast, the knuckles have knocked and the door, unlatched, has swung open.

"Hello?" he says. "Sorry, I heard a noise, I thought you might be in trouble . . . "

It's dark inside, and from what little he can make out in the slice of daylight that he's letting in it looks like the room is empty and he's made a mistake. The bath isn't big enough to hide two people, even if they were surprised and are hiding. He pushes the door all the way back so it hits the wall, just to make sure no one is hiding behind it.

There is water all over the floor, and, as Kevo's eyes adjust, he sees it's spilling over the lip of the bath.

He's stuck on the threshold, wondering if the noise he heard came from a second bathroom that maybe leads off one of the open bedroom doors behind him, when there's a change in the water noise, an extra slap of overflow hitting the tiled floor, and he realises with horror that his first instinct was right: the noise was the occupant having a stroke and they are now drowning in the bath while he hovers uselessly in the doorway like a spare prick at a wedding. There's a tiny voice in his head telling him to leave and not get involved because he's outside his parole area.

"Ah shite," he says, springing across the floor.

His feet slip on the wet surface and he cannons forward, unable to stop his knee from whacking painfully into the side of the bathtub, and he only prevents himself from jackknifing face-forward into the bath itself by slapping his hand hard against the tile wall on the far side of the tub.

Kevo looks down and sees it. It, because, although it looks like an old man – partly clothed and far beyond middle age – an alarm starts klaxoning in the deepest part of his back-brain and he knows beyond all doubt that he's leaning over a man-shaped thing that is no longer human.

It's not just the way the hands are – horribly – in constant motion, twisted into the clothes as it snatches and kneads at itself. It's not the way the body seems to judder and glitch beneath the surface of the water in a way that twists his eyes and makes it painful to look at. It's not even that it's making no effort to get out from under the quaking surface of the water and breathe. It's the eyes staring up at him, as still and calm as the rest of the body is twitching and squirming.

There's nothing human in the depths of those eyes. Just a thing. And he realises with a cold, watery feeling in his bowels that the thing is the purest hate he has ever seen. As if the hate can read his thoughts before he can work out what his brain is telling his body, one of the twitching hands lets go of itself and spears up out of the water as Kevo pushes off from the wall and starts to try and run, and grabs his crotch in a grip like a welding clamp.

It takes a moment of shock for him to realise the shriek of

452

pain and horror bouncing off the tiling is coming from his mouth, and then all he can do is ignore the agony and fight like a bastard against whatever it is that is dragging him unrelentingly down into the bath.

Chapter 79

Ill-met

Magda's always been a bit unsure about the big fisherman driving them along the right-hand fork of the loop. There's something almost unsettling in how solid he is, how comfortable a part of the island's ecology he seems. He's nice enough, though, always gruffly cheerful, though he's never looked at her in the way other single guys tend to. She wonders if he's got something going on with the Swedish woman, and then she closes her eyes and tells herself she's a fool, trying to distract herself thinking about gossip when the world's full of the walking drowned.

"Idiot," she thinks, and then realises she said it out loud too.

"Sorry?" Matt says, slowing down to turn into the driveway of the fancy house with the deck at the back.

"Not you," she says. "Me."

"OK," he says. "I'll just ring the bell see if anyone's here."

She watches him walk to the door and stop. He pushes it open and turns and shrugs at her.

"Hello?" he says, knocking on the door jamb.

And then she's horrified to see him go rigid at something

he's hearing from within, and even more shocked to see him run inside.

Matt hears the shouting for help and instinctively runs into the hall. The shout comes again, and he realises it is coming from above, so he goes up the stairs three at a time.

He bursts into the bathroom to see a small, wiry guy straining against someone that's brutally trying to pull him into the bath by his hair. The wiry guy has twisted himself like a pretzel in his struggle to resist the attacker, who's extremely strong and lying flat in the bath. He has his left hand and right foot braced on either side of the tub as his right hand wrestles with the attacker's hands, which are clamped on to his hair in an iron grip, and he has somehow managed to contort himself to get his left knee buttressed in the narrow watery space between his chest and the attacker, whose face his foot is clamped down on, keeping him squashed against the bottom of the overflowing bath.

Kevo sees Matt burst in.

"Get it the fuck off me!" he shouts.

Matt skids across the floor and tries to open the two fists that are clenched on the man's hair. The hands are immoveable.

"My back pocket," says Kevo through gritted teeth. "There's a chib."

Matt reaches round and scrabbles a Stanley knife out of his jeans. As he does so, he realises the drowned man fighting in the bath is Walter John. He fumbles, sliding the stubby blade out of the chequered metal handle and takes a fast breath, steeling himself for what he's going to have to do. Then he leans in.

"No," shouts Kevo. "Don't stab him. Fucksakes, he's been under for a good ten minutes, he's dead already – cut my hair, do it in a oner, then run like buggery!"

Matt slashes at Kevo's hair with the razor sharp blade. Walter John's hands slam back into the water, clutching a big hank of it just as the newly untethered Kevo kicks down on his face and boosts himself out of the bath, bounces off Matt and sprints for the door. The impact knocks Matt sideways and he loses his footing on water-slick flooring. He flails for something to stop him falling and takes the sink with him as he goes down hard, bursting it from the wall and snapping it off the chrome pedestal it sat on. Water jets from the broken pipes, and by the time he gets to his feet Walter John is out of the bath and running at him with a speed and intensity that is nothing like an old man's. Without thinking, Matt picks up the sink and swings it two-handed, smacking a brutally heavy porcelain haymaker into his head. The force of the impact spins Walter John and topples him, but Matt is out of the door so fast he doesn't see him hit. He slams it shut behind him, and then he tries to take the stairs too fast, loses his footing again and tumbles awkwardly forward, pinwheeling towards the ground floor. He grabs wildly at the banisters to stop himself from breaking his neck. There's a crack and a splintering noise as his momentum snaps the banister loose and he falls untidily to the bottom landing, holding it in his right hand. He lies there on the rucked-up hall carpet for a moment, stunned and taking an inventory of himself to see what he may have broken.

Magda sees someone fly out of the front door, and for an instant thinks it's Matt and he's OK, and then she sees it's Shanna Nisbett's bloody ex, and knows he's not. She's in the passenger seat, but she has time to reach over and slam the central locking just in time as Kevo hits the side of the truck and rattles the handle.

"Please!" he shouts. "Help! Open up!"

In the house, Matt shakes his head, trying to clear it, and

just as he decides he's not too busted up to try to stand, Walter John lunges out of the bathroom above, his jaw hanging sideways, broken off its moorings, pouring water and gurgling in rage as he spots Matt below him and launches himself off the landing in a flying tackle.

Matt twists desperately sideways and jabs the broken banister at him, bracing the other end against the floor. Walter John's deadweight hits the wooden stake with a sound like an axe biting into a tree as it passes straight through his body and punches six inches out the other side. Matt scrabbles to pull his legs free of the drowned man and get to his feet.

Magda stares at Kevo, frozen. There's just too much going on for her to know what to do. Then she snaps out of it and scrambles across the gear stick and slides into the driving seat, fumbling the keys, which won't turn because the truck's parked with its wheels cocked so the parking lock is stiffly resisting. She wrenches the wheel left and right, trying to free it.

"Please!" he says urgently, face millimetres away from the glass. "Please wait!"

And then, just as she gets the steering lock freed up and the key turns in the ignition, Matt stumbles out of the door trying to tear free from a drowned guy with a broken jaw who's latched on to him. Kevo sees it and something changes in his face – he turns to Magda and yells, "No! Get out of here. Go, go!"

And then she watches him force himself to turn and run away from her and launch himself at the drowned monster who is, she realises, Walter John. The old man's ferocity makes him seem twice his normal size and obviously more powerful than a bloody vampire because he's not a bit fussed about the jagged stake sticking right through his chest.

She sees Matt turn and try to help him, but the two of them don't seem strong enough to fight him off. He grasps Kevo's throat in one hand and Matt's face in the other as they swing and claw at him.

She should get out of here fast, she thinks. Instead, she yanks the car out of gear, grabs the shovel from the back seat and tears out into the rain.

Kevo's eyes are bulging as he looks sideways at Matt, who's twisting his head from side to side, trying to escape Walter John's grip, which looks in danger of gouging his eye out.

"Kick his legs out," he gasps, flailing his boots at Walter John's knees. His legs seem to be made of iron for all the good he's doing.

"Wha—?" says Matt.

"His legs," says Kevo. "Get him down so—"

Metal blurs past his ear, so close he feels the slipstream, and chunks into Walter John's shoulder. The grip on Kevo's throat drops off and Kevo staggers free in time to see Magda pull the shovel back and sledgehammer it into Walter John's forehead, bludgeoning him back, freeing Matt.

And then they're all running and diving into the pick-up and slamming the doors and locking them, and Matt peels backwards into the road and guns the motor, and they're speeding away into the rain that's coming sideways now – and no one has anything to say for a mile or so.

Then Kevo looks at Magda.

"Fuck was that?"

"Bait shovel," she says.

"Right," he says. Then: "Thanks."

"I'm thinking we don't go into any more houses," says Matt as they pass Shanna's house and stop at the one just past it. He hits the horn and they watch for any reaction.

"Fine by me," says Kevo. "What're you doing anyway?"

"Seeing if anyone else is left who isn't . . . like that guy back there. Drowned," says Matt.

"Right," says Kevo. "So, which of you's going to tell me what the fuck's going on?"

Chapter 80

Boathouse

The first few homes Sig and Evie try are all empty and unlit, most with the front doors hanging open, as if the owners had left in a hurry, and the ones with the doors closed and locked are, Evie confirms, homes belonging to islanders who'd got on the ferry to go to the Modh.

The sixth house Sig tries nearly kills her.

She parks close to the open front door and hops out, jarring her knee, which puts her in a worse mood; then, as she leans in and calls into the hallway, Rex suddenly growls and takes off like a rocket, cannoning past her. As she steps in after him, calling his name, something huge and man-sized erupts out of the kitchen, shocking her to an abrupt halt as it skitters on the lino, scrabbling on all fours and charging her down at an impossible speed. She tries to get out of its way, but the passage has her trapped and it slams into her, throwing her off balance into a glass-topped hall table that shatters as she falls through it.

Rex hurdles her and chases the ram out into the rain. Sig winces, carefully picks herself up out of the ruin of the table and sees she's bleeding from a cut on her forearm.

She limps back to the Defender and gets in.

"What happened?" says Evie.

"Bloody sheep," says Sig. "There's a first-aid kit in front of you."

Evie reaches into the tray beneath the window and hands her the canvas bag, then watches her unzip it and find a large enough plaster to slap on the cut.

"You might need stitches," she says.

"I'll be fine," says Sig. "But I'll tell you what, that's it for going into houses. That ram nearly gave me a heart attack."

They cruise the rest of their route, pulling in to driveways and up farm tracks and honking the horn, but no one ever emerges to greet them or see what the fuss is. And when they get to Sig's, the others are already there, having had similar lack of luck with their search.

"So that's maybe thirty, forty people just . . . " says Evie.

"Drowned," says Sig. She looks at Matt. "You're right. We've got to call them something."

"How about bastards?" says Kevo. "Because that's what they bloody fight like."

"Who are you?" says Evie.

"Kevo," he says. "I'm a pal of Shanna Nisbett."

"The one she was here to get away from," says Magda.

"He saved my life," says Matt.

"Nah," says Kevo, nodding at Magda. "It was her with the bait shovel."

"Shanna was scared of you," says Magda.

"Aye," he says. "And I was scared of me back then too. I was bad, right enough, when I was on the stuff. But I'm off it now. AA and all the bells and whistles. I come to tell her I'm sorry. To make amends. Not to cause injury."

"Step Nine," says Matt.

Kevo looks at him, surprised.

"Aye," he says. "That's the one."

Sig looks out of her big picture window. Tom has slid down into his former position, leaning against the kitchen island with his back to the sea, clutching Ruby, who is grizzling quietly. Evie has the can of formula Sig had found and is rummaging a bottle out of the bag Tom had carried the baby in.

"Anyone know how this works?" she says.

Matt tilts his head discreetly at Sig. She joins him at the end of the table, away from the others.

"Short days, so we got about three hours of daylight, then dark till eight-ish tomorrow," he says.

"So we all bunk down here and head back to the harbour at first light," she says. "Maybe take it in turns to . . . "

"What?" he says.

She shakes her head, smiling bitterly at herself.

"I don't know, Matt. I was going to say, 'keep watch' but to tell the truth I've no idea what we'd do if they find us anyway."

"Why would they look for us?" he says. "We don't know what they are, let alone what they do or why they do it? Far as we know, they only get nasty when we bump into them. No reason to think they're predators."

"Predators?" she says. "Jesus, Matt. Listen to us. Like we have a bloody clue about what to do here."

"Get on the boat," says a small voice behind them. Sig turns to see Tom looking at her over Ruby's head. "Get on the boat."

"We will," she says. "Tomorrow, when it comes."

"No," he says, shaking his head. "Get on the boat now. We have to get on the boat. The boat is safe."

"There isn't a boat yet," says Evie, reaching out to comfort him. "But tomorrow, yeah?"

He shakes off her hand.

"No," he says. "No. There is a boat. We have to get on it."

"Where is there a boat?" says Sig, looking at Matt.

"Don't know," says Tom. "But we have to get on it."

Matt inclines his head at Sig. They get up and walk over to the window, looking out at the wild sea beyond.

"He's not wrong," he says. "We'd be better off the island, no?"

"But the boats that are big enough for that sea," she says, "they're all useless or gone, right?"

He scowls and shrugs, like even he doesn't like what he's about to say.

"I've been thinking about the lifeboat."

"What about it," she says.

"If the ferry doesn't come tomorrow—"

"Matt," she says. "If the ferry doesn't come, someone on the mainland's going to notice the phones are down. I mean, CalMac for a start, they'll be wondering why they're not getting through to the harbour, no?"

"And then what?" he says. "They'll just wait until the weather clears. They won't know what's really going on here. It'll just look like an outage."

"So?" she says.

"So, if the lifeboat isn't swept off the skerries by this sea—"

"It will be," she says.

"Not if it's an anchor chain that's snagged. The boat is built to be unsinkable. It's basically a big float with a motor at one end."

"OK," she says. "And how do we get to it?"

He looks at the door leading to the boathouse at the end of the room.

"You serious?" she says.

"You still got the kayak?" he says.

"In that sea?" she says.

"I don't know, Sig," he says. "I'm flailing here, but yeah, maybe—"

"It's got to be more than half a mile out," she says.

"It's a tandem kayak, right?" he says. "We could do it together, two paddles better than one?"

Sig looks at him. Then back at the wild sea. Then back at him again.

"That's definitely a last resort. We'd have to be—"

Kevo's voice cuts in hesitantly from behind them.

"Er, don't want to be rude or anything . . . but what's this about a bloody curse?"

"Curse?" says Matt.

"*Faan*," Sig swears under her breath, too exhausted to deal with this on top of everything else. She turns back to see Kevo and Magda standing over Evie, who's staring defiantly back at her. The square of tattooed skin lies on the table in front of them.

"It's not real," says Sig, swinging a chair round and sitting opposite them, suddenly beyond exhausted. "We don't know it's connected with anything, it's just . . . supernatural bullshit . . . "

Even she can hear the conviction leaching out of her voice as she speaks.

"Yeah," says Matt. "And what's happening here is . . . not?"

"I'm sorry, Sig," says Evie. "But the water is kind of walking, right?"

"And if it's in the water, then it's . . . everywhere!" says Magda. "Shit. You should have told us."

"Just leave it," says Sig. "Evie, put it in the bin, stop obsessing about it."

She turns to Magda and Kevo, who are looking at her

accusingly, like she just betrayed them. This, on top of everything else, suddenly deeply exhausts her.

"Yeah, I don't know what's going on," she says. "But neither do you. It could be an infection, I don't know, or food poisoning from the fish farm—"

"Food poisoning!" says Kevo. "If what you're all saying's right, this is a fuckton of murderous water zombies, not a touch of diarrhoea!"

They all stare at her.

"You can get some pretty nasty neurotoxins from bad shellfish," says Sig. "It makes people crazy. Could be some kind of mass delusion, bioterrorism ... I mean, yeah, I have no clue, but talking about curses is just adding to the confusion."

She closes her eyes. She sees the faces of the drowned gaping up at her from beneath the water in the harbour. The hands reaching for her on her morning dive. Allie being dragged off the world at the end of the jetty.

She opens her eyes and meets Evie's steady gaze.

"You know what we need?" says Evie. "Soup."

"Don't need soup," says Kevo. "Need a bloody machine gun."

Sig stands at the window, leaning into the glass with her forehead, trying to pretend she isn't getting itchy about the people using her kitchen. If she keeps her eyes closed and does box breathing, maybe she'll find the calm that is so successfully eluding her. She inhales for a four-count and holds it for another four. She turns to see Kevo poking at the still-damp rectangle of tattooed skin with the end of one of her paintbrushes, as if he's trying to see if it moves.

"Hey," she says. "Leave it be."

"Just having a keek at it," he says.

"Well, I'm just going to throw that damn thing away and you're going to take Evie's good advice and have some warm food."

She walks away to the table, picks up the tray with the book and drops it, tray and all, into the swing bin beside Tom, who is still squatting on the floor. She looks up to see they're all watching her.

"Right," she says. "Now you don't all have to keep on looking at the damn thing and spooking yourselves."

She looks down at Tom.

"You need some hot food too." He's looking at the bin.

"I'll get it for you," she says.

Hot food seems to cool things down and ballast everyone enough to sit around the long table and talk about what they'd each seen or experienced. Even Tom takes a bowl of soup, though he eats it crouched on the ground with his back to the kitchen unit so he doesn't have to see the sea. The view of the water still unsettles him. He doesn't listen to the talk flowing back and forth above him. He sits, concentrating on the distant voice in his own head, the one that keeps coming and going, the one that keeps telling him they need to get on the boat and that now is telling him he needs to take the thing out of the bin.

TAKE IT.

He is happy the thing is out of sight. He'd been glad when Sig put it there. And now he's not so sure he should trust the voice.

TAKE IT.

He doesn't tell the others about the voice because he doesn't have the words to explain it. He just tries to ignore it now he doesn't trust it quite as much as he did, and he is grateful when Sig offers him more soup and a square of bread to dip in it. She smiles at him as he nods his thanks and takes it.

"You don't say much," she says quietly.

He shrugs apologetically.

"That's good," she says, touching his shoulder with a soft squeeze. The offhand kindness of it almost betrays him into tears, but then she's gone and he concentrates on the soup and holding Ruby and letting the dog lie next to him, the animal's warmth a comforting thing against his leg.

Talk at the table dies off after an hour or so, and everyone sits round drinking the dregs of the coffee. Given Sig's one-of-everything regime, that means it's being drunk from a mug, a cup, a water glass and a wine glass, but no one seems too bothered as they watch the light fading from what little of the bruised sky they can see beyond the immediate rain sheeting against the window.

"I hate bloody winter," says Kevo. "Starts getting dark as soon as you roll out of bed in the morning."

"Short days," says Matt.

"Yes," says Magda. "Going to be a bloody long night too."

Magda is trembling. She has always thought of herself as tough and resourceful. She had saved Matt and Kevo when she wanted desperately to run away. But instead of that making her braver, it seems to her as if she's just emptied her tank of any remaining courage, and she now feels almost unable to breathe with fear. It's like her brain fusing or the inside of her head unpeeling and making clear thought impossible as she keeps remembering what she'd seen and how what she had done felt, the impact of the spade jarring her hands as she hit the man's skull. She is no longer brave, she knows that with absolute shameful certainty. Something has broken, and however much she might hate the new querulousness in her voice and the racing thoughts behind it, she cannot find a way to reassert her grip.

Sig feels itchy watching them all, not just because there are so many people in her house but because she needs something to do to stop her mind going where she doesn't want it to go.

"Hey," she says, getting up and looking at Matt. "Let's see about that kayak."

She unbolts the door to the boathouse and hits the lights. The cold air billowing up from the seaward opening in the end wall hits Sig, Matt and Kevo as they walk in. Magda follows them and stops dead, staring at the open arch beyond the slipway leading to the open sea beyond.

"What's this?" she says.

"Boathouse," says Matt, looking up at the two-person kayak hanging from the roof above the rectangle of lapping seawater that takes up most of what would, in other circumstances, be the floorspace.

"And this is good, is it?" says Kevo, standing in the door in what Sig realises is his habitual apologetic crouch. "I mean, sorry, but given the circs, you know – given we know there are drowned zombie bastards hiding in the water – it's all fine that we've decided to hole up in a house that not only has a curse in it but has a room full of open bloody sea?"

Matt and Sig exchange a look.

"They're on the other side of the island," Matt says. "In the harbour."

"No. As far as we know, where the water goes, they go," says Magda, looking over Kevo's shoulder.

"We don't really know what they do, do we?" says Kevo. "I mean, it's all fucking make it up as we go along until they bite our faces off or something! And we don't have weapons—"

"Would weapons make you feel better?" says Sig.

"Feel like fucking Rambo, aye," he says.

"That might come in handy," she says, and points behind her.

Kevo turns and sees wetsuits and flippers and lifejackets hanging on the wall.

"In the corner," she says.

He walks across, bends down and pulls out a speargun from where it's propped behind them.

"Magic," he says.

"Okay," Sig says. "You're in charge of that."

"And try not to put someone's eye out with it," says Matt.

"I'll be Hawkeye," he says, turning to walk back inside. "One arrow, one kill, eh?"

Matt grins at Sig as the other two walk back into the house.

"What?" she says.

"Nothing," he says. "And you said you weren't good with kids."

"He's not a kid," she says.

"Well, he liked the toy you gave him," he says. "Nice one."

"Thank you," she says, surprised at the grin they seem to be sharing, as if they just unearthed a relic of a forgotten friendship. "He's probably harmless."

"If you say so," he says. "And we do have more urgent fish to fry, I guess."

Matt looks back at the hanging kayak. He walks down the narrow strip of stone floor on one side of the rectangle of dark sea water, until he's halfway along the hull hanging above him.

"Look, even if we don't need Plan B, we should strap this to the roof of the Defender. Just in case."

"I think we're way beyond Plan B," says Sig. "Okay, grab it as it comes down. Don't let it get wet. Don't want to drip all over the floor carrying it out."

"I love that you're still being houseproud in the midst of all this," he says, reaching for the bellying hull as she unwraps the suspension rope from the cleat on the wall.

"Coping mechanism," she says. "Just trying to keep as much normal in my head, stop the other stuff forcing its way in."

He reaches up on tiptoe, fingertips touching the long keel of the boat as she lowers it.

"Tell me if it works," he says. "Like I said, I'm bloody flail—"

The boat stops abruptly. He falters, nearly losing his balance and falling into the water.

"Matt," Sig snaps. "Get out, now."

He looks at her in surprise.

As if on cue, the sound of Tom yelling in fright ribbons out through the door to the long room. Matt cranes his head to follow Sig's horror-struck gaze.

A head has broken the surface and keeps rising, revealing a hi-viz CalMac jacket as Robbie the ferryman – or what used to be him – strides in up the sloping slipway beneath the water.

"It's Robbie," Matt says in shock.

"Go!" Sig shouts as Robbie's water-filled eyes swivel sideways to see Matt. He veers suddenly towards him, his hands clawing for his ankles.

Sig lets go of the rope and drops the long kayak right on top of him, knocking Robbie off his feet.

Matt runs back along the narrow strip of stone and ducks through the door ahead of Sig. They see Robbie the Ferry burst back above the water and hurl the kayak to one side as he charges up the slipway towards them, and then Matt slams the door and Sig shoots the bolts. A second later, they hear the wet thud of Robbie running straight into the other side of the door.

"That was too close," Matt pants. "What—?"

Sig is staring at the others, who are all backed up against the landward side of the room, gaping at the wall of glass and what is emerging out of the dusk beyond it.

A small crowd of drowned are coming out of the sea and walking straight at the window, eyes dead and hateful, mouths open – some hanging loose, some with teeth bared and gritted, all with water welling out of them. As they approach the lighted room, the illumination catches them so they appear like actors walking out of the shadows into the full glare of the footlights on a storm-racked stage. They're wet from the sea, but more than that they're each covered in a skin of water that seems to fitfully flicker and glitch as if it's palely reflecting a distant storm. It gives the whole crowd a twitchy, out-of-phase movement that's deeply unsettling as they walk into the plate glass where they press against the window and stare in at the horrified watchers within.

Sig's the first to break the spell.

"Magda," she says. "You drive. Kevo, you get the boy and the baby in the Defender."

She grabs Matt.

"You and I get Evie in the back."

The drowned start slamming themselves against the glass. GO!

Sig hears her subconscious yelling urgently at her.

"Move now," she shouts.

"How are you—?" shouts Evie, spinning her chair, but then Matt gets hold of her and lifts her out of it as the seven of them turn and run for the door, funnelling into the narrow hallway and bursting out into the wild night beyond. Sig brings up the rear, pausing to grab the meat hammer from the kitchen knife rack and then pushing Evie's empty chair ahead of her at a sprint.

Tom leads the charge, careering out into the sheeting rain, hunched protectively over the squalling bundle containing his stepsister. He wrenches open the side door of the Defender and hurls himself inside. A beat later, Magda rips open the driver's door and hoists herself up into the seat, fumbling for the ignition and slamming the door shut in the same movement. Behind them, Kevo runs out of the house and slips, falling in an untidy jumble of limbs, barely avoiding skewering himself on the long speargun.

Matt yanks open the rear door of the Defender and unceremoniously dumps Evie on to the floor inside, turning to look for Sig. Evie scrambles herself backwards with her hands, dragging herself up on to the right-hand bench seat. Matt grabs the incoming wheelchair from Sig and shouts at her, "Get in, I'll do it."

He shoves the chair through the door – the space is just too small, but Evie leans back and grabs it by a front wheel and yells at him.

"I've got it, I'll hold it, let's go!"

And then, as he turns, her eyes widen and she shouts:

"Look out—"

Robbie the ferryman flings himself out of the rainstorm and tackles Matt, smashing him hard against the side of the vehicle and grabbing his head by the ears, mouth wide and spewing an endless stream of water as he tries to pull him towards it. Matt headbutts him and rips one ear free, twisting himself out from where the drowned man has him brutally sandwiched against the Defender.

"I've got the bastard," shouts Kevo, stumbling up on one knee and aiming the speargun.

Robbie's head whips round to stare at him in the same moment that Kevo aims and fires.

The drowned man snarls and twists as the spear flies through the air.

Matt grunts as it misses Robbie and punches straight through his calf, pinning him to the thin metal skin of the vehicle.

"Oh ya bastard," Kevo says, voice flat with shock. "Sorry, pal."

Magda leans out the window and yells, "Get the fuck in."

Robbie spins back and grabs Matt's head again. Matt takes his chin with both hands and pushes it up and away, but Robbie's strength is impossible to resist as he lowers his head and pulls it closer and closer to Matt's mouth. Rex hits the back of his knee in a snarling fury and bites and tugs at him, but he doesn't seem to notice, just hacking at the dog with his heel as he concentrates on Matt.

"Rex, move!"

Sig comes round the front of the Defender, kicking up spray as she sprints along the side and then drops into a sliding tackle that takes Robbie's legs clean out from under him.

He goes down hard but manages to keep his grip on Matt's head with his right hand. Sig rolls up on to her feet and backhands his elbow with the meat hammer. There's a sharp crack as the joint goes the wrong way, and Matt wrenches his head free and then yanks his leg forward along the smooth shaft of the spear, gasping as he stumbles loose. Robbie swipes at Rex, who has dived back in and is worrying at his other leg, and then launches himself up at Matt. He is fast, but not faster than Sig's hammer, which catches him in a savage uppercut that sends him flying backwards with such force that both of his feet leave the ground.

Sig grabs Matt and is tumbling him into the driver's side passenger door before Robbie's shoulders splash down in the puddles around the Defender. Kevo leaps in the other side as she jumps forward up on to the driver's step by Magda and grabs on to the inside of the open window.

"Go," she yells. "Rex, come."

Rex runs low to the ground, following the Defender as it rockets forward just as the other drowned spill round the side of the house. The car tilts alarmingly on its spongy suspension as it slews sideways into the road at the end of the drive and guns untidily into the blackness beyond the house lights, rear door swinging open and shut against the wheelchair hanging off the back as Evie struggles to keep a grip on it. Sig concentrates on keeping limpetted on to the outside on the improvised running board afforded by the driver's step.

"Lights!" she shouts at Magda.

"I don't know—" begins Magda, yanking wildly at the stalks sprouting from the steering column. Sig leans in and switches the hi-beams on, then flips the windscreen wipers into action. The headlights reveal nothing but sideways rain and empty moorland speeding past. She holds on for a couple of minutes, until she feels they're far enough from the shore on either side of the island.

"Got to stop," shouts Sig, eyes straining backwards trying to see if her dog is still on their tail.

"Not yet," says Magda.

"Matt's bleeding," Sig shouts. "Do it."

Magda hits the brakes. Sig sees the telltale reflection of the tail lights in the dog's eyes as he catches up with them. She exhales in relief.

"Good dog," she shouts as she opens the middle door and looks at Matt, who has already tourniqueted himself at the knee and is squeezing down on the wound in his calf.

"Think it went straight through. Lucky. Missed anything big," he says through gritted teeth.

"Is he okay?" says Kevo, craning over. "I'm sorry, man—"

Sig snaps her fingers at him.

"In the tray in front of you. First-aid kit."

"Can we not keep going?" says Magda.

"A minute," says Sig, looking at Matt. "Keep the pressure on it."

She jumps back out of the car and runs back and grabs the wheelchair. She collapses it, passes it to Evie. Rex hops in and licks Evie.

"You okay?" Sig says.

"No. But don't worry about me," says Evie, ruffling the dog's fur.

"Good girl," says Sig, slamming the door shut and running back to Matt.

"Sorry about this," she says and sticks her fingers in the bloodied hole in his jeans, ripping the denim open. The hole is clean and blood is welling slowly out, but it's not pumping. She reaches for the small first-aid kit and grabs a wad of gauze and a bandage.

Magda turns the engine off and kills the headlights.

"What are you doing?" says Kevo.

"No point drawing attention to ourselves if we're not moving, is there?" she says, craning her head to look at the road behind them.

Evie reaches forward and squeezes Tom's shoulder.

"It'll be okay," she says, wishing she believed it.

"We need to get to the boat," he says.

"There isn't a boat," she says. "Not yet."

"Is a boat," he says, nodding at Sig. "She knows where it is."

Sig looks up from where she's tightly binding the wound.

"Wish I did, kid. Really wish I did."

"You do," he insists.

The roof light of the Defender is a tiny, dim point in the wide expanse of dark rain-harrowed heather that stretches below the ravens as they roost with their backs protected from the wind by the slab of rock at the top of the high point in the middle of the island. Only when the lightning flashes does the snaking road reveal itself, twisting away like a silver stream on either side of the light.

The thunder rumbles in from the north, getting closer as the rain increases in its miserable intensity, lashing across the crest of the hill behind them. After a while, they turn their heads as one and see the bright headlights lance out again in front of the Land Rover and watch as it traces the thin vein of tarmac that streams across the uneven land below.

The birds would rather not have to move from their shelter since night is not their traditional element and the weather is fouler than they like, but each senses something else moving beyond the normal limits of sight, and they shake the rain off their feathers and launch into the wind, flying towards opposite shores of the island.

Sig is driving now, Magda having edged sideways into the middle seat, straddling the gear stick, suddenly uncomfortably shoulder to shoulder with Kevo.

They pass the junction leading down to the old cemetery, and for a moment Sig's heart stops as she sees eyes in the road ahead catching the headlights and reflecting them back at her. As she slows, she realises it's just a pair of miserable sheep hunched in the ditch at the side of the road and picks up speed again.

"Where are we going?" Kevo says.

"Irvine's house," says Matt from behind them.

"Why?" says Magda.

"Because it's high on the other side of the hill," says Evie. "Probably the furthest from the sea of all the houses on the island."

"Good," says Magda, nodding in approval.

"Sound," says Kevo, peering out at a narrow inlet that the road ahead is starting to skirt.

"Won't be long," says Sig.

"Won't be safe," says Tom. "Water's everywhere on the island. We need to get on the boat."

"Look," says Magda, turning in her seat. "What's a boat if not something always surrounded by bloody water? That makes no sense."

"Not this boat," says Tom, nodding at Sig. "She knows."

"I wish I did. But I—" says Sig as the Defender seems to miss a beat and skip slightly.

"What?" says Matt.

"Nothing," she says. "I just—"

It skips another beat, then it somehow seems to choke, and then she feels the power steering go heavy as the engine just stops dead.

"What happened?" says Magda. "What is it?"

Sig grips the wheel and lets the momentum carry them forward, up and down a couple of shallow rises, and then there's a straight downward incline with a steep upslope ahead and they almost crest that one too, but gravity and friction win out and she stamps on the brakes just as they stop and begin to roll backwards.

"No diesel," she says, looking at the dial. "I just filled it—"

She twists out of the driver's door and looks at the side of the vehicle. The spear that nailed Matt is still sticking out at right angles, silhouetted by the red glow from the rear lights beyond it.

"Of course," she says and gets back in out of the rain. "Thank you, Rambo."

"What?" says Kevo.

"Didn't just put a hole in Matt," she says. "You shot the fuel tank."

"Brilliant," says Magda.

"He didn't do it on purpose," says Matt.

Everyone is silent for a long moment, each peering out into the darkness.

Something thumps on to the hood, startling them.

"The fuck's that?" says Magda. "What the—?"

"It's a raven," says Sig.

The bird steps forward, cocking its head right and left, as if trying to make sense of the mismatched jumble of humanity jammed inside the vehicle. It raps on the window with its beak, three sharp taps, and then it flies off.

"So, that was creepy," says Evie.

"We've got to go," says Matt.

"I'm not scared of a bloody bird," says Magda. "It's the other drowned bastards I'm worried about."

"It's the other bastards the bird's worried about too," says Matt. "It's telling us to go."

"How'd you figure that?" says Magda. "You just pulled that out of your arse?"

"I just know," says Matt. "It doesn't have to make sense. Sig?"

"We'll take turns pushing you," says Sig, looking back at Evie. She turns to Tom. "Evie can hold Ruby and keep her warm and dry if you like."

"Are we going to the boat?" he says.

"We're going somewhere safe," she says.

"Only the boat's safe," he says.

"Let's move," she says.

"No, I'm staying in here," says Magda. "We should sit tight, right Kevo?"

"No," he says. "You know what? I reckon we should do what Sig here says."

"No, no, we turn the lights off, wait till morning. Nobody knows we're here," Magda says. "I just—"

The raven thumps back on to the bonnet and pulls itself towards Magda, gripping on to the wiper blade to hold it steady in the windblown rain. It raps the windscreen again, cocking its head and fixing one beady eye right on her.

She swallows and backs herself into her seat.

"Fine," she says. "Jesus. Let's go."

They stagger into the night as a ragged group along the ribbon of single-track, Magda and Kevo running beside Matt and Sig, who both limp as fast as they can, taking turns with Tom at pushing Evie and Ruby.

Once they're out of sight of the Defender, they're almost running blind; the weather seems to close in even more as the darkness clams in around them. Ten minutes in, the rain's got so hard it feels like sleet on their faces, and the sound of it battering the hood of her waterproof deafens Sig, making it hard to hear Matt next to her.

"What?" she says.

"My turn," he shouts, taking the handles of Evie's chair from her. "Only about half a mile to the turn-off to the Irvines'."

Her leg is already shrieking in protest, but she nods and shouts back.

"And it's all uphill from there."

"You carry the baby. I can wheel myself," shouts Evie, craning round in her seat. "In fact, if you take her I can go faster on the downslopes than you guys. I'm not helpless here—"

Sig clasps her shoulder for a moment.

"I know that. And I'm sorry for—"

"Sig!" Matt shouts.

Magda and Kevo have come to a sudden halt at the top of the rise just ahead of them. They're staring in horror at something hidden from the others on the other side of the dip.

Kevo turns to them as they catch up, face white in the darkness. Tom looks into the dip.

"We need to get to the boat," he says.

"We're in the middle of the bloody island," says Magda. "No boat's going to save us here. We should have stayed in the Land Rover."

Chapter 81

Bärsärk

The crowd of the drowned at the bottom of the dip move slowly but relentlessly towards them through the sheeting rain, and as they move closer Sig sees again that each one wears its wetness like a slick skin over clothes, faces and staring eyes, a close-fitting shroud of water that judders constantly like the surface of a pot coming to the boil. Each one quivers at a rate slightly out of phase with its neighbour, which makes the whole group seem to be glitching its way forward through the pounding rain. The fact they aren't running at them is not comforting. It just seems like they know they don't have to, that they'll get them in the end — an end that is now pre-ordained and inescapable.

Evie stares at them, white-knuckling on the wheels of her chair, resisting an inchoate impulse building within her that threatens to give in to the awful pull the crowd radiates and let it tug her forwards, careening down the slope despite herself. The most frightening thing about the waiting figures is not that they almost look like zombies or the undead or something out of a movie, no matter what Magda says: what's

481

truly terrifying about them is that they almost look normal. She knows them. She recognises almost all of them – parents or grandparents of kids she knows from school. Friends of her parents, people she'd say hello to in the shop. Just people. Squint your eyes a little and they could so easily be a bunch of ordinary folk who've got a bit wet in the rain. But their near-ordinariness is part of their danger because she can feel the illusion of familiarity tugging at her, telling her to drop her guard, selling the lie that these people have not ever and so could not now be wishing her any harm. That fiction is like the bait wrapped round a hook, and she can feel the urge to believe and to give in pulsing out of the glitching crowd in magnetic waves drawing her towards it.

"Run!" Sig shouts, her words snatched away by the wind.

"Why?" Magda sobs, suddenly dropping to her knees. "What's the point?"

"The point is if we stop, we lose," Sig says. "They win."

"But we don't know what they want," shouts Magda. "We don't know why this is happening!"

"They want us to stop," Sig says. "They want us to be like them."

Magda points at the crowd ahead of them.

"We are like them," she says. "Look at us. We're half-drowned as it is. We've lost, we've—"

"We haven't lost!" Sig says.

"How d'you reckon that?" says Magda. "How exactly do you bloody reckon that?"

"Because we're still fighting," says Sig.

Magda retches out a sour gout of laughter.

"Fighting? We're not fighting. We're running around in the rain shitting ourselves, like a bunch of headless chickens."

"They want the book," says Tom. They turn to stare at him. He clears his throat.

"How the hell d'you know that?" says Magda.

"They told me," he says.

"Who?" says Sig.

"I don't know," says Tom. "But they just say throw the curse at them. And run."

"So we're screwed," says Magda. "Because Sig left the curse in the kitchen bin!"

"Not really," says Tom, pulling the book from his pocket. Sig stares at him.

"I know," says Tom. "But I thought it was important."

"So the reason these bloody things are after us is you brought that thing?" Magda shouts, eyes darting between Tom and the crowd of the drowned.

"He told me to," says Tom.

"Who?" Magda says. She knows she should keep calm, be brave like Sig, but she's suddenly too tired to keep a grip on the panic and just wants to let it out, let herself scream and lash out at someone.

"The voice in my head," says Tom. He looks at Sig. "The voice in my head said bring it."

"You made these monsters chase us just because of a voice in your head?" Magda chokes, eyes wide in disbelief. "Who are you anyw—"

She steps towards him, fizzing with fear and rage. Sig slaps her. She pulls up in shock.

"Leave him alone," says Sig, "He's just a kid. He's doing as well as he can. Like we all are."

She turns to Tom, keeping one eye on the waiting crowd of the drowned.

"You heard the voice too?" she says. "I thought it was just me."

"Guys!" says Evie. "This really isn't time for a blether."

"You really heard him?" says Sig.

He nods. Evie's eyes dance between the pair of them.

"Fucksakes," she says, bouncing with frustration. "I'm going to give it to them!"

She snatches the book from Tom's outstretched hand.

"No!" shouts Sig.

The crowd of drowned lurches forward, heads lifting as if they smell something on the wind, suddenly moving faster, as if the scrap of tattooed skin is drawing them in for the kill, like sharks sensing blood in the water.

"We don't have time to stand around talking!" says Evie. "You guys run!"

She jerks her chair forward, wheeling herself one-handed towards the waiting crowd, letting the incline of the slope take her, holding the book high above her head.

"Here," she shouts. "Here it is. Here it—"

The chair stops short, throwing her forward, making her lose purchase on the curse as she grabs the armrests to stop herself slipping off and faceplanting on the wet tarmac. The booklet skitters on to the road in front of her.

"What the—?" she chokes, head whipping angrily round to look behind her.

Sig has the handles of the chair gripped tight.

"No," she says. "No. You don't do that."

She spins the chair and points it uphill.

"Get her out of here." She points at Tom. "You give her the baby to hold and you push like hell."

"Sig!" Evie says, slapping her hands away. "I'm not a fucking trolley! You can't just decide—"

"Please. You're my family," says Sig. And maybe because it's the first time she's said it out loud, the first time she's admitted it to herself, it somehow catches in her throat and comes out hoarser than she means. "I'm sorry, Evie, but I told your grandparents you'd be safe. I gave my word."

"But—" Evie begins, instinctively grabbing the baby as Tom thrusts the bundle into her lap.

"No," says Sig. "No buts. Nobody else I love is dying because I broke my word."

Evie stares back at her, her eyes wet. "Okay."

"Go!" Sig shouts, and she turns to face the crowd slowly boiling towards her.

Everything now becomes as inescapable as the horrors in her dream, and so inevitable and all-encompassing that she can feel the coming end bleeding over the boundaries of all of her senses. She can smell the sadness and feel the unavoidable doom glitching faster towards her like a wall of cold air charging ahead of them through the rain.

Everything in her wants to turn and run after the others.

She steps forward and snatches up the book. And though it somehow hurts and twists her eyes to look directly at the blankly malevolent incoming faces of the drowned, she forces herself to stare them down. Most of them she recognises, which makes them seem all the more sinister.

She holds up the book.

"Is it this?" she shouts. "You want this?"

All the heads move as one again, staring at the small square of folded skin she waves above her head.

GIVE IT TO THEM.

"You want it?" she repeats, her voice ragged.

All the eyes drop from her hand to stare straight into her face, and all the mouths in their awful rictuses open, showing their teeth in expressions that quiver unnervingly between desperate hunger and something closer to fear.

Sig feels her bad leg begin to shake, like it's trying to make her run away against her will. She tries to swallow the cold ball of terror rising in her throat and braces herself.

If the end's coming, she thinks, best to do it like getting into the winter water.

Do it fast and get it over with.

She cocks her arm.

"Then you can have—" she begins.

Everything goes strangely slow as all the straining, waterlogged mouths shriek at her, a vicious punch of sound that she can actually see coming as it vibrates the raindrops, making the air and water between them fizz and pop. It hits her full-face and she flinches away despite herself, shaking the stinging hail of water spray out of her eyes as they suddenly surge forwards—

—and something blacker than the surrounding night swoops in from behind her, so close that its wing brushes her shoulder. A raven's beak snatches the falling book, snapping shut on it with a sound like a church door slamming.

The surge falters and stops as the raven flaps slowly in mid-air, stationary, at chest height, looking ominous and bigger than its actual size, seeming to defy the laws of gravity.

Then it whips its head sideways, opening the folded rectangle of skin out – and that's when Sig knows she's hallucinating because she sees the tattooed swirls begin to pulse and move and then start to slide off the skin flap, the lines somehow visible as a deeper wetness in the downpour.

Sig stares, forgetting to breathe as they writhe like standing streams of moonlit silver, roiling and interlacing until they make an outline she can make sense of, a three-dimensional outline of a deep chest, then a muscular torso, at the same time sprouting further tattoos that trace onwards, up and round arms and a neck and head. She sees the legs appear and shift to brace the thickening body taking up a defensive position between her and the horde of the drowned as the unmistakable outline of a double-headed battleaxe drops and hangs loosely from the man's right hand.

The storm breaks in a peal of thunder that detonates right overhead, and a lightning flash highlights the wide eyes and bared teeth of the waiting drowned. For a moment, nothing moves, and then the raven bucks and soars away and the tattooed man turns to point at her, his long beard whipping its own trail of spray through the downpour as his mouth opens wide and he shouts.

"*Springa, dotter!*"

And though he calls her daughter, his face is not the weakly pious face of her own father; his face is the face she sees in her recurring dream, the strange face, the known face, the familiar stranger that she always sees as a reflection of herself as she leaps through the window.

In the strange slow-motion she seems to be seeing everything in, she is sure she glimpses both the ghost of a smile and a spark of angry jubilance in his eyes, as if she too is someone else, someone he recognises and has always known.

"*Springa, dotter!*" he roars again, and then he does smile as he jerks his chin towards the road behind her. "*Spring nu, skoldjungfru! Sät dig i säkerhet vid stenbäten!*"

Sköldjungfru. Shield-maiden. The almost-forgotten words out of her childhood games make her grin back at him, and then she sees his smile become a snarl as he turns back and leaps towards the crowd that is now almost on him, axe blurring as he scythes into them, chopping right and left in a frenzied bladestorm. She pauses just long enough to see that the axe passes through the bodies leaving no wound, flinging wide fans of what would have been arterial spray had the blade been cold iron; in this case, they are thick gouts of water. The bodies begin to build up around the berserker now lost in his battle frenzy.

Sig does not wait to see the end.

She turns and tries to sprint away after the others, her

had leg making her lurch and waver with each step, but she overrides the pain and powers on, eyes finding the distant wheelchair and the bobbling figures running with it.

Stenbåten. She knows where they can find safety.

There's only one stone boat on the island.

Chapter 82

The stone boat

Matt's limping as badly as Sig as he hurtles lopsidedly, pushing Evie through the sleeting rain. Magda and Kevo are just ahead of them, stumbling blindly alongside Tom, who has Ruby wrapped in the space blanket, holding on with both hands, as if he's carrying a big silvery rugby ball. He hears Sig shouting behind him as she closes in.

"Matt! Get them to the old cemetery. The old cemetery!"

It makes no sense, but as soon as he hears it he knows without a shred of doubt that she's right. He can see the others running pell-mell down the slope towards the junction.

"Magda," he shouts. "Go left, left! Get on the cemetery, get on the island."

Tom turns to see what he's shouting about, and in doing so he loses his footing on the rain-slick road surface. He goes down hard but manages to curl himself protectively around the baby and roll. Magda has already grabbed Kevo's shoulder and has pushed him into the junction.

Sig catches up with Matt. Her bust-up knee feels worse than ever, like she's running on rusty knife blades, but she ignores that for now.

"I'll do this, you get the kid," she shouts. He lets her grab the handles and take over pushing.

"Let me freewheel on the down bit," shouts Evie. "I can go faster."

Matt scoops Tom off the ground as they pass and takes a firm hold of the baby.

"Come on!" he shouts.

Tom snatches a look at Sig, his face a flash of white in the darkness.

"You were right," she shouts, "we need to get on the boat. The cemetery is the boat. Go!"

He pelts on after Matt and Ruby, feet pumping, breathing hard.

"OK. Let go," shouts Evie as the slope dips.

"Sure?" says Sig.

"You're slowing me down," Evie yells over her shoulder. "Watch."

Sig lets go of the handles and sees Evie begin to get up speed as she freewheels ahead of her. Sig has a stitch in her side, and her knee feels like it's near bursting or shattering, but she powers through it, trying to keep up with the runaway wheelchair.

Evie hits the bottom of the dip and for a moment it looks like the plan has worked, but the front wheel hits a pothole and the wheelchair tips and lurches sideways, throwing Evie on to the ground as it cartwheels to a clattering halt on the upslope.

"Evie!" Sig shouts as she runs to the spreadeagled body. Evie lifts her head.

"Ow," she says.

Sig runs past, grabs the chair and rights it, then hurries it back to Evie. She kicks on the brake.

"Anything broken?" she says.

Evie looks over her shoulder.

"Get out of here," she says.

Sig looks back up the road. She can't see clearly through the curtains of rain sweeping across the moor, but there are definitely people coming after them. She grabs Evie under the armpits and drags her towards the chair.

"Sig," says Evie. "There's no time!"

"Sure there is," Sig pants, glancing behind her and realising how fast the crowd of drowned are moving. She manhandles Evie up to the chair and the girl grabs on, heaves on the arms, and yanks herself up and in. Sig kicks off the brake and starts pushing her uphill as fast as she can, Rex running alongside. It's punishing work, but Evie helps as much as she can, and then they're up and over and on the flat, and there's about three hundred straightish metres to go to the stepping stones that cross the burn to the island at the head of the narrow estuary, where Sig catches a glimpse of the others carefully walking across as fast as they can. Rex stops and spins and runs back towards the incoming crowd of the drowned, barking angrily at the black and white spaniel running low to the ground just ahead of them.

"Rex!" Evie shouts, craning round to see him disappearing over the lip of the downslope. "Don't!"

Rex stretches out into a full-blown run and hits Milly like a torpedo, latching on to her throat and sending them both rolling and tumbling into the ditch in a yelping ball of snarls and fur.

"He'll be fine," grunts Sig, wishing she believed that. Her legs are pistoning and the chair is now going so fast the wheels are throwing up a trail of spray that makes a temporary track on either side of her. She grits her teeth against the pain her sprint-hobble is causing and drops her head, bulling forwards, determined to punch through it all.

"Sig," says Evie, still looking behind them. "Sig! It's in the water!"

Something in the girl's urgency makes her snatch a look back, despite the fact it'll slow her down.

The water spray coming off the left-hand wheel seems to have a life of its own because it's not dropping away as she powers forward.

It's keeping pace and growing taller, as if it's racing her and catching up.

She's only halfway to the stepping stones, and the spray is getting higher with each revolution of the hurtling wheels. She swears and tries to find every last available bit of strength in her body to will it to go faster, but when she risks another backward glance she sees in horror that the wheel-spray is morphing into the increasingly well-defined shape of a running man made from water, just like the unknown Viking from her dreams did, except this man has a familiar shape to him and he's chasing her, effortlessly keeping pace just an arm's length behind. All she can do is run till her trip-hammering heart bursts or she feels him grab her. She runs so fast she can feel the knee joint within the chafing leg brace begin to come loose as the scar tissue and the mended tendons approach the limit of their tolerances.

"Come *on*," she shouts, though she has no idea who she's shouting at and then realises it's herself. "Come on!"

Matt has got Tom and Ruby across the stepping-stones to the cemetery and turns to see how far away Sig and Evie are. He heads back and starts running towards them.

"No!" Sig shouts – and then she sees the second crowd of drowned come over the rise behind Matt, heading straight for her. As she stutter-steps, her knee finally seems to blow out and she loses her grip on the chair and pitches forward, barely managing to get her hands in the way as the ground punches up towards her face. She tries to roll and comes up untidily on her one good knee, fists already bunching as she roars defiance at the running man behind her and tries to tackle him and slow him down, but he just runs straight through her. As she passes through his watery body, she tastes the faint saltiness of unshed tears, and as she twists her head to watch him sprint onwards and take over pushing the wheelchair she recognises the familiar shape of him. Then her already badly tilted world pitches one notch further off-true and locks itself into place, a new place now wholly unfamiliar but also – as she recognises the last impossible thing – known and inevitable.

She drags herself to her feet, checks over her shoulder and winces into her shoogle-footed trot towards the stepping stones. She's sandwiched in a rapidly closing gap. There are still drowned closing in on her from behind, and there is the new crowd of drowned coming towards her. Given the slowness of her uneven progress, one or the other will catch her before she makes the safety of the stepping-stones. There's an inviolable certainty to the physics of this which she can see, but she clenches her teeth to contain the sob that's trying to punch its way out and makes herself run anyway.

Sig sees the running man get Evie to Matt, who stares at him and then grabs the girl out of the wheelchair and limps with her across the stepping-stones.

Evie's safe.

Matt's safe.

That's enough, she thinks, but the stubborn core of her won't let her do the thing she wants to do, which is to stop the pain in her leg and the ache in her lungs and just sink to the ground and let the inevitable happen. And then she sees the running man flicker through the rain towards her, and she does stop and does the last thing, because if the drowned are going to get her she wants this one last thing one last time. The painfully familiar water-man runs into her arms, and this time he's solid and he knocks the wind out of her as he tackles her and sweeps her off her feet and turns for the cemetery and runs.

"You," she gasps.

YOU'LL BE SAFE ON THE CEMETERY.

"Why didn't you tell me?"

I DID. YOU WEREN'T LISTENING.

"Was that you with the axe?"

NO. THAT'S HIM.

She looks back and sees the Viking slashing his way through the drowned who are chasing them, thinning the crowd as they get closer and closer. The other crowd of drowned ahead of them reaches the stepping stones, blocking their way.

"Stop," she says. "It's too late."

IT'S ALL RIGHT.

He doesn't run towards the stepping stones. Instead, he runs straight through the deeper water of the widening burn. Just as they reach the edge, a panting Rex swims energetically past and hauls himself on to the islet ahead of them. He shakes himself dry and Sig allows herself to be carried up on to the top of the cemetery where she is put back on her feet.

"Don't go," she whispers, suddenly somehow more scared of him going than anything that had happened in the last terrifying day.

SIT. YOUR KNEE IS HURTING YOU.

She lowers herself to the ground and then feels him settle behind her back, arms round her, holding her up. She feels the familiar weight of Rex as he steps up and curls himself into her lap. She looks down and sees the dog has his head craned back, looking at something over her shoulder. He whines happily and wags his tail.

494

GOOD DOG.

The remaining drowned arrive and stack up on the other side of the burn, staring and reaching towards them, but none of them step into the water. They just stand there, familiar and unfamiliar, glitching eerily in and out of phase.

"Why aren't they coming across?" says Kevo. He is braced in front of Magda, holding the useless spear gun the wrong way round, like a club. They are standing next to the others, who'd found a place to make a stand, with a couple of tilting headstones as a barrier in front of them, lower down the slope.

"They can't," says Matt.

"Who are they?" Sig breathes.

YOU KNOW WHO THEY WERE.

"Then, what are they now?" she says.

THE WALKING WATER. THE WELL'S VENGEANCE.

The Viking catches up and walks out of the sheeting rain and into the back of the crowd, his watery tattoos glistening silver against the bluer cast of the clear water of his body, and begins cutting his way through the drowned as calmly as a mower scything grass.

Fans of water trace the relentless arcs of his battleaxe as he slashes his way forward over the bodies of the fallen, who lie there unmoving as the pale lightning playing beneath the water that had sheathed them fades and dies.

"And who is he?" Sig says.

THE GUARD.

When the Viking has finished working his harvest, and all the drowned are still and stretched out on the heather, he turns and lopes off into the darkness.

"Wait, where's he going?" says Magda.

HE'S HUNTING. STAY HERE UNTIL HE'S DONE.

"He's looking for others," says Sig.

"We're safe now," says Tom.

HIS NAME IS TOM.

"Yes, Tom," Sig says. "Just like you told us we would be."

HE WAS LISTENING.

"Don't rub it in," she says.

"Who are you talking to?" says Evie.

Matt sits down next to Evie and beckons the others around him.

"Everyone huddle up together," he says. "We'll make a roof out of the space blanket. Share the warmth, keep as dry as we can. Then maybe we get through the night without exposure. Tom and Ruby go in the middle."

"Sig?" says Evie, looking up the slope towards her.

"I'll be fine up here," she says. "I'll keep a watch and wake you if they come back."

THEY WON'T.

Matt gives her a strange look as he unwraps the space blanket and then nods as he and everyone else reach up and pull it over their heads.

"They can't hear you," Sig says quietly, "and they can't see you."

NEITHER CAN YOU. NOT REALLY. THAT'S WHY YOU'RE NOT LOOKING DIRECTLY AT ME.

"But I can feel you."

TOOK YOU LONG ENOUGH.

She can feel his smile, just beside her right ear. She leans back against it and closes her eyes.

"What now?" she says.

WE WAIT FOR THE LIGHT.

"Evie saw you, I think," she says.

FOR A MOMENT MAYBE.

"Can Matt see you?"

IT'S WHY HE'S KEEPING THEM AWAY FROM US.

And then there's only silence as she pulls the hood of her coat up and allows herself to just be happy and feel the warmth of the dog in her lap and the man behind her. She decides not to think about all the ways in which what she is feeling is neither rational nor possible. The only thing she is determined to do is stay awake and not miss a moment of this fugitive happiness.

The rain eases towards dawn. The group huddled beneath the space blanket have somehow slept, kept warm by their enforced closeness.

Sig comes awake with a shiver, feeling like someone just called her name, and then she feels the presence at her back and relaxes, remembering.

"I didn't mean to fall asleep," she says, teeth beginning to chatter with the cold.

YOU SHOULD SEE THIS.

She looks down at the sharp point of the island where the outflow of the burn forks around it and leads out to the sea beyond. The heather is still strewn with the bodies of the drowned; in the grey light of dawn, they look more sad than frightening, more like discarded rags than the monsters of the night before. The water figure of the Viking is wading into the sea, though it seemed as if he was flowing back and becoming a part of it rather than submerging a solid body beneath the wavelets. As the first rays of the sun reach him, he turns and looks right at Sig with a wide smile and raises his axe in farewell.

"Jag ska, sköldjungfru," he shouts. *"Lev ditt bästa liv och var glad!"*

"Where's he going?" Sig whispers.

WHERE WE ALL GO IN THE END.

"Where's that?" she says.

HOME.

She watches the Viking walk into the West until the last waves close over his head, or maybe he just became one wave amongst a multitude because there is suddenly no sign he had ever been there at all.

Two ravens fly low over the point where he disappeared and then tilt, their wings almost like a salute as they turn and flap lazily back to the island.

"And you?" she says.

THE SAME.

"Don't go away," she breathes. "Please. Not again."

She hears him laugh, gentle and warm in her ear, and for a moment she feels the invisible embrace tighten around her.

IDIOT. THIS IS HOME. I TOLD YOU THAT A LONG TIME AGO.

She watches the ravens pass overhead as she listens to the dawn breeze nickering through the heather-tops around them.

"I forgot to believe you," she says quietly. "I'm sorry."

WELL. YOU'LL ALWAYS KNOW WHERE TO FIND ME.

The unswallowable void lurches up behind her breastbone again, choking her words.

"I don't know how to do this. Not really."

YOU'LL FIGURE IT OUT. EVERYONE DOES.

She leans back and closes her eyes, enjoys the warmth of his smile on the back of her neck, and feels the void fill with it and go away. Then, exhaustion takes her into a happy drowse that becomes sleep, and when she finally opens her eyes again the heat is still there, but now it's just the sun.

And instead of the deep chasm of loss she had feared falling back into, and perhaps because the world that is beginning to uncloak and gild with daylight has more layers than the one she had so firmly believed she was trapped in, she is surprised to find that this is enough – this far deeper world in which she can finally breathe easy.

She drops her head, and it feels like a great weight is sloughing off her shoulders, like a waterfall.

"Sig?"

Evie's voice breaks her out of the spell and she looks up to see Matt standing over her and the girl looking up from lower down with a concerned look on her face.

"What?" she says.

"You suddenly looked very alone up there," says Evie.

Sig lets Matt grab her hand and hoist her to her feet.

"I'm not," Sig says. And when Matt relaxes his grip, she doesn't. She keeps a firm hold on it as she turns to smile at Evie.

"I've got you, right?"

VARANGIAN: EPILOGUE

He gives the priest at Uppsala the package the merchant's widow had sent, and the priest reads the letter and leaves him to fast for three days before he is allowed to wash himself and enter the inner precinct of the ash grove.

He walks in through the first snow flurries of the year, past the nine desiccated bodies of last year's offerings hanging like dried fruit from the sacred trees. He stands as the priest sits and listens to his story and then asks to look at the curse.

He turns the square of dried skin over in his hands and agrees that Halvdan's offer to sacrifice himself is the only way to guard against it.

All he disagrees about is the nature of that sacrifice.

He tells him to take back the curse and go and bury it at the edge of the world. And since he has brought it in to the north, he must stand watch over it and his people in case it should rise up against them, so that if it does he can protect them as he had failed to protect the ambassador.

He asks the priest how he will know when the curse has been destroyed.

The priest tells him he doesn't know. But he does know he will not be admitted to Valhalla or Folkvangr until he has stood his watch.

He asks for how long.

The priest says he does not know that either, but that the gods have told him the only way to guard against the curse is to mend the oath that was broken.

He tells the priest he does not know where to find the end of the world.

The priest smiles a thin, unreadable smile and tells him that he will consult the birds and tell him the next day.

After one more night of fasting, he returns to find the priest waiting for him in the dawn mist, standing beneath the hanging bodies.

Two ravens watch from the branches above.

The priest tells him the gods have been silent, but the two birds had told him it was not true he did not know the way to the edge of the world, and they had told him that the way there leads through Birca.

He also tells him death comes for all in the end, curse or no curse, and that life lived well and laughed at is the only antidote, even if it is just a brief passage of sunlight between storms.

He thinks long and hard about it, and then he thanks the priest and heads back to the trading post.

The ravens go with him.

He never asks the woman what had been in the letter she had sent to the temple, along with the heavy gift. He never mentions it at all. And she never tells him.

Nor does she tell their children.

All she tells them is that the gods had told her he would always be there to watch over them and theirs and all who followed and settled here, on the low island she calls both first and last land — a place forever on the border between what is and what might be, back to the world, face to the wild ocean.

extras

orbitbooks.net

about the author

C. A. Fletcher has children and dogs. He lives in Scotland and writes for a living.

Find out more about C. A. Fletcher and other Orbit authors by registering for the free monthly newsletter at orbitbooks.net.

if you enjoyed
DEAD WATER

look out for

PARADISE-1

by

David Wellington

WELCOME TO PARADISE
Paradise-1. Earth's first deep space colony. For thousands
of colonists, it was an opportunity for a new life.
Until it went dark. No communication has been
received from the colony for months.
It falls to Firewatch Agent Alexandra Petrova and
the crew of the Artemis to investigate.
What they find is more horrifying than they could have imagined.

1

Three days still before dawn on Ganymede, and the cold seeped right through her suit and into her bones. The only light came from what reflected off the crescent of Jupiter, a thin arc of brown and orange that hung forever motionless in the night sky. Occasionally a bolt of lightning would snap across the shadowed disk of the big planet, a bar of light big enough that even from a million kilometers away it blasted long black shadows across the charcoal ice of the moon.

Alexandra Petrova rotated her shoulders. Rolled her feet back and forth in the powdery ice, just to get some blood moving through her legs. She'd been lying prone for nearly six hours, out on the edge of a ridgeline a long way from the warmth and the unrecycled air of the Selket Crater habitat. Maybe, though, her suffering was about to pay off.

"Firewatch One-Four, I have visual confirmation," she whispered, and her suit's microphone picked up her words and beamed them up to a satellite, which blasted them back down to some operator in a control tower back in the crater, then transferred them over to the nice, cozy offices of Firewatch Division Fourteen. The central headquarters of the Military Police on Ganymede. "Subject is at a range of approximately three hundred meters, headed north-northwest."

She lay as still as possible, not wanting to give away the slightest sign of her location. Just below her on the ridge a man was carefully bounding his way downslope, hopping from boulder to boulder, headed into a maze of narrow little canyons. He was wearing a bright yellow spacesuit, skintight. No faceplate, just a pair of dark goggles. Half the workers on Ganymede wore suits like that – they were cheap and easily patched, and they came in bright colors so that if you died on the surface your body would be easier to recover. A bar code on his back identified the suit as belonging to one Dzama, Margaret.

Petrova knew that suit was stolen. The man inside was a former medical technician named Jason Schmidt and he was – allegedly – the worst serial killer in the century-long history of the Ganymede colony. Petrova had turned up evidence of more than twenty missing persons cases that led straight back to Schmidt. Not a single body had been found, but that wasn't too surprising. Ganymede might be one of the most densely colonized worlds of the solar system, but there was plenty of ice out there that still hadn't ever been explored. The perfect place to hide dead bodies.

"Firewatch One-Four," she said, "I am requesting permission to make an arrest on one Schmidt, Jason. I've already filed the paperwork. I just need a green light."

"Copy, Lieutenant," One-Four told her. "We're just reviewing the case now, making sure you're within your remit. We should be able to clear this any minute now. Stand by."

All the evidence against him was circumstantial, but Schmidt was her man. She was certain of it.

She'd better be. She was staking her whole career on this case. As a lieutenant inspector of Firewatch, she had broad powers to carry out her own investigations, but she couldn't afford to screw this one up. She knew very well she'd only gotten her job and her rank because of nepotism. The problem was, everybody else knew it, too. Her mother, Ekaterina Petrova, was the former director of Firewatch. Petrova had gone into the family business, and everyone believed she'd been given a free ride at the academy based on nothing but her mother's name.

Clearing this case would go a long way to showing she was more than just her mother's daughter. That she was capable of holding down this job on her own merits. The command level of Firewatch had just let all those missing persons cases go – presumably the new director, Lang, felt that a few missing miners from Ganymede weren't important enough to spend resources tracking them down. But bringing Schmidt in would be a real win for Lang as well as Petrova. It would make Firewatch look good – it would show the people of Ganymede that Firewatch was there to protect them. It would be a public relations coup.

She just had to convince someone in Selket Crater to give her final authorization to make the arrest. Which should not have been so difficult. Why were they dragging their feet?

"Firewatch, I need authorization to make this arrest. Please advise."

"Understood, Lieutenant. We're still waiting on final confirmation."

Below her, Schmidt stopped, perched atop a boulder. His head twisted from side to side as he scanned the landscape. Had he noticed her somehow? Or was he just lost in the dark?

"Copy," she said. Petrova crawled forward a meter or so. Just far enough that she could keep Schmidt in sight. Where was he headed? She'd suspected he had some kind of stash house out here on the ice, maybe a place where he kept trophies from his kills. She'd been following him for a while and she knew he often left the warmth of the city and came out here on his own for hours at a stretch. That worked for her. She would have a better chance catching him out of doors – in the city he could simply disappear into a crowd.

This would be the perfect time to act. Take him down out on the ice, preferably alive. Drag him back to a Firewatch covert site for interrogation. She reached down and touched the pistol mounted at her hip. Checked that it was loaded and ready. Of course it was. She'd cleaned and reassembled it herself. There was only one problem. A little light on the receiver of the pistol glowed a steady, unhelpful amber. Meaning she did not yet have permission to fire.

"I need that authorization, Firewatch," she said. "I need you to unlock my weapon. What's the hold-up?" She kept her voice down, even though there was little need. Ganymede's atmosphere was just a thin wisp of nothing. Sound didn't carry out on the ice. Still. A little paranoid caution might keep her alive.

Schmidt finally moved, jumping off his boulder and coming down hard in a loose pile of broken ice chips. He fell on his ass and planted his hands on either side of him, fingers splayed on the ground. He was unarmed. Vulnerable.

"Confirmation still pending. Director Lang has asked to sign off on this personally. Please be patient," Firewatch told her.

Petrova inhaled slowly. Exhaled slowly. Director Lang was getting personally involved? That could be good, it could mean that her superiors were showing an interest in her career. More likely though it was a problem. It could slow things to a crawl while she waited for the director's approval. Or worse. Lang might shut her down just out of spite.

When Petrova's mother had retired from Firewatch a year and a half ago, Lang had made it very clear that she wasn't going to cut her predecessor's daughter any slack. If Petrova had to wait for Lang's approval she might freeze to death out on the ice before it came.

Screw this, she was moving in. Once she had enough evidence to make her case against Schmidt, no one would question her collar.

She got her feet under her and jumped. In the low gravity it felt like flying, just a little bit. Maybe that was the adrenaline peaking in her bloodstream. She didn't care. She came down easy, two feet and a balled fist touching ice, right behind him. Her free hand drew her weapon and extended it in one fluid motion. "Jason Schmidt," she said. "By the authority of the UEG and Firewatch, I'm placing you under arrest."

Schmidt spun around and jumped to his feet. He was faster than she'd expected, more nimble.

At the same moment, someone spoke in Petrova's ear. "This is Firewatch One-Four . . ."

Schmidt came straight at her, like he planned to tackle her. His move was idiocy. She had him at point-blank range. She brought her other hand up and steadied her weapon. It was a perfect shot. She knew she wouldn't miss.

" . . . authorization has been checked . . ."

Schmidt didn't slow down. He wasn't trying to talk her out of it. At this distance he couldn't fake her out, couldn't dodge her shot. She started to squeeze her trigger. If he really had killed all those people—

" . . . and denied. Repeat, authorization of apprehension is denied."

The light on the receiver of the pistol changed from amber to red. The trigger froze in place – no matter how much strength she used, she couldn't make it move.

"Cease operations and return to your post immediately, Lieutenant. That's an order."

Petrova just had time to duck as Schmidt barreled into her, knocking her back into the ice, which burst apart in a shower of snow with the force of the impact. The breath exploded out of her lungs and for a second she couldn't see straight. Struggling to get up, to grab Schmidt, she missed and went sprawling, faceplate down into the snow. It only took a fraction of a second to twist around, get back on her feet, wipe the snow off her helmet so she could see—

But by then he was gone. Of course. And now he knew she was on his tail. He would run. Get as far away as he could, maybe leave Ganymede altogether and restart his murder spree somewhere else. She tilted her head back and raged at the blank stars.

2.

"Lieutenant, please confirm you received last order. Lieutenant? This is Firewatch One-Four, please confirm—"

She walked over to where her gun lay, half buried in the powdery ice. She grabbed it and slapped it back on her hip. The ice of Ganymede was a deep gray brown, but only on the surface. Where the gun had broken through the crust it left a glaring white silhouette.

Just like her boot prints, and the furrow in the snow where she'd been knocked down.

Just like the boot prints Jason Schmidt had left, which headed around a massive boulder and into the shadow of the ridgeline. Bright white footprints standing out against the dark ice. And what was that she saw, from over that direction? It looked like a light. Artificial light sweeping across the dark surface. It must be coming from some structure over there. Some hiding spot.

Maybe a trophy room.

"Lieutenant? Please acknowledge."

She crept around the side of the boulder and saw exactly what she'd expected to find. The light came from an old emergency shelter, basically a prospector's hut. A big metal hatch was stuck into the ice and a light on the hatch flickered slowly on-off, on-off – the universal signal that the bunker behind that hatch was activated, full of air and warmth. Like a chased rabbit, Jason Schmidt had run for a bolt-hole.

It would be crazy to follow him in. To literally walk into his lair, when he knew she was coming. When her gun was locked down.

"Lieutenant? Come in, Lieutenant. This is Firewatch One-Four. Lieutenant, do you copy?"

Petrova slapped a big button on the face of the hatch and the airlock beyond blasted out air, equalizing pressures. She stepped inside and closed the outer door behind her. A moment later, the inner hatch slid open and she looked down into darkness.

"In pursuit, One-Four. I'll check in when I get a chance."

She switched off her radio. It wasn't going to tell her anything she wanted to hear.

Beyond the lock's inner door lay a concrete-lined corridor that spiraled down into the ice. Tiny light fixtures on the ceiling and walls lit up bright as she passed, then dimmed again behind her. Condensation hung in long, stalactite-like beads from the ceiling, spikes of pure water waiting for Ganymede's low gravity to finally bring them plopping down on the floor. At the bottom of the spiral, the corridor opened into a larger space. She expected to see a big room filled with crates of emergency supplies and old mining gear.

Instead the main room of the bunker was open, cleared out. The concrete floor was stained and damp but clear of debris. Dark chambers — caves, basically — led off the main chamber in every direction. This place was huge, she realized. This wasn't just an emergency bunker. It must be an entire mine complex, though it looked like it had been abandoned.

She thought she heard something — a real sound, echoing in the concrete space full of actual air. She crouched down and tried to stay perfectly still. There was no good place to hide, but maybe Schmidt hadn't seen her come in.

She ducked low into a shadow as he stepped out of one of the side caves. He'd shucked his suit down to the waist, the arms and hood hanging down behind him like tails. He had a large crate in his arms and he dumped its contents on the floor without ceremony. "I'm back," he called, in a sing-song voice, like he was calling to pets who'd been waiting for him to come home.

Petrova watched as the crate's contents slithered out onto the floor. Hundreds of silver foil packets. Colorful pictures were printed on each packet, showing a serving of some mouth-watering foodstuff. Pureed carrots. Mushroom stew. Algae salad. Petrova recognized the pictures right away, as would anyone who had spent time on Ganymede. She knew the pictures were nothing but lies. There was food inside the packets, food nutritious enough to keep you alive, but it never resembled the tempting picture. Instead it was more likely to be a thin gray slop grown in a big bioreactor: proteins and carbohydrates excreted by gene-tailored bacteria in a vat of sugar water. It was the kind of food that workers got when they couldn't afford anything better, when they'd run out of luck. The government of Ganymede wouldn't let any of its people starve, but the alternative wasn't much better.

"Come and get it," Schmidt called out, in that same lilting cadence.

She was about to move in and put him under arrest when she caught a flicker of motion from one of the caves. Bright eyes glistened back there, catching the light. The filthiest, most unkempt human being she'd ever seen came rushing out, almost running on all fours. It was dressed in rags and its face was so grimy she couldn't tell its gender or even its age. It moved cautiously as it approached Schmidt, as if it was afraid of him. It didn't say a word, didn't so much as mumble a greeting.

"All yours," Schmidt said, and stepped away from the pile of food packets.

A hint of motion from another cave mouth grabbed Petrova's attention. Then another – soon people were emerging from a dozen directions at once. All of them as dirty and decrepit as the first. They moved quickly to grab silver packets from the pile, then they raced back toward their caves as if afraid someone would try to take the food away from them. They tore the packets open with their teeth, then stuck their fingers inside. They shoved the food straight into their mouths, getting as much of it on their skin and in their beards as they actually ingested. Their faces sagged with relief, as if they'd been starved for days and this was the best thing they'd ever tasted.

Petrova had no idea what was going on. Time to get some answers.

She rose to her full height. "Schmidt," she called out. "Keep your hands visible."

Schmidt winced but at least this time he didn't just come running at her like a bull.

"Jason Schmidt, you are under arrest. Back up against that wall. *Facing* the wall," she ordered.

He shook his head. His hands were up, in front of him, but he wasn't holding them up to show he was unarmed. He beseeched her with them. It looked like he might fall on his knees and beg her for mercy.

She needed answers. She needed to know what was going on. "You," she called, to the nearest of the unwashed people, who was busy licking out the insides of a third food packet. "Is this man holding you prisoner? Do you need help?"

The man — at least, he had a beard — looked up at her as if noticing her existence for the first time. He dropped the foil packet and stumbled towards her. His hands clawed and patted at the air, seemingly at random. Despite herself, Petrova took a step back as he came closer. His mouth opened but the sound he let out wasn't a word. Just a raw syllable, cut loose from any kind of meaning.

"Do you need help?" Petrova repeated. "Are you trying to ask for help?"

"He can't do that," Schmidt said. She jabbed her pistol in his direction and he shut up, lifting his hands higher in the air.

The victim came closer still and grabbed at Petrova's arm.

She pulled away from his touch and he grabbed for her helmet, instead, grasping one of the lamps mounted on its side. He let out a crude fricative, his mouth opening wide, spittle flying everywhere. She had to shove him, hard, to get loose.

Someone else hissed like a snake. All of Schmidt's other victims were making sounds now, raw noise, just the roots of words.

"What's going on?" Petrova asked. "What did you do to these people?"

Were these the missing persons she'd been tracking? She'd assumed Schmidt had murdered them all. But if they were here, alive, apparently kept captive—

They were moving now, all of them. Lumbering toward her, their hands describing shapes in the air, or clawing at nothing. Their faces were contorted in strange expressions she couldn't understand. They spoke only in meaningless monosyllables. *Ph. Kr. La.*

They grabbed at her, clinging to her legs, her arms. Petrova had to dance backward to get away from them. They weren't particularly strong – now she saw them up close she could see how emaciated and sickly they looked under their coating of dirt – but there were a lot of them.

"Get back," she told them. "Stay back! Firewatch!"

"They don't understand," Schmidt called.

Schmidt – she'd lost track of him. As the clawing, swiping people came at her, she'd forgotten to keep an eye on him. She twisted around and saw him creeping backward up the ramp, toward the surface. His hands were still up but he was getting away.

One of the victims growled, raising her voice as she bashed at the back of Petrova's suit with weak fists. She yelped like a dog.

Petrova pushed her away, harder perhaps than she should have. She was getting scared, she could feel it. She was afraid of these poor wretched people – she needed to get a grip.

She needed to get the situation under control. Well, she knew where to start. Schmidt was all but running up the ramp, away from her. She dashed after him and smacked him across the back of his neck with the butt of her pistol. "Down!" she said. "Get down and stay down, motherfucker." She hit him again and this time he fell down. "What did you do?" she demanded, as he tried to get up. She hit him again. "What did you do?"

Schmidt rolled on the floor, rolled until he was lying on his back. He lifted his hands to his face. She realized he was sobbing.

What the hell?

She retrieved a pair of smart handcuffs from a pouch at her belt. Moving fast, she grabbed Schmidt and shoved his face up against the concrete wall. She touched the cuffs to his hands and they came to life, twisting thick tendrils of plastic around his wrists and fingers, locking them in place. He made no effort to resist.

"Oh, thank God," he moaned. Quietly. His eyes were clamped shut. "Oh, thank you."

"What the hell is wrong with you?" she asked.

"It's over," he said. "It's finally over."

"What did you do to those people? What's wrong with them?"

"It's acute aphasia, it's . . . it's—"

"They can't talk," Petrova said. "I got that. Why? Did you . . . did you do something to them?"

"I *saved* them," Schmidt whined.

She stared at the back of his head, unable to comprehend. She had no idea what was going on. Then she glanced down at the pistol in her hands. The light there remained a steady, unchanging amber. Great.

"Tell me everything," she said. "Then I'll decide what to do with you."